P9-AQL-792

0  00  30  03000

MAIN

# COLORADO TWILIGHT

*Other Five Star Titles*
*by Tess Pendergrass:*

Colorado Shadows

# COLORADO TWILIGHT

*Book 2 of the Colorado Trilogy*

## Tess Pendergrass

**Five Star • Waterville, Maine**

Five Star First Edition Romance Series.

Published in 2001 in conjunction with Martha Longshore.

Set in 11 pt. Plantin.

Printed in the United States on permanent paper.

**Library of Congress Cataloging-in-Publication Data**

Pendergrass, Tess.
    Colorado twilight / Tess Pendergrass.
        p. cm.—(Colorado trilogy ; bk. 2)
        ISBN 0-7862-3301-X (hc : alk. paper)
        1. Women pioneers—Fiction.  2. Colorado—Fiction.
    I. Title.
    PS3566.E457 C63 2001
    813'.6—dc21                                    2001023899

This one is for Mom and Dad,
Who taught me what love is all about.

As always,
I want to thank all the friends and family
who have been so supportive of my writing,
especially my grandmothers, Ann and Terry.
Thanks also to my best critics, Katy and Barb,
who do their best to keep me in line.
Thanks to Auntie Jo for going horseback riding
in the Rockies with me
and to Dan for feeding me while I wrote this.
I love you all.
I couldn't do it without you.

# *Prologue*

January, 1877

"You swore you'd never leave me. You lying son-of-a-bitch."

Jordan's fists clenched as she fought the desire to tear Frank's portrait off the wall and smash it over her knee. She was shaking again. Maybe from anger. Or fear. Maybe from the cold. Since Frank had gone, she couldn't seem to get warm.

Jordan had more recent portraits of Frank, portraits she'd done herself over the past nine years. But this one that her Aunt Rue had painted of him at eighteen had always been her favorite. With his smooth face more a result of youth than shaving, Frank stood straight and terribly serious in his Union uniform. Yet Rue had captured the soul behind his dark eyes. Those solemn, searching eyes promised to listen, to care.

They were eyes to believe in. To rely on.

"Damn you."

The kitchen door opening behind her made her start, ashamed. But if Aunt Rue had heard Jordan's outburst, she gave no sign; she merely shifted her tray of bread and cheese so she could pat Jordan's shoulder. A tall, slender woman, her dark hair cut unfashionably short, the older woman's eyes were full of sympathy.

"I'm glad you've come down, dear. Everyone's waiting for you in the parlor."

*I can't face them. Make them go home.* But she couldn't say that.

"I know, Aunt Rue. I'll be there in just a moment."

Jordan watched her aunt slip through the parlor door and fought the urge to flee back upstairs—or, better yet, out into the frigid New England winter, escaping the house and all its memories. She would run through the snow until the cold burned out her lungs, until her legs gave way and she collapsed into the smothering whiteness . . .

Jordan shook herself. She couldn't do that to Aunt Rue and Uncle Hal or to Frank's parents. If living took more courage than dying, she'd just have to find it somewhere. And she'd have to face the friends and family gathered in her parlor. They loved her. They only wanted to help. And she didn't want to be alone any more than she wanted company.

She glanced at herself in the hall mirror, pulling down her black veil. It made her feel like a fly trapped in a spider web, but it also hid her red eyes and blotchy cheeks. Perhaps it would protect her from the sympathetic eyes waiting in the parlor.

"Oh, Jordan, you poor darling." Her cousin Nicolette, soberly elegant in chocolate and gold silk, greeted her at the door. Nicky's eyes glowed with tears. "You look so thin and pale."

"I'm all right."

"Of course. How brave you are."

With a quick hug Nicky passed her on to Frank's cousin Simon and his wife. Singly, or by twos or threes, each person in the room approached her to offer a heartfelt comment or gesture of sympathy.

None of it penetrated the numbness in her heart, and it was a relief to slip away from Frank's great-aunt Sarah to stand alone at the window. Lamplight reflected off the glass, but she could make out the darkness beyond, the soft shimmer of unbroken snow.

"Jordan?"

In the window's reflection she recognized Wiloughby Braddock, Jack and Simon's baby brother, Frank's youngest cousin. His thick, wheat-colored hair was already rumpled, and in his somber black suit, his face earnest in grief, he looked younger than his twenty-four years.

"May I have a word with you?"

"Of course, Will." She turned from the window to face him.

"I'm sorry about Frank. He was like a brother to me." He blanched, and she knew he thought of her first husband, Jack, who had been his brother. "What I mean is, I understand what you're feeling."

Jordan managed to keep her composure. "Thank you. I know you miss him, too."

"He was a real hero to me, Jordan. At least you know he died like a hero. That's some consolation."

"He should have waited for Simon and Jeanie to catch up with him before he went out on that ice."

"Joey couldn't have hung on that long," Will reminded her. "The boy would have drowned."

"Then Frank should have let him die." The knife-keen words were out before she could stop them, slicing across the thin cords of her self-control. Again the scene played in her imagination, as if she'd been there herself. The little boy from the nearby farm screaming for help, his hands finding no purchase as he tried to pull himself from the hole in the pond ice. Frank throwing off boots and coat to slide out toward him, the ice cracking and groaning beneath him, finally giving way to plunge her husband into the frigid water beside the boy.

Frank had heaved the child onto the ice. It had held beneath the boy as he'd wiggled to safety, but could not support Frank. Before Simon and his wife could reach the edge of the pond with a rope, the cold had conquered Frank's muscles and pulled him beneath the surface of the dark water.

Jordan pressed her knuckles against her lips, willing herself not to collapse, not to break in front of all these people.

Will patted her shoulder, obviously not believing she'd meant the bitter words. "I know these past few days have been hard on you," he said. "Losing Frank. And you must be worried about the farm."

"The farm?"

"You can't stay here by yourself."

No. Just the thought made her tremble. "I've been staying in town with Aunt Rue and Uncle Hal."

"But someone's got to take care of the place. And come spring, there's going to be planting and plowing. I know Frank hired workers, but someone's got to be in charge."

It wouldn't be her. She hadn't sorted out the details, but she couldn't come back to live here, as much as it would hurt to leave. And she couldn't stay with her aunt and uncle forever. They had raised her since she was eight, and they loved her as much as their own children, but some day soon they'd have a wedding for Nicky to plan. Henry Junior was once more home from college in disgrace, and Pete and his bird dogs kept the house in a constant uproar.

Rue and Hal had enough to think about without finding room for her. As much as Jordan didn't want to face the future, she didn't want to return to her childhood, either.

"I know you haven't thought about these things," Will was saying. "But it's like when Jack died. You're all alone again."

"I have thought of it, Will, thank you." She couldn't take the edge off the words.

"Well, it's true. You don't have anyone to take care of you."

"I'll be all right," she lied, willing him to stop talking, to leave her alone.

"I want you to marry me."

She almost laughed before she realized he was serious, and then she almost laughed anyway, the absurdity touching off a fight with hysteria. "Oh, Will." What could she say that wouldn't hurt his feelings, so wrapped up in foolish honor? "That's sweet of you."

"You're part of the Braddock family, and we take care of our own. Frank promised to look after you when Jackson was sent west, and Frank would want us to look after you now."

She could remember years ago scolding Will to wash behind his ears before coming in to Christmas supper. And he was going to take care of her?

"I'm not the helpless child I was when Jack died," she reminded him. "I've been a widow before. I'll manage."

Will opened his mouth to persist, but she cut him off with a smile and a shake of her head. "Besides, Nicky would kill me."

"Nicolette?"

"She's got her cap set for you, Will. Haven't you noticed?"

He flushed crimson to the roots of his hair, and Jordan could see the effort it took him not to glance over his shoulder to where Nicky stood by the fire, in the perfect spot for the flames to pick out the highlights in her golden hair.

"You . . . you don't really think I have a chance with her?" he asked, failing utterly to act as if he didn't care about the answer.

Jordan's amusement died, crushed by an overwhelming envy for Will's youth, hope, and dreams for the future. "Don't be a fool, Wiloughby. She's had a crush on you since she was ten. Now go say something witty to her and stop worrying about me."

"But what will you do?"

"Travel." The word sounded certain, so certain she could almost believe it herself. "Frank left enough money to hire someone to run the farm. I might even sell it. I've always wanted to see the West, but there has never been time. I'll take my paints. It will be like a great hunting expedition, an African safari."

She felt a flicker in her chest of something that might almost have been excitement.

"Jordan, that doesn't sound very practical." Will's concern jolted her back to dark, cold New England. "Who will you travel with? Where will you go? You don't know anyone west of Philadelphia—"

"I know people who do," Jordan cut him off. "That man who went to law school with Simon. What's his name . . . He started a practice in Texas, didn't he?"

"Denver."

"Denver. I could go to Denver first. And Uncle Hal has a brother in San Francisco. I'd make out all right."

Of course she would. She was a survivor, whether she liked it or not. And the idea of getting away, seeing new places, meeting new people who didn't feel her grief, loosened the tightness in her chest just a little. She wouldn't be running away from Frank's memory, not if she took her paints. Frank was so much a part of her art. That would be the part of him she'd want to take with her.

"Jordan—"

"Go talk to Nicky, Will." She looked over to where her cousin held court, plying her charms on the men within range. "If anyone needs looking after, it's her."

# Chapter 1

November, 1877

"It shouldn't take you long to paint this, Jo-jo. Blue for the sky, yellow for the grass—and not much of that. No wonder civilized people stay in the East. Much more of this desolation, and I'll lose my mind."

*Much more of your chattering . . .* Jordan held her tongue. She would have been perfectly happy to take Nicky's place at the window, staring out at the passing plains. However monotonous they might seem to her cousin, their newness and immensity drew her like wine.

But she couldn't sit by the train window because Nicolette became ill sitting on the aisle, and Will refused to allow Jordan to take his seat across from Nicky, since that would mean she would have to sit next to a stranger.

Jordan glanced at the man slumped in the seat across from her. He slept, his hat dipped low over his eyes, his long legs twisted out into the aisle to allow her as much room as possible. He seemed clean enough, though his black duster gave off a faint, acrid smell when the breeze from the window brushed toward her.

The glimpse she'd caught of his face when she, Will, and Nicky had taken their seats had shown his expression to be reserved, but pleasant enough. Hardly a threat to her person or her propriety.

13

But she wouldn't embarrass Will by arguing. She'd be rid of Will and Nicky soon enough, once they reached Denver.

The air from the window touched her again, mocking her with its chill. It was already November. She could hardly travel through the Rockies in the dead of winter. She'd be stuck in Denver until April—if she was lucky and they didn't get late snowstorms.

She took a deep breath, forcing her frustration out with the old air. If only she hadn't told Will that Nicky had a flame for him. Aunt Rue had insisted she couldn't plan the wedding without Jordan's help, and Jordan couldn't refuse Aunt Rue anything. If only she hadn't asked Simon to contact his old law school friend for her. Leland Hedgepeth had not only offered to welcome her into his home and write letters of introduction for her to his friends all over Colorado, but he had also offered to provide Simon's newly-graduated, about-to-be-married, baby brother Wiloughby with a job in his law firm.

As a result, Jordan hadn't been able to leave Connecticut until the newlyweds were ready to move.

Not that she minded the company. She loved Nicolette, for all her youthful egotism, and Will, for all his seriousness, but this was supposed to be *her* adventure.

"Oh, look!" Nicky cried, something out the window finally catching her fancy. "There's someone chasing the train. On a horse!"

Will twisted in his seat to peer back down the length of the train. "We must be on an incline or we'd be moving too fast for him to be gaining on us like that."

"Maybe it's train robbers," Nicky suggested. "That would liven things up."

Jordan leaned into her cousin, trying to see. "There's only one."

"The others might be on the other side of the train," Nicky said, refusing to let Jordan spoil her fun.

Jordan narrowed her eyes. "He's carrying a white flag."

"You're right." Will winked at his wife. "Maybe he was afraid somebody might think like Nicky and take a shot at him. But why's he chasing the train?"

No one had an answer, so they watched in silence as the lone rider passed their car, making his way toward the engine. He was lost to Jordan's view as he moved up the train, but Will let them know when he'd reached his destination.

"He's at the locomotive now. I think he's shouting something at the conductor. There, someone's out on one of the platforms. He's reaching a hand to the man on the horse. Wait . . . they're pulling him onto the train."

In a moment the horse appeared out their window again. Now riderless, he slowed to a confused trot and was soon left behind them. The return of the empty plain, an endless vista beyond the window, was anticlimactic.

"Maybe he was a soldier escaping from an Indian attack," Nicky said, disappointed the excitement was over.

"Maybe he's carrying a supply of medicine to treat an outbreak of cholera in Cheyenne," Jordan suggested dryly.

Nicky made a face at her.

"He's a railroad employee." The soft southern drawl came from the stranger sitting next to Will.

Jordan started. She hadn't noticed so much as a flicker of movement from the man, yet he'd gathered his legs back in front of his seat, and she could make out the glint of his eyes beneath the shadow of his hat brim.

"Or perhaps he has family on the train," the man continued. It seems you'll get to meet your train robbers after all, miss."

Will's eyes narrowed at having a stranger address his wife

in such a manner. Jordan hoped he'd get used to it. Men would always find excuses for introducing themselves to Nicky. Few people could resist her when her head tilted just so, her eyes sparkling like aquamarines.

"Why, what do you mean, sir?"

"The train is slowing." Jordan could feel it, too, could hear the change in the engine's roar, the crescendo of the slowly-applied brakes. "I suspect our good conductor has been given the choice of stopping the train safely or being de-railed where the outlaws have pulled up the tracks."

"We're just coming into Cheyenne," Will grumbled, but Nicky giggled delightedly at the game.

"Is it Jesse James, do you think?" she asked, playing along, "or Sioux Indians? Maybe you'll be carried off by an Indian chief, Jo-jo."

Jordan couldn't respond to her cousin's teasing. They weren't scheduled to reach Cheyenne until four o'clock. It couldn't be much past two-thirty.

She glanced at the stranger to find him watching her. Un-shaded, his eyes were a golden hazel, steady, studying her with a directness that would have been rude in any creature but a cat. He was like a cat, she thought, in his grace, the al-most casual collection of his muscles.

More dangerous than she had thought. And serious about the train robbers.

He nodded, reading her recognition. "They're obviously making an effort to avoid unnecessary injury," he said in that same soft drawl that might have been discussing a game of lawn tennis. "If everyone remains calm, there's no reason to be afraid."

That's why he was watching her and not Nicky. Jordan looked down at her hands, brown gloves clasped above som-ber brown skirts. That's what he saw. A drab little matron, afraid of her own shadow.

The knowledge hurt, and the hurt angered her.

She met the stranger's gaze once more. "I've been informed the dangers of the West include floods, blizzards, wolves, Indian wars, brush fires, and tornadoes. A couple of fools with guns hardly seem worth fretting over."

She hadn't convinced him.

"We're just coming into the station," Will insisted, scowling. "And I'd advise you to quit frightening the ladies, sir, or find yourself another seat."

The train shuddered to a final, jarring stop. The stranger made no reply to Will, but they all followed his gaze toward the window. Nothing but dead, desolate plain stretched toward the horizon.

"Cheyenne must be through the other window . . ." Will began, but the restless shifting and muttering of passengers from the other side of the aisle indicated their view was much the same.

The door at the front of the car slammed open, admitting a biting breath of cold air and three dust-coated men with bandannas secured below their eyes. The largest wore a beard and boasted a scar across his weathered forehead, but the other two looked scarcely older than boys.

The slightest of these, no taller than Jordan, paused by her seat and touched a finger to his hat brim.

"Afternoon, ladies. I apologize for the inconvenience, but we've got boys fixing the tracks as we speak, and you should be on your way again in no time." His speech had the tang of the West but none of the crudeness Jordan would have expected of an outlaw. "In payment for our services, we are asking a donation from each passenger. A small enough price for averting derailment, as I'm sure you'd agree."

He spoke amiably, his pale green eyes disingenuously

wide. If not for the long-barrelled pistol he pointed almost apologetically at the dark stranger and Will, Jordan could have thought his concern wholly genuine.

And perhaps he himself thought it was. Perhaps it was the perfection with which he played the gentleman bandit that sent a shiver of fear up her spine, or perhaps it was something strange behind his eyes.

She watched the big, bearded man roughly harassing the passengers across the aisle to give up their valuables, but the youthful outlaw beside her seemed in no hurry as he gestured for his other young partner to bring forth a bag already weighted with loot from the first-class compartments.

"Look here," Will sputtered, but his indignation choked him.

"If you'll all put your hands where I can see them?" The outlaw waited until they complied. "I'm going to ask you, one at a time, to collect any money or jewelry you may be carrying and pass it to me. You first, sir," he said to the man across from Jordan. "Please be especially careful of how you open that coat of yours. Set a good example for the ladies."

The stranger's long hands, much darker than his pale face, gave Jordan an impression of harnessed strength as he slowly pulled aside the folds of his duster. Careful to show the outlaw his empty hand, he reached into an inner pocket.

"Slow," the outlaw ordered.

The man nodded. For a half-second, Jordan thought she saw the stranger's eyes turn flat and yellow as a predatory beast's, and her heart thudded off-beat with fear. But when his hand withdrew from his coat, it held only a clip of tattered bills which he dropped carelessly into the outlaw's bag.

"Thank you, sir." The outlaw looked to Will, paused, then glanced back at the other man. "And if it's not too much trouble, sir, I surely do admire your hat."

Silence filled the railroad car.

Jordan could feel Nicky quivering beside her, the reality of outlaws much less delicious than the pretense, but she didn't dare reach a hand to her cousin, for fear the movement might startle the outlaws. She stared at the stranger, willing him to relinquish his hat. He'd said if they'd all cooperate, there'd be no reason to fear. But his hesitation was taking much too long. The older outlaw had already finished fleecing the passengers on his side of the car.

Unexpectedly the stranger's eyes caught hers. She might have imagined his nod.

"Why, of course," he drawled, as carefully polite as the green-eyed outlaw. "It's yours, if you like." He lifted his hat by the crown and held it out.

The outlaw started, his pistol snapping into sharp aim at the stranger's forehead. "Jesus Christ! You're Preacher Kelly."

The outlaw's young companion, eyes the color of washed-out denim, leaned forward to gawk at the man. "He's a preacher, Pauly?"

"Son-of-a-bitch, Teapot, you know we don't use names." The outlaw rolled his eyes in comic exasperation, but his awkward confederate blanched bone white. The end of the green-eyed man's gun barrel now wavered somewhere above his partner's abdomen.

"Oh, oh, I'm sorry, Pau . . . I mean, Boss. I mean, I didn't mean—"

"I'm not a preacher," the man called Kelly said, diverting the bandit leader's attention. Gawky Teapot slumped visibly as Pauly swung his gun away from him, back toward the passengers.

"Naw, he's a gunfighter, Teapot," the outlaw said. "Fast as Wild Bill or Bat Masterson, they say. Maybe faster. I saw your face on a wanted poster in Laramie."

"A misunderstanding," Kelly said, with no hint of irony, but the outlaw laughed.

"Yeah." Pauly cocked his head, eyes excited as a boy contemplating playing truant from school. "I hear you don't carry."

The gunfighter shook his head. "My guns are in my baggage."

"I guess you know what you're doing, but Jesus. There are some boys as might take it into their head to kill a man like you, even without you being armed."

"A coward who would shoot an unarmed man wouldn't hesitate to shoot an armed man in the back."

Pauly nodded, a man sympathetic to the hazards of the trade. "You're right there. Honor's a rare thing these days. Well, it's a pleasure to meet you, Mr. Kelly. You go ahead and keep your hat." He turned to Teapot, who jumped back a step. Pauly jerked the loot bag away from him and dug around until he came up with Kelly's money clip. "And this, too." He tossed it onto the gunfighter's lap. "I won't take what's yours without I prove myself to you first, and I guess I'll have to wait for that chance."

"Boss, this is takin' too damn long. Let's move," the bearded man rumbled from his post by the far door.

One bare glance from Pauly's green eyes was enough to silence the bigger, older man. But Pauly nodded to him. "We're coming."

He turned to Jordan, touching his hat brim once more. "Ma'am, if you please. All of you," he added, waving the gun at Will, careful to keep the barrel from pointing toward the ladies.

She heard Will pull his wallet from his pocket.

"And that watch," Pauly urged him.

Nicky's fingers fumbled with the catch on her handbag, and Jordan found her own hands no steadier. Their money tumbled into the bag, insignificant compared to the fat purses of the cattle barons in first class, but more than they could afford to lose.

"Your jewelry, ladies."

Jordan unpinned the brooch from her throat. Lapis lazuli. Frank had said it matched her eyes. She yanked on the matching earrings.

"And your rings."

She tugged off her right glove, willing back tears. She could wire home for more money. She could travel for a hundred years, if she wanted, on the profit she'd made from selling the farm, even without the money she'd been carrying. She could buy a hundred brooches more lovely than the one she'd just lost. She carried Frank in her heart, not her jewelry.

She slipped off Jack's engagement ring, studded with tiny diamond flakes, and the fire opal with the silver band that had been her grandmother's.

"Your other hand, too, ma'am."

She looked up, startled, into those boyish green eyes. "You can't want my wedding band."

"I'm sorry, ma'am." His lips pressed together in sympathy. "If I let one person keep a ring, the next is going to want to keep his daddy's gold watch, and the next is going to give me a story about the hundred dollars in his wallet going to buy a coffin for his dear, departed mother."

She pulled off the glove, but her fingers curved into a fist she couldn't open.

"It's not worth much. It's just a plain band." And not high quality gold. Just what Jackson could afford on a lieutenant's paltry salary. When she'd married Frank, he hadn't offered her a better one. The first hint she had that she might learn to love him.

"Your husband will understand, ma'am."

"I don't think he will!" Her voice echoed shrilly, but she didn't care. The recklessness that had started her on this crazy journey shook her, and for a second she thought she might be as dangerous as the angel-eyed boy beside her with his foolish gun. "This is worth nothing to you, and it's all I have left."

"We won't give you our wedding rings," Nicky spoke up beside her. She'd already taken hers off, but now she clutched it to her breast, her eyes flashing. "That's barbarous! We've given you all our money, now leave us alone."

Pauly looked at her, his face gone blank. "If you don't choose to give me those rings, ma'am, I'll take them from you."

Nicky's eyes widened. She pressed closer to the window. "Don't you touch me, you dirty beast. Will, don't let them touch me!"

Will's scowl darkened, and he hunched forward, despite the gun barrel pointed at his chest. "If you touch my wife, you'll answer to me for it."

The outlaw didn't seem offended. "Maybe in hell." The barrel lifted to a spot between Will's eyes, Pauly's finger playing with the trigger.

"You're right, it's only a ring," Jordan said, her voice thin with fear, but audible. "Just an object, after all." She pulled on the ring. She hadn't taken it off in ten years, and for a heart-stopping second she thought her knuckles had swollen too much to let it pass. Desperately, she tugged and twisted. Another second and her distraction might lose Pauly's interest, turning his attention back toward Will. But with a jerk, the ring slipped free, the sting of scraped skin nothing compared to the emptiness swelling in her heart.

"Nicky?" She turned to her cousin, holding out her hand. Nicky's lips pursed mutinously, but she'd seen the danger to her husband clearly enough. She gave Jordan her rings, her eyes sparking.

"I hope you choke on them," she spat at Pauly.

The click as he cocked his pistol snapped loud in the compartment. He sighted down the pistol at Will, the outlaw's body suddenly limp in parody of a drunken cowboy. "Bang." He laughed, a frighteningly infectious, youthful laugh, as he winked at Nicky's suddenly ghostly pale face. "I don't intend to eat them, ma'am."

He moved forward, but before Jordan could hand him the jewelry, another hand caught hers. Kelly used no force, but she knew she'd been right about the steel in those long, dark fingers.

"Ma'am?" he requested.

She could feel Kelly's panther's eyes on her, though she kept her gaze on his hands. Gunfighter's hands. A killer's hands. But it was easier to pass him her wedding ring than it would have been to give it to Pauly. She couldn't watch him put the jewelry in the bag.

"Thank you, ma'am." Pauly's voice brought her head up to face him once more. "We prefer to avoid bloodshed." He said it with simple sincerity, this slight young man poised on the knife edge of violence. "Good day to all of you."

He moved on, Teapot and the bearded man in his wake, vulture and loon to his deadly sparrow hawk. When the compartment door closed behind them, Will slammed his fist into the wall.

"Bastards! If I'd had a gun . . ."

"If you'd had a gun, you'd be dead," the gunfighter, Kelly, said flatly. "And most likely so would I and your companions.

It's not cowardice to avoid a battle you can't win."

"You'd know about that, wouldn't you?" Will snapped, still hot with rage and embarrassed by his fear. "You were cozy enough with them, I guess you didn't have anything to be afraid of. A gunfighter who doesn't carry guns. I guess killers prefer to confine themselves to innocent victims."

The low, feral growl that whispered through the compartment must have been Jordan's imagination. Or perhaps it was the steam engine preparing for action once more.

"If I'd had a gun," Kelly said in that same, calm voice. "Those outlaws would be dead. And most likely so would you and your companions."

"Will," Jordan warned softly, but he didn't notice.

"Easy to brag, now that the danger's over," he said. "But I guess that's what southerners are best at, isn't it? Bragging. One of you worth ten of us, eh? I'm surprised you didn't take those three bandits on with your bare hands, *Preacher* Kelly."

Jordan did hear a growl. It stopped as the gunfighter pushed a boot under his seat, swirling the edge of his duster to reveal a gray carpet bag. A banked fire flickered behind his hazel eyes.

He still didn't raise his voice, but the drawl thickened. "That's Lieutenant Colonel Elijah Kelly, retired, to you, suh. And the guns of the southe'ners I fought were as deadly as the guns my boys had."

Will flushed, fiery red even against his ruddy cheeks. "You fought for the Union?"

"I did."

"So did my brothers and my cousins," Will said stiffly. "One died at Gettysburg. I hope you will accept my apologies for my rudeness."

"No apology is necessary, suh." Jordan thought the gunfighter looked nearly as embarrassed as Will. "There, I do believe we're about to be on our way again."

Metal squealed suddenly, and their passenger car jerked out of its inertia to join the slow sinuous stretch of the train accelerating once more.

"Isn't the conductor going to send someone to see if we're all right?" Nicky asked, breaking her unusual silence. "I bet someone checked on the passengers in the first class car."

Jordan smiled. Nicky would be fine. "I bet none of those wealthy ladies' husbands offered to lay down his life for her wedding ring."

"My brave, foolish Wiloughby," Nicky said, reaching impulsively for her husband's hand. "Don't you dare get yourself killed over something so silly as that."

His pride visibly restored, Will clasped her hands tight. "As long as I'm around, darling, no one is going to touch so much as a hair on your head."

Jordan looked away. Despite her happiness for her cousin and brother-in-law, sometimes the envy burned deep.

The gunfighter was watching her, that measuring gaze that she couldn't quite call rude.

"There are many kinds of courage," he said.

Her stomach still churned with fear and the loss of her wedding ring. "Yes, there are, and the greatest don't come from holding a Colt revolver in your fist." Let him take that as he pleased, she didn't much care.

But she caught only the edge of a smile as he tilted his hat back down over his eyes and his long body once more slumped in his seat. " 'Be strong and let your heart take courage, all you who wait for the Lord.' But sometimes Mr. Colt's courage is closer to hand."

She didn't know how to reply to that, so she held her tongue. He had done nothing to deserve her anger. In fact, he had done everything in his power to diffuse young Pauly's hair-trigger tension and prevent violence. He hadn't denied the outlaw's description of him as a gunfighter. He might even be a wanted man. But he'd tried to lessen her fear and maybe had just given her a compliment.

She opened her mouth to apologize, but his head had already tilted toward his chest, which rose and fell in a deep, slow rhythm.

She tilted her own head back, staring at the compartment roof, the fingers of her right hand worrying the bare place where her wedding band had rested. She remembered clearly Jack holding her nerve-chilled fingers in his warm ones, his eyes sparkling with love and fear and mischief as he slipped the ring on her finger.

And her wedding to Frank. She hadn't been able to meet his eyes, her stomach sick, half afraid Jack would burst into the church to denounce her for betraying him. Using that ridiculous fear to cover the impossible hope that he would do just that, that the news of his death had been a misunderstanding, that the body the army had sent home from Fort Kearny six months before belonged to some other poor soldier . . .

She had spoken the wedding vows clearly, a condemned woman still not believing the sentence, putting her head on the block with the calm certainty the executioner's axe wouldn't fall. Then Frank's hand had touched hers, his fingers on Jack's band, the calluses new and strange against her skin.

She hadn't thought of the wedding night until that moment, cocooned in her grief, letting others take responsibility for a life she no longer wanted to live. In that instant, the knowledge of what was happening, what she had committed herself to, became all too clear. She hadn't run only because her limbs had frozen in sudden terror.

Then she had met Frank's eyes, full of concern for her, those cavern-deep dark eyes inviting her to stay. And suddenly she hadn't wanted to run . . .

A jolt banged her head against the seat back, and her eyes flew open, the memory of squealing brakes echoing in her ears.

"The tracks?" she asked, surprised to find her voice thick with sleep.

"Cheyenne," Will said. "For certain this time."

Now she heard the other passengers' voices rising, the thump of boots as men shrugged into overcoats and fumbled for small bags. City noises rang from outside the window, shouts, the creaking of wagon wheels, the whistle of another train.

"We'd better hurry," Will said, rising. "Thanks to those dam —" He glanced at Nicky. "—darned thieves, we may not make our train to Denver, and I don't think we've got money for another set of tickets."

He helped Nicky to her feet, then offered a hand to Jordan. Only then did she notice that the gunfighter, Elijah Kelly, was gone.

Will saw her look. "He left as soon as we started to slow down. Maybe he was afraid the law would be waiting for him."

"Oh, Will." Nicky giggled. "Wasn't he just deliciously dangerous, though?"

Jordan bent down for the carpet bag under her seat to hide a sudden burn of disappointment, the feeling surprising and disturbing her. She couldn't pretend it was only regret that she hadn't thanked him for his calm handling of Pauly the Bandit King and his cronies. Kelly's hypocritical nickname and violent profession repelled her, but some part of her had noticed the grace in his movements, the magnetism in his eyes.

Frank's death had left her lonely and scared and, obviously, more vulnerable than she had thought. What disturbed her was not that she had found a man attractive or even that she wanted to be found attractive. What disturbed her was her desperation, the knowledge that never again would anyone love her the way Frank had loved her, the knowledge that she would grow old alone.

Lost in her thoughts, she almost ran over Nicky, who'd stopped in front of her on the train platform.

"You wait over there." Will shouted to be heard over the noise of the trains and the crowding passengers. "I'll find someone to unload our trunks and take them to the Denver train."

He led them out of the crush of people, but Jordan still felt overwhelmed by the whirl of activity breaking around them. The wind, blowing unhindered across the high prairie, bit at her cheeks and ears with malevolent glee.

"How could Will just leave us here?" Nicky complained as they turned their backs to the wind. "We'll freeze to death. Let's go find our train."

"Nicky, wait!" Jordan grabbed her cousin's sleeve. "He'll be back as soon as he can. We don't want to get lost."

"I bet that's our train over there," Nicky said, pointing to a southbound train, the smoke from its black engine streaming close along its back.

"Nicolette . . ."

Nicky reached out a delicately gloved hand to stop a man dressed in a Union Pacific Railroad company uniform. He turned with a snarl, but then caught sight of her wide blue eyes and the deep gold curls the wind had whipped from under her hat.

"May I help you, miss?"

"Is that the five o'clock train to Denver?" Nicky asked, her voice sweet as honeysuckle on a summer's day.

"Why, yes, miss. You're on your way to Denver?"

"We are." Nicky nibbled her lower lip. "I just don't know how we're going to get through that crowd to the train with our bags." She turned her head to wink at Jordan.

"Let me, miss," the man said eagerly. "I'll get you to the train safe and sound."

"Nicky, we've got to wait for Will," Jordan said, reaching for her bag, but the railroad employee had already whisked it away.

Nicky made a face. "Oh, for heaven's sake. You wait if you want. I'm going to the train before I lose my toes to frostbite."

She whirled to follow in the railroad employee's wake. Jordan quashed her impulse to chase after them and wring Nicky's neck. Will was Nicky's husband; her cousin should be the one freezing here on the platform so Will didn't have an apoplectic fit when he came back with the trunks.

"Sparrow? Ma'am?" a voice called from behind her.

Someone else looking for a lost soul. It would be easy to lose your companions in this crush. If she followed Nicky to the train, Will could wander Cheyenne for hours without guessing where they'd disappeared to.

She glanced beyond the train station at the hastily erected frame buildings and dusty streets that constituted Cheyenne. A booming train stop, but hardly a metropolis. Maybe it wouldn't take him hours, but that wasn't the point.

She clutched her arms closer to her chest as the wind snatched at her coat. With her luck, Will would take the trunks directly to the train, find Nicky, and they'd both sit there wondering where she'd gotten herself off to.

"Sparrow?"

The voice came from behind her right shoulder. She

jumped, stumbling as she turned to find herself face-to-face with Elijah Kelly, the cat-eyed gunfighter.

"I'm sorry to be so forward, ma'am, but I couldn't get your attention."

"What?" She wasn't sure what he'd said; she was absorbing the fact that she had to look up at him. She was nearly as tall as most men, taller than many, but Kelly stood at least six feet. He was so tautly slender she'd expected him to be shorter. He was standing impossibly close to her, to be heard over the noise. She felt almost enveloped by his swirling duster.

"Isn't that what your friend called you? Sparrow?"

"Oh, no, she said 'Jo-jo'." Jordan laughed, though the humor felt bitter. She must look like a little drab bird, in her brown traveling dress, with her mousy hair and plain features. Well, perhaps a large drab bird. "Jordan Braddock."

She stuck out her hand before it occurred to her that a lady probably did not offer her hand to a gunfighter. He took it with southern courtesy, his hands now hidden in thick leather gloves. But she still felt the warmth as his long fingers wrapped hers.

"My pleasure, Mrs. Braddock."

"I'm glad you caught me," she said, trying not to notice that he hadn't released her hand. "I meant to apologize to you for being rude earlier. I guess the outlaws frightened me, after all. I wanted to thank you for handling them so well. I'm sure that Pauly the Bandit King would have shot Will on the slightest provocation. There was something strange about his eyes . . ."

*Shut up, Jordan.* She was babbling. She never babbled. But Kelly seemed to have forgotten he held her hand, and she didn't want to be rude again by jerking it free. And though she was speaking to the turned up collar of his duster, she knew he was watching her with his unblinking panther's eyes, and she almost felt like a sparrow waiting for a great black tomcat to pounce.

God, even her thoughts were babbling.

"You handled Pauly and your friend Will quite ably by yourself," the gunfighter insisted. "I'm afraid my presence did more to give our outlaw friend an excuse to show off than to discourage him."

Jordan tilted her head to meet his gaze. What was she afraid of? She'd never see him again. "Is your reputation really so terrible, Mr. Kelly? I must confess I've never heard of you."

His mouth curved only slightly, but the change in his eyes was remarkable. The color in them deepened, and they sparked with purely human wickedness.

"Why, I'm crushed Mrs. Braddock. I'm as fast on the draw as Wild Bill Hickok. Mr. Pauly said so himself." His white teeth glinted briefly through his smile. "Don't believe a word an outlaw or a cowboy says, Mrs. Braddock. They're naturally dramatic. I did have a bit of trouble out in Laramie, but as I said, it was all a misunderstanding. The marshal assured me that all of the wanted posters will be destroyed."

He wasn't telling the whole truth. Not that she thought he was lying, but she felt he was trying to distract her from something.

Perhaps it had worked; she'd almost forgotten he still held her hand. "Indeed. I hope the rest of your journey is less eventful than the portion we shared, Mr. Kelly." She stepped back to give him a hint and pulled gently on her hand. "But I must be on my way. I wouldn't want to miss my train."

"Of course. I'm sorry to detain you. I meant to speak with you before I left the train, but I had to get *him* off before a porter noticed him."

His left hand gestured down to what she had taken on the train to be a gray carpet bag. A bag which hadn't been there beside him when she'd first turned around to face him. A carpet bag with its dark-fringed ears lying back along its head, its silver eyes staring up at her, as human as Kelly's.

A wolf. She'd met a flesh-and-blood gunfighter, and he'd brought a wolf on the train. Her nephews- and nieces-in-law would have writhing fits of jealousy. She wouldn't tell them that her mouth dropped open, leaving her speechless.

The silver and gray creature was panting despite the chill —from the stress of the crowd and the noise, Jordan guessed —showing long, gleaming teeth. But it was his paws that caught her attention.

"My, what big feet you have," she murmured, mesmerized by his inquiring eyes.

The gunfighter turned her hand, bringing her attention back to him. She didn't want to take her eyes off the wolf, but he struck her as being less dangerous than the man in front of her.

Kelly curled her fingers over her palm, pressing them tight. "I am sorry I could not do the same for your friend Nicky, but her husband is alive to buy her another."

Jordan looked down at her dress. A modestly cut cocoa brown silk with pale cocoa trim suited for traveling, suitable for a respectable matron of any age. She wore no sign of mourning. She'd left all her black back in Connecticut with the graves.

"How did you know . . . ?"

He'd released her hand, and she raised it close to her, uncurling her fingers one by one. There in her palm sat a familiar plain gold band, with the funny dent in one spot from the time she'd caught her hand in a carriage door. Her fingers suddenly shaking from more than the cold, she pulled off her left glove and slipped on the ring. It slid over her scratched knuckle without even a tug.

She closed her fingers into a tight fist. She knew her face burned from repressed tears as she raised her eyes again.

"How can I thank you, Mr. Kelly? I—"

But he had already turned and slipped away. She could see the path of his black hat through the crowd, but before she could give in to the impulse to rush after him, a hand grabbed her arm.

"Jordan, I've got the trunks. Where's Nicky?"

She turned, hardly recognizing Will in the rush of emotions pouring through her. "What?"

"Jordan, where's my wife?"

"She got cold and went on to the train. It's right over there."

The anxious pallor disappeared from Will's cheeks, replaced with wind-bitten ruddiness. "I'm glad she got out of this wind. What a godforsaken spot." He caught sight of Jordan's face and paused. "You must be freezing. Come along to the train."

"Just a minute, Will. I've got to find . . ." But as she turned back to look toward the station, she knew she'd lost him. Just as well. She couldn't possibly have thanked him. It was just a ring. She'd said it, and she'd meant it. And yet . . .

She pressed her fist against her chest and covered it with her gloved hand, the one still warm from the gunfighter's touch.

# Chapter 2

May, 1878

High, icy clouds streamed across a frost-blue sky. The sun burst through frequently, dazzling on the ice that hadn't yet melted from the corners and crevasses of the train platform, but the frigid yellow ball made no change in the air temperature, which Jordan estimated to be somewhere just above freezing. With the brisk breeze, it felt even colder.

"I should have waited a month," she muttered, clutching her overcoat closer with one hand, the other firmly on the handle of her paint box. "Maybe two."

But another month in Denver would have snapped her fragile hold on her sanity. With Nicky by turns glowing and petulant with her pregnancy, complaining to Jordan every time Will neglected her, and Will thinking Jordan had nothing better to do than care for Nicky and look up law precedents for him, the past six months had felt like years. Not to mention that Leland Hedgepeth, Simon's old law school friend and Will's new employer, had an unmarried (and to Jordan's mind, unmarriageable) partner whom Lenora Hedgepeth insisted on sitting next to Jordan at every dinner party she held.

No, freezing to death was preferable to another month in Denver.

"Ma'am?"

She glanced around to see a teenage boy beside her, his tawny hair slicked down, his freckles sharp in his winterpale face.

"May I get your bags for you?"

"Yes, please. These are mine." She had two large bags and an easel. Altogether they probably weighed as much as the boy, but he hefted them with ease.

"To the Colonel's, ma'am?"

Jordan pulled a letter from her coat pocket and checked the address. "Is that the Grand Hotel?"

"Yes, ma'am."

"Then that's where I want to go."

She followed the boy off the train platform and into the streets of Oxtail, Colorado. Situated nearly equidistant between Cheyenne and Denver, the town had taken longer than Greeley, farther east, to establish itself as a permanent settlement. Leland Hedgepeth had told her the train had reached Oxtail only the previous spring, and she could easily pick out the signs of new construction—a solid brick bank, a block-long mercantile store, the freshly whitewashed Episcopal church down the street. They would soon make the older, clapboard businesses look out of place.

They didn't outshine the Grand Hotel, however. Obviously long established, its elegant three-story facade and smart front porch would hold their own against the newest buildings of the train station boom.

The boy led her up through the front door of the hotel and into the reception area, which consisted mainly of a wide, sweeping staircase carpeted in forest green and a long reception counter with a darker green marble top. Behind the counter, a plump woman with an emerald cap on her gray hair sorted mail into rows of boxes while a white-haired, white-mustached gentleman in a matching white shirt and gray suspenders thumbed through an account book.

"Colonel, this lady wants a room," the boy announced.

Jordan stepped forward, offering her hand before the frowning Colonel could chastise the boy for ruining his elegant atmosphere. "Colonel Treadwell? My name is Jordan Braddock. I have a letter of introduction from—"

"Leland Hedgepeth," the Colonel finished for her, his smile causing his mustache to dance. "My pleasure, Mrs. Braddock."

He took her hand and pressed it heartily. "How is Leland, that old scoundrel? I got a note from him yesterday morning telling me to expect your visit. A painter, are you? The loveliest painter I've ever seen, I must say. I met Albert Bierstadt when he passed through Colorado last year, and he was nowhere near as easy on the eyes."

Jordan blinked, searching for a reply, but the Colonel had turned another frown on the boy behind her.

"What? Still here, lad? Don't just stand around. Take up the lady's bags."

"Which room, sir?" the boy asked, uncowed.

"Thirty-one. Third floor in the back." The Colonel's smile returned to Jordan. "It's another flight of stairs, but those are the newest rooms. And you'll have a lovely view of the mountains."

"Thank you," Jordan managed to breathe before the Colonel launched in again.

"I understand you won't be staying with us long. Want to see our Rockies up close, eh? They rival the Alps, my dear, and I can say that with all honesty, having visited the Alps myself in 'forty-five. Leland says he's recommended Battlement Park. Don't know why he sent you all the way north to Oxtail instead of having you get off the train in Longmont. You'll have to go back south to Longmont to take the road

36

west into the Park. That's the best route into the mountains."

"I told Mr. Hedgepeth I wanted to see the foothills and the prairie as well as the mountains." She had only caught a glimpse of them on the trip to Denver, but their spare beauty pulled her almost as much as the mountains did.

"Eh? And quite right you are, my dear. We've got our own scenery, not quite so grand, perhaps, but we like it. I can see you're a woman of perception. Necessary in an artist, isn't that right? But Leland wanted me to arrange for your transportation. We'll make sure you see all there is to see between here and Battlement Park!"

The gray-haired woman turned around, an envelope still in her hand. "You're traveling all by yourself, dear?"

Jordan nodded, her head still spinning from the Colonel's merciless verbal barrage. She could imagine his tenacity in battle.

"Mr. Hedgepeth thought it would be safe," she hastened to explain. She had been surprised by the lawyer's assistance in quelling Will's objections to her traveling on her own, but she intended to make full use of it. "I'm not a young girl and am well suited to looking after myself—"

"It's just like that English lady a few years back," the gray-haired woman interrupted. "I did think that was so courageous. Traveling about by herself. You know the one I'm talking about, Colonel. It was in all the papers . . ."

"Isabella Bird," the Colonel said, his own eyes misting. "Ah, yes, a lady indeed. Brave and determined, but as refined as your finest china, Mrs. P. I had the great pleasure to meet her in Denver that fall."

Mrs. P. smiled at Jordan. "What a great adventure. I'd go with you myself, dear, if I was twenty years younger."

Jordan managed a return smile, a knot of uncertainty loosening in her heart. She knew that no one back home, except

Aunt Rue, understood her decision to leave Connecticut, and even Aunt Rue might not approve of her gallivanting about the wild countryside without an escort.

The idea frightened her more than a little. She had been forced to learn independence early, when her parents had died, but she had never been truly alone before today. Still, the long, cold winter in Denver had chilled more than her bones, and she was afraid of succumbing to worse than boredom if she didn't do something to dispel the phantoms around her heart.

The Colonel closed his account book with a flourish. "Mrs. Pepperill, can you watch the counter for me for the rest of the morning?"

"Of course." Mrs. Pepperill stuffed her last envelope in room twenty-five's box and brushed her hands together. "Celia can see to poor Mr. Frederick's tea, and there's nothing else that needs to be done before this afternoon."

Colonel Treadwell was already shrugging into a neatly tailored pearl-gray coat. "Thank you Mrs. P. As always, you're indispensable. Come along with me, Mrs. Braddock."

He advanced around the end of the counter, and though he must have been an inch shorter than Jordan, he swept her along like a favorite granddaughter.

"It's lucky you came by so early this morning, my dear," he said, leading her out through the front door and into the street. "I usually have a horse available to let to travelers such as yourself, but my best gelding's come down lame and my mare's got a young foal this year. But if you've a mind to pay a reasonable price for an excellent riding horse, I know just where to take you. The Jacksons have the best horses in the state."

"Riding horse?" Jordan thought she might not have heard him right. "That's really not necessary, Colonel Treadwell. I thought, I mean, isn't there a stagecoach—"

"No trouble at all, Mrs. Braddock," the Colonel assured her. "My pleasure to see you suitably outfitted." He swung into the yard of Treadwell's Livery Stable, bellowing, "James! Leroy! My buggy! Come along, boys, I don't have all day."

As the two stable hands set to hitching up the Colonel's vehicle, Jordan tried again. "Really, Colonel, a stage-coach—"

"No stage between here and Longmont any longer," the Colonel answered blithely, his sharp eyes on the stable hands. "Just the train. And you've already done that on your way up here."

"Perhaps I might rent a buggy, then, or find a ride with a farmer headed that way? I have too much baggage to carry on a horse."

"We'll send it on," Colonel Treadwell stated, with military confidence in the deployment of supplies. "Your luggage will be waiting for you in Battlement Park. Don't need much for a couple days' ride. Here we are, Mrs. Braddock. Allow me."

She took his offered hand and allowed him to assist her into the buggy. The Colonel scrambled up beside her and clucked to his horse, a handsome roan who set out at a proud trot.

"Ah, what a glorious morning," the Colonel stated, turning the horse's head toward the mountains. The brisk breeze kissed his cheeks and nose with color. "A drive is just the thing for a morning like this. I wholeheartedly agree with Mrs. P. If I were twenty years younger . . ."

Jordan listened to the Colonel's words just closely enough to nod and murmur in the right places, content to let him dominate the conversation while she readjusted her plans. A horse. It hadn't occurred to her that anyone would think she planned to *ride* to Battlement Park.

Once she and the Colonel arrived at their destination, she could explain to him and his friends that buying a horse was out of the question. She rode adequately, but she much preferred to travel by buggy or wagon. Perhaps the Jacksons could rent her a buggy as well as a horse. If not, she could always take the train back south to Longmont and then the coach service from Longmont to the hotel in Battlement Park.

To ride off on a horse through unknown country . . . What would Will and Nicky say? What a foolish, reckless, terrifying idea. She might encounter bears or wolves. Her horse might spook. What if the weather changed? What if . . .

Her own smile stopped her. She tried to frown, but her lips wouldn't cooperate. She was sure the fluttery feeling in her stomach was the result of purely justified fear. And yet for the first time since arriving in Colorado six months ago, she found herself anticipating the future, pressing back regrets and grief for a few precious moments.

She fought down a laugh. She didn't want to take the train to Longmont like a responsible, respectable widow. She wanted to let the brisk, wintery breeze blow away her caution, let danger and adventure crack some of the ice around her heart. She wanted to experience life. She wanted to find out what happened next.

Elijah clutched his duster closed and turned his face from the wind that sang down the mountains like an icy siren calling for a lover. Another time he might have heeded the call, turning his horse's head into the keenest gust, burning his senses with the sharp scent of pine, the blue blaze of sky, daring the heedless mountains to take him.

But not today.

His horse's feet knew the way as well as he did, following the narrow path through the newly-green brush. As he topped the small rise, Elijah's hand dropped from his coat, the wind losing its bite as it flowed into the grassy depression below.

Achilles' pace quickened, whether from the horse's own desire or an unconscious direction from him, Elijah wasn't sure. Before them, smoke streamed from a ranch house's chimney pipe. Almost supper time. Elijah's stomach tightened, though he wasn't hungry.

His eyes took in the familiar details: the sturdy barn and stable, painted red to suit Maggie's Kentucky tastes, the pair of young horses waiting in the paddock, the apple trees just unfurling their shocking green leaves.

Distracted by the view, he had no chance to defend himself against the attack when it came. A fury of motion burst from behind a boulder in the path ahead, an enormous explosion of silent fur that sent adrenaline pumping to Elijah's heart and caused Achilles' eyes to roll white with fear. The gelding's scream shredded the rushing wind. He reared and twisted, his spine suddenly elastic. Elijah grabbed the saddle horn in one hand, reins in the other, struggling to stay seated until the gelding's forefeet once more hit the ground.

Before Achilles could lift off again, Elijah fought the gelding's head down, only sheer strength preventing the horse from taking flight down the path. Once the gelding recognized the source of the attack, he slowly stopped struggling against Elijah's hands, but his sides heaved with remembered panic, and his eyes burned with killing fury.

Meanwhile, the perpetrator had jumped to the side of the path, prepared for any sudden movement on the part of horse or rider. His tongue hung at a ridiculous angle from the side of his mouth, and his eyes shone in mad delight at the success of his ambush.

Elijah couldn't yell for fear of spooking his horse again. And the wolf knew it. Elijah settled for a fierce glare. The beast's tail jerked back and forth as it laughed.

Elijah nudged Achilles forward. Out of the corner of his eye, he could see the wolf's tail stop, his eyes darkening in disappointment at Elijah's bowing out of the game. But then he sprang back into movement, dashing past the skittish gelding and bounding ahead along the path.

He stopped and looked back, ears pricked, anticipation replacing the momentary madness in his eyes. Another bound and he turned again. He whined, more piercing than the wind.

In response, Elijah let Achilles move into a slow trot, though it jarred his bones down the incline. The wolf raced ahead, his hind legs seeming to outpace his front, looking as though he might bowl himself over at any moment. At the bottom of the hill, he skidded to a stop, turning impatiently to wait for the horse.

"All right, Loki," Elijah conceded, giving in to his laughter. "It feels good to be home, doesn't it? Go on ahead."

The wolf's ears flattened, and he dashed down the path toward the ranch, as undignified as any cub.

Elijah envied him that. The word "home" still burned on his tongue. He had no home. Even before the war, he had stopped thinking of South Carolina as home. His brief visit last fall had confirmed that. And this ranch . . .

He knew he could gallop down to the ranch house with as much heedless certainty of his welcome as Loki. Yet he held Achilles in check, letting the familiar surroundings absorb him slowly. For if the welcome came all at once, effusive and sincere as only the Jacksons would welcome him, it might overwhelm him with the knowledge that he didn't belong.

He couldn't have said exactly when that knowledge had

begun to hurt. But each time he returned to Oxtail, he became more aware of it.

Impatiently, he shook off the heaviness that had settled around his shoulders. He liked his life the way it was. And even if he didn't, he couldn't change it, so there was no sense in sentimental melancholy. He loosened his hold on Achilles, letting the gelding leap forward into a gallop.

By the time he reached the ranch house, Loki had already terrorized the chickens and treed one of the cats. Elijah found the wolf dancing beneath an apple tree, a little gray tabby dangling her tail just out of reach of his gleaming canines.

"Leave Dallas alone, you big oaf," Elijah advised, dismounting. Loki grinned. Elijah didn't trust the wolf around the chickens, not when he was as playful as this. But he didn't fear for the tabby. By this evening, she would be curled up between the wolf's paws in front of the stove like the old friends they were.

Elijah left Achilles hitched to the porch rail and knocked at the door. No answer. He checked the porch window. A pot sat simmering on the stove, untended.

"Loki, where's March? Where's Maggie?"

Loki ignored him, making another futile leap for the cat's twitching tail.

"Loki, find Maggie."

With a sigh, the wolf dropped back to the ground and shook himself. Sending Elijah a disgusted look, he crossed the garden from the apple tree to the porch. Apparently by chance, he passed close enough to Achilles to annoy the gelding, but not close enough to get kicked, before he trotted across the yard toward the barn.

Leaving Achilles tethered to the porch, Elijah followed, uneasy despite his belief that Loki would sense if there had been any trouble. Outside trouble. He almost turned back to the house, the untended pot nagging at him. At this hour, Maggie was probably here alone. If anything had happened, if she had miscarried again . . .

Then he heard voices from the barn and laughter, punctuated by a bark from Loki. He reached the barn door, and the wind pushed him through into the dimness and warmth.

"Elijah?"

Maggie appeared from the gloom of an open stall and ran to him, hugging him fiercely. He couldn't remember exactly when that had started, either, and it still surprised him.

"Oh, sorry," she added, backing away and swiping at the straw she'd left on his coat.

"Maggie . . ." His eyes took in the half-full wheelbarrow, the pitchfork leaning against the stall door, and her loose braid, strands of red hair plastered to her cheek. "You haven't been mucking stalls?"

Her cheeks flushed, but not from embarrassment. "That's a fine greeting after all these months, Mr. Elijah Kelly."

"Where's Lemuel? Does March know about this? The doctor said—"

"The doctor said I could cook meals and do laundry. Mucking stalls is no harder than laundry, and a hell of a lot more enjoyable. Leave Lemuel out of this. He had errands in town. And as for March—"

"We've just had this discussion," March's voice interrupted. Elijah hadn't seen him emerge from the stall, but he stood leaning against it, his hand resting on Loki's head. "There's no need for you to have your head taken off, too, 'Lije."

Maggie turned her glare on her husband. "March agrees that it's perfectly all right for me to muck out the stalls, as long as I take it easy."

March's hands clenched. "That's not exactly what *I* said,

Maggie. I know you want to spend time with the horses—"

"That's right," Maggie said, as sweetly as if he'd just agreed with her. "Besides, Dr. Markham said if I got through my third month, the baby should be fine. I'm almost to my fifth month now." Unconsciously, she put a protective hand over the swelling of her belly.

"He *said* it would be a good sign," March corrected, but a smile tugged at one corner of his mouth. "What he didn't say was how *I* was supposed to survive these next few months trying to rein you in."

"I'd say you're up for the job." Maggie eyed him speculatively. "You've got good hands, and you know how to use them."

Elijah choked back a laugh. March blushed like a schoolboy caught kissing a girl in the cloakroom.

"Where's Achilles, Elijah?" Maggie asked, composed, though her eyes sparked with at least temporary victory. "I'll bet he could use a good rubdown. Unless you've shot him?"

"Not yet. He's hitched to the porch."

"Since March is so worried about my health, I'll let him take care of that old nag." Maggie smiled like a cat.

"Achilles is a damn good horse," March objected.

"He bites," Maggie and Elijah reminded him in chorus.

"Among other things," Elijah added.

"I could have taken care of that years ago," March said, unruffled, "but Lucas thought it was funny. It didn't seem right to correct his horse after he died."

"He's never tried to bite *you*," Maggie muttered.

"He's a good working horse."

"And you're welcome to him," Elijah broke in. "Just tell me where my horse is, and you can have that one back."

"Hallo, there! Where is everybody?" The jovial bellow carried from the yard, above the keening wind.

45

"Sounds like the Colonel," March said, startled.

"Damn!" Maggie swiped at her skirt, rearranging the straw and dirt. "Well, if people come calling without warning, they just have to take what they get."

She swept toward the barn door, but March laid a hand on Elijah's arm. "You did get that business in Laramie cleared up?"

Heat crept up Elijah's neck, but his voice stayed cold. "Colonel Treadwell has no reason to come looking for me. I wouldn't bring any danger here to you and Maggie."

March's clear eyes darkened. "For God's sake, 'Lije. If you need help, you come to us. We owe you—"

"You don't owe me anything!"

March dropped his hand, his fist clenching. "You're family, 'Lije. We'd call on you if we had trouble. Don't make me feel like I'm not as much a friend to you."

The sudden tightness in Elijah's gut loosened a little. He nodded, briefly. "I'm sorry." Then forced a smile. "Of course, the last time I asked for your help, I ended up with Achilles."

March grinned back. "What are friends for?"

As March started to follow his wife, Elijah cleared his throat. "Before you go out there . . . you didn't get your shirt buttons straight."

March's face burned fiercely beneath his sun-browned skin, but Elijah didn't allow himself a laugh until his friend's frantic fumbling revealed his shirt correctly buttoned after all.

He dodged March's fist with ease and slipped outside, using his hat brim to protect his eyes from the sudden glare.

A buggy sat parked in the middle of the yard. Beside it, Colonel Treadwell spoke animatedly to Maggie, his hand gesturing toward the barn. Behind and a little to the side of

46

them stood a woman.

She wore a deep blue traveling dress and a stylish, but conservative blue hat trimmed with black. It surprised him that he remembered so vividly the fine line of her jaw, and her hair, the color of polished cedar by autumn firelight. And he remembered that calm with which she held herself apart, the calm of a storm about to break.

She glanced toward the barn. Her eyes widened when she saw him, and though he was fifty feet from her, he knew those eyes were a deeper sapphire than her dress. Perhaps she uttered a noise of surprise, for at that moment the Colonel also glanced toward the barn. His wind-reddened face darkened in a scowl.

"Kelly." The word was a curse. "I see you haven't done us the favor of getting yourself shot yet."

# Chapter 3

The gunfighter smiled, but his stride turned predatory as he stalked closer. "Colonel. Always a pleasure, suh." He touched the brim of his hat. "Mrs. Braddock, am I correct? It is truly a pleasure to see you again, ma'am."

Jordan found herself once again offering her hand to a gunman, despite the frown of disapproval on the Colonel's face.

"Mr. Kelly."

This time he merely pressed her hand briefly and released it. Yet he still left an imprint of warmth on her palm. She remembered correctly, then, the silky steel of his voice, his appraising stare. Unaccountably, she wished herself back in Lenora Hedgepeth's parlor, laboring on the rose she was needlepointing for a pillow cover.

"You know this man?" the Colonel asked, indignant.

A gust of wind caught her, and she shivered. "Yes, we met on the train to Cheyenne last fall." Her left hand tightened into a fist, and she felt the pressure of the ring on her third finger. "He did me a great service."

"Humph." The Colonel maintained his glare at the gunfighter. "You'll do well to steer clear of the likes of that one, Mrs. Braddock. He's got the devil in his soul."

Looking into those dangerous eyes, she could well believe it.

"One of these days he'll step out of line and give me the excuse I need to see him swinging from the end of a six-foot rope. Mark my words—"

"Colonel Treadwell!" the flame-haired woman, Maggie, interrupted him fiercely. "Elijah is a guest here on our ranch, and if you wish to accept our hospitality, I expect you to treat him with respect."

The Colonel's brow wrinkled in distress. "Margaret, my dear, I've tried to tell you time and again—"

"Colonel Treadwell, good to see you again, sir."

Jordan had seen the other man pass them to collect the big bay gelding tethered in front of the house. He blended so perfectly into the ranch surroundings that she'd hardly noticed him, but his quiet greeting expertly diffused the escalating tempers.

And when he turned his smile on her, the warmth in his sky blue eyes drew a return smile from her.

"March," the Colonel greeted him gruffly. "Allow me to introduce Mrs. Jordan Braddock. As I was just telling your wife, Mrs. Braddock is looking for a good, sensible horse to take her to Battlement Park. Mrs. Braddock, March Jackson, the best horseman in Larimer County. March breeds top-notch horses."

"March and Maggie breed top-notch horses," Maggie said under her breath to Jordan.

"This one's certainly a handsome fellow." Jordan reached out a hand to the muscular bay March led.

She saw the twitch in the gelding's lip, but was no match for the horse's whipcord swiftness. His teeth flashed for her hand like a snake striking. March was faster. He jerked down on the bit with a speed and strength that caused the beast's nostrils to flare in pain and shock. But Jordan could still see murder in the horse's eyes.

Almost as an afterthought, she jerked back her hand, her

heart jumping in her chest.

*This was a bad idea.*

"Are you all right?"

The question came in a chorus. Jordan forced a faint smile to her lips. "Yes, yes. I'm fine. I'm sorry I startled him."

Maggie scowled. "You didn't startle him. He's a mean son-of-a-bitch."

Jordan could tell the woman's profanity offended the Colonel, but she appreciated it. Maggie's matter-of-fact statement kept her from turning and running back the way she'd come.

"I'll put him away," March said.

"Why don't the rest of us follow and get out of the wind." Maggie put a hand on Jordan's arm, leading her toward the barn. "I'm sorry about Achilles. He's like that with everybody. March would never allow one of *our* horses to act that way."

"He's *not* mine," Elijah asserted from behind them, his voice tight. "That horse is a menace."

"For once we're in agreement," the Colonel said, hurrying to hold the door for the ladies. "I don't know what your cousin ever saw in that animal, Margaret. I can assure you, Mrs. Braddock, that I wouldn't have brought you here if I didn't have the fullest confidence in the temperament of March Jackson's horses."

The sweet scent of hay and the strong odor of horse assaulted Jordan's nose as she entered the barn. The Colonel closed the door behind them, and the sudden cessation of the wind seemed to raise the temperature fifteen degrees. March Jackson already had Achilles' saddle and bridle off and was rubbing him down. The gelding stood quietly, apparently docile, but Jordan thought his eyes gleamed with anger that she'd escaped his teeth.

*Definitely a bad idea.* "Mrs. Jackso —"

"Maggie, please," Maggie insisted, steering her toward the row of stalls at the stable end of the barn.

"Maggie." Jordan glanced back over her shoulder. Achilles still watched her. So did Elijah Kelly. She was starting to feel a trifle stalked. "I have a confession to make. I'm an adequate horsewoman, I suppose, but I may have gotten myself in over my head. Perhaps I should just take the train back to Longmont after all."

"Nonsense, Mrs. Braddock," the Colonel began, but Maggie cut him off with a wave of her hand.

"That's up to you, Mrs. Braddock—"

"Jordan."

"Jordan." Maggie's smile was as warm as her husband's. "This is your expedition."

Jordan missed a step at Maggie's words. Yes, it was hers, wasn't it? For a moment she lost contact with her surroundings, trying to remember the last time she'd acted on her own without considering what other people would think. She had almost always done what she wanted—Frank had supported even her wildest whims. But Frank had always been there to ask, to rely on.

Her throat tightened against a sudden wave of grief. *Oh, God, Frank. I miss you.*

And then she was back in the barn, hearing Maggie's voice again. "And this one is my mare, Ari. Her full name is Aristotle, but the purists among us thought that was too masculine."

The buckskin mare in the next stall pricked her ears at the sound of her name, pushing her dusky muzzle over the door toward her mistress. Maggie stepped forward, blowing into the mare's quivering nostrils. She murmured something Jordan couldn't hear and brushed the mare's dun cheeks with her fingertips.

She motioned Jordan forward. "Ari has the heart of a lion and the soul of a philosopher. *She* doesn't bite."

Jordan stepped up to the stall door warily. The mare watched her with interest, but Jordan saw no malice in the soft brown eyes.

"Hello, there." She showed the mare her hand, then tentatively reached over to pat the horse's neck. Ari pushed slightly against her palm.

"She likes to have her ears scratched."

Jordan moved her fingertips to the base of the mare's ears. Ari sighed. Jordan scratched harder. The horse stretched her head forward in oblivious delight.

"There you go," the Colonel said, his confident voice filling the stable. "What did I tell you? They'll set you up with a fine horse, Mrs. Braddock."

Jordan tried scratching Ari's chin. She liked that, too. "You mean they have another horse just like this?" she asked.

"No," Maggie said. "Ari's one of a kind. But we do have a horse I think would be just right for you, if you decide you'd like to ride. A nice coffee-colored bay. A little shaggy yet, from winter, but generally gentle and exceptionally smart."

"Maggie!" Elijah Kelly had faded into the shadows along the stable wall, but his voice brought him sharply back into Jordan's focus. "You cannot give away my horse."

"I'm not in the business of *giving* horses away," Maggie said, her stern voice almost hiding the mischief in her green-flecked eyes. "And I don't know what you're talking about. What about your horse?"

The gunfighter's eyes flattened. He wasn't playing. "If he's recovered, I want him back."

"He? Recovered?"

"From his pneumonia." Though the words were clipped, the southern accent had intensified. "And I don't want to hear that he's too old and slow for me. He's gotten me out of more tight places with his brains than his speed."

"Ohhhhh." Maggie drew out the word with exaggerated enlightenment. "You mean Rover."

Jordan choked. Glancing up, she saw that the gunfighter's eyes had finally sparked with reluctant humor.

"Your horse is named Rover?" she asked, almost managing to say it with a straight face.

"I promised my son he could name him." He crossed his arms defensively. "He was four at the time."

Maggie laughed. "For once you got what you deserved."

Elijah shook his head, trying not to grin at the redhead. Even the Colonel allowed a chuckle to escape.

Jordan once more found herself forcing a smile. Oddly, she had assumed the gunfighter didn't have a family. It didn't matter, but it was unexpected. The surprise seemed to have spoiled her laughter.

"Rover's recovering nicely," Maggie admitted. "But you can't have him back until the weather warms up. He *is* getting older, Elijah." Her face softened at the look in the gunfighter's eyes. "But he's got some more good years in him—if you don't get caught in any more blizzards. You can live with Achilles for another month or two."

"Easy for you to say."

"In any case, I wasn't talking about Rover. I was talking about Smoke." Maggie turned back to Jordan. "She's a good little mare, sensible for her age. And she won't let you get lost."

Jordan couldn't be embarrassed that her fears appeared so obvious. Maggie's warmth was too open.

"You think Smoke's big enough?" March asked, closing a

stall door behind Achilles and strolling up to the group. "She's a little small for me."

Maggie glanced sharply at Jordan, apparently noticing for the first time the disparity in their heights. "She may be nearly as tall as you are, March, but she's a lot more delicately built." She frowned suddenly, looking Jordan up and down once more. "Delicate." Then she smiled. "I'll bet she weighs less than I do right now."

Jordan shared in the infectious laughter, though her cheeks pinkened at the reference to Maggie's pregnancy. One no more talked about such things in mixed company in Denver than one did in Connecticut.

"You've got a point there," March said with a slow smile for his wife. "And Smoke will do right by her, that's for sure. Prince and the mares were down in the lower pasture this morning. If they're still there, I can have Smoke back in half an hour."

"Just about dinner time," Maggie said approvingly. "You and the Colonel will stay for the midday meal with us, of course, Mrs. Braddock? Good." She winked at Jordan, knowing she hadn't given her time to reply. "It's been a while since I've gotten to hear all the gossip from Denver. Then after dinner, if Smoke's to your liking, we'll fix you up with a saddle and bridle and settle on a price. You'll want to sell her back to us on your return to Denver, I expect, so you'll hardly know it cost you anything."

"Let me haggle the price for you, Mrs. Braddock," the Colonel said, his eyes narrowing. "That Margaret's a shrewd businesswoman, for all her pretty smiles."

Maggie laughed, taking the Colonel's arm and leading him toward the barn door. "You'd better bargain for yourself, Jordan. Once Colonel Treadwell gets a taste of the molasses cake I baked this morning, he'll be butter in my hands."

When Jordan moved to follow them, Elijah Kelly pushed away from the wall to walk beside her. She felt relieved that he didn't offer her his arm.

"What takes you to Battlement Park, Mrs. Braddock?"

An ordinary conversational opening, yet he sounded genuinely curious.

"The wind." The oblique honesty of her own answer surprised her, and she hastened into a more conventional explanation. "My brother-in-law, Will, the one you met on the train? His employer suggested I see Battlement Park. He said it has many stunning vistas to paint. I'm an artist, you see."

He hardly seemed to have heard. "The wind?"

"Like the leaves." She laughed, trying to sound frivolous. "Just blown about like a dried leaf, here and there, waiting to see where I end up."

"I don't think so." He stopped, looking out toward the greening foothills, forcing her to stop, too. "Here along the Front Range, the wind generally blows down from the mountains, not up into them."

She frowned, annoyed. "It was just an analogy."

He glanced at her, the thin spring light slanting across his hazel eyes. "No, I think maybe it is the wind taking you into the mountains. It calls to some people. But it doesn't blow you along. You have to fly against it, Sparrow."

She had no reply to that. She didn't intend to explain to a stranger that she wasn't going to fight anymore, that she didn't care where she went or how she got there as long as the journey helped block the memories of thin ice and black water, cold death, and missing Frank.

So she said nothing, simply wrapping her coat closer against the cold and stepping forward once more toward the ranch house.

*Dear Aunt Rue,*

*Tomorrow I ride from Oxtail to Longmont, the first stop on my journey to Battlement Park, on my new horse, Smoke. Horse? I hear you ask, and well you may. She's a pretty little thing, despite being as shaggy and compact as an Indian pony. And she's young—about four, according to the woman I bought her from, so she's got the look in her eye of one who will run for home if I turn my back on her. But Maggie Jackson says she can travel forty miles a day if needed, won't step in a prairie dog hole, and if I get caught in a late spring blizzard, she'll carry me safely to the nearest barn.*

*I am enclosing a sketch of Smoke and one of me in my new riding outfit (don't you dare show it to any of the relatives). Imagine my consternation when Mr. Jackson led out my new horse with her borrowed bridle and Mexican style saddle. I am expected to ride cavalier fashion! Apparently this is how Miss Isabella Bird, an English lady who came through Colorado in seventy-three, travelled, and as a mature widow traveling alone, I am supposed to be as eccentric as Miss Bird. Perhaps they're not far wrong.*

*I thought at first it was a joke, until Mr. Jackson's sister Harriet (they call her "Harry"!) arrived from the far pasture wearing a pair of blue jeans like the boys wear at home. Since I had nothing suitable in my wardrobe for riding straddle, Maggie insisted I borrow her split-skirt riding dress, with bloomers as you see in my sketch. She is in a family way, and so will have no use for it for months. She must be four inches shorter than I, but the bloomers are so baggy that they cover my ankles, and the skirt is still longer than the one worn by the redoubtable Miss Bird.*

*Miss Harriet also insisted I borrow a pair of Mr. Jackson's blue jeans!! in case the weather turns colder again. I had to roll up the bottoms and tie the waist with a rope. I would rather freeze than be seen so! I suppose if it gets cold enough, I can wear them over the bloomers and under the skirt.*

*Colonel Treadwell, the proprietor of the hotel at which I am staying, says his right shoulder, which took a bullet wound in the war, predicts clear, warmer weather coming. I pray he is right!*

*Maggie and Miss Harriet are like no other ladies I've met, even in Colorado, although I have heard stories of women who run their own ranches and even rope steers. Do you remember the gunfighter I mentioned meeting on the train last fall? He is a good friend of the Jacksons'. Miss Harriet fair threw herself into his arms on seeing him. And Maggie swears worse than Henry Junior. But she has a good heart, and in only one day I've grown very fond of her.*

*Well, it appears I am going to have my adventure, after all. And much to my surprise, I find I am quite enjoying it, irascible Colonels, gunfighters, horses and all.*

*Give all my love to Pete, Henry Junior, and Uncle Hal.*

*Yours always,*
*Jordan*

Jordan set down her pen and glanced out the window. Colonel Treadwell had not exaggerated when he'd boasted of the view from her room. At three stories, the Grand Hotel was the tallest building in town, and Jordan could see easily over the web of streets and houses behind it to the foothills and mountains beyond. The sun had just set, leaving the peaks of the Rockies tipped in cold rose fire, snowy monarchs against the slate-blue sky.

She had already relinquished her paints and easel, along with most of her baggage, to the Colonel to send ahead to Battlement Park, so she didn't feel guilty that she didn't have her colors out, mixing blue and gray or red and silver, trying to match the beauty of the night.

She glanced at her letter again. To her eye, the handwriting looked cramped, ashamed of all the details she had so carefully left out. That she was worried about Will and Nicky barely speaking to each other. That it was a relief to send her supplies on ahead so they couldn't remind her that she hadn't started a painting since arriving in Colorado. That she didn't seem to care if she never painted again.

Jordan turned down her lamp to watch the stars appear.

They blinked on one by one as though a cosmic lamplighter danced drunk across the night, faster and faster, until the lights spread across the whole sky, settling like a diamond-studded cloak across the backs of the mountains.

No, she couldn't tell Aunt Rue about her painting, nor about the emptiness that clutched her this time of night. A few people still moved about in the streets below her, and she knew nearly half the rooms in the hotel were filled. Yet she felt as though she could stretch her arms across the whole expanse of the night and never touch another living soul, never find a spark of life to warm her fingertips.

Muffling a curse, she rose to draw the curtains closed. Her skirt caught the edge of the sketch pad that lay on the desk, sending it to the floor with a startling clap of noise. She snatched it up, smoothing out the page that had crumpled when it fell open—a picture of Nicky, her expression distracted as she bent over the tiny booties she knit, almost as though she could already hear the pattering feet of her unborn child.

Jordan turned the page. There was Will, his eyebrows pinched in a frown over a legal text on Leland Hedgepeth's extra desk. Further back were Aunt Rue and Uncle Hal, sketched just before she left Connecticut. And her young cousin Peter, down on one knee, his arm around Beryl, his best retriever bitch.

Lord, she missed them. Even Nicky and Will, and she'd only left Denver that morning. It seemed like ages ago. Flipping forward, she found her sketch of Colonel Treadwell. She'd put him beside a cavalry saddle, a flight of fancy. And she'd done a quick line drawing of Maggie with Ari and one of March fighting down a fire-eyed Achilles. All from memory, but not bad.

One more page . . . She'd put the subject in partial profile, almost unconsiously turning his penetrating stare away from her, toward some distant goal she couldn't see.

She'd felt reluctant to sketch him, and her reluctance showed. She'd captured his features adequately—the sharp cheekbones, the sharp, dark eyebrows that emphasized the paleness of his skin, the strong angle of his jaw, the concentration of his eyes, fringed with dark lashes.

Yet the sketch remained flat and lifeless. Flat and lifeless, because her drawing of it lacked honesty.

She had evaded the most essential aspect of Elijah Kelly's features, the life that burned beneath his skin. She had left out the mobility of his expression as a portrait painter might leave out the unsightly mole on a wealthy patroness' cheek. Why? Because it frightened her? Or because it reminded her of something she'd lost and could never regain?

While she stared at the sketch, her fingers found the pencil on the desk in front of her. She sank back onto her chair and brushed the pencil experimentally beneath the gunfighter's cheekbone. There. And the movement of his eyes. And the hint of lines around his mouth. It should be fuller here, thinner there.

The pencil sketch pulled her in as her painting hadn't pulled her all winter. An addition here, subtraction there, her heart beating with the steady rhythm of purpose, but fast with the hint of her fear. And her hands moved more surely with the fear, for what was art without danger?

Her hand paused and a smile almost touched her lips. A perfect danger it was, too. She could let herself be drawn into the illusion, to brush a finger against that cheek, smoothing the shadow. She could match the predatory appraisal of that gaze. For the moment of creation, he had no home, no family, and she was not a drab little widow, but a creature of power and freedom, stretching her wings.

And when she was finished, she would return safely back to rest, settling back into herself, with only a brief memory of flight. No harm done. She'd never see Elijah Kelly again.

The Colonel's weather shoulder had been right, Jordan noticed, as she stepped onto the hotel porch. The rays of the low-hanging sun touched her with warmth this morning, the chill air refreshing rather than daunting.

She half wished the cold mountain wind still blew, keeping people off the streets. She felt like an exotic stork with her legs sticking out up to her calves beneath her borrowed skirt. The ridiculous bloomers didn't make her feel any less exposed.

"Glorious morning," the Colonel boomed expansively, pausing to pull a heavy gold watch from his waistcoat pocket. "And starting it in fine time. You'll arrive in Longmont well before suppertime, Mrs. Braddock, even with stops to refresh your artistic eye."

Mrs. Pepperill approached her other side and handed her a package wrapped in brown paper. "Here you go, dear. Some rolls, cheese, and a little ham for your dinner. Just drop it in your saddlebag and nibble when you get hungry."

"Thank you."

"Fine thought, Mrs. P.," the Colonel jumped in. "Always have your eye on the important details. I could have used you in 'sixty-four. Well, Mrs. Braddock, time for us to be off."

"Safe journey, Mrs. Braddock," Mrs. Pepperill called to Jordan. "I hope you'll visit us again and tell us all about your adventure."

"Thank you, Mrs. Pepperill. If I get the chance—" Then she had to turn away so her feet could find the stairs as the Colonel pulled her along in his wake.

He led her along the sidewalk toward the livery stable.

Rushing to match steps with Colonel Treadwell, she had no time to notice whether or not the people they passed were staring at her.

They turned into the stable yard. The two young men from the day before were already at work, hair curling damply about their freshly washed faces. At the sight of the Colonel, one of them ran into the stable and led out a sturdy little bay mare, already saddled.

"Here y'are, Miz Braddock," the stableboy said brightly. "Nice horse."

"Yes, she is," Jordan agreed, with as much conviction as she could muster.

"Yep. She had a hankerin' to kick out the stall door last night, but I didn't let her. Strong legs on that filly. I'll hold her while you mount up, ma'am."

Jordan abruptly dropped the hand she was raising toward the mare's nose. She didn't know whether to laugh or run. "All right, Smoke. If you don't kick or bite, neither will I. Do we have a deal?"

The mare's nostrils twitched, her eyes big and alert. Cautiously, Jordan raised her hand once more. Smoke's lips gently lifted the bit of carrot she found on Jordan's palm. Jordan released her breath.

"Okay, let's go."

The Colonel took the package of food from her hands and tucked it into one of the saddlebags. They already bulged with her sketch pad, a change of clothes, toiletries, and the borrowed pair of March Jackson's blue jeans.

The stableboy led Smoke to a mounting block. Jordan had practiced mounting and riding in her new outfit at the Jacksons' the afternoon before and managed to climb into the saddle without mishap.

"A fine, brave sight you are," the Colonel approved, taking the reins from the stable hand. "I wish I could be there to see your first view of Battlement Park. You will find enough there to paint to keep you busy a lifetime."

He led Smoke toward the street. With the saddle strange between her legs, Jordan felt like a toddler led about by her grandfather on her first pony ride. Except that growing up she'd had neither pony nor grandfather.

"In fact," the Colonel continued, "if you have the inclination, I could do with a mountain vista for the hotel lobby. What would you charge for an oil painting about yea big? I could pay a hundred dollars. Make it a hundred and fifty! Make your trip profitable as well as edifying, eh?" He beamed, pleased with his plan, as he passed the reins over Smoke's head into Jordan's hands.

"I . . . I . . ." Jordan quashed her sudden panic, not knowing if it came from having sole control of the horse or from the fear that she might never find the heart to paint again. "I'll certainly keep your generous offer in mind, Colonel."

"I understand," an unmistakable drawl interrupted them, "that the Earl of Dunraven paid Albert Bierstadt fifteen thousand for a painting of Longs Peak."

He sat easy in his saddle just outside the stable yard, his hat low over his eyes, holding the malevolent Achilles to an almost uncanny stillness.

Colonel Treadwell's good humor vanished. "Kelly. What are you doing here?"

"I'm here to offer my services to Mrs. Braddock as a guide to Longmont and Battlement Park."

Jordan's heart fluttered like a mouse whose eye catches the faint moon-shadow of an owl's silent wing. So much for never seeing Elijah Kelly again.

# Chapter 4

"Nonsense!" The Colonel sputtered, indignation turning his ears red beneath his fine white hair. "You're not welcome in this town, Kelly. We have no use for your kind of trouble."

The gunfighter sat immobile, but Achilles shifted, his nostrils flaring. Elijah's right hand lay lightly on his black-clad thigh, free to draw a six-gun, if he'd worn one. Jordan could see the stock of the rifle attached to his saddle. She wondered if Colonel Treadwell would have dared challenge him if he really believed Elijah had come to town looking for trouble. She glanced at the fierce little man. Probably.

"I'll remind you that Oxtail has a marshal now, Colonel," Elijah said, without rancor. "Since he doesn't seem to object to my presence, I'm afraid you'll have to endure it a little longer."

"Very well." Despite his words, the Colonel gave no sign of giving ground. "But I will not stand for you harassing my guests. You will allow Mrs. Braddock to leave without further incident. Alone. She has no use for a guide."

"Thank you for your offer, Mr. Kelly," Jordan broke in, wishing March Jackson were there to separate the two men. "But Colonel Treadwell is right. I'll be perfectly fine on my own. As long as I keep the mountains to my right, I can hardly get lost on my way to Longmont, and I understand there is only one road from there to Battlement Park."

For the first time, the gunfighter turned his eyes on her,

startling her heartbeat into a faster rhythm. Something in her sensed danger each time she met those piercing eyes. If only she could take heed of it, instead of relishing the shiver of excitement at the warning.

"I'm sure you could find your way to Longmont without incident, Mrs. Braddock." More sure than she was, apparently, but she didn't interrupt. "However, there is a chance you might run across some unsavory characters, and I would feel more comfortable if you had an escort."

"Nonsense," the Colonel repeated. "Coloradans have nothing but respect for the fair sex, as you'd know if you spent more time with people like the Jacksons and less time raising hell—pardon me, Mrs. Braddock. Isabella Bird travelled all about the territory, by day and night, through mining camps and wilderness, without an escort, and never once was she treated as anything less than a lady."

"Miss Bird was in her forties," Elijah reminded him. "And though from all accounts handsome, I doubt her beauty rivalled Mrs. Braddock's."

Flames engulfed Jordan's cheeks, the more so since he had said it so matter-of-factly, without any apparent intent of flattery. He'd calculated his words to give the Colonel nothing he could reply without insulting Jordan, something as impossible to the Colonel's nature as flying.

"Surely you've heard about the trouble in Laporte a fortnight ago, Colonel." The gunfighter pressed his advantage. "Colorado is changing. The more prosperous the people of this state become, the more attractive they are to men with few scruples and little love for hard work."

"You'd know about that, Kelly."

The gunfighter's mouth didn't soften as he smiled. "I don't take what isn't mine, Colonel. And you know well enough that Mrs. Braddock will be safe in my company."

"Do I?" The Colonel's chin notched upward, his mustache twitching with animosity. "Tell that to the mother of that little bastard Henna Culbert is raising for you."

Elijah's face paled to white, his lips thinning in tight fury. His eyes, no longer searching, turned flat and hard as stones. "Would you care to repeat that, Colonel?"

If Jordan hadn't quite allowed herself to believe Elijah Kelly capable of murder, the taut threat in his voice convinced her. Colonel Treadwell blanched, but he put a hand up to stop her as she moved to urge Smoke between him and the gunfighter.

"I apologize," the Colonel said, and Jordan admired his dignity, for he seemed to speak from true shame rather than fear. "That was uncalled for. Whatever I may think of you, Kelly, I can assure you I would never do anything to embarrass Henna Culbert or young Wolf. He's a good boy."

Elijah's head inclined, and he shifted, looking almost as embarrassed as the Colonel. "I know."

Achilles shuffled his feet, heaving a breath of released tension which Jordan found herself echoing. The Colonel stepped back, his antagonism dissipated for the moment. He looked up at Jordan, and she saw deep lines around his eyes that she hadn't noticed before.

"If Elijah Kelly says he will take you safely to Longmont and Battlement Park, he will. I've never known him not to be a man of his word." His mustache twitched again. "But I don't think you need an escort. You'll be safe on the road, and my friends in Longmont will see to your comfort there. But it's up to you, my dear."

Jordan nodded. She didn't need an escort, not from a self-confessed gunfighter on a mean, spoiled horse. She glanced at Elijah. Especially not from a gunfighter with a face as compelling as the devil's and the gall to call her beautiful.

65

"It would be a terrible inconvenience to you, Mr. Kelly."

"Not at all, ma'am. I never find it inconvenient to travel into the mountains, and I have no pressing business here until late next week."

Obviously only a firm, confident "No, thank you" would convince him. "I appreciate your generous offer, Mr. Kelly—"

"Then we should be going. We'll want to have time this afternoon to rest the horses."

*No, thank you.* But he'd already moved Achilles into a brisk walk down the street. She couldn't just yell after him.

She turned to the Colonel. He gave her a little smile, patting Smoke's neck. "I hope you find what you're looking for in Battlement Park, my dear. I wish I could accompany you myself. You'll be safer from brigands with Elijah Kelly along, I suppose, but even keeping to his word, he can still be dangerous. Take care."

She didn't take time to explain to him that she wasn't going anywhere with Elijah Kelly. "Thank you, Colonel. For everything."

Clutching her reins tightly in her fist, she nudged her mare forward. She turned for a last look at the Colonel, forcing a brave smile, but whirled back around when Smoke broke into a jarring trot.

Jordan grabbed for the saddle horn, steadying her seat. She caught her balance and tightened her knees, using her legs to ease into the horse's rhythm as she'd seen her cousins Peter and Henry do. Of course, they'd had English hunting saddles, not this bulky Mexican saddle designed for roping cattle. After several more painful thumps to her rear, she gave up and pushed Smoke into a canter for the brief distance it took them to catch Elijah.

He had passed the last houses straggling along Main

Street, heading out into the short-grass prairie.

"Let yourself lean forward a little," Elijah advised, "and don't push your boots so far into the stirrups. Back straight." He turned Achilles' head down a little track that branched off from the main road. Smoke followed without waiting for a signal from Jordan.

"This will take us up past the hogbacks, into the foothills," Elijah explained. "We have time; you may as well see the scenery. We'll parallel the mountains until we reach Longmont. Then we'll turn west, straight up into them."

*We* are not going anywhere. "What was the trouble in Laporte?"

He didn't look back at her, his eyes on the terrain before them. "Masked outlaws robbed the general store. They killed the French proprietor and raped his daughter. They must know the mountains fairly well; the posse lost them within five miles."

Jordan's stomach clenched at the senseless death and violence, but the thought of outlaws in the mountains didn't frighten her—at least, not any more than traveling with Elijah Kelly did. The bandits would be planning another robbery, not wandering the hills hoping to run across helpless women.

"And that's the reason you offered to guide me to Battlement Park?"

"The main reason."

She waited, but he didn't elaborate. "Then why didn't you say something yesterday afternoon? Why wait until this morning?" She should stop asking him questions and start telling him to get lost. Politely, of course.

He turned in his saddle to look back at her, surprising her with the humor in his eyes. "I thought if you had time to think about it, you'd tell me to get lost."

Much against her best intentions, she found herself smiling back at him. "Very perceptive of you."

"You've got good instincts, you just don't trust them. I didn't want to give you time to second-guess yourself."

*And what if I told you all my instincts are screaming for me to run in the other direction whenever I see you?* "And you know all this about me, having known me for how long?"

"Six months."

Her lips tightened. She would not let him think she was amused. "Having exchanged all of a hundred words." *I don't need a guide, Mr. Kelly. Just say it, Jordan.* "Let's see, I'm now riding what is apparently a half-wild mare into the wildest mountains in the country with a gunslinger I don't know anything about. I'm not overly impressed with my 'instincts'."

So low as almost to be silent, his laughter tickled inside her ribs. "Perhaps you're right, Mrs. Braddock. Perhaps you ought to be wary of your instincts at that." His eye caught hers for an instant. "But I intend to encourage them, all the same."

Instinct or not, she didn't believe he intended her harm. He had done her a great service, returning her ring. His friendship with the Jacksons and Colonel Treadwell's grudging respect for his word spoke well of him. Yet she couldn't begin to fathom his motives for traveling with her. She doubted they sprang solely from altruism. She couldn't put from her mind the words he'd spoken to Colonel Treadwell. Did he really think her vain enough to believe he would find a drab widow of almost thirty beautiful?

She was eight kinds of fool for getting herself into this situation. She'd only be more of a fool if she let pride prevent her from turning around and riding back to the train station in Oxtail.

"Stop." Elijah's quiet command echoed her thoughts. She

pulled Smoke to an abrupt halt, causing the mare to shake her head in objection.

*I'm going back.* She opened her mouth, but shut it again when Elijah raised a warning hand, his concentration focused on the terrain before them. Up ahead, a scrubby growth of some prickly shrub marked a bend in the trail as it wound its way up the long slope of the hogback ridge that lay between them and the foothills. Nothing else of any size broke the monotony of grass and rocks, and Jordan couldn't see anything about the bush that explained Elijah's rapt attention.

"Give it up." His voice, loud and sharp, startled her. "You may as well come out from behind there. I can see you."

Smoke took an abrupt step back, responding to Jordan's convulsive clutching of the reins. She hadn't noticed the way the bush complemented the curve of the slope, providing plenty of cover for a man on his belly. Though she still saw no sign of life, she could suddenly feel the ambush ahead of them deep in her bones.

She wanted to ask Elijah if they shouldn't be running away, but she didn't dare distract him.

"This is your last warning." His voice was quieter now, almost casual. Achilles' nostrils flared, catching the scent of danger.

Jordan wondered why the man lying in wait didn't answer. Or shoot at them, for that matter. In a fluid motion she almost missed, Elijah lifted his rifle from its holder. She heard a decisive click as he threw the lever.

At the sound, the bush rustled ahead of them and a head popped up over the top. A gray head with eager silver eyes, long white teeth showing in a grin of excitement.

For a long, breathless moment, Jordan was caught between instinctual fear at the surprise and relief that their ambusher didn't have a gun. Smoke experienced no such hesitation. Jordan felt the mare twist beneath her. She grabbed hold of the saddle horn, but she'd already lost her seat. Her boots slipped free of her stirrups, and with shocking suddenness she found herself flat on her back in the dusty horse trail.

"Mrs. Braddock, are you all right?"

She looked up into the gunfighter's anxious face, pale against the black brim of his hat, and almost laughed. She couldn't breathe, and every rib along her spine felt bruised.

"Nothing broken," she managed to gasp.

And then he was gone. She lay for a moment, unbelieving, as the sound of Achilles' hoofbeats raced away from her. With tears of pain stinging her eyes, she raised herself up on her elbows.

Smoke ran with an agile surefootedness that Achilles couldn't hope to match as they pounded down the hill. But once the two horses hit flat prairie, the gelding's huge strides easily outpaced the little mare's jackrabbit dash. Within half a mile, Achilles had caught up and ran alongside the mare, enabling Elijah to reach the loose reins.

He'd gone after her horse. He'd just left her there, battered and winded, lying in the dirt.

"So much for chivalry." The words were easier now, the fire in her chest subsiding to a painful burn. But her breathing still sounded strange, ragged and uneven.

No, not *her* breathing.

Slowly, she turned her head to find herself nose to nose with the wolf from behind the bush.

"Hello, there. Remember me?" she asked faintly.

He sat barely two feet away, ears swiveled forward, his silver eyes fixed on her. At her words, his head tilted and his mouth dropped slightly, letting his long tongue loose in a controlled pant. His front legs were crouched, his muscles tensed, but Jordan had spent enough time with Peter's dogs to know he was inviting her to play. He posed no immediate threat.

"Loki!" Elijah's voice came strongly, despite the distance. "Come here." The wolf turned his head, but seeing his master still at least a quarter mile away, he ignored the call and focused his attention back on Jordan.

"A troublemaker, are you?" She sat up, wincing.

"Loki!"

The wolf's ears twitched. Apparently recognizing that Jordan had no interest in a game of tag, he eased down onto his forelegs, his mouth stretching open in a huge yawn.

"Well, Loki, it's a pleasure to meet you." She held out her hand, hoping he wouldn't eat it. The wolf snuffled her fingers, his nose tickling slowly up her arm. Jordan slid her hand forward and tentatively scratched his chest. She heard the faint swish of his tail against the grass, and he raised his head slightly, his eyes narrowing.

"I'm sorry." Elijah brought the horses to a halt about ten feet away. Smoke's nostrils flared, her eyes fixed on the recumbent wolf, but she seemed to have run off her panic. "I wanted to catch Smoke before she made it back to the Jacksons'. I forgot that Loki might frighten you."

He dismounted fluidly, ground tying Achilles, Smoke's reins still attached to the gelding's saddle.

"He did frighten me," Jordan admitted. "But then I remembered him from the train station."

"Wretched beast."

As the gunfighter approached, the wolf wriggled closer to Jordan, laying his muzzle along her arm, rolling his disarming silver eyes back toward Elijah.

Jordan laughed. "He's saying he just stayed here to protect me."

"He could have gotten you killed."

Hearing the harshness of Elijah's tone, the wolf heaved himself to his feet. Head low, his long, lanky body mere inches off the ground, he crept toward the gunfighter.

"Go on. Get out of here." Elijah waved him off. Loki shuffled away into the grass, lowering himself silently to the ground, his chin on his paws.

Crouching beside her, Elijah saw Jordan's expression. "He's got to learn not to do that."

"Were you really going to shoot at him?"

Air burst from Elijah's lungs in a sound that wasn't quite laughter. "When I cocked the rifle, he thought I was going to shoot something for supper. I meant to trick him into showing himself so he wouldn't scare the horses. I didn't want to shoot him until I saw you leave your saddle."

His eyes, barely a foot from hers, showed a mixture of humor and concern. "Now that you've been assured of the monster's safety, will you tell me whether or not you're all right?"

"Sore, but I'm fine. I can breathe again." Or she could until he smiled at her that way. She looked away, brushing her hands on her skirt. "I just feel a little stupid for falling off my horse."

"Don't be silly. That was a fine acrobatic piece of work, getting your feet out of the stirrups and not breaking a wrist landing."

She took the hand he offered and climbed shakily to her feet. "Don't make me laugh; it hurts."

"Plenty of things that are good for you hurt. You should laugh more often. Here, hold still." He brushed at the dirt coating the back of her outfit.

His nearness disturbed her, and she moved away, stretching her shoulders. Loki sat up as she neared him, tail swishing once more.

"I've ruined Maggie's riding dress thanks to you," she

scolded, scratching behind his ears. "Bad wolf. Bad, bad wolf." He closed his eyes in ecstasy.

"He does look like a wolf, doesn't he?"

Elijah was checking the cinch on her saddle. He glanced at her without meeting her eyes. "Many people make that mistake. But he's just a dog."

She looked down at Loki. He grinned with mad innocence.

"You're a terrible liar, Mr. Kelly."

He met her gaze now. "A liar, Mrs. Braddock?"

"Yes."

"I'm not accustomed to having my honor questioned, Mrs. Braddock." But his drawl was amused.

"Loki's no more a dog than you are."

"He's a northern breed. Brought down from Canada."

Jordan snorted. "Mr. Kelly, my cousin's a dog fancier. He knows just about everything there is to know about dogs. I may not know much about horses, but I know enough about canines to tell the difference between a dog and a wolf. That —" She pointed at Loki. "—is a wolf."

"A wolf?" Elijah frowned at the animal in question. "Fancy that. No wonder Achilles hates him so much."

Loki stood and shook himself, his skin rippling loose over his bones, then trotted over to Elijah. Still frowning, Elijah scratched his chin. "You're not forgiven." Loki's ears twitched.

"How did you end up with a wolf?"

"He's not mine." The gunfighter absently dropped his other hand and rubbed the wolf on both sides of his muzzle. "He's my son's. I just . . . watch after him."

She couldn't ask him about his son, not after what Colonel Treadwell had said that morning.

Elijah didn't seem to notice her embarrassment. "And he

is part dog—you can tell by those ears and the way he holds his tail up." Loki's tail waved in response, and he growled in pleasure at the attention, throwing himself to the ground to mouth Elijah's boots. "A large, foolish dog with absolutely no sense of dignity."

Elijah looked up from the wolf's impish play. "Are you ready to get back in the saddle?"

She'd happily forgotten she'd have to do that eventually. She looked at Smoke. The mare stood more or less calmly by Achilles' side, her intelligent eyes watching Loki's antics with more disdain than fear.

"It's not that far back to Oxtail. I could walk."

Without bothering to comment, Elijah led Smoke to a level section of the trail.

Each one of Jordan's ribs ached. "There's no mounting block."

"Then it's a good thing she's a small horse. I'll help you." Elijah crouched by Smoke's stirrup. Out of excuses, Jordan set her foot in the cupped hands he offered.

"Grab the horn."

She did. As she swung herself up, he boosted with his hands. The momentum nearly carried her over the other side of the saddle. She clutched at the saddle horn and Elijah held her boot, helping her right herself. Only belatedly did she realize that Maggie's split skirt had bunched under her arm as she mounted, leaving her entire right leg exposed. She fought with her skirt, the movement making Smoke dance.

"Here, let me help you."

"No!" Her face flamed as Elijah moved around the front of the mare, in view of her exposed leg.

"Stay calm. I think it's just those bloomers that are bothering Smoke."

Jordan glanced down. Billows of white cotton fluttered in

the morning breeze. It occurred to her that her ridiculous undergarments were more likely to arouse laughter than anyone's inappropriate desire. With another firm tug on her hem, she slid her skirt down over the foolish garment.

"Did I say something funny?" Elijah asked.

She could only shake her head as the laughter bubbled up. She was a mature widow, for heaven's sake—too sensible to get skittish over being alone with a man. Elijah Kelly no more had designs on her than she did on him. If he wanted to play the chivalrous knight for a day or two, why shouldn't she enjoy it?

His company had certainly been entertaining so far. She'd have plenty of stories to tell the nieces and nephews when she got home to Connecticut.

And Peter would never forgive her if she met a wolf and didn't take the chance to sketch some pictures.

Missing the sound of hoofbeats behind him, Elijah reined in Achilles. He turned to see Smoke and Jordan halted in the shade of a stand of ponderosa pine. Jordan had her sketchbook out, her pencil flashing over the paper with sure confidence. He had become used to the transformation in her countenance as she sketched furiously or simply sat and held the picture in her mind.

Or perhaps she merely listened to the mountains. Watching her, Elijah thought Jordan found particular pleasure in the silence surrounding them, a soul-deep silence made only more profound by the liquid call of a meadowlark and the rustling of the wind.

"Guide her to Battlement Park? What on earth for?" Maggie had asked him at supper the night before. "She seems like a sensible, competent woman to me. I'm sure she'll be fine."

Harry had snorted, her nose crinkled in scorn. "Sure,

she's about as competent as . . . as a rabbit. Didn't you see her on Smoke, Maggie? She sits a horse like a sack of potatoes. If anyone could get lost between here and Longmont, it would be a helpless eastern lady like her."

She'd turned to Elijah. "She obviously needs a keeper. I just don't see why it has to be you, 'Lije.''

Since he had no answer to that question himself, he'd side-stepped it. "Lem and March haven't had their turn. Why do you think it's a bad idea, Lem?"

Recognizing his tone, the big black man shook his head with a smile. "You'll do what you please, Preacher. I'd say you're the one needs a keeper. Praise the Lord it ain't me."

"I doubt she's in any danger, 'Lije," March said quietly from the other end of the ranch house's sturdy table. "I know Yves Sevier's murder still bothers you. If anyone could have tracked those men, it was you and Old Renard. It's not your fault they got away. But if it will make you feel better to see Mrs. Braddock safely to Battlement Park, you ought to go."

At the memory, Elijah let out his breath in an explosive sigh, glancing back down the trail at the woman in question. March's consistent belief that he had a noble reason for his actions could sometimes be as annoying as Colonel Treadwell's automatic assumption that he rode into Oxtail looking for people to shoot.

But March knew him better than anyone did, even his own brother. And that business in Laporte still bothered him. He was a good tracker. Robert Sevier, the dead man's brother, wily and tough as the fox that had earned him his nickname of Old Renard, was better.

That the six outlaws had lost their trackers so quickly and so thoroughly could only mean they knew the mountains as well as Old Renard himself and that they worked together with a discipline not usually seen in outlaw gangs. What bothered Elijah was not that he had not had the chance to avenge Yves Sevier and his daughter. Yves was dead. Old Renard had said he would take Marie back to her mother's people in the Dakotas. There was nothing Elijah could do for them.

What troubled him was the thought of those killers hiding in the mountains planning their next attack. He was not a righteous man. He had killed his fellow men and would probably do so again. If there was a final judgment, he would pay for that, however justified any particular killing might have been.

But he had felt the wild holiness of the mountains the first time he had entered them. There, violence was a natural, elemental force, as much so as beauty and peace, without the taint of man's cunning and greed. Men who used the mountains to prey on the innocent offended him like finding maggots in fresh meat.

But he couldn't say with total honesty that any of that had anything to do with why he had volunteered to escort Jordan Braddock to Battlement Park.

"I'm sorry. I'm holding us up again." Jordan had stuffed her sketchbook back in her saddlebag and urged Smoke up the trail to where he waited. "Those trees, they're just so . . . not beautiful. Not exactly."

She glanced back at them, searching for inspiration. "Not like the trees back home are, anyway. I've always thought maples were the most beautiful of trees, so green in spring, such vivid colors in the fall. But . . . even our conifers look, I don't know, 'civilized' compared to your pine trees out here."

She turned back to him, wrinkling her nose in frustration at the inadequacy of her words. "You can set a faster pace, to reach Longmont before dark. Don't worry about me. It's my fault we're so late."

"We'll make it. No need to push the horses." He pretended not to notice her relief, just as he had pretended not to notice that she could hardly stand when they had dismounted to eat Mrs. Pepperill's provisions.

She would be painfully sore tonight, more sore tomorrow. But she already rode with more poise and confidence than she had that morning. A fact which pleased him out of proportion to the accomplishment.

And only twice during the long ride today had he glimpsed the ghostly pain that played around her eyes—the look that had haunted him so deeply when he met her on the train that he hadn't been able to dismiss her from his thoughts for weeks. The look he had seen the previous morning when Achilles had tried to bite her and she'd half made up her mind to give up her adventure and return to Longmont by train.

Even this morning, riding into Oxtail, he'd been afraid that his offer, his challenge, would not be enough to provoke her into the foothills, that she would give in to the chill that he could almost see wrapping itself around her.

Why it should matter to him, why he should want to chase the pain from her eyes for even a short time, he couldn't have said, except that it had something to do with the courage she'd shown in front of the train robbers. And something to do with the strength he'd sensed in her. And something to do with the way she'd looked at him in the ranch yard the day before—without Barnett Treadwell's censure, without Harry's hero worship. As though she saw him honestly, as a man. As if that was enough.

He breathed deeply the scents of earth, of fresh green grass, of sturdy pines. Maybe for today it was.

# Chapter 5

Jordan knew her outfit looked even more ridiculous this morning than it had the day before. Dirt still smudged the back of the dress, and her bloomers were decorated with horse hair. But if anyone stared at her as she walked the short distance from her hotel to the Longmont Trust, she didn't notice. She was too focused on walking without groaning in pain.

She never wanted to see the back of a horse again, much less get on one, but it felt a little better to walk. As her muscles stretched with the exercise, she lengthened her stride, easing out the soreness that had settled into her thighs overnight.

She stepped into the Longmont Trust building, breathing in the universal bank smells of sterile propriety, money, and efficiency. Her boots ticked smartly on the wood floor, cutting through the rustling murmur of patrons and bankers. She waited in line at one of the open windows. When she reached the front, the clerk offered her a brief, professional smile.

"How may I help you, ma'am?"

"I believe I have some money waiting for me. Mrs. Jordan Braddock." She'd telegraphed Leland Hedgepeth from Oxtail, asking him to arrange to have some of her funds sent to Longmont. She'd spent all of the money she'd carried with her on Smoke, a doubly sore subject with her at the moment.

"Wait just a moment, please, ma'am."

The clerk hurried into the back to find one of the bankers, his manner conveying briskness without urgency. He caught the ear of one of his superiors. The banker, a balding man with large round eyes, nodded. They spoke some more.

A rhythmic ticking invaded Jordan's consciousness as their conversation dragged on. Tick, tick, tickety, tick, over and over. She glanced around, prepared to glare at the source of the annoyance, then realized it came from her fingernails on the marble counter top. She clenched her fist, stopping the noise, but her irritation at the delay remained, surprising her. She certainly felt no impatience to return to Smoke, or to the hotel's indifferent cooking. That left Elijah Kelly, with his surprising smile and patient acceptance of her inept horsemanship.

She snorted, disgusted with herself, and turned from the counter to watch the other patrons. Women in fashionable dresses waited at the two other windows. Businessmen in conservative suits spoke with bankers at low tables. Even cowboys and laborers apparently trimmed their beards and put on clean shirts to enter these hallowed walls—one of the former stood in line at the window at the far end of the counter.

As if feeling her eyes on him, he glanced her way. Ash-blond hair fell across his forehead, framing green eyes that stared boldly back at her. Jordan glanced away, unaccountably disturbed.

"Here you are, ma'am."

Jordan jumped at the clerk's return. He pushed a small stack of bills across the counter toward her, along with a receipt.

"We'll just need you to sign for this, and you can be on your way."

Jordan murmured her thanks, quickly signing the paper and tucking the money away in her handbag.

"I hope you enjoy your stay in Longmont, ma'am."

She looked up to respond with a perfunctory pleasantry of her own, but the clerk's expression silenced her. He had frozen in place, his eyes wide, his lips parted in fear.

Before she could react, a rough hand grabbed her arm, pushing her hard against the counter, preventing any struggle.

"This here's a holdup," announced a thick voice as rough as the homemade whiskey on the speaker's foul breath. "You give me all the money you got handy, and this little lady don't get hurt."

The man holding her thrust a fistful of canvas sacks past Jordan's ear and slid them across the counter toward the clerk. Jordan gasped as the hard edge of the counter dug into her rib cage. The jab behind her ear could only be a gun. She couldn't swallow the bitter fear that filled her throat.

"Hurry!" her unseen captor bellowed. The clerk fell back, his hands clutching the empty sacks.

"All the rest of you get down," another voice ordered.

The holdup man swung around, using Jordan as a shield, though it wasn't necessary. The other patrons, including the young cowboy Jordan had noticed earlier, were quickly complying with his partner's demand, dropping to hands and knees.

"All the way down!" Her captor's accomplice stood just inside the front door, a readied shotgun in his hands.

The man holding Jordan turned back to the clerk. "And don't you think about running out the back way, you yellow toad. I've got a man out there who'd be happy to make a window of your belly. Now get moving!"

The clerk stumbled backward. He tossed a bag to the next clerk, and the two of them began stuffing money into their sacks.

"We don't want any trouble," the balding banker said, keeping his hands above his head as he came around from behind his desk. "We'll give you anything you want, just don't shoot anyone."

"That's right, you'll give us exactly what we want." Jordan's captor laughed. "What's the matter? Blood bad for business? Discourages the customers, does it?"

The banker blinked, round eyes bulging. He caught Jordan's gaze, and she saw fear for her in his expression.

The robber released his hold on her arm to slide his hand around her waist. Almost casually, he squeezed. Jordan gasped, the pressure combining with her fear to leave her breathless. For a second she swayed, lightheaded.

The robber's gun clipped sharply against her jaw.

"Now don't you faint on me, missy. You're gonna walk outta here with me."

Jordan couldn't control the trembling in her legs. She remembered Elijah's story of the shopkeeper and his daughter in Laporte. These men were going to kidnap her, rape her, and probably kill her. She'd die before ever reaching Battlement Park, the first goal she'd looked forward to since Frank's death. Tears of fear and self-pity stung her eyes, embarrassing her. Elijah had thought she was brave.

"Take me instead." The trembling voice belonged to the balding banker behind the counter. "Leave this lady alone."

Her captor's laughter rang through the bank. "Keep making me laugh, little man, and maybe I won't get it in my mind to shoot you."

"I mean it. I won't give you any trouble."

"I don't think so, Baldy. You wouldn't feel half so nice in my arms as this little piece." He squeezed Jordan again. "You'd better hurry up back there. I suddenly can't wait to take my loot home." His hips moved suggestively behind Jordan, and she gagged on her disgust and terror.

"Don't worry. I don't plan to kill you. I like my women lively." The robber chuckled, enjoying her fear. She could feel his breath nearing her ear. Before he could continue, an explosion of noise knocked them both against the counter.

As her head turned, Jordan saw the bloody hole in the chest of the robber's accomplice by the door. The slender blond cowboy she'd noticed earlier was on his feet and was swinging his six shooter from the dead man toward her.

She screamed, even as her left fist jabbed up over her shoulder to connect with her captor's lowered jaw. As his head went back, hers went down. The impact of the bullet toppled the robber backwards, pulling her down with him. She heard the sickening smack of his head against the floor an instant before she landed on top of him.

As the pressure of his arm loosened, she rolled away, desperately untangling herself from him, anticipating the crack of his gun. One glance at his still form showed she need no longer fear him. She couldn't even make out his features through the blood and bullet-smashed bone. One hole between his eyes, one just above his ear.

She screamed and screamed, but no sound came from her throat, as though she were trapped in a nightmare.

"Ma'am, allow me to help you to your feet."

Her shattered memory couldn't place the impossibly familiar voice until she'd taken the hand offered and found herself face-to-face with the green-eyed cowboy. She realized why his gaze had disturbed her earlier. She *was* trapped in a nightmare. She was staring into the angelic face of Boss Pauly, the train bandit.

Without his bandanna mask, his chin freshly, if unnecessarily, shaved, he looked even younger than she remembered. Those ice-green eyes couldn't have failed to see her recognition, but he bent low over her hand, brushing his lips against it. Too shaken to move, or even to fear, she simply stood, waiting.

"Sparrow." Elijah's voice spoke near her ear, his presence accounting for the second bullet in her captor's head. His hand gripped her elbow. His touch released her from her immobility, and she trembled. His grip tightened, and if he was surprised when she sagged against him, she didn't turn to see it. She heard a clatter as the gun he held hit the floor, and then his arm was around her waist, his long body supporting her as though she had no more substance than a willow sapling bending against him.

"Mrs. Braddock, are you all right, ma'am?" The balding banker made his way around the counter and hurried to her side. "Please, come sit down. I'll get you some tea."

As it became obvious no one else was going to die, the other patrons and bank employees broke their silence. The building rang with shouts and arguments and nervous laughter. One woman sobbed desperately. Jordan felt surprise that it wasn't her.

"No, thank you," she managed. "I'd just like to get outside, please." To breathe air that didn't smell like blood.

Pauly, the bandit, reached for the arm opposite Elijah, but the banker pushed in beside her, turning a dark glance on the young man. "You might have gotten Mrs. Braddock killed, sir, not to mention our other patrons. It's a miracle that bast . . . that *outlaw* . . . didn't shoot her."

The planes in Pauly's face sharpened. He rolled lightly on the balls of his feet. "Only a fool would shoot his best protection."

Jordan had just seen the results of Pauly's lightning hands and pinpoint accuracy with a gun. She didn't want to see another demonstration. She jumped in before the banker could open his mouth. "No, please. I wasn't harmed. He risked his life to save mine. Thank you, Mr. . . ."

"Jones." Pauly's eyes turned back to her as he flicked a non-existent hat brim with elaborate courtesy. "Lucifer Jones."

The banker stiffened beside her.

"And there was no risk to me, ma'am," Jones continued. "I knew I could take them. If you're all right, ma'am, then I guess I ought to be about my business."

"Yes," Jordan agreed faintly. "I'm fine, thank you."

"Then good day to you, ma'am." He mimed tipping his hat again, then bent to retrieve the revolver Elijah had dropped. "Your gun, Mr. Kelly."

"Thank you, Mr. Jones, but that does not belong to me." If the bandit's tone was almost theatrically respectful, Elijah's voice had no intonation at all. "It belonged to that man by the door."

Jones tucked the gun into his belt, glancing toward the corpse. "I doubt he'll have much use for it after today."

His arm still around her waist, Elijah turned Jordan toward the door, the banker on her other side. Her spine tingled, protesting the idea of turning her back on the man calling himself Lucifer Jones, but she didn't dare turn her head, for she knew those flat green eyes followed them all the way out to the sidewalk.

"Lucifer Jones," the banker muttered as the heavy doors closed behind them. "He has a reputation, that boy, and it's not a good one."

"An outlaw?" Elijah asked, his tone clipped.

The banker shrugged. "I don't doubt it, but nothing that can be pinned on him—yet. He'll swing eventually, though, you can bet on it. What arrogance. He knew he could take them. Why, he might have shot Mrs. Braddock instead."

"He didn't," Jordan reminded him, despite her discomfort at defending the young man she still thought of as Pauly. "And if he'd asked my choice, I would rather have risked being shot in there than be carried off by that wretched animal and his friends."

Elijah's arm tightened around her once more, and she couldn't find the desire to object, any more than she could find the courage to look up into his face while her hip was pressed against his, her shoulder tucked against his side.

"There's the marshal." The banker's attention turned up the street toward a stocky man in a stiff new bowler. "News travels fast in this town. I'd better go talk to him. That is, if you'll be all right, Mrs. Braddock."

"I'll be fine, thank you. And thank you for trying to help me."

The banker shrugged, embarrassed. "I'm afraid I'm better with numbers than with gunfights. I'm relieved no one got hurt."

He hurried up the street toward the marshal, and Elijah turned her in the opposite direction, toward their hotel.

"Shouldn't we stay and talk with the marshal?" Jordan asked.

"Do you want to wait and talk with him?"

"No. I want to sit down somewhere. But . . ."

"That banker seems like a sensible man. I'm sure he can tell the marshal all the details."

Jordan nodded, the movement of Elijah's hand just beneath her ribs distracting her for a moment from her train of thought. He'd loosened his arm, giving her room to walk, but he'd left his hand on her waist, a warm, steadying pressure. She could feel his touch with every nerve, and the rest of her senses seemed equally expanded. The eggshell blue of the sky, the town smells of dust and horses and garbage, the jingle of harnesses and the laughter of a child seemed more distinct, more clear, more significant than she'd realized before entering the bank.

She risked a glance at Elijah's face, and that, too, seemed clearer, sharper. The definition of his eyebrows, the hint of mahogany in his dark hair which had escaped her notice. His eyes focused on the street ahead, providing her with the profile she'd sketched in Oxtail. Her fingers itched with the desire to touch his jaw as they'd smoothed the shadows her pencil had drawn.

She glanced away quickly, missing a step. This winter, chilled to the heart by loneliness and grief, she had half welcomed the idea of death creeping in to steal her away. Now faced with death's sudden, violent face, she found herself clutching for life with both hands.

She should be stepping away from Elijah Kelly's side, away from the touch of those long, strong fingers. Instead, she found herself smiling, wondering how shocked he would be if she surrendered to the impulse to touch him. She was giddy from her brush with danger, something she would not have guessed about herself. She'd have to be careful. Might she just as readily have leaned on Lucifer Jones for comfort?

She stopped abruptly.

"What's wrong?"

"Pauly the Bandit King. That's what the banker can't tell the marshal, Mr. Kelly. That man who shot the bank robbers, he was the one who held up our train last fall. I'm sure of it. I recognized his voice," she added, knowing it sounded far-fetched. "And I'm sure he recognized me."

"I recognized him, too."

She turned in surprise, dislodging his hand from her back. "You recognized him? Then why didn't you wait for the marshal?"

His mouth tightened. He didn't look at her. "He saved your life."

"Yes." Jordan crossed her arms over her chest, fighting down a flash of guilt. "He did save my life, probably. I don't mean to be ungrateful. But . . . I don't know how to say it, Mr. Kelly, but that young man is dangerous. He would have killed you or Will or anyone else on that train without hesitation. I don't know why he chose to rescue me today, but I don't think he would have given any more thought to killing innocent bystanders than he did to killing those two bank robbers."

"He could hang for hijacking a train."

"Or a judge might be lenient on him for his actions today."

Elijah didn't look at her, and Jordan's stomach twisted. Of course she didn't want to see her rescuer hang, but how could she look the other way? "You don't think he's dangerous. You think I'm being silly."

"No. I think you're right. He has the eyes of a killer."

"And you'd just let him walk away?"

When his eyes met hers, their hard flatness gave her no more information than his soft drawl. "I may be a disreputable man, Mrs. Braddock, but I live by rules as unbreakable as yours. I'm going to get the horses ready for our ride to Battlement Park. You do what you have to do."

He nodded to her and strode away toward the hotel. As she watched him go, she couldn't guess whether the sense of doubt and disapproval that hung about him was directed toward her or toward himself.

Much the same as her own disappointment.

She turned away to find Longmont's marshal.

Jordan hadn't spoken to Elijah in over three hours, and he could feel her silent anger like a knife in his back. Loki had run off ahead of them, tired of the human foolishness, and Elijah almost wished the wolf would ambush them again to relieve the tension.

They were winding their way up the canyon of the Little Fowler River, the horses carefully traversing the narrow, twisting road that snow and spring rains had ravaged, leaving it barely passable to the one wagon they'd met so far this morning.

When restlessness or expediency had driven him west, Elijah had seen the great canyons which lay beyond the Rockies, fissures in the earth both narrower and deeper than the one they traveled now. Canyons that glowed with color, as though some god or devil had painted them with blood and fire. By comparison, the canyon of the Little Fowler looked more like a crack in a flawed granite block that a huge stonemason had discarded.

The walls reached skyward with heavy purpose, gray and wrinkled, relieved only by the occasional green of a determined ponderosa pine clinging to a tiny patch of earth. Below them, the Little Fowler itself roared past, swollen and brown. But even now, at its spring height, it seemed more a flooded mountain stream than a river when compared to the Arkansas or the Rio Grande or the Colorado.

And yet he loved this canyon. Loved the solidity and power of its rock. The untamed ebullience of its river. The tenacity of its trees—the pines that climbed the rocks and the willows that clung to their precarious existence beside the treacherous waters. And just when he least expected it, a turn in the canyon or a bend in the sunlight would fire the canyon walls with their own blush of passionate color.

But today the rocks remained stubbornly gray, the river, flooding the few stretches of low road, became merely an annoying obstruction, and Jordan Braddock's continued silence was giving him a headache.

He glanced back at her, just in time to see her shifting in her saddle, her mouth a thin, hard line. A flare of anger throbbed behind his temple.

"We'll rest here." He swung off Achilles without looking back again. She could get off her own horse if she was too proud to admit she hurt and needed to stop.

The water swirled past the trunks of the willows just below them. A steep track made by other travelers or by runoff from further up the cliff led down to the river, and he led Achilles down for a drink. He came back for Smoke, taking his time watering her, giving Jordan a chance to stretch her aching legs.

She surprised him by sliding down the gravel-slick path after him, crouching on the other side of Smoke to splash some of the frigid water on her face.

"How did it go with the marshal?" It sounded awkward and argumentative, but he had to say something to break the silence between them.

She didn't look at him as she rose to her feet. "He wasn't very helpful."

He'd guessed that when she'd arrived back at the hotel with her face a mask of brittle annoyance. "I'm sorry."

"I'm sure you are, Mr. Kelly." She looked at him now over Smoke's bent neck, her sapphire eyes hot with sarcasm. "I'm sure you had no idea what his reaction would be."

"He didn't take you seriously."

"Why should he take me seriously? I'm just a silly, empty-headed city woman. He took great care to explain to me how I was hysterical, understandably so, of course, after my encounter with a gunman, and that I should run along home and not worry my pretty head. He assured me that all the bad guys were dead, their heads blown to bits by the good guys. I guess that makes you a good guy."

At least she was talking to him. "Why, thank you for your vote of confidence, ma'am. I'm touched."

Her eyes burned more brightly the angrier she got. Or maybe she was trying not to smile. She held herself with such firm control, he couldn't tell for sure. He wondered if she let go of that control when she painted, if that fierceness in her eyes seeped out through her fingertips. He wondered if she'd let him watch her paint.

"He didn't even glance at the sketch I did for him. If you had come with me—"

"It wouldn't have made any difference." He let Smoke take another step into the river. "He's probably heard my name. I don't think my word would mean much to him."

That much was true. A frontier lawman he could have convinced, one of those men as comfortable with a gun as he was. He knew most of the officers in the mining camps and cattle towns of Colorado, Texas, Wyoming and beyond. He'd ridden with them in posses, or against them, on opposite sides of a range war, but practical men didn't hold grudges.

But a new breed of lawman had come west with the farmers and the schoolteachers and the bankers and the financiers. The sort of law based on rules and order rather than individual cases and necessity. The sort of law that had no use for a man with a reputation with a gun, regardless of which side of the line he walked.

Jordan ran a hand along Smoke's neck, her gaze still fierce. "You know, the man in back of the bank was shot, too. The marshal thinks Pauly—Mr. Jones—went out the back way and killed him. It couldn't have made it any worse for you to come with me. Why didn't you?"

"I told you. He saved your life."

"Then *I* owe him something. Not you."

His fist clenched on Smoke's reins. "I told you I would see you safely to Battlement Park. I wasn't there when you needed protection." Failure tasted familiar in his mouth.

"But, you . . ." Frustration tangled her tongue. "You couldn't have known those men were going to rob the bank. I should have been safe. That's ridiculous. You can't keep someone safe from everything." Her voice rang with the pain of experience. "It's just not possible."

"I know that." He couldn't expect her to understand when he didn't fully understand himself. But he knew that Pauly, or Lucifer Jones, or whatever the man chose to call himself, had understood enough to know that Elijah could not turn him in after he'd saved Jordan's life. He owed Pauly a debt of blood. It didn't matter that he could not have been expected to protect Jordan from an improbable bank robbery. If she had died in that bank, he would never have been able to forgive himself.

The simplicity of it overwhelmed him. Standing there in Maggie's old riding dress, she echoed the willows behind her. Still in their drab winter garb, the river merciless against them, they clung to life, their limbs graceful as the promise of spring. She wouldn't ask for protection, any more than the willows, and yet the strength and spirit he saw in her spoke to him. He would be lessened if that spirit was gone.

She snorted as she realized he'd finished his explanation. "And men say women are illogical."

Elijah allowed himself a slight smile. "There is nothing logical about humanity. 'For the wisdom of this world is folly.' "

"How convenient for you." Her smile twisted with annoyance, but at least she smiled.

Smoke lifted her head, indicating she'd finally had enough water. Elijah turned her toward the path, gesturing Jordan to climb up first. "It's possible I owe another debt to our Mr. Jones. Those may have been the same men who robbed the general store in Laporte last month."

She glanced back at him. "You knew them. The man who was killed and his daughter."

"Yves Sevier was a friend of mine. A good friend. I don't have so many of those that I lose them lightly."

She looked down at him for a long moment, her mouth a hard line across her face. "If you're right, if those were the same men . . . If you'd told me that, I wouldn't have gone back to the marshal myself. Those men deserved to die."

"Mrs. Braddock, those men deserved to die in any case."

At the grim reminder in his voice, an echo of fear flickered across her eyes, but she said nothing, turning away to scramble up the last few feet to the road.

Loki waited for them at the top of the little path, his tongue drooping out the side of his mouth, eyes bright with mischief as though daring Elijah to guess what he'd been up to.

"There you are," Jordan exclaimed, crouching to rub the sides of Loki's jaws. "Where have you been all morning?" The wolf gazed up at her in adoration, sparing a smug glance for Elijah.

"I'm sure you'd rather not know." Elijah frowned at Loki. He led Smoke over to where Achilles waited, but he watched Jordan and the wolf. He couldn't hear what she said to him, but Loki's eyes had slitted closed, his ears laid back in pleasure. She bent forward, and Loki's tongue flashed too quickly for her, catching her across the lips and nose.

"Ugh!" She fell back on her bottom on the damp, rocky ground, laughing, which only encouraged Loki to follow, washing her face with his tongue. "Ugh! Get away, you brute!"

Elijah moved forward to help, but she'd already grabbed the loose skin at Loki's neck and heaved him aside, lifting herself to her feet at the same time.

"Bad boy," she scolded, rubbing his neck. The wolf threw himself to the ground with his paws in the air.

"Shameless," Elijah said in disgust as Jordan leaned over to rub the soft white fur of the wolf's exposed belly.

Jordan shook her head. "You've done a marvelous job with him. Not all of my cousin's dogs are this well-behaved."

"It's none of my doing." Elijah relented and bent down to add his scratching to Jordan's. "His heart's always been more dog than wolf. But as he's grown older, he's become more reserved around strangers."

Jordan laughed. "I'd hate to see him friendly."

"No, I mean I've never seen him take to someone so quickly. In fact, I've never seen him this friendly with anyone, except Wolf."

"Wolf?"

"My son."

"Oh." Her laughter died. She gave Loki a last scratch under the chin and rose to her feet, her eyes averted from his.

His throat closed with shame as he remembered Treadwell's words of the day before about his bastard son. But it was anger that brought him to his feet and turned him away from her toward the horses, anger at himself for feeling the shame. His forgotten headache returned with a wrenching throb.

"We'd better get moving." His voice sounded nearly normal. "It's still a long ride to Battlement Park."

"Mr. Kelly?"

He glanced back. Pink stained her cheeks, but her gaze found his.

"I'd like to apologize for my behavior earlier. For being

angry with you for acting as you believed right. I'm a new-comer here, and I've no right to judge you before I've even had the chance to know you."

He knew she meant his son, as well as Lucifer Jones, though she couldn't say it. He wished she'd left him angry. When she looked at him like that, as though his feelings mattered to her, he almost believed she'd put him under the same spell she'd woven over Loki.

"Does that mean you intend to chance knowing me, Mrs. Braddock?" He knew his tone was dangerous. She tempted something dangerous inside him.

He moved a step forward, expecting her to back away. She didn't. Her chin tilted up, her eyes defiant, though whom or what she was defying he couldn't guess.

"I believe I do, Mr. Kelly. You lost your friend in Laporte not long ago. I know almost no one in Colorado. Perhaps we could both use a friend."

She stuck out her hand. He stared at it a moment before joining it with his, feeling her fingers light as bird bones against his palm. The moment hung in the cool mountain air between them. He could see her steady heartbeat along her throat.

"Perhaps you're right. But I fear hawks are rarely good friends to sparrows."

She wrinkled her nose, breaking the spell. "If you're trying to frighten me, Mr. Kelly, it's a bit late for that. You've promised to escort me safely to Battlement Park, and if we ever get moving, I expect you will."

He dropped her hand and moved to hold Smoke's bridle for her. A smile touched his lips. "People rarely surprise me, Mrs. Braddock. You seem to make a habit of it."

Using one of the boulders that dotted the road, she scrambled onto the mare's back. "It's not a conscious habit. I have no idea what you expect from me."

Elijah swung himself into Achilles' saddle. "I expect you to tell me next time you need to stop for a rest. Understand?"

She grimaced. "I understand." She shifted in her saddle. "I can't decide whether it's better to rest or whether the pain would be over faster if we didn't stop and just got to Battlement Park as quickly as possible."

He laughed. "You'll make it. I promise." He nudged Achilles into a fast walk, moving out ahead of Jordan and Smoke on the narrow road. As it wound higher up the cliff above the river, he found it difficult to keep from smiling. Even the thought that he was enjoying her company when he preferred riding alone couldn't quench the pleasure he felt in it. The air smelled too sweet and his headache had almost disappeared, only a headache after all and not something worse.

As Achilles picked his way around a granite outcrop that curved the road away from the cliff, a flash of movement in front of them caught Elijah's eye.

He groaned in exasperation. "Loki! Don't even think about it!"

And then his world exploded in noise and pain.

# Chapter 6

Smoke's high-pitched bugle echoed Achilles' scream as the thunderous gunshot reverberated off the canyon walls around them. Jordan heard her own voice join Smoke's as she jerked on her reins, trying to prevent the mare from skidding off the road in her terrified attempts to turn around. Smoke threw up her head, screaming again, her lone voice no longer matched by Achilles'.

Jordan's eye didn't catch Achilles' fall. All she saw was the suddenly empty road in front of her.

"Elijah!"

The blood pounding in her head drowned out her shout and the sounds of falling rocks. She threw herself off Smoke's back, her foot catching for a second in her stirrup. She hung on to the reins until she regained her balance, then dropped them, not caring if Smoke ran all the way back to Oxtail.

Faster than she, Loki brushed past her, plunging over the edge of the road.

"Hold it right there, lady!"

She didn't even look around to see the man who had barked the order. Hardly more cautious than Loki, she ran to the cliff edge and looked down toward the water, her mind blank of fear or prayer. Achilles had rolled half into the river. Jordan's breath left her in a strangled gasp at the sight of the great bay gelding broken on the rocks below, his blood-spattered neck twisted at an obscene angle.

"I said stop right there, lady!"

Her feet left the road, searching for purchase on the steep slope beneath as her eyes swept the swirling gray-brown river.

*Elijah.*

Loki had found him. The wolf stood over the still, black form that had wedged against a distorted pine tree halfway down the slope. Elijah had been thrown from his saddle during the fall, but had Achilles crushed him on the way down?

*It's all my fault. It's all my fault.* No matter that the words made no sense, they repeated in Jordan's head to the rhythm of her fluttering heart.

"Lady!"

She couldn't breathe, but her feet kept moving, picking their way across the treacherous rubble of the slope. Ten feet from the gunfighter's body she lost her footing and half-slid, half-scrambled the rest of the way.

"Elijah?" *It's my fault.* She'd hardly had time to offer her friendship, and already he'd been killed. Again, she had offended the fates, and they would continue to punish her for it by killing anyone she cared about. *Oh, God, it's all my fault.*

At the sound of her approach, Loki's throat bristled. His low growl faded into a high-pitched whine when he recognized her.

Jordan reached for Elijah's head, turned away from her toward the river. "Elijah?" Her fingers found his cheek warm and rough to the touch, but he made no response to her voice or the contact of her hand.

"Get away from him, lady." The voice shouted in frustration from above. "I ain't gonna hesitate to shoot you if I got to."

Grabbing a twisted limb of the pine beside her for support, she turned to look up at the road. The barrel of a rifle pointed straight at her head, and behind the rifle a man in a shapeless brown hat knelt on the edge of the cliff. Against the bright sky, she couldn't make out much of his face except for the brindle of his graying beard.

"I said, move away. I ain't gonna let that scoundrel take a shot at me from behind your skirts."

Fury and horror made Jordan's legs shake. "He's not going to shoot you, you goddamn fool! You killed him." Beside her, Loki began to growl again.

The man lifted his eye from his rifle sight to squint down at her. "Damn. You sure about that?"

"Of course I'm sure." Her voice squeaked on the edge of hysteria. "I've already had two husbands killed. I know a dead body when I see one."

"Damn. Well, you'd better make your way back up here, Mrs. Kelly. Guess I'm gonna need a rope." The face disappeared.

Loki scrambled past her, his huge teeth bared.

"Loki, no!"

The wolf stopped to look back at her.

"No. Don't you get yourself killed, too." Her voice cracked. He wouldn't listen to her. Intent on his quarry, he was already turning away.

"I'm not . . . quite dead." The unsteady voice froze them both.

Jordan's feet slipped again as she spun around, and she sat down hard. "Elijah?"

Only a thin rim of gold showed around his huge pupils, but they focused on her face. "More or less."

"Are you all right?" Stupid question. "Where do you hurt?"

"Huh." He tried to pull his left hand out from behind the tree and dropped it heavily again. "Everywhere."

"Are you shot?" She lifted his other hand. It moved faintly

in hers. Loki crept up beside her and laid his head on the gunfighter's stomach.

"I don't think so." His breath wheezed harshly. "I think the bullet . . . Achilles?"

She shook her head.

"Bastard."

Jordan glanced behind her up the slope. "He's coming back."

Elijah choked on bitter laughter. "I meant Achilles."

She glared down at him until his breath returned. "I told the man who shot him that you were dead."

"It only feels that way." He shifted, trying to sit up, but fell back again with a grimace. "I may have a broken rib. But I suspect that won't matter when our friend returns with his rifle. Can you reach Achilles? Get my rifle or the guns in my saddlebags?"

Jordan rose to a crouch, her eyes searching out the dark form of the horse twenty feet below.

"Hey, there! Miz Kelly!" The man had returned. Those twenty feet might as well have been twenty miles. "I'm gonna toss down the end of this rope. You tie it around his waist, and once I've hauled him up, I'll send the rope back down for you."

"Mrs. Kelly?"

The amusement in Elijah's strangled whisper infuriated her. He wouldn't be laughing long once their assailant found out he was still alive.

"A misunderstanding," she growled. But a misunderstanding that might prove useful. She bit her lip as a desperate idea blossomed in her mind. "Do you know that man?"

Elijah blinked against the brightness of the sky. "I don't know. I don't think so, but he's fairly fuzzy from here."

Jordan's knees shook as she stood. She had to get Elijah up

that slope. He obviously had some kind of head injury as well as his broken rib, and she could do nothing for him where he lay. She couldn't help him by herself.

"Now, Miz Kelly, I know you're upset, but you gotta grab the end of this rope."

She looked up at the man on the road. "How do you know my name?"

"Eh?"

"I said, how do you know my name? How do you know who I am?"

The lines on the man's forehead crinkled. "Why, I didn't, lady. I recognized that no 'count husband of yours. I seen him in Longmont and set up here waiting for him. I recognized him from this here wanted poster." He waved a wrinkled yellow handbill. " 'Ee-lijah Kelly, wanted for attempted murder. Armed and Dangerous.' I expect they'll be glad to see him up there in Laramie, though the bounty is more for him alive."

He spat off to one side at the injustice.

"I've got some good news for you." Jordan crossed her arms over her chest. "He's not dead after all."

"Shii-it!" The man dropped to his stomach, his rifle bouncing on the rocks along the road edge. "Get away from him, lady. I mean it."

"Do as he says," Elijah ordered, his voice taut.

"No."

"Damn it, move!" She heard Elijah shift behind her, trying to leverage himself up to push her away, but the sound of the rifle lever being thrown froze him.

"I'm not going to move," she repeated, surprised at how cool and calm her voice sounded, "because I've also got some bad news for you. You've got the wrong man."

"What?"

"You've shot the wrong man."

"Like hell I did."

"How dare you!" Jordan gave her indignation free reign. "You've shot our horse. You've well-nigh killed my husband. And now you're calling me a liar?" She didn't have to feign the fury as her voice rose. "My husband's name is Zechariah Kelly, and he may be the brother of the no-good gunslinger you're after, but that is no fault of his. My husband is a man of God!"

"He's a preacher?"

Jordan cringed as she realized that not only had she lied and probably blasphemed, but she'd gotten the idea for Elijah's new profession from his ridiculous nickname. If their attacker had heard of Preacher Kelly . . .

But the man above them lowered his rifle slightly. "You ain't gonna trick me. He ain't no preacher."

"I'm a Methodist, suh. Strictly speaking." Elijah's voice, weak as it was, reached their assailant's ears. But his whisper was for Jordan alone. "He's not going to buy this. You're going to get yourself killed."

The man shifted. "I'm a Baptist."

"I hope you won't hold that against me, brother."

Jordan grimaced. Trust Elijah to find the situation amusing.

"This ain't right." The man retreated back behind his rifle. "This don't say nothing about no brother. That there's Ee-lijah Kelly, and I ain't letting him get away."

Hearing doubt in his voice, Jordan played her last, desperate card. "It doesn't say anything about a wife, either, does it? Take another look at that poster you've got there. Look real hard. And then you look at my husband. Take your time. You'll see they're two different men."

For a long moment the man didn't move. Then he shifted,

and the handbill rustled against the gravel as he unfolded it with one hand. He peered at it closely, then glared down at Elijah. Jordan held her breath. She'd yet to see a wanted poster with a decent portrait on it, but this one had obviously been good enough for the man to recognize Elijah in the first place.

"Hell." The man's face twisted in indecision. "He does look smaller than the man in this pitcher. And a lot older, too."

"My brother's always been known as the handsome one in the family," Elijah drawled.

"Hell, I don't know."

"One more thing," Elijah said, finally managing to shift himself into a sitting position. "I'm not armed. 'For all they that take the sword shall perish with the sword.' I have a rifle for hunting, but I suspect it is beyond repair." He gestured toward Achilles' body.

"Yeah?"

"I'll show you."

"No!" The man waved his rifle at Jordan. "You take his coat off for him. If either one of you makes a funny move, I'll shoot you both, see if I don't."

"I'm going to have to stand up," Elijah said.

"Put your hands on that there tree and keep 'em where I can see 'em."

"Right." Elijah reached up for the branch Jordan held. His face twisted in pain, but when she moved forward to help him, he shook his head. "Move back. If he gets nervous, I don't want him to shoot you by mistake."

With both hands on the pine branch, he pulled himself to his feet. The little tree shook with his effort. He raised his arms out to his sides, careful to keep his hands away from his coat.

"Slowly," he murmured to Jordan.

Jordan bit her lip, knowing any sudden movement would frighten their attacker into shooting. She edged between Elijah and the pine tree. The broad expanse of his back shielded her completely from the man with the gun, but she felt no relief. At any moment a rifle bullet might tear into Elijah's heart and leave her alone.

Alone with a murderous gunman. She lifted trembling hands to Elijah's duster.

She reached around his shoulders to grasp each side of the front of his coat. Even standing on tiptoe, she had to flatten herself against his back to reach all the way around. His dark hair tickled her nose, and she could smell dust and horse and sweat and wool mixed with the musky scent of his skin.

For an instant, she shook with the desperate desire to bury her face in the back of his duster and hide there. Hide from the fear, from Achilles' death, from memories and from the future.

Her fingers wrapped around the edges of Elijah's coat, and she pulled it back, lifting it over his shoulders and letting it slide slowly down his arms.

"Well, I'll be. You *ain't* armed."

"No."

Jordan felt the rumble of the word in his chest.

"Well, okay, Reverend Kelly. You tie that coat up with this rope, and I'll pull it up first. You don't mind if I take a look-see through your pockets?"

Elijah shook his head. The motion made his foot slip, and Jordan grabbed his arm. The muscles trembled, but as she moved beside him, she saw that his face showed no indication of his pain. He took the duster from her and wrapped their attacker's rope around it.

"Once I get that coat up here, then I'll send the rope back

down for you and then for your missus, Reverend."

"Thank you, friend," Elijah said, watching until the duster swished up onto the road and the man's face disappeared. Then he turned to Jordan. "Let him help you up first. I'm going down to Achilles."

"You'd never make it down there. You're hurt, remember?"

"I've got a broken rib, not a broken leg. I've made tougher climbs."

Jordan glanced down the slope at the horse, water swirling up his side almost to the saddlebags. The saddlebags. Of course. She turned on Elijah, her nerves snapping.

"Are you crazy? What do you think you're going to do, go down there and get your guns? And then what? Your sixshooters are no match for that rifle. And there's no cover down there. He'll just sit up there on the road and shoot you full of holes."

Her breath came hard and fast, and she found her hand balled into a fist. "I'm not going to let you go down there and get yourself killed."

"And just how are you planning to stop me?" His hint of amusement infuriated her.

"Let me see. A good punch in the ribs ought to do it."

His mouth twisted, and then laughter shook him. He had to grab the pine limb to keep his balance.

"You don't think I'd do it?"

He shook his head, squinting with the pain of laughing. "No, I'm sure you would." He met her gaze, his eyes still more black than gold. "You've already put your safety at risk to save my life, Sparrow. Not many would have done that. I promise you I won't recklessly throw your gift away."

She finally was the one to glance away, unclenching and clenching her fists.

"But I do need to retrieve my saddlebags and my violin. If

there's anything left of it."

"I'll do it." Exasperation harshened her voice. "Don't be an idiot."

He looked away from her, his lips narrowing. "I can't just leave Achilles like that."

"You're going to have to," she said. "We can't move him, and even if we could, there's nowhere to move him to."

"I know," he said brusquely. She had thought the gelding's death hadn't affected him; once again she'd misjudged him. "I know. I—" He sighed. "Thank you. Are you sure you can get down there safely?"

Jordan snorted derisively, careful not to look down the twenty-foot slope of rock and rubble. "I've made tougher climbs, too."

When she'd been nine years old.

The rifleman's voice interrupted them again. "All right, Reverend Kelly. Here's the rope. You jes' tie it around your waist, and I'll haul you up. I've already got it hooked to my saddle."

Elijah let go the pine branch to reach for the rope and loop it beneath his arms.

"Your ribs." Jordan hadn't recognized that problem before. "He can't pull you up that way."

But Elijah waved her away. "I'll take the weight in my hands as much as possible and walk up. As long as I don't breathe, I ought to be all right."

Jordan didn't laugh, but she didn't argue. Perhaps she was getting to know him better after all; he planned to do things his way, and that was that. As the man above started his horse forward, tightening the rope, Elijah leaned back, leveraging himself against the slope. He started upward, Loki beside him. His feet slipped on the loose stones, and once he fell to his knees, the rope tightening abruptly around his chest. But he struggled to his feet again. Jordan could hear the harshness of his breath.

When she couldn't bear to watch any longer, she started down toward the river, toward the broken, dead horse. Horror had numbed her; her emotions were blank as she set about the grim task of salvaging Elijah's belongings from Achilles' body.

She rummaged through the gunfighter's saddlebags, pulling out his gunbelt. Even while hitching up her skirt and buckling the belt over her hips, knowing the gunman might look down any time and see her, she felt nothing but the driving of necessity.

She found Elijah's violin case a few yards from the horse's body. One side was dented, but flipping open the buckles along the edge, she found the violin itself appeared miraculously unharmed. She ran a finger across the strings, the dissonance drowned by the rush of the river.

A violin. No, she didn't know this man at all.

The rope dropped once more, and she began tying Elijah's belongings to it, the violin case first. She found Elijah's hat among the rocks above the horse and stuffed it into the saddlebags, sending them next along with the soaked rifle and the bridle she slipped over Achilles' foam and blood-flecked muzzle. He couldn't bite her now. She brushed at her eyes and moved to the saddle. Death came as suddenly and inexplicably in the West as it did anywhere.

After the saddle, the rope returned for her. She looked up the long slope at Elijah and the other man.

What was she doing here? What had possessed her to travel out into the western wilderness with a notorious gunfighter? Her hands stung from climbing down the cliff. Her feet were nearly frozen from clambering around Achilles in the river, and the man she had to trust to pull her back to safety had only recently been shooting at her. Well, maybe he hadn't been shooting at *her,* but she'd had more bullets fly past her today then she cared to count, and all she wanted was to go home to Aunt Rue's for a hot bath and a cup of peppermint tea.

She wrapped the rope around her waist and grabbed tight. Undoubtedly it would rub her hands raw by the time she reached the top of the slope. Her only consolation was that the day could hardly get any worse.

She waved her readiness to the men waiting above, and the rope tightened around her. Leaning back for balance, she had little difficulty picking her way up over the rocks, though it seemed at least four times as far going up as it had coming down.

The two men waiting at the top helped her onto the road. But it was Loki she reached for, digging her hand into his neck fur for comfort.

"Miz Kelly." Their attacker touched his hat brim. His height surprised her; he was nearly half a foot shorter than she. Ropy muscles thickened his arms and legs, and his coffee-dark eyes were set deep in a face browned and wrinkled by the sun. "The name's Billy Calhoun. Pleased to meet you."

Since she couldn't say the same, she said what was on her mind. "Mr. Calhoun, you owe us a horse."

Calhoun frowned. "All I got is old Rosy and my pack mule, and I cain't spare him."

"You should have thought of that before you pulled the trigger on that rifle," Jordan said, examining the man's horse.

Old Rosy resembled her master, short and squat, her gray muzzle as grizzled with white as his. But she looked as tough as the pack mule.

"We'll make do with Rosy, and you'll have to make do with your feet."

She heard Calhoun spit. "Lady, I'm sorry about your horse, but I ain't giving you Rosy."

"Mr. Calhoun owes us nothing," Elijah's low voice interrupted. "Shooting Achilles was the result of an understandable mistake—"

"A *mistake?*" Jordan was sick and tired of the "code of the West." It was time for some Yankee practicality. "It was a deliberate attempt at murder! What do you think you're going to do, Mr. Kelly? Walk to Battlement Park with a head injury and a broken rib?"

"We've still got Smoke, Mrs. Kelly," he replied, his calm words a warning. Anger had made her forget the dangerous charade they were playing. Calhoun hadn't made a mistake at all, and the sooner they were rid of him, the less likely he was to realize it.

"Yes, of course we still have Smoke," she said, surprised to note that the mare still stood where she'd left her by the side of the road. "You're right, Zechariah. Please forgive me, Mr. Calhoun, for my lack of charity."

The man's weathered face reddened. " 'Course that's all right, Miz Kelly. It's jes' that Rosy's about all the friend I've got." He glanced at the old mare and shuffled his feet. "I'll tell you what I can do. There's a grassy clearing 'bout a mile back up the canyon. I'll help you carry all your things up there, get you settled down for the night. Tomorrow I can bring help from Battlement Park."

"That's very kind of you," Jordan said, now eager only to escape the man. "But it's not necessary. We plan to push on to Battlement Park tonight. Mr. Kelly—my husband—needs medical attention."

"Why, you ain't going to make it to Battlement Park

tonight, Miz Kelly."

She looked to Elijah. "You said it wasn't that much farther."

He shook his head. "Look at the sky. This incident has cost us at least two hours. Mr. Calhoun's right. With only one horse we'll never make it to Battlement Park before dark. We had better find a place to camp for the night."

Jordan's eyes closed only briefly as she promised herself that she would never again doubt that things could, indeed, always get worse.

# Chapter 7

Calhoun dumped a last armload of wood beside the fire. Flames sent smoky curls of ash up toward the gap of dusky blue visible between the canyon walls. "That ought to last you through the night. I'll be taking my leave, 'less there's anything else you need."

Jordan fought back the impulse to ask Calhoun to stay. Despite the fact that she'd spent a good portion of the afternoon at the wrong end of his rifle barrel, his presence added some sense of human companionship to their desolate location.

Not that the meadow was not as lovely as Calhoun had promised. Ringed by pines that shielded them from the road, it offered not only a park-like carpet of green grass, but also a sense of quiet and privacy.

Yet she could feel the empty wilderness stretching out around her, feel it reaching inside her to touch her soul. Every so often a tremor of terror caught her unawares at the thought of what she would do if Elijah's injuries were worse than she thought, and he died. She would go mad if she had to spend a night in this empty silence alone.

Even the companionship of a murderous mountain man was better than that. Besides, for the past hour and a half Calhoun had put aside his murderous tendencies and acted the perfect, if rough-edged, gentleman. He'd not only helped them haul their belongings to this camp site, he'd built a fire and donated a rabbit and some potatoes to their supper, which he'd cooked with simple skill.

"I think we're settled for the night," she said, offering him her hand. "Are you sure you want to travel now? It's nearly twilight already."

"I know this road like I know my own nose," Calhoun assured her. "I been hunting these mountains longer'n I like to remember. Don't know that I'll be back next winter, though. With prices on elk meat like they are in Longmont, hunting barely keeps me in coffee these days. 'Course, bounty hunting doesn't seem to be doing me much better."

He shrugged off the disappointment. "I'll see you get some help come tomorrow."

Elijah rose from his seat on a log by the fire. Loki remained lying by his side, glaring balefully at Calhoun. The wolf had refused to leave the gunfighter's side since his fall.

Elijah shook Calhoun's hand. "I was kicked by a mule once. Wasn't any worse than this. Of course, I was younger then."

Calhoun grunted. "Just be sure to keep that fire going. It'll be a cold one tonight."

He swung himself up on old Rosy, and with a tug on the pack mule's lead, they set off toward the road.

Elijah shook his head as Calhoun disappeared behind a tree. "That's a dying breed."

"A killing breed is more accurate," Jordan retorted.

The echoes of Rosy's and the mule's hoofbeats faded, merging into the ceaseless roar of the river. Jordan could feel the shadows deepening around them as the sky darkened above. She shivered. Calhoun was right. It would be a cold night.

"I'll get the blankets."

Elijah had bought blankets in Longmont that morning,

calling them a necessary precaution for entering the mountains at this time of year. But they were only emergency supplies. Jordan dragged the two rough wool blankets from their pile of gear and wished they'd packed real bedrolls and maybe a couple of pillows. But comfort was secondary to her concern about warmth.

She'd cleansed the blood-caked lump she'd found on the back of Elijah's head, and he'd shown no more ill effects from it, but she still feared that the head injury combined with the cold might send him into shock.

As for herself, she wasn't sure she'd ever get warm again. The terror and anger and grief she'd felt during the long day had worked into her heart and frozen there. The echoing emptiness of the canyon filled her soul with the knowledge of its own frailty. She could feel the life flickering in her like a flame that one good gust of wind might blow out.

Elijah's voice broke the silence. "While you're over there, could you get me a clean shirt?"

"Of course."

She opened the stiff buckle on one of Elijah's saddle bags. In among his leather shaving kit, an extra pair of socks, blue jeans she'd never seen him wear, and a packet of gunpowder, she found his two extra shirts. One was wrapped around a small silver box, like a snuff box, though she'd never seen him use tobacco.

She pulled out the other shirt. It was bleached a harsh white, but the cotton, softened through frequent washings, felt like goose down against her finger tips. She wrapped her icy hands in it, bringing the shirt closer to her face. Despite its fastidious cleanness, she thought she caught Elijah's scent in the fabric.

Involuntarily, she imagined running her hands over the shirt while he wore it, feeling the hard, warm muscles beneath the cotton. And if she pushed aside the fabric, she could feel the skin itself, a fire to burn warmth into her fingers. She shivered, but not from the cold.

She took a deep breath of crisp mountain air, clearing her head of foolishness. Tears stung her eyes. It shouldn't surprise her that she wanted a touch of human comfort this evening. Anything to combat the cold and the fear that had sunk into her bones. It had been nearly a year and a half since Frank's death, but she still wasn't used to being alone.

Of course, she'd met other attractive men during the past year and hadn't fantasized about touching them. But then she'd never been stuck out in the middle of nowhere with one after being shot at twice in one day.

She buckled Elijah's saddlebag, gathered up the shirt and blankets, and turned back to the fire. It was fifty feet away, and yet suddenly she felt its heat.

Elijah stood before the flames at an angle to her, a knife between his teeth and his shirt in his hands. As she watched, he tore a long strip off the shirt, notched the material again with the knife and tore off another strip. But it was the lack of shirt on his back rather than what he was doing with the one in his hands that caught her gaze. The muscles in his arms and shoulders rippled beneath his bare skin as he worked. Skin darker than she'd expected, a tan that glowed in the firelight and suggested he wore his shirt less consistently than he wore his hat.

He must have sensed her stillness, for he glanced in her direction. He pulled the knife from between his teeth.

"I thought I should wrap this rib if I want to get any sleep tonight. The shirt was ruined anyway."

"Very sensible." Jordan made her feet move forward again, trying not to stare, hoping she wasn't too obviously not staring. Her brief moment of fantasy had seemed harmless enough when she knew she'd never see the gunfighter's bare skin. Now, it made her face flame. She dropped her burden by the fire.

From the corner of her eye, she saw Elijah sit down on his log, tucking his knife back in his boot. Loki settled against the boot with a sigh as the gunfighter lifted his left arm experimentally, seeing how much use he could make of it before his rib protested.

Jordan unrolled their blankets and arranged them on opposite sides of the fire—not far enough apart, she could hear Aunt Rue objecting, given the tendencies of even the most chivalrous gentleman. Another glance at the gentleman in question showed her Elijah had managed to wrap a strip of cloth once around his chest, but his face looked gray from the effort.

"Oh, for heaven's sake," she muttered, brushing her hands on her skirt. He was in no condition to assault her, even if she asked him to. "Here, let me do that."

He glanced up at her, the firelight picking out flecks of gold in his hazel eyes. For a second his gaze reminded her he was a gunfighter. Then he shrugged and handed her the strip of cloth he held.

"I don't seem to be getting very far by myself. I would be grateful for your assistance."

Jordan moved behind him, looking doubtfully at the dirty, torn cloth she held. She'd have to tie several strips together to make them hold his rib in place, but she supposed they'd do.

"I've tended a broken bone or two in my day," she said, working several short strips into one long one. She crouched down to get a better look at his back. "Living on a farm, someone's always falling out of an apple tree or having a run-in with an ox."

The mundane words allowed her to run a professional

hand against his rib cage, probing the bruise she found. "And Frank and I always seemed to have a horde of nieces and nephews running underfoot, getting into trouble."

She felt a knot beneath her fingers, but no movement. "Of course, a kiss and a piece of pie cured as many of their bruises as a bandage did. I think you've got a broken rib, all right, but it doesn't feel too bad. If you avoid throwing yourself off cliffs for a week or two, you should be fine."

She slipped the end of the makeshift bandage around his chest, trying not to notice the scent of his skin or that it felt firmer and more supple than she'd imagined.

"You never had children of your own?"

Her fingers fumbled with the cloth, but the wave of grief and regret she expected didn't come. Perhaps because she heard no pity in his voice.

"No." She looped the cloth again around his chest. "I . . . no." She didn't talk about such personal things with anyone. And yet the words came. "Jack and I . . . Jack enlisted in the Union Army near the end of the war. When it was over, he was sent out west with his cavalry unit. We were . . . careful. He didn't want to miss the birth of his first child. He died a month before his discharge. And then Frank and I, we planned a family. But it never came."

They'd stopped talking about it eventually. She knew that at some point Frank had given up any hope of having children. But she never had, not until the day he'd died.

"In four days, my son will be thirteen." The soft-spoken words surprised Jordan almost as much as her own confession had. "I never knew I had a son until he was nearly a year old."

Elijah shifted as she reached around him again. "The life of a gunfighter is no life for a child. Wolf's grown up with a real family, in a real home. Now, he's no longer a child." His voice faded, mixing with the smoke from the fire. "I'm beginning to wonder if I had it wrong all those years. Maybe the life of a gunfighter is no life for a father."

She couldn't see his face, but she felt the tension in his back. She tightened the last wrap she'd made around his chest, then tied the ends of the cloth together.

"There. It doesn't look pretty, but it ought to stay in place." She stood, but her hand rested tentatively on Elijah's shoulder. "We all have our own regrets."

She could see his face in profile now, and his lips turned up wryly. "And life is never quite what we expect it to be." He shifted over on the log, making room, and Jordan found herself stepping over it to sit beside him.

The fire turned his eyes to mirrors of gold. "I've made so many mistakes in my life that if I lived to a hundred and ten I could never hope to put them right. I don't know if God can forgive me for all of them. I have not. But a worse sin than any would be to stop living for fear of making more."

"I suppose."

He smiled as he shrugged into his clean shirt, a smile more predatory than amused. "What I said is just as true for grief, Sparrow. You can't stop living for fear of being hurt again."

"What do you mean?" Jordan asked, suddenly, unexpectedly, defensive.

He studied her with his unnerving stare. "When I first met you on that train, and later at the Jacksons' ranch, I thought you were so carefully controlled because you were afraid to let out your feelings, that your grief might explode and destroy you."

Jordan could think of no appropriate reply for a statement so utterly presumptuous and at the same time so painstakingly impersonal.

"But I think I misjudged the situation," Elijah continued, undaunted by her silent indignation. "I think the danger is not that your grief will explode, but that it will crush you. I thought you came to the mountains running away. But I was wrong, wasn't I? You came looking for something, looking for a reason to keep fighting the pain."

Jordan's hands clenched in her lap. "Do you have a point to make?" she asked. "With these gunfighter platitudes?"

The intensity faded from his eyes. "I just don't want you to overlook the possibility that you may have already found what you were looking for."

Heat flushed her cheeks. "And just what do think that is, Mr. Kelly?"

His mouth twisted, and he looked back toward the fire. "I mean this place where we are now. The heat from this fire in front of us, the cold breath of the canyon behind. The unending flow of the river, the unfeeling light of the stars. This peace that you've fought so hard against ever since we stopped here."

Jordan glanced up, but the firelight had blinded her to the stars. "You mean this emptiness? This brutal emptiness that doesn't care whether we live or die?"

"Peace is never empty. Only peace can show you what's inside your soul. And what you'll find there is that it doesn't matter that the mountains don't care whether you live or die. It only matters that you care."

Jordan shook her head. "Maybe that's true for you. I'm not that strong. It matters a great deal to me to know there are people who care about me."

"But you do know that. Your family back in Connecticut, your cousin and her husband in Denver, even people you've just met like Barnett Treadwell and Maggie and March Jackson care what happens to you." His soft drawl was almost hypnotic. "Maybe you had to come up here, away from all of them, to discover that you care, too."

She felt an unexpected smile touch her lips. He had an odd idea of what to say to make someone feel better, and yet he'd pushed back the emptiness, just a little.

"You're quite a philosopher, Mr. Kelly."

"I see. We're back to 'Mr. Kelly'?"

"Since we're no longer married, it seems appropriate."

He raised an eyebrow. "Perhaps it was a result of my injuries, but I have a memory of you calling me by name just after my fall this afternoon."

She frowned at him. "I thought you were dead."

His smile reached his eyes. "So in order for you to call me by my given name, I have to be either married to you or dead?"

"Thus far, they've proven to be much the same thing."

She thought she'd managed to make it into a joke, but his eyes darkened. "Is that what you meant this afternoon, when you said my fall was all your fault?"

"What? I didn't say that."

"You muttered it several times. Perhaps it's another one of those things you only say to dead people."

Jordan stared, horrified. She hadn't thought she'd spoken the thought out loud.

"Your husbands' dying has nothing to do with you. And Calhoun shooting at me certainly didn't."

"Of course not." Jordan fought to control her composure. She forced a laugh. "You got shot *before* I became Mrs. Kelly, remember?"

To her surprise, it was Elijah who flushed and turned back toward the fire. "Of course. I only meant that . . . you and I were traveling together, and I had made a promise to take care of you. You might not have much faith in such promises."

"I'm perfectly capable of taking care of myself."

"I know." He glanced at her sideways. "I knew that before I offered to guide you."

Awareness prickled through her, kindling a warmth more thorough than the flames. Her head told her he had meant nothing by the remark, but something primal within her responded anyway. She had merely to ask him why, then, he had come with her, and when he answered . . .

She parted her lips, but the words didn't come. She was afraid of his answer, as afraid that it would be what she suddenly wanted to hear as she was afraid it would not be.

He laughed softly, breaking the moment. "And it's a damn good thing you can take care of yourself. So far I've needed your help more than you've needed mine. Of course, if it weren't for me, you'd be in Battlement Park now, missing out on this camp fire and the smell of the pine trees."

Jordan shook her head mournfully. "I'd be stuck in some nice, warm cabin with a real bed. Poor me. Instead of frigid, muddy river water, I'd have hot water for a bath. And for tea."

Elijah laughed. "And elk steak and fresh bread to look forward to for breakfast in the morning."

"And a lamp for sketching by."

"Or maybe fried eggs and griddle cakes."

"A book to read."

"Biscuits and gravy. Or hominy."

Jordan jabbed him in the shoulder. "Would you quit talking about food!"

"I thought you said you weren't all that strong," Elijah complained, rubbing his shoulder. His eyes glinted. "I was right yesterday."

"About what?"

"You are even more beautiful when you laugh."

The sudden surge of reaction that rippled through her was

as shocking as a headlong plunge into a glacial lake. His words, so easy to say, cracked a barrier she hadn't even realized she'd erected, and for just a moment they tore her apart in a rush of fear and desire.

For just a moment she rejected the self she'd become, a staid, sensible widow who'd make do with memories of passion. Agonizing hunger choked her, hunger to be cherished, held, loved. Hunger to be touched. Hunger to have a hungry mouth press against hers.

Elijah's mouth.

She turned away, shocked by her response, biting the inside of her cheek until she tasted blood, fighting for control. Feeling his eyes on her, she could almost picture the image he'd used earlier in the day, she as the sparrow, he the hawk searching for her soul. And when he found it, he could pluck it from her in a heartbeat.

She hoped he couldn't see her shaking.

"I'm tired." Her voice sounded dead in her ears, at odds with her raging pulse. "We've got a long walk tomorrow; I'd better get some sleep."

"Yes."

Jordan could feel the cold night air rushing into his place beside her as he stood. A sigh of pain escaped him. She rose, ready to offer an arm. "Your rib?"

He wasn't looking at her, his face knotted in a fearful grimace. "My head."

Jordan swallowed down the fluttering fear that she'd overlooked a crack in his skull when she'd bandaged the back of his head.

"That's a nasty lump you've got," she said, forcing herself to remain calm. "It's probably going to give you headaches for a few days. I don't have anything to give you for it, but I'm sure once we get to Battlement Park we can find some medicine that will ease the pain."

The lines in his forehead eased with sudden relief. "I'd forgotten about that tree connecting with my skull. I'm sure it will feel better by morning."

Jordan didn't think his forgetting the injury was such a good sign, but she kept her peace. There was nothing more she could do for him that night. She hoped there was a decent doctor in Battlement Park and that Elijah would be all right until they could reach him tomorrow.

While Elijah fed the fire, she adjusted her blanket a little closer to the flames and crawled between the folded halves. A rock jabbed sharply into her hip and thigh. She shifted onto her other side. Another jab. It took her another moment of fruitless shifting to realize the rocks that plagued her were in fact Elijah's revolvers, still hidden up under her skirt.

Thrashing around under the blanket, she managed to unhook the gunbelt and slip it down her legs. She brought it up to her chest. Firelight flickered on the metalwork decorating the revolver stocks. She wrapped her right hand around one of the guns, its weight alien, yet fitted to her palm. Death sat waiting in each chamber of the revolver while the pulse in her thumb beat against the hard metal.

Uncoiling her fingers in revulsion, she sat the gunbelt beside her and turned to see if Elijah had noticed. He had slipped across the meadow to check on Smoke. He'd put on his coat, hiding the white of his shirt. She could make out only the bulk of his form and the gleam of his eyes as he turned to make his way back to the fire.

She looked back at the guns, as reluctant to touch them again as she would have been to touch a rattlesnake preparing to strike.

"Your gunbelt," she said, lifting it by the buckle.

He materialized out of the night, his black duster swirling

around his knees as he knelt to take it from her. "Thank you." As he lifted the belt, his hand rested lightly on each revolver, the fingers slipping over the smooth stocks with easy familiarity, and she almost wished she hadn't returned the belt. If he'd worn his guns this afternoon, either he or Calhoun would be dead. Perhaps both.

"I haven't yet regretted taking these off," he said quietly as he rose, as though once again reading her mind. "Though there was more than one moment when I would have liked to have repaid Calhoun for what he did to Achilles."

As Elijah moved to his side of the fire, a chill ran up Jordan's spine. For most of the day she'd managed to forget that the man she rode with was a hardened killer. But the tone of his voice left her no doubt that he would be willing to kill a man over a horse.

And the fact that she had felt that same killing anger while unsaddling the dead gelding only made the chill worse.

She scooted back down into her blanket, wrapping it tightly under her chin as she turned her back to the flames. Blackness surrounded her, kept at bay only by the fire's delicate wings of light. Elijah had told her there were few bears and fewer wolves in this area anymore. But it wasn't wild animals that she could feel stalking her.

She lay with her eyes wide, listening to the sound of her heartbeat, the thin thread that kept her from falling into the darkness. She heard Elijah settling into his blanket, heard him murmur something to Loki. Tears burned in her eyes. Tears of exhaustion and fear and regret.

Elijah's words echoed in her memory. You can't stop living for fear of being hurt again. He thought the mountains might restore her life to her. Being shot at? Looking death square in the eye once more? Seeing the brutality that men held within them? Lying in the darkness with nothing to protect her from the demons of grief who came after her in the night. Wishing herself in Elijah's arms, wrapped warm against the darkness, his hands against her face, his breath a promise against her cheek.

She tugged the corner of her blanket up over her face and curled more tightly against the cold. At least she could take comfort in the fact that this time things really couldn't get any worse.

# Chapter 8

Bear.

Abruptly wakened, Jordan's imagination clearly pictured the great, gurgling beast snuffling about the camp. She couldn't run. She couldn't even get up; she was too cold. Maybe if she just stayed quiet, her eyes closed tight, he wouldn't notice her. She listened for the thud of heavy, clawed feet stalking her bedroll, for the frothy snorting of the rabid beast's breath on her neck.

Nothing.

It might have stopped to eat Smoke before it got to her. But she didn't hear any crunching, either. It might be watching her even now, waiting with evil glee for her to move. But she was too tired to move. She knew she needed to stay awake, to stay vigilant, but as the silence stretched out, her exhaustion dragged on her, whispering that it didn't care if she *did* get eaten by a bear, as long as she got to sleep first.

Just as she drifted back toward shadowy dreams, the faintest of sounds drove sleep away for good. A rustling sound behind her. A moan.

Her eyelids flew open. The world was no longer black. Starlight silvered the grass around her. She could pick out the trunks of the trees that hid the river. The soft cold light intensified the returned silence, and Jordan's pounding heart was suddenly the only sound she could hear.

A muffled curse barely reached her ears. A low whine followed.

Loki. Jordan's eyes closed again as she loosed her breath in a sigh. Trust a canine to pick the dead of night to start a game. Her cousin Pete used to sneak his dogs into his room, and the tyrants would wake him at all hours of the night, knowing he had to respond to their demands to keep them quiet or risk his parents' wrath.

At least Loki had chosen Elijah as his victim. For now.

Turning her head, she saw that the fire had burned down to a few red embers. No wonder she was cold. Clutching her blanket about her, she managed to stand and make her way to the woodpile Calhoun had collected. She wanted to relieve her bladder as well, but looking out into the star-shadowed trees, she decided that could wait until dawn.

Her handful of kindling caught quickly, and she added some larger pieces, warming her fingers over them. Elijah hadn't made a sound while she worked, and she guessed he'd fallen back asleep. She glanced over the fire to see Loki lying with his head on the gunfighter's chest, his silver eyes gleaming back at her. His ears pricked forward, and he whined again, a sound that sliced across Jordan's nerves.

"Shhh." She put a finger to her lips. "Let him sleep. Come here, and I'll play with you if you like."

The wolf's ears drooped, and Jordan stifled a laugh. "I'm that irresistible, am I?"

The wolf whined again, barely audible, and suddenly his expression of misery reminded her of how he'd acted when Elijah had fallen over the cliff.

"Mr. Kelly?"

He didn't answer. Of course not. He was asleep. But Loki's gaze still pleaded with her. She watched the gunfighter's chest, but couldn't see whether it moved or not. Fear ran a dread finger along her spine.

She clutched her blanket closer and moved around the fire. She'd probably scare him half to death, creeping up on him in his sleep. But a greater fear overrode her fear of embarrassment.

"Mr. Kelly? Elijah?"

He made a noise, something between a gasp and a chuckle. "Am I dead, then?" he asked, his soft voice flooding her with relief. "Or are we married? I can't keep track."

"I heard a noise." He could be amused if he chose. At least he was alive.

"Loki won't let anything sneak up on us. Go back to sleep."

She almost turned away, but something in his voice didn't sound right.

She moved forward again, around the glare of the fire, and saw his face. Even the ruddy firelight couldn't hide his pallor. His lips pressed together in a thin line against pain. Or cold. Even as she watched, an uncontrollable shudder shook his body.

"My God." She dropped beside him, catching the hand that tried to push her away. His fingers chilled hers. "You're freezing."

"I'm fine." He jerked his hand away. "Thanks to your tending the fire, I'm warming already. Go back to sleep."

He shuddered again.

"You're sick."

"I said I'm fine."

"Yes, you're fine. Just fine." Fear sharpened her tongue. "Chills, clammy skin, fingers like ice are all perfectly normal."

Jordan shrugged her blanket off her shoulders.

"What are you doing?"

"Keeping you from hypothermia."

"I said I was fine. Leave me alone."

A year and a half ago, his harsh order might have daunted her. But she would never forget the feel of Frank's frigid cheek beneath her fingers. She would not lose Elijah to the cold.

Loki shifted as she lay the body-warmed wool over Elijah's own blanket, then the big wolf settled back into place, doing his own part to heat his master.

"We don't have any tea, but I can boil some water." Jordan rose to her feet, needing words to ward off her panic. "It won't taste like much, but I think something hot inside you will help, whatever is wrong."

"Malaria."

"What?"

The gunfighter managed to sit up, pulling the blankets tightly around him. "It's malaria. The chills won't last long. I'll soon be more than warm enough."

"How do you know it's malaria?"

"I first caught the fever during the war. It earned me a medical discharge in 'sixty-four." He paused while the chills racked him again. "It plagues me now and again. Don't concern yourself. It hasn't killed me yet."

In the face of his calm, Jordan's fear receded a little. "But malaria . . . don't you have something to take for it?"

"There's a box of quinine pills in my saddle bags."

She dug her fingers into her palms to keep from strangling him. "Don't you want me to get you some?"

"I can get it for myself. In just a moment." He met her gaze, saw her expression. The harsh lines around his mouth softened slightly. "Please, would you fetch my quinine, ma'am? I'm in your debt."

*"Men."* It took her less than a minute to find the pill box

wrapped in his clean shirt in his saddle bag. She returned to Elijah's side. "I don't understand why you would rather die than ask for help."

"I didn't want to disturb your sleep."

"I think it's too late for that."

She opened the box. A single dark pill fell into her palm. It smelled faintly of licorice and something bitter.

"That's the last?" Elijah asked, sounding only faintly surprised. "I hadn't realized I was so low."

"It's not enough?" Of course not. How could one pill be enough?

"Someone in Battlement Park will have quinine on hand." He took the little pill from her palm. "This will do until we get there." His face twisted in disgust as he swallowed.

"Can I get you anything else?"

"No. Go back to sleep. The quinine will take care of my chills and reduce the fever later. I should be fit to travel by breakfast time. You'll need your rest."

She dug her fingers into the fur behind Loki's ears. "I don't feel much like sleeping anymore."

"And I've got your blanket." At the sudden realization, he began shrugging it off.

"No." She grabbed one hand. The contact felt different this time, reminding her how long it had been since she had touched another person's skin. "Please, keep it. You're already starting to feel warmer."

"Or you're beginning to feel colder." His eyes darkened, resting on the gooseflesh that prickled her bare forearms. He shuddered again, his hand clenching involuntarily on hers.

"I'll be all right," she said. "I'll sit here next to Loki. The fire will keep me warm enough."

It was in his eyes to fight her, but he couldn't rouse the energy. "You'll take your blanket back when the fever comes?"

She nodded.

With a ragged sigh that scared her as much as his shivering, he lay back down, his black lashes fluttering closed against his pale skin. Jordan scooted closer to the fire, drawing her knees up to her chest. She was close enough to Loki to rest a hand on his side. The steady rise and fall of the wolf's ribs comforted her.

In the darkness, its silence cleansed by the voice of the river, time faded away. She couldn't have said how long she stared into the fire before the fever hit, nor how long the fever time lasted, with Elijah so hot she could feel the temperature against her skin from inches away.

The fever brought a vision of hell, the firelight casting demonic shadows across the face of the insensible devil lying beside her. The hungry flames within him burned hotter than those at her back as she fought to cool him with cloths she soaked in water from the river. She knew there were long periods when he didn't recognize her; occasionally her touch even seemed to frighten him. But he didn't have the strength to escape her.

When the fever finally subsided, just as a dawn she'd forgotten would come was brushing the sky overhead, she almost cried with relief. Her shoulders ached, and scratches traced her arms from fighting through the brush to the river. Her arms shook with exhaustion and tension.

And still the malaria had not run its course. Even as Elijah's skin cooled to the touch, it dampened with sweat. And suddenly, the threat of hypothermia returned as the sweat chilled in the frigid dawn air. Jordan struggled to wrap him once more in the blankets he'd discarded during the fever, her ice-cold fingers making him shudder when they brushed against his skin.

When he finally settled into a fitful sleep, Jordan huddled once more close to the fire. The smoke stung her burning eyes, and she buried her face in her knees. All around her she could feel gray. Gray dawn light, gray canyon walls, gray shadows against gray grass.

She almost smiled, even as tears of exhaustion and self-pity trickled down her cheeks. She should be enjoying this brief moment of peace. Things would undoubtedly get worse.

Cruel sunlight pierced Elijah's eyelids, dragging him up from a half-forgotten dream of misery. He tightened his eyes against the light as he assessed his situation. His ribs felt like someone had been hitting him with a hammer all night, the knot on his head throbbed and itched, and his mouth tasted like fuzzy, bitter licorice. Which meant he probably hadn't died. He allowed himself a brief moment of disappointment.

Against his better judgment, his eyelids fluttered open. Morning sunlight streaked across his face; the sky glowed watery blue above him. The river chortled not far away, and unseen birds chittered happily. The whole world seemed renewed in the glorious spring morning.

Elijah shut his eyes and willed himself back toward oblivion.

"How are you feeling?"

The devil had a sweet, sweet voice, but he knew better than to give in to temptation. There were very good reasons why he did not want to be conscious at the moment.

"I know you're awake. I should also warn you that I'm the only thing standing between you and a tongue bath from Loki."

He tried to smile at her, but the sunlight hurt. She might not look like the devil, but she'd sure been through hell. It wasn't her hair, dampened and combed and twisted into a knot behind her head. Or her skin, freshly scrubbed and a rosy red from the icy river water.

It was in the muscles stretched tight along her jaw, the blue smudges beneath her eyes, the haunting fear she hid behind a fierce glare that burned almost as bright as the sunshine.

"Here, try this."

As he struggled to sit up, Jordan handed him a tin cup filled with a hot liquid of dubious origins.

"No offense, ma'am," he said, sure he was about to offend, but unable to stop himself, "but it smells like burning cat hide."

"Boiled rabbit skin," she agreed. "It was the best I could do. There's some willow bark, too, though your fever looks gone for the moment. Drink it."

The injuries and the malaria had weakened him. The cup was at his mouth before he realized it. The hot tin burned his lip. The liquid burned his tongue. But it didn't burn badly enough to stop him from tasting it.

It occurred to him that perhaps he had died, some time ago, and had arrived in hell without noticing.

"I'm sorry I don't have anything better," Jordan said. "It would be good if we could reach Battlement Park before your fever returns. Do you think you are well enough to ride?"

Apparently he looked lively enough for some of the fierceness to fade from her voice.

Familiar guilt crawled around his skin like gooseflesh. He had offered her protection and instead had forced her to spend a night freezing in the wilderness taking care of him. A night which must have brought back all her soul-chilling demons with their icy reminders of death.

And he hadn't cared. He couldn't remember much of the

night before, but he remembered knowing that her quiet murmurs of comfort, her gentle touch with the cold rag had come from fear that she would have to face down death again rather than from any feeling for him. It hadn't mattered. All that mattered was the soft voice that sounded as though he meant something to someone, the soft touch that felt as though someone cared.

He would give anything to have her touch him like that now. And this morning it wasn't the innocent wanting of a sick man.

A damn fool, his father had called him when he'd joined the Union army instead of attending seminary. Apparently his father had been right.

He gulped down the rest of the liquid in the cup, the bitterness almost enough to atone for his more immediate sins. It certainly distracted him from them.

"I can ride," he said, offering the empty cup to Jordan. "Smoke should be watered first."

"I'll have her ready in a few minutes." She took the cup. He thought she was almost as careful as he that their fingers not touch.

He watched her lead Smoke across the meadow, her head bowed in thought, strands of hair escaping her knot to trickle down her back, those fanciful bloomers puffing beneath her skirt. He'd always thought the idea that a woman's bared ankles might incite a man's lust ridiculous, but he was having a hard time remembering that this morning.

A damn fool was right. Yesterday he'd been perfectly happy to enjoy her company and appreciate her beauty and intelligence in an appropriate manner, and he'd do the same today. She wanted a friend. He knew better than anyone that his life had no room for anything more.

With a curse, he pushed himself to his feet. Friend or not,

he was glad she wasn't there to see him stumble, his legs weaker than he expected. It was going to be hard to ride while she had to walk. It still surprised him how weak a bout of malaria left him.

Maggie Jackson had asked him after the last attack if he wanted to die, because if he continued to forget his quinine pills, the malaria just might kill him. The idea hadn't frightened him.

He looked down at his open shirt and the careful wrapping around his ribs. He tasted the bitter bark at the back of his throat. He looked up at the searingly blue sky.

Today, he didn't want to die.

Billy Calhoun met them after they'd gone less than a mile. Good as his word, he'd brought an extra horse, a boxed breakfast, and a small, German man in thick round glasses who turned out to be a doctor on holiday.

"My lungs," he explained to Jordan in a soft, crisp voice as he prodded Elijah's side. "The city air, it is not good for them. Ja, Mr. Kelly, you have cracked ribs. One, maybe two."

Dr. Gottfried proceeded to wrap Elijah's chest, clean the bump on his head and, by some magic, pull a box of quinine pills from his shiny black bag. With a minimum of fuss, they were treated, fed, and in the saddle once more.

Jordan was almost disappointed at the ease of it all. She had prepared herself for things to slide from worse to worse.

Her fears of the night before, the wild panic of knowing herself small and alone in a savage, cold universe seemed a child's fear of the dark in the bright light of a mountain morning. A cloudless sky, picturesque canyon views, a doctor's care . . . all was safe and right with the world, and thank goodness she hadn't said anything too foolish to Elijah when she had thought he was going to die.

As if he'd felt the touch of her thoughts, he turned in his saddle to glance back at her. Jordan favored him with her brightest isn't-this-a-dandy-morning smile and glanced away at the river far below. She'd hoped it would be gone today. That awareness she'd felt the night before. If only he wouldn't look at her with those dangerous eyes.

"Sparrow." Or talk to her. He'd dropped back so he rode beside her. "You don't want to miss this."

She glanced at him, and he pointed ahead. They were riding around a curve in the road, emerging onto a broad ledge above the steepest part of the canyon. Only, magically, it wasn't a canyon anymore.

Jordan gasped in wonder. Spread out below them was a broad valley, but unlike any valley she'd ever seen. Riding through the canyon, she'd forgotten about the mountains, their peaks hidden by the steep cliffs rising above her. Yesterday, the mountains had been a dream. Today, the dream enclosed her.

They marched into the distance, white peaks lifted high above the trees. Close, so close, they gathered around the green bowl below like a convocation of saints, beautiful and terrible, watching over Battlement Park with solemnity and steadfastness. Mist rose from the snow fields high on their slopes, shadowing them in icy haloes.

The park itself might have been a painting of an English countryside, a carpet of lush spring grass, trees scattered about as if by design to create the prettiest picture, the river, swollen as it was, almost lazy across the flat valley bottom.

"Oh," Jordan said, unable to put words to what she saw. How could she ever have thought she could paint this? She could never do it justice. Yet her heart pounded at the idea of trying.

The sound of Billy Calhoun spitting brought her back to herself.

"Damn vacationers. No offense to present company. Pardon the language, ma'am. The place is going to look like Denver afore long."

Leland Hedgpeth had told her that Battlement Park was a swiftly growing resort, much like the larger Estes Park across the nearest mountain ridge. Yet the few rough-hewn buildings near the river seemed insignificant compared to the grandeur about them. Farther up the knee of the closest mountain to the north stood a much larger building, still rustic in character, but with a grand porch all along the front and cabins scattered about it up into the trees.

"That must be the new hotel," Elijah said.

"The Fox and Hound," Dr. Gottfried confirmed. "Run by an Engländer. I believe Herr Calhoun has arranged lodging for you there, nein?"

"That was unnecessary," Elijah said. "I'm sure we can make our own arrangements."

Jordan didn't personally care who made the arrangements. The thought of a comfortable bed—or at least one without rocks in it—was almost enough to tear her eyes away from the scenery.

"That was very kind of you," she told Calhoun.

"It weren't any trouble," Calhoun said, and she thought he might be blushing, though it was hard to tell under his ragged beard. "They wasn't busy. Early in the season yet. I ain't staying around till it fills up, neither."

"We won't hold you up any further," Elijah said. "Why don't you and the good doctor continue ahead. We'll stay and enjoy the view a while. I want to extend my gratitude for your help once more. I don't expect we'll see you at the Fox and Hound?"

Calhoun grimaced. "Wouldn't stay there if my life depended on it. I hear they got goosedown pillows." He spat again.

That did it.

"I have all summer to enjoy the scenery, Mr. Kelly," Jordan reminded him. "And I can't wait to get to it. After a long, long nap."

"I'm sure you don't want to arrive at the hotel immediately," Elijah said. He looked odd to her. She wondered if his fever was returning.

"I'm sure I do," she said, nudging Smoke back into a walk. "And if they've got good English tea, they may never get rid of me."

"Herr Wayne will drown you with tea," Dr. Gottfried assured her, somewhat dolefully. "It is the English cureall. Ah. See there? Herr Wayne rides us to meet."

Tea-swilling, English country gentleman would not have been her first impression of Herr Wayne. The man on the trim blood bay hunter cantering toward them wore neither neat mustache nor tweed coat, and he couldn't have been any older than she. His hair, the color of autumn wheat, was bare to the sun, but his kelly green coat was impeccably fashionable, his boots shone like ebony, and he rode with a military bearing, one hand on his reins, the left free on his fawnclad thigh.

He didn't hurt the scenery a bit. Jordan couldn't stop the smile that played on her lips. A mountain paradise, a handsome English host, hot tea, and goosedown pillows. Things were definitely looking up. Perhaps she had left disaster behind her for the moment.

"Herr Wayne," Dr. Gottfried greeted the man. "I haf just been promising your visitors a cup of your good tea."

"Indeed, Doctor?" The hotel proprietor brought his

hunter to a prancing halt a few yards away. His relaxed smile was ingenuous, but his eyes were sharp.

"I will do my best to ensure they are not disappointed. However, having the acquaintance of Mr. Malachi Kelly, I could not pass up the opportunity to ride out personally to welcome his brother, the good Reverend Zechariah and his wife."

# Chapter 9

She should have known. Disaster hadn't forsaken her. Disaster had simply been waiting for the right time to pounce.

"You know my brother, suh?" Elijah asked, nothing in his voice to indicate there was anything disastrous in that. " 'Better is a neighbor that is near than a brother far off.' This is indeed a pleasure."

"I am enjoying it immensely."

It was obvious to Jordan that Wayne knew Malachi Kelly well enough to know he had no minister brother named Zechariah. Elijah knew Wayne knew. And as they sat poised for anything, Wayne a gold mirror image to Elijah's dark, Jordan didn't have a clue what they were going to do about it.

"You have the advantage of me, Mr. Wayne," Elijah said finally, as though it were not a matter of life and death.

"Ach! How rude of me!" Dr. Gottfried thumped a fist on his thigh. "Frau und Reverend Kelly, this is Herr Major Anthony Wayne."

"Anthony Wayne?" Jordan gulped, sliding helplessly from the melodramatic to the ridiculous. "Like Mad Anthony Wayne, the Revolutionary War general?"

"You can see why I prefer to be called Tony."

"Mr. Wayne," Elijah interrupted, "allow me to introduce you to . . . my wife, Jordan Kelly."

"A great pleasure, ma'am." Somehow Wayne angled his hunter so that he could take her hand and press it lightly with his lips.

Jordan hoped he interpreted her blush as being in response to his kiss. She had no idea how they were going to
remedy this situation, but having Elijah call her his wife was
not something she had any intention of becoming accustomed to.

"I am pleased to make your acquaintance, as well, Major
Wayne."

"Tony, please." His eyes shifted between her and Elijah
and back again. "I consider Mal a good friend. The two of
you may be sure of your welcome at the Fox and Hound."

Jordan glanced at Elijah. He raised an eyebrow. Whatever
scrutiny Tony Wayne had subjected them to, they appeared
to have passed. Unless this were some kind of elaborate trap.
Surely in his present condition Elijah didn't pose enough of a
threat to require a trap.

"Thank you for your kind welcome, Major Wayne." She
stressed the word kind.

"Tony."

"Tony."

"Jolly good!" His broad smile filled with good cheer.
"Shall we ride down to the hotel? You'll have your cup of tea
within the half hour, or I'll know the reason why, Mrs. Kelly.
I know the good doctor would be bereft without his morning
cup."

Dr. Gottfried smiled a tiny, pinched smile, much too polite to roll his eyes. The hotel proprietor gave him a hearty pat
on the back as they started down the road into the park.

"Good mountain air and a spot of tea. It will mend you
better than all your potions, doctor."

"Ach, Herr Wayne, you are too good to me. Too good by
far."

Jordan fell in behind them, simply because there seemed

no other alternative. The tea, the scenery, the down pillows, had all lost their ability to engage her mind. From one desperate, amateur bounty hunter, her ruse had spread to include a doctor and a hotel proprietor. Three men thought she was married to a preacher. Two men. God only knew what Tony Wayne thought.

She shook her head, but it continued buzzing. All she'd wanted when she left Denver was to escape the winter ghosts and attempt to paint. That would have been quite enough adventure for the summer.

No wonder Elijah hadn't wanted to ride down into Battlement Park with Calhoun and the doctor. Perhaps he'd planned to turn tail and run back to Longmont with her.

Not a bad thought.

She glanced longingly back the way they had come. But even if they could miraculously slip away from their escort, they couldn't take Tony Wayne's horse—horse stealing was certainly a hanging offense, whatever Elijah had or had not done in Laramie. It was unlikely Elijah could ride all the way to Longmont in his condition, anyway.

" 'Tony?' " Elijah's low, amused voice by her shoulder snapped her head around. "You never even call me Zechariah."

Smoke danced as Jordan's temper flared. "You go ahead and find it funny," she hissed. "He could turn you over to Billy Calhoun at any moment."

Elijah gave Tony's back a speculative glance. "I don't think he will. And I expect Calhoun will leave Battlement Park by this afternoon. Once he's gone, we can confess our predicament to Tony Wayne."

Jordan blinked. Of course they could, since the man knew who Elijah was anyway. They could drop their temporary roles, and she could stay in Battlement Park just as she'd planned. Elijah would also have to stay put at the Fox and Hound, at least for a while, to recover. Something fluttered in her stomach.

Fear. Ridiculous. She had no reason to fear Elijah's company. Or his leaving.

"I would feel better if I knew what Wayne's connection to Malachi was."

While her mind had wandered, Elijah's had stayed strictly on track.

"Don't tell me your brother is an outlaw, too."

"I'm not an outlaw. The wanted posters in Laramie were the result of a misunderstanding." He waved it off, but Jordan was startled to realize that she could see through to the real discomfort beneath his nonchalance. "And no, my brother is not an outlaw. He's simply . . . difficult."

"Unlike you."

He laughed, easy, almost boyish laughter that surprised her and eased some of the knots in her stomach. His amusement ebbed to a sly smile.

"You should know, Sparrow. You're the one who married me."

Elijah swung his leg off his borrowed horse, doing his best not to twist his ribs. The landing jarred through him, taking his breath, and he stood for a moment with a hand on the horse's neck, waiting to be sure he could walk without collapsing.

He hadn't lied to Jordan. He didn't think the hotel proprietor would turn him over to Billy Calhoun. But he'd learned to be careful where he put his trust. He didn't know what Tony Wayne's true motives were, and he didn't care to show how weak he really was in front of the man.

He strolled over to the stairs, giving himself an extra moment by appearing to admire the hotel. It was an impressive building. Constructed of rough-hewn logs, it had a rustic look, but the plush-cushioned cane chairs on the porch, the large glass windows and lace curtains, and the elaborately carved door breathed luxury.

"It's lovely," Jordan said, pausing beside Elijah. He caught her quick glance and saw she understood exactly why he'd stopped. She was giving him extra time. He didn't let people read him like that. "I'm surprised to come across a resort like this in such a remote place."

"Jes' brings in more of the damned rich gawkers," Calhoun growled. "Beg your pardon, ma'am."

"I think my father couldn't think of anywhere farther to send me," Tony Wayne said, almost managing to sound amused. "He certainly ran back home soon enough after building it, I expected it to succumb to my benign neglect posthaste, but much to my chagrin it's become rather a popular place.

"We get a respectable clientele, though it's not quite so grand as the Earl of Dunraven's English Hotel in Estes Park."

"Vhat is it with English lords and Colorado resorts?" Dr. Gottfried muttered, shaking his head.

"Dunraven's an Irish lord," the Englishman answered mildly. "And I'm just a second son. Still, we both know beauty when we see it."

With a wink, he moved toward Jordan, but Elijah took her arm before Wayne could reach her. Instinctively cutting off the Englishman, he hadn't counted on his own reaction to Jordan's nearness.

After their night in the wilderness, she smelled of Ponderosa pine pitch and sweat and horse, a hint of lilac soap, and some soft, warm scent he knew came from her own skin, a scent that had him wanting to brush aside the tendrils of hair that caressed the nape of her neck and lean in so he could smell it better.

Chagrined at the unwelcome turn of his thoughts and the immediacy of his physical pain, he was surprised by the slamming of the heavy entrance doors to the hotel.

"Come back here!" The male voice rasped with anger. "I'm not through with you, you ugly harpy."

"Don't you dare talk to me like that—"

"I'll talk to you any way I damn well please. You tell that no-good—"

The voices stopped.

A woman stood frozen at the top of the stairs. Not old in years, but aged by sorrow, Elijah thought. Creases lined her mouth, and her blue eyes and blond hair both looked faded, like bright clothes that had been washed too many times. She held a bucket of soapy water with slender, redknuckled hands.

The man behind her was older, perhaps fifty. His thick, dark hair and broad mustache were grizzled with gray, but other than the gut pinched in by his broad belt, there was nothing soft about him. He was shorter than Elijah, but his thick arms and wide-legged stance gave him the bulk to intimidate, even without the six-shooters on his hips. His dark eyes glared down at the group on the stairs.

Tony Wayne took the steps two at a time to stand beside the woman. He reached for the bucket. "Are you all right, Philomena? What is the problem, Marshal Cox?"

Elijah should have noticed the star on the man's black, pin-striped shirt right away. But he'd learned to keep his attention on the eyes of anyone as angry as the marshal obviously was, especially an angry man carrying guns.

"It's nothing, Mr. Wayne," the woman said, pulling the bucket out of his reach.

"That's right." The marshal spat over the porch railing. "Nothing. That brat of hers. Thought he'd borrow my horse without asking."

"It was a joke," the woman said, sending the contents of the bucket after the marshal's spit. "Polydorus didn't mean any harm."

"A joke?" The marshal's eyes narrowed. "We'll see how hard the boy laughs with a rope around his neck."

The woman's eyes flashed with a spirit Elijah wouldn't have guessed she had. "Who's going to put it there? You?"

"Philomena," Tony Wayne interrupted. "Why don't you go on back to your work. I'll take care of this. Marshal Cox, does the boy still have your horse?"

The marshal and the housekeeper glared at each other until she disappeared back into the hotel. "Naw. It's back."

"Then there's no harm done. Just a bit of youthful high spirits." Even the Englishman's heartiness couldn't make the words sincere— taking a man's horse went beyond high spirits, even if the man weren't a town marshal.

"That brat's going to get what's coming to him. Mark my words." The marshal shrugged in disgust, apparently willing to let it go for the moment. Elijah got the impression the man's current anger was more habitual than actively dangerous.

"I was about to escort our new visitors in for a cup of tea," Tony continued. "Why don't you join us?"

"No. Thank you." The marshal's expression indicated he'd rather sip cyanide. Something in Tony Wayne's jovial smile suggested to Elijah the Englishman had counted on that.

Marshal Cox's gaze flickered over the visitors, pausing abruptly at Elijah.

"You." The fingers of Cox's right hand flicked on his hip

just above his gun. "That the man you was going to bring in, Billy?"

"Yep. That's him." Elijah's eyes didn't leave Cox, but he knew Calhoun flushed. "I shoulda noticed he didn't wear no guns."

Cox moved to the edge of the stairs, using the extra height to force Elijah to look up at him. Elijah struggled to keep his expression relaxed.

"You're the brother of that bastard Elijah Kelly?"

Definitely habitual anger. But he couldn't imagine why it was directed at him—the him who had suddenly become his alter ego.

"If you are calling into question my brother's parentage, suh, that doesn't sit well with my memory of my good mother."

Jordan's elbow dug into his bad rib as Cox's eyes narrowed still further. Elijah sucked in the pain and tried again.

"What do you have against my brother, Marshal?"

"I don't like outlaws in my town, Preacher."

"Very commendable," Elijah said, fighting to produce an affable, pastoral smile, "but my brother doesn't happen to be an outlaw. Mr. Calhoun must have been carrying that wanted poster around for quite some time. That business in Laramie has been cleared up."

"You say." Cox shrugged. "But if I see him around here, I'll shoot first and ask questions later. You let him know that, if you correspond with him. Good day, Mr. Wayne."

He stomped down the stairs through the middle of the small group, acknowledging none of the rest of them. But as he passed Jordan, barely glancing at her, the hairs on the back of Elijah's neck rose. It was nothing his conscious mind could latch onto. Certainly nothing like Tony Wayne's overt flirting. There wasn't lust in that glance. More like . . . contempt.

Jordan pulled free, and he realized he had been grasping her arm too tightly. He mentally shook himself. What with his malaria and everyone threatening to kill him, he was probably just a little oversensitive.

He had other things to worry about. Like his head was beginning to hurt again. Like his stomach still hadn't recovered from Jordan's rabbit-hide tea. Like he had gone from single gunfighter to married preacher in less than twenty-four hours, and the prospects for switching back again any time soon were looking decidedly slim.

"Why does Battlement Park need a town marshal?" Jordan was asking Tony Wayne as he held the hotel door open for her.

Elijah had been wondering that himself. The town had grown in the two years since he'd last been here, and the Fox and Hound was certain to draw a good tourist business, but a mountain resort was not the sort of location that generally drew large numbers of rough-necked cowboys needing a little law to keep them in hand.

"Precautionary measure," Tony said. He held the door for all of them. Elijah guessed it was so he could watch their reactions to the front room of the hotel as they entered. He didn't blame the man for wanting to show it off.

The huge, open fireplace in the center, the thick hunter green rug covering much of the polished wood floor, the two-story windows at the back of the room that looked out on a mountain scene out of a fairy tale—all were designed to impress. Yet the paintings of fox hunts, and the rustic side tables and chairs with their bright patchwork cushions lent the room an air of charm rather than ostentation.

"The dining room is just off this room to the left," Tony said, waving that direction. "My office is at the end of that hall. The guest rooms run down the hall to the right. When the weather is warmer, we take our tea out back on the veranda, but for today, we can sit by the windows. The next best thing."

Jordan took the seat Tony held out for her.

Elijah moved to sit to her right, but the hotel proprietor jumped in, the perfect host. "No, no, sit here, Reverend Kelly. You must sit facing the window. I'll have my back to it. I've seen the view often enough. Though you never get tired of it."

Elijah took the chair to Jordan's left, managing a smile, though his back itched. He couldn't remember the last time he'd sat with his back to a door. Of course, backing against the huge windows would not have felt much better.

For a flash of an instant, he envied the men who settled around him without any concern or need for caution—and who could face all that bright sunlight without feeling sick to their stomachs. He had at least another twenty-four hours before his next bout of fever. It wasn't fair for his head to pound like this already.

"I'll see to the tea," Tony said, but before he could leave the table, a young woman wearing a black dress and starched white apron appeared from the hallway bearing a large silver tray.

"We seen ya comin', sir," the maid said, her bright smile and country accent clashing with the English uniform.

"Splendid!" Tony said, his own jovial smile making the girl blush. "Set it here, Lily. Would you do the honor of pouring, Mrs. Kelly?"

Jordan was staring out the window, something haunting in her eyes. Hunger, Elijah thought. Hunger for the beauty. But fear, too. And grief, that desperate grief that caused his own heart to ache.

"Mrs. Kelly?" Tony tried again.

Elijah nudged Jordan's foot with his. She started and turned to frown at him.

"Major Wayne has asked if you would like to pour the tea, Mrs. Kelly."

"What? Oh!" She colored, remembering where she was and who she was supposed to be. "Of course." She reached for the teapot and for a topic of conversation to cover her disorientation. "What exactly is Marshal Cox a precaution against, Major Wayne?"

"Tony." That ridiculously cheerful smile.

"Tony." The red ran higher up her cheeks, unaccountably annoying Elijah. She passed the teacups and saucers.

"Theft, I would think, nein?" Dr. Gottfried said, dropping two cubes of sugar into his tea. He saw Elijah's glance. "Almost I can drink it this way."

"Try a splash of this, Doc," Billy Calhoun suggested, pulling a small, dented flask out of a holder on his hip. He took his own advice, then passed it to Dr. Gottfried. The doctor took a delicate sniff that wrinkled his nose and made his eyes water.

"Ja, just what is needed. Flavor!" He poured a tablespoonful in his cup and offered the flask around.

Seeing the dismay on Tony's face and the disapproval on Jordan's, Elijah couldn't resist. " 'Give strong drink unto him that is ready to perish, and wine unto those that be of heavy hearts.' "

"Indeed." Tony said. Elijah had to hand it to the man, his smile only became more determined. "But as for Marshal Cox, I would hire someone a little more . . . inconspicuous to combat theft. No, I—that is, Battlement Park—has taken the step of hiring a marshal, at least temporarily, because of an unfortunate rash of robberies and other criminal activities in the area since last summer."

"Like the trouble in Laporte?" Jordan asked.

"Precisely." Tony pushed back his chair and rested his teacup on his knee. "I believe the same band of brigands is responsible for a number of such incidents in this part of Colorado. Laporte was the first time murder has been done, but I don't expect it will be the last. The violence has been increasing."

"You've had attacks here?" Elijah asked.

"No. Not yet. But with the decline in the cattle business locally, nearly everyone in the park relies on tourism for a portion of their livelihood. And that depends upon safe travel for the tourists, as well as their expectations of being safe once they arrive. I don't intend to wait around for my clientele to be frightened away."

"You might be interested to know that Mrs. Bra—" He caught himself with surprise. He never slipped like that. It must be the headache. And Calhoun's rotgut was doing nothing for his stomach. "Mrs. Kelly was involved in foiling a bank robbery in Longmont just yesterday. The men involved will not be causing anyone any more trouble. They may very well have been part of your gang."

"Our Mrs. Kelly? A scourge on malefactors?"

Jordan glared at Elijah, but there was humor in her eyes. "Hardly. Though any moment I might—"

"Good show!" Tony banged his free hand on his knee, then had to grab his saucer to keep his cup from flying away. "We'll hope they were our men. If not, I have . . . other cards up my sleeve."

Elijah heard an evasiveness in Tony's voice he knew he ought to be paying attention to, but he had just noticed that the room had begun to spin. Almost imperceptibly at first. But it was definitely picking up speed. He tried to focus on the Englishman's face, but it wouldn't stay still long enough.

The floor tilted up toward him. He managed to catch himself, but his chair was no longer stable . . .

"Mr. Kelly?"

The slender hand, firm on his arm, slowed the spinning enough for him to regain his balance. Those clear blue eyes held him steady.

"I'm more tired than I thought," she said, rescuing him once again. "Perhaps we should have Major Wayne direct us to our rooms."

"Tony, please." The Englishman rose from his chair with alacrity, almost tilting over the table. "How thoughtless of me to hold you here, after the night you've spent. Doctor, Mr. Calhoun, please finish your tea while I show the Kellys to their lodging."

He pulled out Jordan's chair for her. Elijah managed to force himself to his feet to follow them. It seemed to him the English major marched double time back across the huge entrance room.

Jordan glanced over her shoulder as Tony dragged her along, concern on her face, but Elijah nodded her on. The sooner they reached a bed, the sooner he could collapse.

"I do have a surprise for you, Mrs. Kelly," Tony was saying as he whisked Jordan out through the front doors.

"Our rooms, Major Wayne?" Jordan said, with what Elijah couldn't help finding rather charming concern for his own welfare.

"Tony, Mrs. Kelly." He led them down the front stairs. "When I heard we were going to have an artist staying with us, I thought, 'I have just the thing. Knock her right over.' "

"Mr. Wayne . . ."

"Tony."

"Tony."

Elijah reached Jordan's side just in time to catch her rolling her eyes. The sight pleased him immensely. He really was feeling light-headed. *An artist.* Jordan an artist. *I have just the thing.* The words stuck in his head, and he couldn't figure out why . . .

"Our rooms . . ."

"Are not in the hotel." The hotel's proprietor led them up a rock-lined path through a stand of pine trees. "When I realized my father was going to strand me here, I looked into what brought people to Estes Park. Many visitors preferred to rent cabins from the local inhabitants rather than stay at the English Hotel, so I thought, Tony, my boy, here's an opportunity the old Earl missed. Build your own cabins and rent 'em out!"

The path led up, and Elijah dropped behind again, trying to catch his breath. A snapping in the trees turned into Loki, checking in. The wolf gave Elijah a very dog-like grin and disappeared again, nose to the ground.

"A cabin?" Jordan asked. Elijah wondered if it was the thought of being alone in a cabin with him that made her sound so strangled. He wanted to assure her that he was incapable of importuning her for anything more than to beg her to shoot him and put him out of his misery. Except he didn't have the energy to form the words. Were they ever going to stop walking?

"Here we are."

" 'O give thanks to the Lord, for he is good!' " Elijah exclaimed.

"It does rather inspire one, doesn't it?" Tony agreed, visibly pleased. Jordan was giving him a look. But as she took in the scene before them, her face changed, and he looked, too.

The cabin itself was built in the same style as the hotel, rustic, but far from spare. Yet it blended into the woods behind it, leaving the view open beyond its front porch. It was the same view as from the hotel's great room farther down the hill, yet it seemed even more magnificent from this angle. The mountain to the north towered above them, its ice fields lit by sunfire along the sheer granite ridge that had given Battlement Park its name. A meadow stretched beneath the mountain's bulk, a stream braiding through it. A doe and two tiny fawns picked their dainty way across the lush grass, as if put there just to make the picture perfect.

" 'He maketh me to lie down in green pastures' and all that," Tony said. "Wouldn't you say, preacher?"

Elijah gave in to weakness, rubbing his fingers deep into his temples. The man's infernal cheeriness was enough to give anyone a headache.

"Thank you so much, Major Wayne. Tony," Jordan corrected herself with a bright smile. Elijah suspected this particular distraction was meant to protect Tony rather than himself. "This will be lovely. Already Battlement Park is more extraordinary than I could have imagined. It's all an artist could dream of."

"Your paints and other luggage arrived yesterday," Tony said. "I've had them put in the cabin already."

Elijah's headache evaporated in an instant of clarity. That was it. No one had told Tony Wayne that Jordan Kelly was an artist. But paints had been sent ahead for Jordan Braddock. Jordan knew it, too. She paled.

"Please, Mrs. Braddock, I'm sorry." Seeing her distress, the Englishman grabbed one of Jordan's hands in both of his and patted at it ineffectually.

Good, Elijah thought. It kept the man from being able to reach for a weapon. His own knife was in his boot, where it would take no more than a moment for him to retrieve it.

"I didn't mean to frighten you," Tony continued, and his glance at Elijah included them both. "With such an unusual first name, it didn't take much guesswork to figure out that Mrs. Jordan Kelly must be Mrs. Jordan Braddock. Colonel Treadwell from the Grand Hotel sent a letter with your baggage, describing you and recommending you to me. I must say, you're even more lovely than he suggested."

"The question is, what are you going to do about our deception, Major Wayne?" Jordan asked. Elijah was pleased to note her immunity to Wayne's flattery.

"Do?" The Englishman looked genuinely puzzled. "I expect you'll have to continue it, at least until we can get confirmation from Laramie that Elijah Kelly is no longer a wanted man. Billy Calhoun's a decent man, and I could probably talk sense into him, but I'd rather not tangle with Napoleon Cox without official notification behind me."

"You don't intend to turn Mr. Kelly in?"

"I assure you, Mrs. Braddock, that was never my intention."

"He'd have done it first thing this morning, if he'd planned to," Elijah said. He leaned against a pine tree, an easy slouch that he knew made him look dangerous. In this case, it also kept him from making a fool of himself by collapsing onto the forest duff. "The question is, what does he want?"

"Ah." Tony Wayne dropped Jordan's hand with a faint smile. "One of the few things your brother has told me about you is that you two are nothing alike."

"True enough," Elijah agreed. He wanted to tell Jordan to move away from Wayne, but he didn't want to up the stakes.

"No, actually." The Englishman's smile broadened. "I've seen that exact expression on his face any number of times. Look, if you are anything like Mal, you won't believe a word I say until you can check it for yourself, but I don't want anything except to help out a friend.

"When Billy Calhoun arrived last night with his story of shooting the wrong Kelly, I knew that Mal didn't have a preacher for a brother. I suspected Calhoun had got the right man and that you'd somehow bamboozled him, but I had to discover for myself whether or not you were really Mal's brother before I went out on a limb for you.

"The family resemblance is really quite strong."

"That is true." Elijah sighed, pushing himself away from the tree. If Tony Wayne was trying to bamboozle *him*, it was working. And he simply didn't have the energy to worry about it.

"I'd say I'm surprised to find a friend of Mal's in Battlement Park, but I'm quite honestly surprised to find a friend of Mal's anywhere."

Tony smiled again. "Oh, he's . . . difficult. I grant you. But he's been a good friend to me. And I'll make sure you're not bothered for as long as you need to recover."

"Thank you, Tony," Jordan said again, her relief palpable, giving Elijah a strange feeling he didn't know whether he liked or not. Or maybe that was his headache returning. "He really can't travel like this. In fact, he should be in bed right now."

"I'm not an invalid," Elijah growled, but the strange feeling only intensified.

"Oh, no, of course not." Her sarcasm was not tempered by the amusement in her eyes.

"I'll see you settled in," Tony said. "Follow me."

"Thank you for the total destruction of my reputation," Elijah muttered to Jordan as they obeyed their host. "I am managing just fine."

"You can hardly stand up," she said sternly, taking his offered arm. "You belong in bed, and you know it."

It was the malaria. It had to be. He couldn't resist. "If you insist, Mrs. Kelly. Are you going to tuck me in?"

Her snort of laughter surprised them both. "Watch it, Mr. Kelly," she said with a wicked glare. "I've been widowed twice already. I could arrange for one more."

# Chapter 10

Jordan was charmed. The brightly colored pillows on the plain wooden chairs, the braided rug in front of the fireplace, the small fire that someone had already set, driving the lingering spring chill from the room—it might have been a cabin from a fairy tale. It bore no resemblance whatsoever to the conditions Colonel Treadwell had told her the indefatigable Isabella Bird had faced in Estes Park just a few years previously. No wind would dare whistle through these carefully caulked log walls.

She could easily picture herself enjoying a mountain evening here, warming her toes at the fire. Tony undoubtedly had a supply of cocoa she could pilfer. As for the daytime, she would be out before dawn to watch the sunlight kiss the tips of the mountains. And she would stay out until twilight, lingering on the porch as the stars flickered on, one by one.

She had been in Battlement Park barely an hour, but the mountains and the meadows already called to her soul. She could spend the whole summer here. And the fall.

Except she couldn't stay.

"There's a bedroom just through that door there," Tony was saying, "and another, sort of attic room, up those steps. I took the liberty of having your things put up there, Mrs. Braddock, since I didn't know how badly injured Elijah would be."

"I can't stay here." She realized she still held Elijah's arm. Maybe she'd even been picturing him sitting by the fire beside her. She dropped her hand and moved a safe distance away.

"Of course, you will stay here," Elijah said, his voice telling her he'd withdrawn even further than she had.

She felt an odd lurch in her stomach, a sensation that was becoming familiar, unable to guess the motives lurking behind those fathomless eyes.

"It's one thing to play a part to help a friend," she explained. "But it wouldn't be proper—"

"You've done enough for me. I would never ask you to risk your reputation."

Couldn't she be practical without hurting his feelings? "Of course. I didn't think you would. But that means I can't stay here with you."

"I didn't imply you should." The southern drawl was clipped short. "This is my problem, not yours. There is no need for you to discommode yourself on my account. Once I leave for Laramie this afternoon, you will be free to resume your real identity."

"You can't leave!" Though it would surely be a relief to have him gone. To have his inevitable departure over with. She ground her teeth and plowed on. "You can barely stand. Dr. Gottfried said that even with the quinine, you will probably have at least one more bout of fever."

He shrugged, slouching against the door frame. "I'll sleep before I leave. I've survived the fevers before."

Flat and cold. Calculated to infuriate her. But she could be as stubborn as he. "And next time, you're welcome to crawl off into a mountain snowbank to die. But it won't be on my conscience. Today, you are staying here. I can stay at the hotel tonight and leave for Denver tomorrow."

Maybe later in the spring Denver wouldn't be quite so bleak and depressing.

"I don't think my travel plans are your concern."

Jordan straightened. "That tone of voice might scare a drunken cowboy, but it doesn't scare me." Too much. "I don't even need to argue with you. Once you get into bed, you won't be able to get out."

He pushed off the door frame, replacing his hat on his head. "You do have a point there."

Jordan's fists clenched. Killing him had been a joke outside, but at that moment, she thought she might be capable of it.

"Please, please, this is all unnecessary," Tony interrupted. "No one needs to go anywhere. You will both stay here."

Elijah adjusted his hat. "Mrs. Braddock has been through enough on my account. I won't injure her good name."

"I wouldn't think of asking you to. I have taken care of that little problem, as well." Tony flashed his dazzling smile. "Mrs. Braddock will have a chaperone."

"A chaperone?" Jordan echoed. The whole situation was slipping out of her control. Of course, it had left her control as soon as the deception had slipped out of her mouth the afternoon before.

"It's too complicated," Elijah said, voicing her thoughts. "And dangerous. There's no advantage to having another stranger know we're lying about who we are."

"But she's not a stranger," Tony said, rubbing his hands together with delight at his own ingenuity.

Jordan's mind skipped around this pronouncement. She knew no one in the area. Did Elijah have a wife? Colonel Treadwell had called Elijah's son a bastard, but that didn't necessarily mean he didn't have a wife. Or a mistress.

Or a sister. She resisted the urge to roll her eyes at herself.

"This is a pleasant surprise," Tony insisted.

Jordan looked at Elijah. He obviously couldn't think of

any way this would be a pleasant surprise, either.

"Perhaps we should both leave this afternoon," Elijah said dryly. For the first time since entering the cabin, Jordan knew they were in mutual accord.

But a giggle behind her told Jordan it wouldn't be that easy. A very feminine giggle. In fact, a curiously familiar giggle.

She couldn't avoid turning around forever. The door to the downstairs bedroom was open now, and the surprise emerged.

"Nicolette!"

Her cousin rolled her eyes, managing to look coquettishly cute despite the pronounced curve under the midriff of her cornflower blue dress.

"Oh, for heaven's sake, Jo-jo. Who else do you know in Colorado?"

*Dear Aunt Rue,*
*You will be wondering why it has taken me so long to write you.*

Actually, she probably wouldn't be. Had it only been a week since Jordan left Oxtail? It felt like a month.

*Dear Aunt Rue,*
*Henry Junior will be pleased to hear that I have become a much better horsewoman since writing to you last.*

How silly her fear of Smoke seemed now. After all, the worst the horse had done was throw her flat on her back. She should have seen it as a warning to run back to Denver—and been grateful for her narrow escape.

And how she had worried about what people would think of her in those bloomers! How on earth could she tell Aunt Rue she was posing as the wife of a gunfighter who was posing as a minister? Mild-mannered, jovial Uncle Hal would have an apoplectic fit.

*Dear Aunt Rue,*
*You know how I promised to take care of Nicky for you? She was languishing in Denver and needed some fresh mountain air, so I've brought her to Battlement Park with me.*

Aunt Rue was much too shrewd to believe that.

Jordan put her head down on her arms. A definite mistake. Exhaustion pulled at her eyelids. She was seated at the corner desk in the main room of the cabin, and in general it would hardly be conducive to sleep. It was too far from the fire to be warm, and the quaint slatted chair was possibly the least comfortable seat she'd ever endured. But at the moment she could probably have slept standing. In fact, that would probably have been more comfortable.

She lifted her head and picked up her pen again, stifling a groan. She couldn't lie to Aunt Rue, and she couldn't tell her everything, either. But if she didn't write, Aunt Rue really would worry. And if Will wrote to her aunt about Nicky before Jordan did, Rue would panic.

*Dear Aunt Rue,*
*I am safely here in Battlement Park. I must tell you that Nicky met me here. She says that Will cares more about his work than he does about her, and she won't go back until he promises to do better for her. You know how Will's pride will react to that. But I will get her back to Denver soon, you may count on it. The fresh air and quiet mountains are a balm to me, but I think Nicky already misses the hustle and bustle of the city!*
*There is so much beauty here, Aunt Rue. You would love the view from the bedroom I share with Nicky. The sharp granite ridge that gives Battlement Park its name cuts into the blue of the sky like a knife, and the Park, the name they give*

*these high mountain valleys, is a quilt of every color green you can imagine. I am eager to unpack my paints.*

Jordan froze, staring at the words, waiting for lightning to strike her down.

*I hear you lecturing me that I should be out painting already. "There is no excuse for wasting your God-given talent, Jordan. There will always be apples to dry and laundry to wash. You are procrastinating!" The eighth deadly sin! But I have been busy with Nicky, and my gunfighter*

*My* gunfighter? For heaven's sake!

*and Mr. Kelly, the gunfighter who led me out here, has been ill with a bout of malaria. I have been helping Dr. Gottfried make sure he is comfortable.*

Two more attacks of fever since they had arrived on Wednesday. The first had frightened her. She would not even have known it was happening if not for Loki. His low, eery whines from downstairs had woken her the second night after they arrived.

Elijah had told her he wouldn't need her, that the quinine would take care of him. But she'd slipped out of bed and gone downstairs anyway, just to check. The fever had been so high, he hadn't even known who she was. It was past dawn before it finally broke and she could leave him to his sleep.

The second attack had been nearly as mild as he had predicted. He had ordered her to leave him to his misery. But she had known she wouldn't sleep, so she'd sat up in the main room, sure the ever-attentive Loki would let her know if Elijah needed her.

This morning she was feeling that lack of sleep, along with her worry for Nicky. She had to convince her cousin to return home before the pregnancy advanced much further. Those concerns only added to the strain of pretending to be someone she wasn't, living in the same cabin with a man whose very life might depend on her ability to deceive Marshal Napoleon Cox. She was a terrible liar.

Which brought her back to Aunt Rue.

*I assure you that Nicky and I are both healthy and doing well. Nicky looks wonderful, and has not been sick a day with her pregnancy. Lenora Hedgepeth complained all winter how unfair that was! I have enclosed a sketch. She says she's not that big, yet, but I assure you, she is!*

*As ever, my love to Pete, Henry Junior, and Uncle Hal.*

*Yours always,*
*Jordan*

Jordan folded the letter, creasing it carefully. She would take it down to the main lodge later in the morning for Tony Wayne to send out with the other mail on the coach for Longmont. Meanwhile, she could try to slip into bed upstairs and have a little nap before Nicky woke up and . . .

"Jo-jo?"

No such luck. She turned in her chair to see Nicky's head, golden hair tousled by a good night's sleep, peeking over the stair railing.

"Jo-jo, are you up already? I stole your pillow. I cannot get comfortable with just one. We need those extra pillows Tony promised."

"We can pick up some pillows when we walk down for breakfast."

Nicky's curls bounced as she shook her head. "Oh, I don't feel up to walking all the way down to the lodge this morning. Would you just bring me back some toast?"

"There's bread in the pantry. I can toast you some of

that." Jordan pushed herself heavily to her feet. Among its other amenities, the cabin had a small closet well-stocked with tea and coffee and other necessities. She'd put a half-loaf of leftover bread in the breadbox the afternoon before.

"But that's stale!" Nicky protested. "I want it still hot from the oven. With fresh butter. Oh, my feet are freezing out here!"

"Then put on some—"

But Nicky had already disappeared back upstairs. Jordan could hear the creaking as her cousin settled back into bed. She realized her fist had clenched, crushing her letter.

Fresh bread. More pillows. Fetch Doctor Gottfried to check Elijah once more. Warm tea with milk, but not too much. Let Loki out. Let Loki in. Nicky's feet would ache. After sweating all night, Elijah would need new bed linens.

Jordan retrieved her coat from a peg by the door, stuffing the letter in her pocket. She wrapped up in the bright red scarf one of her nieces had knit her for Christmas several years ago, fingering the odd, lumpy knots. She'd only packed it because it reminded her so fiercely of the family she missed, but she'd discovered quickly that she was grateful for its warmth on these crisp mountain mornings.

Opening the front door, she knocked against her easel, which leaned beside the door frame with her paints. She'd attempted to paint the view from the porch yesterday, but that had been a disaster, with Tony or Dr. Gottfried dropping by every few minutes, and Nicky or Loki needing attention every other. She would have to escape company before she would get any painting done. She should ask Tony to have her equipment brought down to the lodge.

Jordan sighed and closed her eyes, shaking her head at herself. If she had to live with Nicky much longer, she would turn into her. Without the dimples and golden curls to ameliorate the effect.

She grabbed the paint box in one hand and hefted the easel under her other arm, managing not to make too much noise banging out the door. The frosty air, laced with the scent of pine and glaciers, shocked her lungs. But it was so still, so quiet that she barely felt it on her skin.

She trudged down the path toward the lodge. The easel banged against her side, bruising her arm and ribs. The cold burned her lungs. Yet in the sweet, clear air, not yet warmed by the sun that touched the mountaintops, she felt her exhaustion and grouchiness ebbing away like an unpleasant tide.

Instead of heading straight for the lodge, she picked her way down the side path to the stables, where she hoped to find a safe place to leave her tools. Safer than the cabin, where she had to see them every day. She pushed the guilty thought from her mind.

As she reached the stable door, she saw the hotel housekeeper walking toward her, leading a horse. The gelding's head drooped, and his neck was damp with sweat. He'd obviously been ridden hard. In the gray morning light, the housekeeper looked even more drained of life than usual, her skin almost the same sallow beige as her faded hair. Jordan felt a stab of pity.

"Let me get the door for you," she offered. Her voice made the woman jump, her eyes briefly blooming with fear.

"I'm sorry," Jordan said, setting down her easel to struggle with the door. "I didn't mean to startle you. You've been out riding this morning?"

The woman's eyes remained bright, but antagonism replaced the fear. " 'Course not. This is a guest's horse. What would I be doing riding about? I got work to do."

Unlike some people, was her unspoken conclusion. She led the horse into the stable, with Jordan following in their wake.

"Here, boy!" the housekeeper called, with more vigor than Jordan would have expected. "I haven't got all day."

A stableboy hurried out of the gloom, straw sticking up out of his hair.

"I got 'im, ma'am. Oats, like usual?"

"Just do your job, boy. And comb your hair. You think this is a saloon?"

"No. 'Course not."

"Are you sassing me, boy?"

"No, ma'am."

The woman turned on Jordan, resentment and nervous deference warring in her eyes. "What do you want? Ma'am?"

Jordan struggled not to feel like an idiot. "Nothing, Mrs.—"

"Jones."

"Mrs. Jones. I was just looking for a place to—"

"I expect you need more sheets for that husband of yours."

Jordan took a calming breath. "That's true. If you'll show me where to get them, I'd be happy to—"

"I can do my job," the other woman snapped. "I'll take care of it while you eat your breakfast."

She moved toward the stable door, obviously expecting Jordan to follow.

"I'll have breakfast after I see to my horse," Jordan said, feeling a guilty pleasure at the housekeeper's disapproval. "As long as you're seeing to the linens, Mrs. Braddock would like some more pillows."

It still felt odd to refer to Nicky as Mrs. Braddock. Even odder than referring to herself as Mrs. Kelly, though Nicky's marriage was at least real, if not perfect.

"I'll see to that, too," Mrs. Jones said, her gaze darting around Jordan as though suddenly not quite able to settle. She looked paler again, and her movements seemed uncannily graceless as she slipped back out into the morning.

"Can I help you, ma'am?"

The stableboy was back. He barely came up to her shoulder.

"That horse Mrs. Jones brought in needs to be dried off," she said, wondering if he had someone to help him. "It's dangerous to leave them wet like that."

"I know, ma'am," he said, grabbing her easel. "Don't you worry none. I'll take good care of him. I'm just letting him have a drink while I help you. My ma'd tan my hide if I let a horse suffer."

Mrs. Jones. After their recent unpleasant encounter, Jordan could easily imagine the woman tanning the boy's hide. This must be the young troublemaker Marshal Cox had complained of, the one who had "borrowed" the marshal's horse.

"What's all this stuff you got with you, ma'am?"

"That's my easel and these are my paints."

"You're the painter, ma'am?" He gazed up at her hopefully.

"Yes, I'm a painter." She hoped she still was.

"You're preparing to paint this very morning? Terrific! Major Wayne and me, we got your saddle all fixed up so's you can carry your stuff more easy-like. I'll help you get it packed!"

He hefted the easel under his arm and trotted down the row of stalls toward the far end of the stable.

"You don't need to . . . I didn't plan . . ."

By the time she caught up with him, he already had Smoke out of her stall and was dragging over the old Mexican saddle

Jordan remembered with so little fondness. The boy's head barely reached the horse's withers, but he managed to throw the heavy saddle over the mare's back with surprising ease.

"Here, let me show you." He pulled over a stool and got on it to lift the easel up. "We added these straps to the back and side of the saddle here."

His fingers flew, fastening the awkward easel to the saddle. He unhooked the easel's backboard and strapped it on separately, sort of like a table on Smoke's rump. Unorthodox, but secure. And the fastenings were positioned not to crumple the canvas under its oilcloth covering.

"My ma's got a painting over our fireplace. Grandpa calls it frippery, but I think it's right nice."

Jordan felt a flash of sympathy for Philomena Jones, striving to create a gentle household for her son in the rough West. Whatever her faults, she'd raised a well-mannered, likeable boy. He might have his wild moments, but she'd never known a child who didn't.

The boy reached for her paint box. "Major Wayne and me, we knew you'd want to get up into the mountains for your painting. This ought to make it nice and easy for you."

It would, too. She'd worried about how she'd carry all her equipment on Smoke. She probably wouldn't have been able to do it at all without the ingenuity of Tony Wayne. And this stableboy.

"It's wonderful," she said sincerely, though her stomach was twisting uneasily at the erosion of her justifications for not painting. "What's your name, son?"

"Ben."

"I'm amazed, Ben. This looks like it will work out perfectly."

"It's all ready for you to try out," the boy said, fairly bouncing with pride. "I'll hold her for you, ma'am. You can use my stool."

"Oh, but I've got breakfast—"

"There's hardtack and jerky in the saddlebags, for emergencies," Ben said, delighted to surprise her once more. "And a blanket and some water. Major Wayne don't want none of his guests coming to harm while they're here at the Fox and Hound."

"I'm not dressed for it." A weak objection. She'd put on those silly bloomers to keep warm this morning, and the skirt of her blue cotton dress was fuller than was stylish this year.

"You'll be warm enough, once the sun hits the park," the boy said.

But she had Nicky and Elijah to think of.

A weak objection. Mrs. Jones was taking care of Nicky's pillows and Elijah's bed linens. And it wouldn't absolutely kill Nicky to eat day-old bread if she didn't want to walk the hundred yards to the lodge to get fresh.

Her excuses were slipping through her fingers, leaving her clutching only the cold ball of her real fear, the real risk. She couldn't fail at her painting unless she went out and tried.

"Let's see if it works, ma'am."

Yet she couldn't disappoint the boy. He'd put so much effort into helping her. She patted Smoke's neck and stepped onto the little stool. Her skirts proved almost as awkward as she feared, but once she got settled in the saddle, they draped nearly to the middle of her calf, and the bloomers amply covered the rest.

"Is it comfortable, ma'am?"

"It's fine." Deceptively so. An hour's ride ought to remind her just how uncomfortable the darn saddle could be. An hour's ride. Nobody would even miss her. She could ease into it. An hour would prove whether or not Tony and Ben's contraption worked without giving her time to unpack her paints. Still . . .

"I don't even know which way to go."

Ben cocked his head at her as he led Smoke out through the stable doors. "Why, ma'am, you could go *any* way."

She stared at the boy. She could, couldn't she? As long as she didn't get lost. She took the reins from the young stable hand with a surprising tingle of anticipation. She wouldn't mind just a ride. Wouldn't mind it at all.

"Thank you, Ben."

"I'll see you when you get back, ma'am."

A path led back behind the stables, and she turned Smoke onto it. If she passed the lodge, someone might hail her. If she passed the cabin, Nicky might catch her. Of course, then she couldn't get lost or fall off Smoke and break an ankle or get eaten by a bear . . .

Another horse suddenly appeared around a bend in the path ahead, and she almost jumped out of her skin from nerves and guilt. She found it wryly ironic that she was relieved it was only Billy Calhoun on old Rosy, his pack mule plodding behind them.

"Miz Kelly," he greeted her, snatching his battered hat off his head.

"Mr. Calhoun! I thought you'd left Battlement Park several days ago."

"I meant to do some hunting, ma'am, but the game is skittish this spring. So're the ranchers, for that matter. I ain't aiming to be taken for one of them outlaws ever'body's all het up about. Thought maybe I oughta head south, try my hand at mining for the summer, so I'm heading for Longmont. Hate to go down to town."

He spat off to the side of the trail. "Not that I reckon I blame you for wanting to see the back of me."

Jordan reddened. "That's not what I meant at all, Mr. Calhoun—"

She stopped, seeing the unexpected glint of humor in the mountain man's eyes.

"That's all right, Miz Kelly. I wish I'd never taken that shot at your husband. My bounty hunting days is over."

"I'm glad to hear that," Jordan said sincerely.

"Even if I'd gotten the right man, I reckon I couldn't a lived with myself if I'd killed him." Calhoun watched her face closely. "No, the real Ee-lijah Kelly ain't got nothing to fear from me. But I couldn't say the same about that there wolverine Cox. If you take my meaning, ma'am."

Jordan struggled to keep her composure. "I believe I do, Mr. Calhoun."

"Then I'll be on my way, ma'am. Good day to you." He plunked his hat back on his grizzled head and nudged Rosy forward.

"Good day, Mr. Calhoun." Jordan eased Smoke to the side to let him pass. "And thank you."

"Ma'am."

Jordan watched him pass around the next turn in the path toward the stable. She took a deep breath, willing her arms to stop shaking.

Calhoun knew. Or guessed. But he wouldn't speak. She didn't doubt the mountain man's word. Elijah was safe, but for how long? How long before Cox made the same guess Calhoun had? How long before Elijah could leave Battlement Park? How long before he would be forced to?

Jordan urged Smoke forward. She wouldn't think of that this morning. She was finally riding into the mountains that had called to her since her first sight of Battlement Park. She intended to make the most of it.

The path she followed led through the woods between the

lodge and the cabin. Smoke's hooves thudded mutedly on the needle-strewn earth, and Jordan could hear both their breathing in the morning silence. The path needed maintenance after the long winter, but sure-footed Smoke had no trouble negotiating the sudden drops and protruding tree roots.

They broke into the meadow below the Fox and Hound just as the sun poured its glory down into the park, gilding the grass with gold and turning the creek into a ribbon of diamond. A bird trilled somewhere out of sight.

Jordan's chest tightened as the beauty cascaded down upon her, the brilliant snowy mountain, the dazzling sun, the fervent green of the trees. She tilted her head up, breathing it in, letting it flow around her. She thought her heart might break with the pure, cold wildness, and she didn't care.

Smoke slipped, jolting Jordan back to herself. The path turned mucky as it crossed the meadow, requiring more concentration, but it was passable. With each step of her horse's feet, Jordan felt civilization falling away behind her. Civilization and responsibility and regret. And humanity and warmth and safety.

She remembered Maggie Jackson calling this Jordan's adventure. Standing in Maggie's barn with friendly faces all around, adventure had sounded wonderful, something that might even dispel some of the darkness around her heart. Today, despite the brightness of the sunshine, the hairs on the back of her neck prickled. A result of her encounter with Calhoun, undoubtedly.

It was an eery feeling—as though she'd stopped hunting adventure, and adventure had begun stalking her.

An hour's ride. That's all she could spare. Maybe that's all she would be able to stand.

# Chapter 11

Despite the unease Jordan had felt that morning riding into the wilderness, she had no warning of danger when it came. There must have been a sound, a change in the movement of the soft air, a scent that would have shouted a warning to some primal part of her brain.

But all she heard was the sigh of the wind across the grass, the lazy buzz of bumblebees in the first gold and white flowers of spring. All she felt was the warmth of the sun on her shoulders, the hard granite of the stone on which she sat. She smelled only sweet cold water and quickening earth.

One moment she was half aware of the peace around her, half lost in her own thoughts. The next, ninety pounds of bone and muscle struck her shoulder, knocking her off her stone seat and onto the ground. The world might have spun around her. She didn't know. All she could see were the huge white teeth inches from her nose.

The instinct for self-defense urged her to connect her fist to her attacker's big, wet nose, but she was too stunned to move. Besides, one huge paw rested squarely in her abdomen, making breathing her number one priority.

She settled for a scathing glare into the silver eyes gleaming above hers.

"Loki!" She heard the rattle of reins and saddle, heard boots hitting the ground. "You wretched, filthy beast."

Murder laced the edges of Elijah's voice. Loki must have

heard it, because he dropped to his belly, trying to force his nose under Jordan's neck. He whined.

A black hat and black duster filled the sky above her. The sun shone behind them, so she couldn't see Elijah's face.

"The angel of death must look just like that," she gasped. Loki whined again. Almost unconsciously, she wrapped an arm around his furry bulk. "I should probably let you kill him, but I've grown rather fond of him."

"Death is too good for him," Elijah growled. Despite his cracked rib and recent fever, he hauled Loki up by the scruff of his neck. He dragged the wolf aside and dropped him. "Pulling out his teeth one by one sounds much more satisfying."

He reached down for Jordan's hand and pulled her up with the same ease he had the wolf. "Are you all right?"

"We seem to ask each other that question with alarming frequency." She tried breathing. Her lungs filled with only minimal pain. "I think I just need to sit down a minute."

He helped her ease back onto her stone seat. Some long-ago glacier had scraped its surface nearly flat, and now it rested about two feet above the rest of the surrounding mountainside, creating a bench for looking down over the forest into the park below.

"I apologize." Elijah snapped his fingers, and Loki crawled closer to them. "I didn't intend to disturb you. I only wanted to make sure you hadn't come to harm. Tony said you told the stableboy you'd only be gone an hour."

"What time is it?" Jordan looked up into the dazzling sun, past its zenith. "I'm sorry. I didn't mean to worry anyone. I lost track of the time."

Elijah's hand on her shoulder kept her from rising. "Don't. You stay here as long as you like. I'll leave you alone in just a moment."

The tightness in his voice told her he was trying not to let her know what trouble he was having catching his own breath. Now that the sun no longer shone in her eyes, she could see the dark circles under his.

"Are *you* all right? You shouldn't be out riding. You shouldn't even be out of bed."

He raised one sardonic brow. "Thank you, nurse. I think I'll live."

He settled beside her with his accustomed grace. But she knew he never would have sat without asking if he didn't need the rest. She decided not to mention that fact.

"I can see why you forgot to come back," he said, taking in the view. The park stretched out below them in shades of jade and emerald. Beyond the valley, the towering gray and white peaks marched away into a haze of snowblindness.

"I'm sorry I worried you," she said. That was too personal. "Worried everyone."

Amusement touched his eyes with gold. "I wasn't too worried," he confessed. "The stableboy said you'd taken your paints."

"It was all his fault." She tried on one of Nicky's pouts. Apparently she got it right, because Elijah rolled his eyes. "He talked me into it."

His grin turned dangerous. "Are you that easy to influence? I'll have to keep that in mind."

She looked him up and down. "You don't have Ben's dimples."

"And I don't think anyone could talk you into something you didn't already want to do." The teasing left his eyes. "I could tell that you wanted to get out, but I didn't know how to make it happen. Next time I'll just recruit Ben. What have you been working on?"

His gaze caught her easel standing a few yards away. Jordan flushed. There was no hiding the utterly blank canvas.

He laughed. "I see. Painting can also be a good excuse when you need to get away."

Jordan felt her answering smile slip. To her horror, tears stung her eyes. She dipped her head. Loki's greeting must have knocked her hair pins as well as her breath loose, for her hair fell in a curtain across her face.

"Did I say something wrong?"

She shook her head, forcing back the tears.

"What is it?"

"Nothing!"

"Sparrow?" His finger brushed her temple, easing aside her screen of hair, pulling it back over her shoulder.

She shook his hand away. Couldn't he just leave her alone?

"I warned you against befriending a hawk," he reminded her. "We have sharp eyes and we're hard to shake."

"And stop that, too, damn it!" She glared up at him, catching the surprise in his eyes.

"Stop what?"

"Reading my mind!" Despite the sincerity of her demand, she also saw its ridiculousness. Elijah obviously did, too. They stared at each other for a long second before bursting into laughter.

"It's not funny," she growled.

"What's not funny?"

"Don't pretend you don't know!"

And then they were laughing too hard to speak. It didn't last long. Jordan's mirth died away as she took in the wonder of hearing Elijah laugh helplessly, letting go for a moment of the control he wrapped so tightly around him.

Then he caught her watching him, and his laughter faded, too. He reached out with his thumb to brush the moisture from her eyes.

176

"If I can ever read your mind, I can't now. I don't know what's hurting you, Sparrow. Will you tell me?"

It was the kindness that undid her. More tears spilled from her eyes. She brushed them away herself.

"It's too much," she said, her voice strange with emotion. She waved at her easel and then at the scene before them. "Trying to paint this is like trying to capture eternity or infinity or both in your fist."

She pulled her hand through the air, catching nothing. "I don't know how to explain . . ."

She stood up, turning slowly around. "Even your eyes can't take it all in." She turned faster, impatient with the limitation. "Just a piece at a time. A tiny piece. How do you even comprehend how much more there is, just at the edge of your vision?"

Her eye caught his, and she stopped, suddenly remembering her audience and feeling absurd.

"It's overwhelming," he said.

"The clouds." She looked out at the view once more. "You think, I can just paint that one mountain. It's been here, been the same, as long as I've been alive. As long as people have walked these hills. But when you look, it's changing, right under your eyes. The clouds running their shadows across the snow. A mist coming off a pool of water. An eagle hanging still for just a minute above the trees.

"And this is no better." She dropped to a crouch to point out a delicate yellow flower, its petals curling back in a motionless dance. "This lily. How can you paint it without the scent of the grass around it? It would be like picking it and putting it in a vase. Killing it."

Elijah's hand reached out, dark against hers, though she did not have the smooth, white skin of a lady. Too much farm work. And you couldn't paint in gloves.

Her thoughts were babbling again as she tried too hard not to notice the way Elijah's fingers felt against hers. He pulled her over to sit on the rock again.

"My father had—has still, I suppose—an inexplicable fondness for German philosophy." He was looking out at the mountains with a distant expression, but he still held her hand. "I never became fluent in German. Another way I failed my father. But I do remember reading an essay by Schiller on the difference between the beautiful and the sublime."

He still smelled of gunpowder, but she could also smell the sweet soap Tony had stocked in the cabin. No, she didn't smell it, didn't notice his hand on hers, didn't find herself hypnotized by his southern drawl. She couldn't paint—what did she care what Elijah Kelly smelled like!

"I don't remember much of Schiller's argument, but beauty . . . beauty is something that makes you feel good." He stopped. "Well, that's not exactly what he said, but it's what I understood at age twelve. Beauty is seeing a flower and thinking, isn't that lovely, and moving on. The beautiful is pleasing, agreeable, safe.

"The sublime, on the other hand—" He glanced at her, and the intensity in his eyes brought her back into focus. "The sublime is *not* safe. The sublime is both beautiful and terrible at the same time. It is something that fills us with awe, awe so deep that it is frightening, even as we recognize its sheer wonder."

"Yes." Jordan didn't notice that she was squeezing his hand. "That's it, exactly. This . . ." She waved her hand at the mountain panorama. "This isn't beautiful. It's awesome. And it terrifies me."

"I don't know if I got this from Schiller, or from my father, or if I made it up myself," Elijah said. "But I always thought . . . Never mind."

It turned out that Elijah was the one who tried to pull his hand away, but Jordan clutched it tighter. "Tell me."

"It will spoil my image as a hardened gunman." The exaggerated drawl and the dangerous smile couldn't hide his embarrassment.

"Unlike owning a horse named Rover and having a wolf who likes to have his belly scratched."

"Your logic, as always, is inescapable." When he turned his head toward the mountains, his eyes paled to pure gold. "I always thought the sublime was what happened when you caught a glimpse of God."

Or one of his angels, Jordan thought, a brush of wings in the sunlight between her eyes and the mountains, a touch of grace between her fingers and Elijah's. Beautiful and terrible at once. She knew why people clung to each other in the face of such terrible beauty. She could not have let go of Elijah's hand if she had wanted to.

She never knew how long they sat there like that, holding a tiny candle of life alight against the wildness of immortality. Only a moment, perhaps, a heartbeat stretched to eternity by their complete presence in it.

Then a bumblebee buzzed past her ear. Loki sighed. A breeze tugged a wisp of hair across her eyes. Her hand was hers again, back in her lap, and Elijah was a gunfighter she barely knew.

She glanced at him, caught him watching her. No, she knew him better now. She knew he didn't show those unguarded eyes to everyone. She had learned much about Elijah the man, which made Elijah the gunfighter only more alien to her.

With the wrenching suddenness of Loki's sneak attack, loss slammed into her throat, suffocating her. She had to stand, had to move to her easel, fiddle with her paint box. She couldn't let the pain out. It would kill her.

Grief sucked at her, grief that the tears it brought couldn't soothe.

Her hands shook as she pulled out her palette knife, her turpentine, the linseed oil, her pots of paint. White for snow. Black for shadows. Never black enough for the shadows in her heart.

"Sparrow?" Elijah's voice was as light as the touch on her shoulder. She meant to turn away. But instead she turned into his chest, and his arms wrapped around her, gentle enough to hold her there, and she sobbed against him.

"I'm sorry," he said. "I'm sorry."

"Sorry?" She looked up at him. She wanted to reach out and brush away the remorse in his eyes. "You didn't do anything."

"What is it then?"

She managed to turn away from him, to make herself leave the false security of his arms. "It takes me like that sometimes, so I can't bear it."

"Your husband. Frank."

"Oh, God, I wish he was here." It was probably not something to say to a man who had just been holding her in his arms, but it kept him from touching her again. She didn't know what she might have done if he had touched her again.

"I miss him." His smile. His hands, burned dark by the sun, the nails cracked from hard work. The way they sometimes understood each other without speaking.

"And I hate him." The words burst from her, shocking her. "I hate him! How could he have left me?"

"You know he didn't want to," Elijah said quietly, no condemnation, nor pity in his voice.

"I know."

He offered her a handkerchief, as black as his duster. She couldn't help it. A strangled laugh escaped her, shocking her more than her previous outburst.

"White shows the dust." His amused drawl helped to steady her.

She blew her nose in a very unladylike manner and took a deep breath of mountain air. "Thank you very much, kind sir. I think I'll go hide under a rock now."

He laughed. "No need, ma'am. I think I'd rather you paint."

She looked down at the chaos of her paint box. "What?"

"Whatever you like."

That wasn't the question she'd asked, and he very well knew it. But the smile in his eyes kept the shadows at bay.

She looked out at the mountain that had confounded her all morning. The afternoon light had changed it yet again, shifting the pattern of the ice on its face. This time, though, she saw the changes with an artist's eye, the change of shape and color. Shape and color she could approximate with her paint. She looked at the ridge on the north side of the peak, with its teeth like crenellations on a castle tower. She could draw that.

She pulled out her pencil to sketch it in. The corner of her eye barely caught the movement of Elijah backing away.

"I won't intrude any longer," he said.

"Stay," she said. She couldn't tell him she couldn't try this alone. "If you'd like to."

"I don't want to distract you."

"You won't." She'd learned on their journey to Battlement Park that Elijah had a way of being that didn't intrude.

She turned back to her canvas, making the first feathery mark with her pencil.

"I didn't mean," she began, her voice as whispery as the

181

sketch. "When I said I wished Frank were here, I didn't mean that I wished you weren't."

"It would be all right," he said, "if you had."

Of course it would, she thought.

The peak would go there, up to the left, the crenellations falling away down its side to the right.

As soon as he was healed, Elijah would leave Battlement Park, and she would never see him again.

Her hand moved more steadily, trusting her eyes.

There was no reason for her to be careful of Elijah's feelings. He was a gunfighter. He had learned not to have feelings. Except that her heart told her he did have them. That he had been hurt. In some past she would never know. And that he could be hurt again.

Some barely acknowledged part of her was more afraid of that than of being hurt herself.

"I'm sorry." She paused, weighing her words. "I didn't mean to burden you with all of that."

"Maybe what the sublime gives us is a glimpse into our own hearts."

She risked a glance back at him. He sat on the flat stone, arms resting on one knee, the other leg stretched out in front of him. But there was nothing casual in the eyes that locked on hers.

"Did you know how angry you were at Frank?"

"He didn't mean to die!" Guilt washed over her. "I didn't mean I really hated him."

"Of course not."

"There's no reason for me to be angry at Frank."

"No." He sat up and stretched out his other leg. "But that doesn't mean you aren't angry. Angry at Frank. Angry at God. At the unfairness of it."

"It is unfair," she said, her voice knife thin. "But I don't think it's any of your business how I feel about it."

She wished she could read *his* mind. His cat eyes glinted, giving nothing away.

"You're right. It's no business of mine. And I can't tell you how to forgive Frank. Or God, for that matter. For putting you through such pain."

"I've been through it before," she said, tasting the bitterness. "I'll survive."

"But I think you will forgive them," he went on, as though she hadn't spoken. "I just wonder if you will learn to forgive yourself."

"For what?"

"For surviving."

Maybe she wasn't going to mind so much when he left, after all.

Jordan turned from the challenge in his eyes to the challenge of her canvas. She looked up at the mountain again. A hint of gold and silver where the sun hit the snow. Gray there, by the rocks. She would need blue for that shadow.

She looked down at her palette with the faintest smile. So much for black and white.

As the light faded, the air seemed to become even clearer, expanding in a living silence around them as they rode, so that the horses' hooves rang like bells on the rocks and padded like cat's paws in the dirt.

Elijah gauged the setting of the sun against the distance back to the hotel. They could make it before full dark. He hadn't realized how long it would take Jordan's paint to dry enough on the canvas for her to risk packing it up to return.

She hadn't spoken to him all afternoon, beyond a few short directions when he helped her strap her gear onto Smoke's back. Yet it didn't feel like her silence on the road from Longmont. Not angry. Focused.

Her intensity while painting had not surprised him. It was the the way she changed, reflecting her work, that kept him watching her. Her painting style shifted like the clouds over the ice fields. One moment she would be calm and quiet, the brush flowing in long, smooth strokes. Then she would tense, her muscles bunching, the brush jabbing and dancing. The ferocity would settle into a dangerous stillness before she attacked, catching an escaping twist of light.

Riding behind her, he could see the physical toll it had taken on her. Her hand trembled slightly as she brushed her hair back from her face. Her shoulders slumped from fatigue. But there was no tension in them. Sitting in silence, waiting for the paint to dry, he'd thought she'd made at least a temporary peace with her ghosts.

He didn't think she was angry with him.

He ran a hand through his own hair, surprised to find that it trembled as much as Jordan's had. The damn fever.

"Are you all right?"

She *would* have to turn right then, to catch his weakness.

"I'm fine."

She slowed anyway, letting his borrowed sorrel catch up with Smoke.

"You have all kinds of advice for other people," she said with only a touch of asperity, "but you refuse to listen to anybody else's. Dr. Gottfried said you needed a few more days of rest."

He had been right. She wasn't angry. Anger might have been easier to take than the amusement in her eyes.

"This is rest," he growled warningly. "I'm not doing a damn thing."

"I think Dr. Gottfried meant bed rest," she replied mildly.

"I couldn't stand another minute in that wretched little

room. It feels like a jail cell."

"Personal experience?"

He grinned reluctantly. "The only time I ever slept in one was as a town marshal in Texas. I'd been drinking, and I passed out cold making my rounds."

He tested a breath of the twilight air. His rib barely protested. "Any room starts to feel like a prison after a while."

"When you could be out in this."

He looked at her, her sapphire eyes darker than the sky behind her. He wanted to tell her she didn't understand. He didn't want her to understand. But he heard his voice explaining.

"My father's house in Charleston. The church. The army. Blackwater, Texas. They didn't want to let me out. I couldn't breathe until I could escape."

"So now you don't have a home to trap you."

Any home would be a trap. No matter how his heart ached when he sat in front of the fire at the Jackson ranch, listening to Lemuel sing hymns, watching March and Maggie share quick smiles.

"My son Wolf's mother died when he was born." The words slipped out before he could stop them. "If I had known she was pregnant, if she had survived . . . I would have tried."

Shame burned on his skin. Surely the woman beside him could see the darkness in his heart, the part of him that had been relieved Annabel hadn't lived.

"You loved her?"

"No." She had been pretty, with that midnight hair and sidelong smile. It had been her humor that brought him back from time to time, made him feel easy with her, as easy as he could feel with anyone back then. "I liked her. She was a prostitute. We had an arrangement. Or I thought so. She named her baby Wolfgang, because she knew how I felt about

Mozart. Henna said Annabel loved me. I never wanted her to."

He thought he'd finally shocked Jordan into silence. But when he glanced at her, he saw her contemplating him with that sharp concern that made him uncomfortably certain that she saw more of him than he cared for her to see.

"Yet you would have tried."

"Not hard enough!" He hadn't meant to sound noble. There was nothing noble in what he'd done. "When I found Wolf, Henna and Jed Culbert had taken him in. They had children already, but they loved him like their own son. They could offer him a family. A home.

"So I left him. A helpless baby, and I couldn't stay in one place long enough to watch him grow up."

He tilted his head to the sky, letting the air cool his face. "I've been leaving him ever since. I'd visit. Never more than a few days. I couldn't bear seeing him. But I kept coming back.

"Until a couple of years ago. I had to stay at the Jackson's ranch for a couple of weeks. I got to know him. I learned . . ." He'd learned about friendship. March and Maggie and even Henna had offered him a family. Without asking him to stay. "I learned I could come back. I've tried. Spent time with Wolf. Thought maybe I was beginning to be a father to him."

He glanced over at Jordan because he didn't know where else to look. "I've missed every single one of his birthdays. I promised I'd be there for his thirteenth. It was today."

She reached over and grabbed his gelding's reins, bringing them both to a stop.

"You told me this afternoon that I need to forgive myself."

"That's different." He pulled her hand from the reins. "What I've done can't be forgiven."

She caught his fingers. He didn't quite pull back hard enough to break her grip.

"I can't forgive you," she said. "You haven't done anything that needs my forgiveness. And you can't forgive me. But if there is a God out there, the one thing I can believe about him is that he forgives us. Maybe we're here to remind each other of that."

Her expression was shadowed by the gathering dusk, but he could still see the light in her eyes. Conscious of her breathing, of the warmth of her skin, of her heartbeat through the thumb she squeezed against his palm, he raised her hand to his lips and pressed it against them.

He closed his eyes against the feeling, like pain, that wrenched at his heart. He opened his eyes, pushing the feeling aside, but his voice broke anyway.

"God would never send someone as good as you are to someone like me."

For a second she resembled the bird whose name he'd accidentally given her, as startled and ready for flight as a frightened sparrow. Her pulse fluttered against his fingers.

He hadn't meant to scare her. But he realized suddenly that she ought to be scared.

It had been so long since he had been with a woman. Been so long since he had allowed himself to want a woman. He had mistakenly believed he had made himself immune to desire. Or at least fooled himself into thinking that he could control it.

He had about as much control over the unexpected, desperate hunger that shook him now as a starving wolf would have coming across an injured fawn.

The image appalled him, but not enough. Nowhere near enough.

He remembered her worrying over him during his fevers. He thought she had even sung to him, trying to calm him, one dark night. He remembered holding her that very afternoon while she cried, just wanting to comfort her. He remembered trying to find a way to stir her desire to paint, the good need to help a friend.

And there in the dusk, gripping her hand so hard he knew it must hurt, though she didn't say a word, it all seemed a calculated strategy to reach this moment. For though he could sense her fear, though she wished nothing more than to have her husband with her again, though she found Elijah's profession as loathsome as he currently found himself, he could also feel, along the nerves that ran from her hand to his, that if he reached for her and dragged her to him, she would let him kiss her.

If he kissed her, kissed her from this desperate lust, he would have no honor left at all. And he didn't even care.

His leg bumped against hers as he nudged his gelding closer to Smoke. She didn't bolt when he dropped her hand. If it was because she was too terrified to run, mesmerized by the hunger in the hawk's eyes, he didn't care. He didn't care.

His hand brushed her neck, her skin luminescent in the fading light. He wrapped his fingers in her thick, dark hair, his fist clenching so tight it hurt him.

"Elijah." She said his name so softly, it reminded him that he had a name, reminded him to breathe. He found he could loosen his fist, release her hair. "Please . . ."

He found he could wait for her to finish. That he could let her go when she did. He could wait for her to say, "please don't."

Or please do.

Heaven help him.

# Chapter 12

*Please.* Jordan didn't know if she breathed the word again or not. She couldn't see Elijah's face in the deepening shadows, just the brush of silver twilight on his cheekbone, the glint from one dark eye.

He was waiting for her to speak. She wanted to say something. But in this silence into which her heart crashed and her breathing broke, she could not open her mouth to tell him what she wanted.

Any more than she could lie and tell him she did not want it.

So she waited, too. And in the silence of their waiting, they both heard the sounds of harness and hoofbeats announcing riders approaching.

Elijah's fingers brushed her neck, her cheek. Then he was reaching for his rifle, moving his horse between Smoke and the trail.

*This is Battlement Park,* she wanted to snap, *not Dodge City,* but she didn't trust her voice. And she knew the irritation stabbing through her had almost nothing to do with Elijah's acting like a gunfighter. What she didn't know was whether she was more angered by his almost kissing her and upsetting the delicate balance between them, or by her own disappointment that he hadn't.

"Who's there?" Elijah's voice sounded steady enough.

"Who the hell are you?" The roughness and belligerence

189

in the reply sounded familiar to Jordan. "Get where I can see you or I'll blow your head off."

"Why, Marshal Cox," Elijah slipped easily into his lazy, dangerous drawl. "I don't think putting a bullet into a man of God would be good for your immortal soul."

"Show yourself, Kelly," Cox growled back. There was no lessening of his antagonism. Jordan couldn't blame him. Elijah sounded just like a gunfighter. It was a good thing she wasn't armed. Putting a bullet into Elijah Kelly would do wonders for *her* soul at the moment.

"Is there something wrong, Marshal Cox?" she asked, riding into the light in the middle of the path.

She could see the riders in the trees now. The one on the trim hunter rode forward, his hatless blond head easily recognizable in the dusk.

"Mrs. Kelly?" Tony asked, relief filling his voice. "We were looking for you. Reverend Kelly went out to find you hours ago. When it started to get dark—"

"Exactly where have you been?" Cox asked, pulling up beside the Englishman, his rifle across his lap.

"Enjoying the scenery," Elijah replied, indolent as ever. " 'The mountains shall bring peace to the people.' "

"Don't mess with me, preacher," Cox warned, the dim light not hiding his snarl. "I'm not feeling too friendly toward outlaws right now. Or their relatives."

"We were up the mountain there," Jordan jumped in, wishing she could give Elijah a discreet kick. Cox was annoying, but, in their current circumstances, he was also dangerous. "I'm sorry we worried you. We were waiting for my paint to dry."

"I have had a guest or two spend a cold night on the mountain," Tony said. "Not pleasant, but they tend to see it as a jolly good adventure over all. But we've had a bit of troubling news."

"Your bandits," Elijah guessed, straightening from his slouch.

"I'm afraid so," Tony agreed. "The day before yesterday an outlaw gang robbed the same Longmont bank that was attacked while you were there, Mrs. Kelly. Perhaps they thought no one would expect it, coming so soon after the previous attempt. They weren't quite right. One of the bankers had a gun. They shot him."

"Oh, God." Jordan thought of the balding man who had offered to take her place as the robbers' hostage. She hoped it wasn't him.

"And just this morning there was a problem between here and Estes Park. The English Hotel sent a man over to warn us."

Gold still glowed on the ice topping the mountains separating the two parks. Whatever had happened, it was close. And it was bad. Jordan had heard the change in Tony's voice, the reluctance to continue.

"Let's ride back to the hotel." Elijah had obviously heard it, too. His attempt to protect her only brought Jordan's back up.

"Tell us," she insisted, as they turned down the path.

"Oh, for Pete's sake," Cox snarled, spitting into the dark. "It was only some damn fancy-pants dogs."

"Five men attacked a fox hunting party in Estes Park," Tony said. "All they got were a few pocket watches and some jewelry. They couldn't have expected much more. But they threatened to kill the whole party, said it was time for the rightful residents to claim the mountains, time for the 'blasted rich foreigners' to get out. Then they shot and killed the entire pack of foxhounds."

Marshal Cox's guttural laugh crawled up Jordan's spine

with her own horror. "I bet them boys was pissing their prissy pink tights."

"It's the *jackets* that are pink," Tony muttered darkly.

The hounds, the banker. It could have been the men in the hunting party. It could have been Elijah and herself. It could have been Tony or Nicky—would the outlaws have the audacity to attack a hotel?

"There has been bad feeling between Lord Dunraven and the ranchers in this area for a long time," Elijah said. "Surely there's no reason to think the attack today is related to the robbery in Longmont."

"Just a gut feeling I have," Tony said. "The same number of men involved. The boldness—the bloodly recklessness I might say—of the incidents are similar.

"The ranchers of Estes Park have never resorted to violence against the earl, even under provocation. Intimidation is more Dunraven's style, I'm afraid. And he's given up the idea of turning the whole area into his own private hunting reserve. It simply wasn't working."

Lights bloomed ahead of them, winking through the ranks of trees. They rode out into a clearing, and Jordan realized they'd arrived at the meadow behind the hotel. The lodge towered above them on its rise, lamps shining from the tall back windows.

"I very much fear it's the same men who attacked Laporte," Tony continued. "And no closer to justice than ever. The brigands wore bandannas as disguise, though the man from Estes Park said the victims all agreed the leader was a young man. They said he had eyes like a crocodile, cold as death."

Jordan's breath caught in her throat. "Pauly the Bandit King."

"What's that?" Marshal Cox turned on her, eyes burning.

"It's possible," Elijah said, his voice tightly controlled, "that your outlaw leader is a man calling himself Lucifer Jones. He has a bad reputation in Longmont. And he robbed a train in Wyoming. I would not be surprised if the same gang committed the murder in Laporte."

Jordan caught Elijah's gaze and wished she hadn't. She could read the self-condemnation clearly in his eyes. *I let him get away.*

She shook her head, but he turned away.

"I drew a sketch of him," she said. "We could send it back to Longmont."

"Give it to me," Cox ordered sharply. "I'll see to it."

They had reached the back porch of the lodge.

"We can leave the horses here," Tony said, dismounting at the base of the stairs up to the porch. "I'll send the stable hands for them."

Jordan would have liked nothing more than to flee inside to a hot cup of tea.

"My paints," she said instead. "I can't just leave them."

Tony took Smoke's reins, a hint of his natural jauntiness returning. "Ben will take care of them for you," he assured her. "He's a bit full of himself, helping out our resident painter. Like me, he can't wait to see the result of your labors, though I'm afraid young Ben's sudden interest in art has more to do with your personal charm than your artistic technique."

"It's a good thing your interest is purely aesthetic," Elijah snapped, edging Tony aside to extend Jordan his hand. "You haven't got Ben's dimples."

Perhaps the teasing was a peace offering, but for the moment Jordan wasn't sure a truce was entirely safe. Ignoring both men, she swung her leg over her easel to dismount. She didn't manage to land gracefully, but she didn't fall on her behind, either.

Indefatigable, Tony tied Smoke's reins to the railing and reached for the easel tied to the saddle. "Shall we take this in and have a look?"

"No!" Jordan held the easel down. "I don't like to show my work to anyone until it's done. This piece will probably take me two or three more days. I'll have to go out again tomorrow."

"I wouldn't let her do that, preacher," Marshal Cox warned, pausing with a foot on the back steps.

*"Let me?"* Jordan asked. No wonder Elijah couldn't resist baiting the man. He drew out the worst in people. "You wouldn't let me do what, Mr. Cox?"

"I ain't got time to be riding around after ladies playing at being artists," he said, still addressing Elijah. "I've got outlaws to catch, and I intend to do it. But there ain't no guarantee I'm going to catch them before they come across your pretty wife all on her lonesome out there."

For a second the marshal's glance hovered over Jordan, not quite acknowledging her existence, and her skin crawled. Elijah moved ahead of her to climb the stairs, and she didn't mind his protection at all this time, putting himself between her and Cox.

"Mrs. Kelly may choose to paint wherever she likes," Elijah said. "She will have my protection."

"You and that rifle?" Cox asked. They'd reached the porch, and the lamplight showed his scornful grin. "Against a band of outlaws."

"I hope I don't have to raise my rifle in anger," Elijah said, prim as the preacher he played, "but I certainly know how to use it. If Mrs. Kelly chooses to continue her painting, she will be safe."

There was no expression on the face he turned to Jordan,

but she knew precisely what he meant. She would be safe, not only from outlaws—and though she'd never seen him use a gun, she somehow had little doubt he could keep her safe from a whole outlaw gang with only his rifle and those killer's eyes—but also safe from him. It was his way of apologizing.

*Apologizing for being human,* she thought, irritated again. But she knew he was right. She had known what it was to share passion with a man she loved, and she had no interest in passion without love. Any more than Elijah wanted a home and family.

"Marshal Cox has a point," Tony put in, taking Jordan's elbow. "Maybe you should wait until we catch these men."

"If Mr. Kelly says I will be safe, I'm sure I will," Jordan said, still keeping her gaze on Elijah's. *Apology accepted.* "I don't think I need to give up my painting. I didn't go far today. I'll stay close to the hotel."

Elijah nodded, almost imperceptibly. The return of the status quo. A good thing. She reminded herself of that several times as she allowed Tony to guide her through the door into the huge entry room of the Fox and Hound.

"Jo-jo!" Nicky nearly bowled her over, throwing her arms around Jordan's neck. "Oh, darling, I'm so glad you're all right."

Her cousin stepped back, her unfeigned relief changing into a pretty frown. "What were you thinking of? Worrying us so. Staying out until the middle of the night like that."

"It's barely sunset!" Jordan objected.

"And well past suppertime," Nicky said. She took Jordan's arm from Tony, steering her toward the dining room. "I'm starved!"

Jordan had to laugh. "You're always starved, Nicky."

Nicky rested her free arm protectively across her belly. "Someone is, anyway."

As they approached the door to the dining room, Jordan caught the scent of roasted meat and fresh bread straight from heaven, reminding her that she'd eaten nothing all day but Ben's emergency rations of jerky and hardtack.

"I suppose Tony's told you all about the bandits," Nicky said. She shivered. "Dreadful beasts."

"Yes." Even bandits couldn't distract Jordan from the delicious smells.

"But has he told you the real tragedy?"

"Tragedy?"

Jordan glanced at Tony, who looked nonplussed, then back at Nicky. Her cousin stopped, eyes dancing.

"Yes, *tragedy*. Tony's throwing a grand party next Friday in our honor."

"Oh." Her response, muted by imminent starvation, was obviously not what Nicky was looking for. Jordan tried again. "How kind." She looked at Tony again. "That's very thoughtful."

"I thought just a dinner party," he said. "Something to celebrate your arrival and Mr. Kelly's recovery."

Jordan turned back to Nicky, who apparently had no intention of moving until Jordan asked the obvious question. "What on earth is so tragic about a dinner party, Nicolette?"

Other than Jordan's dying of hunger while they talked about it.

"Oh, for heaven's sake, Jo-jo!" Nicky shook her head in disbelief. "It's only a week away, and I haven't a thing to wear!"

If Jordan thought of Tony's dinner party at all over the next week—other than when Nicky was in a whirlwind of fuss over having her dress let out or giving Tony advice on the menu—it was only to think how odd the whole idea was, one of the paradoxical aspects of Battlement Park that kept the area's essence just out of her reach.

The park still struck her with wonder. One of the things she rashly struggled to capture in her painting was the peculiar juxtaposition of the park, as smoothly groomed as though husbanded by some mythically proportioned gardener, against the unstructured wildness of the mountains surrounding it. The contrast between the civilized Europeanness of the Fox and Hound, of Tony and Dr. Gottfried and the other newly arriving continental guests, and the rugged frontier mentality of the local ranchers.

Once she started painting, everything that had kept her from it was swept away by the torrent of images and emotions that fought to squeeze through her fingers out the tenuous tip of her brush. There could never be days enough in her whole life to capture all the glory and dread of this stretch of Eden.

She painted mountains, sunsets, a bald eagle in a blue spruce, a bouquet of meadow flowers, the porch railing at the cabin, Loki with his legs in the air, a narrow, glorious waterfall, an old boot she found wedged in some rocks. Each grand view and each small hideaway held a new wonder that reinforced Elijah's comment about glimpsing God.

And each time she went out into the mountains, a gunfighter and his rifle accompanied her to ward off the earthly dangers of violent, grasping men. Just another paradox.

Elijah was true to his silent promise—as she had known he would be—never crossing the bounds of courtesy between them. Neither had he withdrawn into stony silence as she had feared.

For hours at a time, he and Loki would keep an unobtrusive watch while she worked. But when she took a break to let her paints dry or when Elijah firmly interrupted to make her eat, they would talk. Talk about anything. Philosophy and religion or how to make a good stew. Music and art or how to find water in a desert. Horseshoeing and farming and John Donne.

Jordan talked about Aunt Rue and Uncle Hal, about being the big sister to her three cousins. She talked about autumns of leaves painted with fire and winters sledding with nieces and nephews. She talked about the dreams she had had as a girl and how many of the blessings in her life were things she never could have expected.

She listened while Elijah talked about growing up in Charleston. The stories he told were of young boy adventures, of scrapes and near escapes and running wild. But she could hear the loneliness beneath them, the isolation of the oldest son of an anti-slavery minister in that elegant southern city.

When he talked about his later life, it was to talk of his son, Wolf, Wolf's foster parents, the Culberts, and their children, of March and Maggie Jackson. He described for her some of the places he had been, empty plains, deserts in bloom, canyons as deep and black as nightmares, but he didn't talk about his profession or the life he led while he was traveling.

One afternoon, when her painting had succeeded particularly well, and she felt reckless with inspiration, she asked the question that had nibbled at her since she had met him.

"Mr. Kelly, may I ask you a question? Why would a professional gunfighter not wear his guns?"

"Yes."

They were in the meadow she had found her first day riding in the park, Elijah sitting in the thick grass, his back against the flat rock seat. Jordan's nearly finished painting of her mountain was drying on her easel a few feet away. Smoke and Elijah's borrowed sorrel grazed further down the slope, while Loki kept a proprietary eye on them from his nap spot atop a boulder at the high end of the meadow.

"Yes, what?"

"Yes, you may ask."

She could see the hint of a smile at the corner of his mouth. He looked almost asleep, hat tilted over his eyes, arms resting on the rifle in his lap, but Jordan was quite sure nothing bigger than a pika could approach the meadow without Elijah or Loki noticing. And even the pikas had better be careful—Loki had been known to try to snack on the little rabbit-like creatures if they got too bold.

Jordan settled on the rock bench, a careful arm's length from Elijah. He looked prepared to wait all afternoon. Jordan was not.

"All right. I'm asking."

"Asking what?"

She swatted at his hat and missed. "Why don't you wear your guns?"

"I don't like killing people."

"What do you mean?"

"I don't wear my guns because I don't like killing people."

"You're a gunfighter!" She didn't mean to be flippant, but there it was.

He tilted his head just enough to glance up at her. "I make my living with my guns. It's what I'm good at. I'm not good because I have good aim and fast reflexes. I'm faster than most, but I've faced men who were faster. I survive because I keep my cool. I don't shoot unless I have to, and I don't kill unless someone's trying to kill me."

He leaned back against the rock, tilting the hat down over his eyes.

"I've worked as a town marshal, a sheriff's deputy, and a Texas ranger. I've hunted fugitives. I've fought on what I thought to be the right side of range wars. I've guarded train shipments and stagecoaches. I've hired on to protect businesses or towns that thought they needed a gun.

"But I've never taken money to kill."

Which explained nothing at all. Not why he left his Colts back at the Fox and Hound, on a hook on the bedroom door. Not why he had taken them up in the first place. Not why he continued to pursue a profession that must frequently put him in a position of at least threatening to kill people.

Looking out over the same view he saw, the conifers and meadows, the mountains, the pure blue sky, she could almost touch the walls of difference between the lives they had led. The different worlds they had lived in. She saw color and shadow and angles. He saw lines of sight and cover and potentials for ambush.

She wanted to lean over, to rest her hand on his shoulder. She wanted to ask if there were any point of intersection in the worlds they saw.

But she sat quiet and still, letting the afternoon sun warm her back. And after a while she realized that she knew where their two vistas connected, what they saw in the mountains that both could claim.

The heartbreaking beauty.

"Wait, wait. Okay, now. Look!"

Nicky lifted her hands from Jordan's eyes.

"Well?"

Jordan dutifully examined the woman in the mirror. She thought she looked every one of her thirty years. Fine lines feathered the corners of her eyes. Her mouth had a determined set it hadn't had when she was younger; her expression must have been lighter then, when her heart had been lighter.

"You look gorgeous," Nicky said, tired of waiting for Jordan's own opinion. "I wish I had your figure tonight!"

She did still have a trim outline, which her carefully tailored dress flattered. The cutout bodice just below the high collar hinted at decolletage. And her eyes were as deep a blue as the silk fabric.

She'd brought the dress to Colorado to wear in Denver society. For a dinner party at the Fox and Hound, she should be wearing the more modest green taffeta.

"Tell me your hair isn't gorgeous."

"It's certainly . . . curly."

Trust Nicky to find a way to make stylish ringlets of Jordan's notoriously stubborn hair in a remote mountain cabin. All her hair should be pulled back in a respectable widow's knot. And she certainly shouldn't be nibbling her lips to deepen their color.

Not that all the primping in the world would make anything any different. However she looked tonight, she would still be a little brown bird of a widow, and Elijah would still be a solitary gunfighter.

He would be leaving soon, recovered from his bout of malaria and his rib healing nicely. It might even be tomorrow, she guessed, though he had not said. They had talked of many things over the past week, but not that. And not the fact that she suspected he planned to hunt down Lucifer Jones when he left. Cowardly in this, she didn't want to know for sure.

Once he left, she would probably never see him again.

Part of her would be glad to get it over with.

"Jo-jo!"

Jordan turned away from the mirror. She and Nicky could move down here to the lower bedroom after Elijah left. It offered more room—it certainly had been easier to dress down here, with Elijah waiting for them with Tony at the main lodge. And it would be easier on Nicky than taking the stairs.

"I don't know how you managed it, Nicky," she said, the

one honest thing she could say. "I could walk into any party in New England looking like this. Of course, you'd still be the belle of the ball."

Nicky snorted delicately as she tugged a perfect blond ringlet down to brush the deeper gold of her dress. "My cheeks are pudgy."

"You look like a cherub," Jordan said, then couldn't help laughing at Nicky's glare. "An angel, as always."

"I have no shape at all!"

"You certainly do. Mrs. Jones did a wonderful job letting out the waist on that dress for you."

Yet scanning her cousin's outfit, Jordan was startled to see that despite Tony's housekeeper's surprising skill with a needle, Nicky still looked pregnant. Glowing. The softening in her face perhaps making her more beautiful than ever. But pregnant, nonetheless.

Jordan did a quick count. Six and a half months. Worry stirred in her stomach, unexpected fear for her petite young cousin. She'd let Nicky's pique at Will continue too long. It was time to return her to Denver, to proper care.

Almost as if reading Jordan's thoughts, Nicky leaned closer to the mirror, her frown deepening.

"It's no wonder Will doesn't find me attractive anymore. I look like a cow."

"Will loves you."

Nicky whirled on her. "Then why hasn't he come after me?"

Looking into her cousin's glittering eyes, Jordan's heart contracted with guilt. She'd been so annoyed with Nicky's self-indulgent dramatics that she hadn't paid attention to the pain behind them.

"Oh, Nick." She reached for her cousin, but Nicky pulled back.

"All he ever does is work. Morning and night. If I ask for the simplest thing, for him to take me downtown or to read to me when my eyes are tired at night, he says he can't, he's too busy."

"He's just started working in a prestigious, well-established law firm. He needs to prove himself to Mr. Hedgepeth. He doesn't want to be a law clerk forever."

"I know that!" Nicky's eyes blazed. "I'm not stupid, Jo. I'm not even as selfish as you all think I am. But he's not the only one starting somewhere new. I don't have any friends in Denver. Since I got pregnant, he doesn't even want me to go out anymore. But he doesn't show any interest in the baby. He says he's doing this work for us, but do you know what he said when I told him the baby kicked me for the first time?"

She didn't wait for an answer. "He said, 'That's nice sweetheart.' You were more excited when I told you." Nicky crossed her arms over her chest. "Do you think I'm awful for getting upset?"

"No, of course I don't."

"He's wants to impress Leland Hedgepeth. What does it matter if it takes him an extra year to make junior partner? Maybe he's just working so much so he doesn't have to spend time with me."

Jordan took a deep breath, trying to sort out what to say. "You know what I saw when Will was working so hard in the evenings? I would see him bent over those law books, and then you would walk through the room. He would glance up, and his whole face would change. It was as if he lived for those glimpses of you. And I would think, how lucky Nicky is to have someone who loves her like that."

Nicky's snort was spoiled by the tears pouring down her cheeks.

"It's true. Do you know why he wants to make junior partner so quickly?" She pushed on. "It's not because he's trying to impress Leland Hedgepeth. He's trying to impress you. He wants to be worthy of you."

"Bah!" Nicky pulled out a lace handkerchief and dabbed at her eyes. "Why hasn't he come, then?"

*Because he's as pigheaded as you are.* "Because he's just as afraid that you don't love him as you are that he doesn't love you."

"Do you really think so, Jo-jo?"

The look in her cousin's eyes nearly broke Jordan's heart. "Yes, I really think so."

Nicky let her hug her then, snuffling into her handkerchief. Jordan wondered why she hadn't realized before that her cousin's pouting had come from fear and insecurity. She knew Nicky's weaknesses well enough, but she also knew her cousin's deep loyalty and capacity for love.

She hadn't noticed Nicky's pain because she had been too wrapped up in her own concerns. Tonight she had almost missed her chance to comfort her cousin because she had been worrying about what impression her finery would make on Elijah.

She was the silly, vain, selfish one.

It would be good for her to have him gone.

"Oh, for heaven's sake!" Nicky pulled away, holding up her dainty handkerchief, limp with tears. "What a ridiculous piece of vanity."

Jordan rummaged in the chest of drawers, coming up with a sturdy cotton handkerchief, which she passed to her cousin.

"Much better," Nicky said, and she looked better, Jordan thought, than she had all week. "My eyes must be ruined."

"No, they're fine," Jordan said, turning her cousin back toward the mirror. "You're the only person I know who can sob her eyes out and have them sparkle instead of turning red and blotchy."

"Hmph." Nicky patted at them again. "Well, I suppose I won't be completely unpresentable. It doesn't matter, anyway. You're the eligible young widow all the men will be watching."

"Nicky!"

"Rather gorgeous men, too." Nicky smiled in satisfaction, for all the world like a married auntie reassuring her debutante niece.

It was Jordan's turn to snort. "You're incorrigible."

"I am, aren't I?" Nicky put her arm through Jordan's. "Come along, Jo-jo. We have some dazzling to do."

# Chapter 13

They walked arm in arm down the path toward the hotel lodge. Tony had sent young Ben with a lantern to guide their way, though the sun had just dropped behind the western peaks, and the soft colors of twilight only muffled the glow of the lantern's flame.

Tony had taken every effort to create a night of genuine festivity. Ben wore a starched shirt and a green jacket only a little too big for him. He blushed furiously when Jordan told him how handsome he looked.

Jordan could feel sorrow hovering around the edge of the evening, as night hovered around the rim of the park, spilling in with the disappearance of the sun. She couldn't stop it from coming. But she could enjoy the soft twilight while it lasted.

So she let Nicky chatter and answered Ben's questions about painting and breathed deeply of the fresh air, which was cooling rapidly with the sunset.

In the half-light, with smoke-purple shadows merging under the trees, she half expected to be met by a host of fairy tale characters, talking wolves and dancing pixies drawn by Ben's swinging light.

She did *not* expect the fire-eyed stranger packing two six-shooters and a shotgun who stepped into the path in front of them, though she would have been forced to admit he was statistically more probable.

"Where's that son-of-a-bitch, Kelly?" he demanded, the soft southern tenor of his voice more chilling than the words themselves. "They said he's staying up this way."

Clad all in black from his unkempt hair to his cavalry boots, he stood half a head shorter than Jordan, a result of the steepness of the path. But with her mind still half in a misty fairyland, she found it hard to be frightened of him. Or maybe she was becoming accustomed to being confronted by men with guns.

"Heavens, sir," Nicky said breathlessly, her eyes huge and dark in the dusky light. Jordan recognized her cousin's recipe for coping with difficult men. "You startled me half to death. What on earth could you want with Mr. Kelly at this hour?"

"That's none of your damn business."

"Hey, mister! You can't talk to these ladies—"

Jordan grabbed Ben's shirt collar and jerked him back, effectively cutting off his protest. Any man who could be rude to Nicky in her full coquette act wouldn't hesitate to hurt a teenage boy.

"I don't think I like your tone, sir," Nicky was saying, tossing back an indignant curl.

The man's scowl deepened. "I don't think I care."

"Cousin." Putting her free hand on Nicky's shoulder, Jordan followed her brainless debutante lead. "Let's just tell this poor gentleman what he wants to know. He's obviously in a terrible hurry."

"Why, you are right, cousin," Nicky agreed, her eyes glinting. "I should have seen that right away. He doesn't mean to be rude, I'm sure."

The stranger's soft voice started to rasp. "Lady, I'm about ready to—"

"Right up there," Jordan said sweetly, pointing back the

207

way they had come. "Mr. Kelly is staying in a cabin just up this path."

With only a grunt of acknowledgment, the stranger pushed past them, striding purposefully up the hill. Of course, he didn't have their lantern, and the dusk was deep enough now to be tricky. Jordan felt no guilt at all when she heard a crash and a curse as he tripped over a rock in the path.

"Serves him right!" Nicky said gleefully.

"Hurry." Jordan felt the chill of reality creeping in. "We'd better reach the hotel before he finds out Elijah's not at the cabin."

She released Ben, who shook himself indignantly. "I can take care of myself, Mrs. Kelly. I'm not a kid."

Jordan nudged him forward. "That man was carrying three guns. That I could see. I don't doubt your courage, Ben, but our first priority is to see Mrs. Braddock safely to the hotel. Right?"

Ben cast a glance back at Nicky's rounded figure. "Yes'm."

"I can take care of myself, too," Nicky objected, her eyes still shining wickedly, but she retained her grip on Jordan's arm as they hurried down the path.

They didn't have far to go. Panting, but without further incident, they reached the stairs to the front door of the Fox and Hound.

Ben thrust the lantern at Jordan. "I'll run back and see what he's doing."

"Wait!" Jordan pushed the lantern back. "Ben, you've got to check on the horses. What if that man was one of the outlaws? Major Wayne may need to put a posse together."

Ben shifted, weighing this possibility against the excitement of spying. Pride of responsibility and loyalty to his employer won. "You're right, ma'am. Tell Major Wayne I'll have everything ready if he needs the horses."

Jordan watched the boy trot away. She couldn't be sure he'd be safe in the stable, but it had to be better than chasing after their short-tempered accoster.

"Be careful!" she called out belatedly. She just caught the flash of Ben's hand waving back at her as he and his lantern disappeared around the corner of the lodge.

"Do you really think that man was one of the outlaws?" Nicky asked. Breathless, she tramped heavily up the stairs.

Jordan shook her head. "I don't know. He certainly didn't seem concerned about concealing himself."

"True." Her cousin sighed dramatically. "Besides, I could hardly hope to be confronted by bandits twice in one year."

Jordan failed to mention she'd had quite enough of that already.

Light spilled from windows up and down the building as they reached the top of the stairs. Nicky paused to smooth her skirt and try on a flirtatious smile.

"A bandit would have spoiled the dinner party," she concluded, shrugging off the last of her disappointment. "Besides, if he's a hotel guest, we'll see him again. He was cute."

"In a surly, insulting sort of way," Jordan muttered. She decided not to mention immediately that the stranger's not being a bandit wouldn't necessarily salvage the dinner party. She didn't want to ruin Nicky's grand entrance.

Elijah stifled the urge to glance at the ostentatious grandfather clock dominating the west wall of the hotel's entrance room. He wouldn't give Tony Wayne the satisfaction.

The hotel proprietor was leaning against the back of a green overstuffed chair, his jovial face as relaxed as though the women weren't twenty minutes late. But then, he'd predicted they would be at least that.

Elijah had taken a seat by the open fireplace and now regretted it. Though the logs burned low, it was still too hot. But he couldn't get up and move without looking nervous.

Which meant that he was, in fact, nervous or he wouldn't give a damn what he looked like to Tony Wayne. Cheery bastard. He caught himself grinding his teeth.

He didn't like the Englishman's sunny disposition. He didn't like his bringing tea and crumpets into the Colorado Rockies. He didn't like Tony's having the power of knowing his true identity. And he didn't like the man's maddening calm during this interminable wait.

His feet hurt. He should have worn his old boots instead of accepting shoes from Tony. He'd had to borrow a suit from the man, too. The waist on the pants was loose, and the length of the legs and arms just a little short. He felt like a teenage boy in an awkward growth spurt.

The price of vanity. Why couldn't he just come to this ridiculous party in his regular clothes? Because he didn't want to look like an uncultured boor in front of Jordan Braddock. Why couldn't he just decline to come? He didn't want to leave her in the clutches of the insufferably charming Major Wayne.

What was wrong with him? He shut off the thought, understanding instinctively that it was better not to know.

"I could have one of the serving girls bring out a plate of hors d'oeuvres," the Englishman offered blithely. "The other guests are enjoying them in the dining room."

"That's not necessary," Elijah assured him, projecting his best deadly calm.

Perhaps he'd missed the mark. Tony's smile got just a touch wider. "I thought it was the unmarried chaps who were supposed to have the butterflies."

Elijah reminded himself he didn't wear his guns because

he didn't like to kill people.

Tony clicked his tongue. "You look like a pony on derby day."

He didn't like to be *forced* to kill people. Choosing to kill them was a whole different matter.

"I dare say, though, Mrs. Kelly would give anyone butterflies, married or not."

At the reminder of Jordan's precarious position, Elijah sat up, just a little. "Mrs. Kelly's marital status is not a matter for levity, Mr. Wayne."

"No, no, of course not. I have the greatest respect for Mrs. Kelly." Tony looked contrite, but was obviously not cowed. "I must say it's a lesson to me to see a man so conspicuously in love with his own wife. I dare say—"

"If you dare say it, I'll rip your tongue out of your mouth," Elijah growled.

"Jolly good." Tony crossed his arms over his chest, quite satisfied with the results of his teasing. Elijah didn't care as long as the man shut up.

All right. He was nervous. It was the damned formality. He'd spent all week near Jordan, enjoying her company and nothing more. This evening would be no different.

If Tony would just be quiet, he could regain his accustomed cool distance. But before the silence could properly settle, they heard noises on the porch.

Elijah stood, tugging down his waistcoat. Tony's amused smile told him he should have stayed seated, looked bored, anything, but it was too late.

The double doors swung open. Nicolette and Jordan stepped through, and Elijah realized immediately that cool was completely out of the question.

Jordan expected Tony's effusive greeting. She expected

Nicky's tinkling laughter. She expected lights and delicious smells and the popping of a log in the fire. She expected Elijah to wear a black silk coat with the same catlike grace he wore his duster.

She didn't expect her breath to stop when she saw him in it. She didn't expect her heart to thud in her ears in response to the look in his eyes.

"We are the luckiest men in Colorado," Tony was saying, offering Nicolette his arm. "Wouldn't you say, Zechariah? Escorting such beauty for the evening."

Elijah moved with the elegance of an aristocrat—or the instinctive poise of a hunting cat. Jordan found she could smell him even before he reached her, a musky hint of danger. She could hear his soft breathing, maybe even his heartbeat. Her senses sharpened and contracted on this one man.

She had acknowledged it would hurt when he left. Because she had grown fond of him. The friendship they had forged had become special to her. That was all. That she had wanted to look her best tonight, a last flash of color before settling into a brown bird life, had nothing to do with her transitory physical attraction to him the week before.

Had she really believed that? The truth shook her. She had worn this dress, this color and this cut, to put exactly that hunger in his eyes.

When he took her elbow, the heat from his hand flowed up her arm, flushing her face.

Nicky's voice sounded dim and far away. "There won't be too many continental guests at this dinner, will there, Major Wayne? I'll be mortified I didn't have anything more appropriate to wear than this old thing."

"Nonsense!" Tony's voice held the perfect note of shock. "You will outshine the entire gathering. Mr. Kelly, aren't the ladies astonishingly lovely this evening?"

"No." A panther's voice might have a feral purr just like that. "I am not astonished. They are always lovely."

Tony grinned in delight at being out-charmed. "I couldn't have put it better myself, old man. Will you allow us to escort you to the dining room, ladies? I hope you're hungry. The chef has outdone himself."

Having eaten the Norwegian cook's hearty, but plain, fare for almost two weeks now, Jordan didn't think that was saying much. It didn't matter. She doubted she'd be able to taste it, anyway.

"Marvelous. I'm starved," Nicky said, neither recent dining experiences nor etiquette able to dampen her pregnancy-induced enthusiasm for food of any and all kinds. "Our little bit of excitement must have sparked my appetite."

"Excitement?" Tony asked politely, steering Nicky toward the hall.

"Oh, God." Jordan stopped, horrified that she'd forgotten. "That stranger. He's probably on his way down here right now."

Elijah caught her tone. "Who?"

"A perfectly horrible man," Nicky said with a delighted shiver. "Very rude. He wanted to know where you were staying, Mr. Kelly, so we told him. Of course, we didn't happen to mention that you weren't there."

"He wore guns," Jordan said, more practically. "And he's not going to be happy when he gets back from the cabin."

"We decided he wasn't an outlaw," Nicky put in quickly. "He wasn't skulking or anything. I'm sure he'll be along eventually. We don't have to invite him in to supper."

Jordan's fear was even greater than that of outlaws. "Mr. Kelly, he might be another bounty hunter. He's not the type to ask a lot of questions before he starts shooting."

"Er, my dear ladies, what did he look like?" Tony asked.

213

Jordan noticed that Elijah's eyes narrowed at the Englishman's strange expression. Tony almost looked amused.

"He was about my height, I think," Jordan said. She usually had a solid memory for details, but the encounter had shaken her. She glanced toward the doors. "He wore a gunbelt with two pistols and carried a shotgun. He didn't wear a hat. Dark hair. Dressed in black—"

"Navy," Nicky corrected her, fashion sense prevailing over the literal artistic eye. "It looked black because of the dark. His jacket was last year's cut. He wore riding boots. And he was rude."

"A violent temper," Jordan agreed.

"I was afraid of that," Tony sighed, not nearly the alarmed response Jordan thought appropriate to the situation. She looked at Elijah, but his face had gone carefully empty.

His voice was equally blank. "Malachi."

From the edge of her mind, Jordan recognized the name. "Your *brother?*"

The front doors slammed inward with a resounding crash, letting in a swirl of night.

"Well," Tony said brightly. "Speak of the devil."

# Chapter 14

Malachi Kelly might well have been the devil incarnate, standing in the doorway to the Fox and Hound with his shotgun cradled in his hands, his dark hair wild around his fierce face, his green eyes catching the light like a wolf's. Jordan glanced at Elijah, his own eyes a hard, flat gold.

The devil? Not Malachi. She could see the resemblance between them now, but there was no contest which Kelly brother was the most diabolic.

Malachi dropped the butt of his shotgun to the floor. "There you are. You careless son-of-a-bitch."

"I believe you owe the ladies an apology for your language." Elijah's soft tone did nothing to hide the steel behind it.

His brother's sharp green eyes scanned Jordan and Nicky. "Your ladies have amused themselves at my expense. I think we're even."

Elijah's eyes flattened further. "I do not."

"Mal!" Tony interrupted, striding over to clap his friend on the shoulder. "It's good to see you, old man. Let's start over, shall we? Let me introduce you properly to our lovely guests."

His smile was wide and ingenuous, but Tony kept a hand firmly on Malachi's shoulder as he pushed him forward into the room.

"May I present Mrs. Nicolette Braddock?"

"How do you do?" Nicky said politely, but apparently Jordan was not the only one who saw the mischief in her eyes.

Malachi's eyebrows rose. "You mean other than my twisted ankle, ma'am?"

Jordan noticed he only flinched a little when Tony kicked it.

"Fine, just fine, ma'am. Thank you."

Tony turned him toward Jordan before Nicky could properly provoke him.

"And, of course, I am pleased to present your brother's wife, Mrs. Jordan Braddock Kel—"

"Leave it, Tony. My brother doesn't have a wife," Malachi snapped.

"Mal." Tony's teeth clenched behind his smile. "As I explained in my letter—"

"My brother's gotten himself into 'a bit of a pickle.' " His imitation of the Englishman was almost perfect. "One that only serves him right. And I'm supposed to get him out of it."

Elijah's drawl vibrated in the tense air. "I did not ask for your help."

"I wouldn't help you if you did ask," Malachi said indifferently. "But you didn't. Tony did. So you can go back to being your own winsome self, and this woman can quit pretending to be your wife and go back to whatever previous employment she enjoyed."

Jordan discovered with terrifying swiftness that she had never seen Elijah truly angry before. She barely had time to register that he had moved before he held Malachi's shotgun in his hand. She thought he meant to strike his brother with it rather than shoot him, but she never found out for sure.

After a tense moment, Malachi held up a disgusted hand. "Hell, 'Lije, I didn't mean to question the lady's honor. Just yours."

Elijah tossed the shotgun onto a nearby table.

"I see nothing's changed," he said dryly. "You're still a snot-nosed brat."

Malachi shrugged. "And you're still oversensitive."

"Blast." Tony's sharp tone turned them all toward the Englishman, but his attention was on the colorless house-keeper, Mrs. Jones, standing in the shadows by the west hall-way. "Yes, Philomena? What is it?"

The woman's pallid face showed no emotion, but her eyes glittered as they passed over Jordan. She must have heard Malachi's comment about Jordan's marital status.

"I'm sorry, sir." Her voice was as colorless as her face. "I was just wondering if we'll be having an extra guest tonight. We'll need to set another place."

"Yes, yes. You may as well." Tony waved his hand vaguely.

"And you may as well stop skulking around spying on peo-ple," Malachi added. Jordan wanted to be offended by his rudeness, but she'd been thinking the exact same thing.

Mrs. Jones' expression took on its habitual mixture of de-fiance and resentment. "I'm just doing my job."

"Bullshit."

"Mal," Tony objected.

Spots of red dotted Mrs. Jones' cheeks. "I feel sorry for your mother," she said, an edge of steel showing in that jaded voice. "I couldn't abide it if my son were rude to a woman."

"My mother died when I was two," Malachi said, "so my rudeness has never bothered her much. And I don't see why I have to be polite to someone who's lying to my face."

"If I were a man, you wouldn't dare call me a liar," Mrs. Jones said, old antagonism burning in her voice. "My boy would never let you talk to me like that."

"If you were a man, I wouldn't have bothered calling you

anything," Malachi said. "My fists would have done the talking for—"

"Mal!" Tony interrupted sharply. "That's quite enough. Philomena, please set another place at my table."

Mrs. Jones shot a look of malice at Malachi before drifting back down the hall.

"Do you have to act like that, Mal?" Watching his friend's face, Tony breathed out heavily. "I know. If I'd wanted polite conversation, I should have sent for someone else."

"You should have sent for someone else, anyway, because I'm not working with him." Malachi pointed at Elijah.

"Luckily for you," Elijah said, drawing out the words, "though possibly not luckily for him, you are free to work for Major Wayne without fear of interference from me. I suppose he's brought you in to stir up trouble."

"That may be the result, if not the intent," Tony said, foregoing his usual tact. "Let's all have something to eat. It should be hard for you two to insult each other with your mouths full."

He reached for Jordan's arm. "My dear, please allow me to escort you to dinner."

It was much safer than accepting Elijah's escort. Tony's genuine smile warmed her heart without making her stomach dance.

"What the hell is going on out here?"

Jordan took one look at Marshal Cox's face, visibly red even with the hallway lights behind him, and almost groaned aloud. She might have given up on tasting her food, but she didn't want to have to give up on eating it.

"Marshal Cox." Tony's greeting sounded weary.

The marshal's thick arms crossed his chest. "That Jones woman said you had the reverend's brother out here and that he said the reverend wasn't married."

His scowl fixed on Jordan, his dark eyes gleaming unpleasantly as he looked her up and down.

"Reverend?" Malachi choked. "Honestly, 'Lije. Just when I think you can't get any lower."

Tony was faster than the marshal. He had Cox by the arm before the marshal could reach for his gun. Fury quickly replaced the confusion on the lawman's face.

"What the hell's going on?"

Jordan caught Elijah's gaze. "Go," she mouthed at him. He was healthy enough now. Marshal Cox might be strong, might be good with a gun, but he'd never catch Elijah if Elijah didn't want to be caught.

She couldn't decipher the expression that crossed Elijah's face, his eyes intent on hers, but he shook his head.

"Marshal Cox," he said, disarmingly cool. "I believe what my brother means to say—"

"Is that I can't believe you fell for that ridiculous story," Malachi said, with a disgusted glance at Elijah. "I guess it proves he's not as famous as old Wild Bill yet. Not so many have heard of 'Preacher' Elijah Kelly."

Tony was stronger than Jordan had thought. He managed to keep the marshal to a short lunge.

"Let go, Wayne," Cox snarled. "I'm going to take that bastard into custody. Unless he argues about it. And then I'm going to blow him to hell."

"Not in my hotel, you're not," Tony objected. "Listen for a minute—"

"Listen to what?" Cox's face turned a deeper purple. "That's a wanted man. Get your hands off of me, Wayne, or I'll charge you with aiding a known outlaw."

"He may be a scoundrel," Malachi said agreeably. "But he's not an outlaw."

"I've got a wanted poster," Cox said. "The marshal up in

Laramie sure thinks he's an outlaw."

"That's a misunderstanding," Elijah said, obviously not expecting anyone to listen to him.

Malachi reached into his coat—navy, Jordan saw, as Nicky had said—and pulled out a wrinkled envelope.

"Here," he said, thrusting the envelope at Cox's free hand. "This is a sworn affidavit, dated two days ago. The charges against Elijah Kelly have been dropped. I think he should go to jail, myself, shooting an unarmed man. But Si wouldn't testify against him, and if the victim himself refuses to press charges . . . If anyone wants my brother—something I find hard to imagine—it's not Laramie's marshal."

Cox snatched the envelope from Malachi's hand. Cautiously, Tony released him. The marshal checked the seal, then tore the envelope open. He glowered down at the affidavit, his mustache twitching with rage.

"It's a good thing he's just a hired killer and not a confidence man," Malachi said. "You'd undoubtedly have been helping him pass the collection plate. I can see why Tony thought he needed some outside help to hunt down those outlaws."

Marshal Cox was as quick to action as he was to anger. Malachi ducked, but not fast enough. Cox's right hook caught him square in the jaw, sending him thudding back over the nearest chair.

Nicky squealed. Tony grabbed the marshal from behind in a bear hug before he could press the attack. As Malachi rose, his own fists clenched, Elijah did the same to him.

"I will be taking my brother outside for a little fresh air," Elijah said, his voice tight with what might have been anger or amusement or merely pain from his injured rib. "Please go in to supper without us."

Malachi didn't protest as his brother shoved him unceremoniously out the front doors. Tony waited a second longer before releasing Marshal Cox.

"I apologize, Marshal," he said, his face the soberest Jordan had seen it. "Mal doesn't think before he speaks. He's a bit rough, but he's a top-notch tracker. He's been deputized by the Larimer County sheriff and—"

"You knew!" the marshal roared, turning the full force of his boiling fury on the Englishman. "You knew the whole time that man was lying about his identity."

Tony sighed. "I knew there had been a mistake—"

"Mistake?" Cox spat on the floor. "The mistake was thinking you could make a fool out of me. I'll find your outlaws for you. I'll do my job—without the help of that smart-mouthed bastard. But I won't eat at your table."

Jordan felt a stab of pity for the man, even when he stopped beside her, rage mottling his cheeks.

"You've made the wrong enemy," he snarled at her. "You tell that to your lover. Maybe he weaseled out of that charge in Laramie, but I'll get him for something. I promise you that."

He stomped out, slamming the doors behind him.

The three remaining stood still for a long moment, looking at each other. Nicky moved first, walking over to pick up Malachi's shotgun.

"The next person who tries to stop me from reaching the dining room," she said, "gets both barrels."

Tony laughed loudly, the strain easing from his face. He walked over to take Nicky's free arm and offered his other to Jordan.

"Shall we?" He led them toward the hallway. "Don't worry, Mrs. Braddock. With those three out of the way, there will only be more food for us."

Jordan couldn't smile. She could still feel Napoleon Cox's rage.

★ ★ ★ ★ ★

The light from Jordan's lantern flickered pitifully against the thick darkness pressing around her. She could barely see the trees, but she could feel them surrounding her, solid and cool, whispering together more softly than she could hear.

She stubbed her toe on a root and almost dropped the lantern. Hiking her skirt up a little higher, she wondered what on earth had possessed Tony to let her return to her cabin without an escort.

Yes, she'd insisted she'd be fine. This walk hadn't seemed like a scary notion, back in the lights of the Fox and Hound. It wasn't far, and she'd done it so many times, she could probably find her way without the lantern. It was just that the feeble light made the shadows under the trees blacker. It brought to mind bears and wolves and lunatic marshals.

With her free hand, Jordan rubbed the back of her neck. Maybe walking back alone wasn't such a great idea, but she couldn't have stayed at the party a minute longer. Making small talk, laughing politely at Baron what's-his-name's mangled jokes. Her nerves had prickled the entire time, wondering what had happened between Elijah and his brother, worrying about the marshal's threats, her head pounding over the problem of delivering Nicky, currently the belle of the party, back home to Will.

A twig snapped, too close. Jordan almost jumped out of her shoes, even though she knew her own foot had been the one to snap it. She peered into the darkness, anyway, heart pounding, watching for a wisp of movement or the gleam of an eye. Light blinded, she wouldn't see it even if it were there.

She frowned down at the lantern in her hand. She was halfway to the cabin. No advantage in turning back. But she wasn't going to make it if she had a heart attack.

Opening the lantern's door, she blew it out. In the sudden

dark, her ears began to work again. She could hear the trees sighing in a soft breeze, the rustle of some tiny creature in the underbrush, the river rushing through a meadow far away.

As her heart settled into the night rhythm of the park, she found that the light from the stars and the sickle moon gave enough illumination for her to see where the path wound ahead. She'd have to tread carefully, wary of roots and rocks, but at least she wouldn't feel so exposed.

She picked her way forward, letting her breathing match the hush of the wind, her footsteps padding into the needles of pines and spruce. An owl hooted somewhere up the mountainside.

And another sound caught the edge of her hearing. Something like the sighing of the breeze, something echoing the voice of the river. Something as untamed and untroubled and bright as the stars overhead.

The music of the spheres, she thought, somewhat wildly. Then she realized that it was music, pure notes chasing each other through the night. It came from up the path. From the cabin.

As she moved closer, she could make out the melody, quick, but mournful. Violin music. She had forgotten retrieving Elijah's violin when Achilles was killed. The instrument had seemed too alien to the life of a gunfighter, too civilized for the wilderness.

It didn't now. In the dark, with the mountains rising on all sides, the music flowed like the wind through the trees, in eddies and gusts. Into the lonely night it sang, as plaintive as a wolf's howl, as wild as a panther's cry.

Candlelight glimmered in the cabin windows. Softly, she climbed the stairs to the porch. Outside the door, she hesitated.

It seemed thoughtless to intrude on such music, to break

the spell. Yet it also seemed rude to wait outside and eavesdrop on so intimate a song.

Jordan looked back the way she had come. She couldn't do that alone again tonight.

She rattled the handle on the door. The music continued, though perhaps he hadn't heard. Nothing to do but push the door open and step inside.

He had heard.

Elijah stood in the center of the cabin's sitting room, his whole being focused intently on the violin he held. But his eyes caught Jordan's and held them.

He'd thrown his coat over a chair, and his white shirt, open at the neck, stuck to his chest and back with the intensity of his playing. His dark hair showed russet depths in the candlelight, curling damply above his open collar.

Jordan thought she should continue upstairs and leave him to his playing, but she couldn't move, mesmerized by the dark, wild music and the tautly controlled power of the man who played it.

The melody slowed and faded. Elijah lifted his chin from the instrument.

"I didn't expect you back so soon."

"I didn't feel very festive tonight," she said. "You don't have to stop playing. I didn't mean to intrude."

"You didn't," he said, though he set the violin down on the side table by the bedroom door.

"What you were playing, that's just how I feel tonight," she said, her heart still beating to it. "Recklessly melancholy."

Jordan nearly bit her tongue. She *was* reckless. She hoped he wouldn't ask why, hoped he'd laugh. But he did neither.

"I'm sorry," she said. "I'll go."

"Don't." He moved toward her to pick up his coat. "Don't

apologize. I was playing for you."

She snorted, relieved by the humor. "I wasn't even here."

He wasn't smiling. "It seemed safer that way."

And suddenly the five feet between them was much too close. He could have meant anything by that remark. Whatever he meant, she could brush it away. But only if she could break her gaze away from his.

There was nothing safe about the look in his eyes. Nothing safe about the heat rising in her body. Nothing safe in the world, because nothing in the world could make her look away.

"I should go." He picked up his coat and stepped toward the door. Another step closer to Jordan. She could feel the heat of his body, hear the rush of his breath, count the hairs on the back of his sun-browned hand. All in the infinity of a heartbeat.

"Let me go," he said, his drawl soft as a whisper, rough as a cat's purr. "Please. Sparrow. Tell me to go."

"Elijah."

His eyes darkened when she said his name. It was almost as though she could bind him with that word, the way he had captured her with his violin. As though she could hold him, keep him, if only for a moment.

"Elijah," she said again, savoring the sound, as reckless as the music, as bittersweet. "Don't go."

He raised his hand, not quite touching her cheek. The air hummed between them. His eyes burned with gold.

"You don't mean it."

No. She *shouldn't* mean it. A sober widow. An example to her nieces and nephews, a protector for Nicky. A sensible, practical mature woman. Not a giddy, impressionable schoolgirl.

But she didn't feel like a giddy girl. She felt old as the

mountains, wild as the wind, reckless as the stars.

She raised her hand, touched him first, her fingers brushing the roughness of his cheek, the warmth of his neck, clutching his hair.

She could hear the music again, singing in her ears. She could feel the stars shining through the roof of the cabin, through her body, through the world.

Elijah touched her then, his hand mimicking hers, tangling in her hair, cupping the back of her head. Gentle, unstoppable, they pulled each other close. Even when her eyes drifted shut, Jordan could still feel his gaze burning through her.

She couldn't bear it. Couldn't bear touching him and letting him go. Couldn't bear losing him. But that was tomorrow, and this was tonight.

Only a sigh escaped her as she tilted her head. His breath mixed with hers, warm and sweet.

"Sparrow," he whispered. He dropped his coat.

And he kissed her.

# Chapter 15

His groan vibrated through Jordan's veins, and her heart beat so hard that she thought it would break. Maybe it did. She knew her lashes were wet when he pulled back to look into her eyes. He brushed a thumb beneath them.

"Sparrow."

"Kiss me."

His lips barely skimmed hers, warm and soft. And again. Jordan felt herself leaning into him, giving in to the dizziness.

"Elijah." She whispered his name against his lips, and he groaned again, clutching her shoulders, his mouth coming down on hers with a hunger that burned.

He touched his tongue against her lips, and she let him in, the sensation rippling down her spine, between her thighs. His hands found her back, pulled her close.

She felt his heat through the thin silk of her dress, her breasts crushed again his half-bare chest, his hands sliding down her ribs, pulling her hips against the hard length of his desire.

And still he kissed her, savage and gentle, giving and taking, nibbling and teasing, leaving them both gasping for breath, foreheads resting against each other.

"Sparrow," he whispered again, pressing his lips above her brows, at her temples, softly against her eyelids. He could feel her heart beat in rhythm with his, feel her trembling against him.

She knew. He knew she knew exactly what his body wanted, and she didn't pull away. No. More than that. She wanted it, too. The thought nearly drove him mad.

He looked into her eyes and saw the life burning in them, through the sorrow and the fears. The courage and decency he had seen the first time he met her, the light he had glimpsed through the pain in her heart stunned him like sunlight exploding off a snowbank. Beautiful and terrible.

"Sparrow," he whispered, his voice ragged. "Let me go. You deserve better."

Better than a rootless gunfighter with a broken soul. Better than hands that had killed. Better than a man who had failed everyone he had ever cared about.

She took his head in her hands, keeping him close. She kissed him, feather light.

The flash of a bird's wings. Or an angel's.

"Most of us should just be grateful we don't get what we deserve," she said, her voice deadly serious, but with the glint of humor in her eyes.

He shook his head. "I promised to protect you."

She silenced him with another kiss, this one deeper, demanding. She brushed his lips with her tongue, and he felt himself falling.

"I don't want your protection." Her words were a whisper against his mouth. "I want you. For tonight if that's all there is."

Her eyes, darkened with desire let him see the truth in what she said. "That's all there ever is, Elijah. This moment. It's never enough, but it's all we get."

And suddenly he wanted to run. As far and as fast as he could. Because he knew with absolute certainty that it never *would* be enough. He could never get enough of her.

It would be better to leave now and spare himself the agony of losing her.

But he couldn't let her go.

Reckless, she had called his music. Nothing so reckless as the way he kissed her now, as though he could touch her very soul with the heat pouring through him, the brush of his lips, his tongue as intimate as if they were already lovers. Lovers. His breath caught as she melted against him.

He ran his thumb from her lips, over her chin, down the pulsing length of her throat. His fingers skirted the edge of her decolletage as he brought his hand down to cup her breast, catching her soft moan in his mouth. He brushed his thumb across the skin-warmed silk, feeling her nipple harden to his touch.

Bending his head, his lips found the bare skin just above his thumb, and she gasped, arching against him.

Raising his head, he pressed his cheek against hers, so flushed it burned.

"Sparrow." He whispered against her ear. "If you don't tell me to go . . ."

A spark of reason flickered in Jordan's brain, warning her to run. But when she pulled back to look into his eyes, the desire that burned there melted her bones. Yet it only matched her own. Reason left her, and she found she didn't particularly want it back.

"I'm not going to tell you to go."

With a wrenching groan, Elijah gathered her against him and lifted her off her feet, carrying her into the bedroom behind the stairs. A single candle burned beside the bed, caressing the planes of his face, firing the gold in his eyes.

His hands found the buttons down the back of her dress. She thought it should feel strange, letting him see her bare skin, touch her, knowing he would soon be touching her in the most intimate way possible. She should be nervous, afraid, ashamed.

The silk whispered off her shoulders.

She should be *terrified*. A man she had known for mere weeks. A man who was not her husband. A gunfighter whose eyes burned hers with his hunger, whose hands felt like fire as they tossed aside her corset and caressed the bare skin beneath.

Yet she knew her hunger burned just as brightly, knew her hands brushed flames up his chest as she lifted his shirt over his head.

She wanted him. This man whom she did not understand, but who was no longer a stranger. As the last of her underclothes slipped to the floor, she wanted that desire that darkened his eyes, wanted the need that pressed against her through his pants.

She ran her fingers down his chest, lowering her head to lick his nipples.

Elijah groaned again. He lifted her head, his kiss as shocking and fierce as her own response. He pushed his hand between their bodies, between her thighs. She cried out, her legs giving way beneath her.

He lowered her to the bed, stroking her. Her ragged breath, her wetness, the mindless need in her unfocused eyes nearly undid him. He kissed her as he touched her, kissed her belly, her breasts, the hollow of her shoulder. He could feel the heat rippling off of her, feel the tension building beneath his fingers.

He stroked her deeper.

"Please." She pulled his hand away, pulled it up to hold it against her chest.

"Sh." He brushed his fingers over her breast, teasing it. "Let me pleasure you."

"Please." Her voice shook. "I need all of you." Her hand brushed across his need, making him gasp.

"No." He had trouble making the words. "I won't endanger you."

She stilled beneath his hands. "Elijah, I . . . there's no danger. You don't need to worry about that."

In the dim glow from the candle, he could see the old pain in her eyes of her two childless marriages. If he could have changed that for her then, he would have. He would have done anything to drive all sorrow from her heart. Brought back her husband and sent her home to him if it would erase the grief from her soul.

She was reaching for the buttons of his pants, her light touch loosening his last frayed threads of self-control. He wrenched off the pants and lay on the bed beside her, pulling her close. Wanting to comfort her. Wanting more than that. Wanting to tangle his hands in her long, dark hair, spread it down across her breasts. Wanting to bury his face in her neck, hear her gasp when he licked her ear. Wanting to run his hand from her shoulder to her knee, feeling every inch of soft, soft skin.

Jordan moved beneath his hand, wanting his touch everywhere at once. Wanting to touch him everywhere at once. Wanting to tell him with her body what she couldn't say with words.

That it felt right. That it felt right to be there with him. That it felt right to share his warmth, to touch and be touched, to cry out his name when his hardness slipped between her thighs. That when he entered her, it felt as natural and necessary as breathing, as if they were meant to be a part of each other.

Their hunger was too great to take it slow. It drove them against each other as though they might starve before they had their fill, as though this touch, this fire, could burn away the shadows and free them to the light. They clung to each other, only that anchor keeping them from spinning away into the night.

And when it was over, they clung to each other still, their heartbeats as entangled as their bodies. Elijah rolled, pulling Jordan on top of him, pulling the bed's quilt up over both of them. In that cocoon of warmth, they held each other as though they would never have to let go.

The bittersweet call of a morning bird woke Jordan. She lay against Elijah's side, his arms still clutched around her, though she could tell by his breathing that he was asleep.

The candle had burned itself out, but she could see his face in the cool pre-dawn light from the window. She had seen him asleep before, fitful dozes fighting the malarial fever. He had seemed vulnerable then. Perhaps that was when her heart . . .

But she had not seen him at peace. The very angles of his bones seemed to have softened, making him look younger. Heartbreakingly innocent.

She would remember that, along with his gunfighter's stare and his dangerous smile.

She had to get up. She had not meant to sleep. If Nicky came back to the cabin to find Jordan not safe in her own bed . . . It didn't bear thinking about.

She slipped her feet out from under the quilt and, gently as she could, untangled herself from Elijah's arms. He mumbled a protest, but she pulled free without waking him.

Even with her heart aching, she smiled. The lethal gunfighter with his lightning reflexes sleeping like a newborn puppy. More soundly than Loki who gave her a flash of his silver eyes and a thump of his tail before settling back into sleep at the foot of the bed.

Jordan gathered up her scattered clothing. There was an

afghan draped over the back of the chair by the door. She'd put it there to keep herself warm when Elijah was sick. She wrapped it close around her shoulders and crept out into the cabin's sitting room. She padded to the stairs and climbed them with care, avoiding the creaks in the center of the steps.

The ceiling of the upper bedroom triangled with the slope of the cabin roof. Even with the two beds tucked into the eaves, there was not much space. And with only two tiny windows at each end of the room, it was much gloomier than it had been downstairs.

Jordan felt for the trunk at the bottom of her bed and draped her clothes over it. She knew she would not sleep again, but if she were in bed when Nicky returned, she could avoid her cousin's cheerful party report for a few hours.

She had tossed her nightgown over the footboard of the bed the morning before. The mountain air was definitely bad for her sense of propriety.

Pushing down a bout of hysterical giggles, she pulled on the nightgown and grabbed her bedcovers. They didn't move. Jordan reached out to see what they had snagged on and had to stifle a scream when her hand found something big and warm lying in her bed.

She took a shaky breath. Nicky. Her cousin had returned, the party ending before dawn after all. Yet she hadn't raised an alarm over finding Jordan missing. She must not have noticed. She had claimed wine was the one thing that made her queasy with her pregnancy, but she must have had some as the evening went on and simply fallen into the wrong bed. Jordan would take hers.

As she pulled back, a strong hand grabbed Jordan's arm. For the second time in as many seconds, she choked back a scream.

"It's just me, Nick," she whispered shakily.

"Sh!" Nicky's hand, a ghostly blob in the gloom, beckoned her closer. Her voice barely carried to Jordan's ear. "You have to share this bed with me."

"Why?"

Nicky shushed her again, raising a frantic finger to her lips. "There's someone in my bed," she hissed.

A thousand scenarios flew through Jordan's head, none of which made any sense at all.

Nicky pulled aside the covers. "Get in," she ordered in a fierce, but almost soundless whisper.

Jordan did as she was told, finally understanding how her nephews had felt, forced to share the narrow bed in the farmhouse loft when they came to visit. This was a larger bed. It was big enough for two adults. If one of them didn't happen to be pregnant.

"What is going on?" she hissed back at her cousin.

"Visitors," Nicky said. "There was some kind of trouble in Hogsblood. I guess they got lost coming over the mountains, and they bumbled into the Fox and Hound sometime after midnight."

"From where?" Jordan's mind had been working fine when she woke up, but it seemed to have gone downhill from there.

"You know, that place where you met that general. Catlick or Horsefeathers or whatever. You were the one who went there, for heaven's sake."

"Oxtail?" Why would Colonel Treadwell have come to Battlement Park? Or maybe it was March and Maggie Jackson. But Maggie had been pregnant. Trouble?

"Tony sent them up here with me. They didn't have any money with them, and I think Tony was afraid they'd sleep in the woods if he tried to offer them a room free, and with all these mad bandits running around like . . . well . . . mad bandits, he—"

"Nicky." Jordan wondered which of them was losing her mind.

"The boy's downstairs on the settee, and the girl's asleep in your bed."

Jordan tried not to whimper. "Who *are* they, Nicky?"

"Zechariah's—I mean, Elijah's—son and a young lady— and I use the term loosely," she added with a bit of asperity, "who's some kind of friend of the family, looking after the boy."

"Oh." She tried to grasp that and failed. It didn't matter, she had been wrong about not being able to fall asleep. All the strain had worn her mind out, and she was dozing off already. She could worry about Elijah's son and the young lady in the morning. At least she'd woken up before they had.

A very unladylike curse escaped her lips. They had come into the cabin sometime after midnight. When she and Elijah had been asleep. Together. In his room.

"Don't worry," Nicky whispered, more gently now. "They think you've been asleep here the whole night. I didn't let the girl have a light up here. I said I didn't want to wake you."

"Didn't it occur to you I might have been eaten by bears?" Jordan hissed, thinking even as she said it that that might have been an improvement over her current situation. "Or kidnapped by bandits?"

Nicky snorted daintily. "Oh, for heaven's sake, Jo-jo. I saw the way you and Elijah were looking at each other last night."

"Nicky!" Jordan's face burned, but she couldn't stop. "How could you even think—"

"Would you rather have had me rouse a search party?" Nicky asked dryly. She waited. "I didn't think so. Now let me get some sleep."

Things could not get worse. Jordan stopped herself short.

Oh, sure they could, even if she couldn't see how at the moment.

She had slept with a man who wasn't her husband, who planned to leave her as soon as he could. She had acted like a fool and a hussy, and her cousin wasn't even shocked. *Why not?*

She could have—could still—be exposed as a loose woman, lose the respect and protection of polite society, be ostracized from her friends, cause a scandal in her family, disgrace Aunt Rue and Uncle Hal . . .

Worse than that, worse than all of it, her actions could have shamed Frank's memory. That his widow could act so. People would think she hadn't loved him, that she'd made a fool of him, and she couldn't bear that.

What if Frank came back and found out what she'd done?

But he wouldn't. The thought sank heavily through her mind. It hurt. It hurt in a sad, aching way that told her that her heart had finally accepted that Frank really was not coming back.

Tears welled in her eyes. Tears of grief and love. And grace. Whatever the world might think, she had not betrayed Frank. Her heart would never have let her. She could never have slept with a man she did not love, and she could never have loved another man while Frank was alive.

Which meant . . .

She closed her eyes, and the tears spilled over her cheeks. "Oh, God." It was less than a whisper.

No.

She had found him attractive, dangerous, compelling. His company had kept the ghosts at bay. His friendship had helped her to paint again, and she was grateful for that. None of that was love.

This ache in her heart could not be love. She could not

lose another person she loved. Elijah would leave. She had no doubt about that. He would disappear into the vastness of the West . . .

Her mind caught on that thought.

Elijah would disappear into his gunfighter's life. She would never hear from him again. Never see his alarming smile again. Never hold him again.

But he would be alive. She would know he was out there, self-reliant as the mountains, guided by nothing but the wind. She would never lose him to death as she had her parents, Jack, and Frank.

Maybe that knowledge would be enough.

Elijah woke to full watchfulness, as he always did, but this morning he woke with the knowledge that something was deeply wrong. The room's details were visible in the morning light, but he could tell the sun had not yet risen clear of the mountains.

He listened for the echo of a sound that might have alerted him. Birds sang undisturbed in the trees outside. A faint snore, like the rustle of leaves, came from the end of the bed. Loki didn't sense anything worth waking for.

Of course, Loki had proven able to sleep through floods, gunfire, saloon brawls and having his tail yanked soundly by young Tucker Culbert.

Elijah hushed even his breathing. No sound, or lack of sound, to indicate anything out of the ordinary. No change in the air to indicate a storm.

Still, he would not be able to get back to sleep. He might as well get up and prowl around a little, satisfy himself that all was safe.

That Jordan was safe.

Jordan. For a second he thought the whole night might

have been a dream. But his pillow still held the faint lilac scent of her hair. And a whiff of turpentine.

And he was definitely not wearing his nightshirt.

He suddenly knew what felt wrong about the morning. Jordan's absence from his bed. From his arms.

He had expected to awaken to remorse this morning. To the shame of having hurt someone he cared about. Again. Jordan's grief, her great heart, had made her vulnerable, and he had taken advantage of it. She had not even been able to bear to wake him before escaping upstairs.

He had expected this guilt, tightening around his throat like a noose. He had not expected to remember the warmth of her flesh with every nerve in his body. He had not expected to long for the chance to watch her awake, to rouse her to the dawn with a kiss. He had not expected to want to greet the day with her laughter. He had not expected to want to bury his face in the pillow and breathe her in.

He had not expected this aching emptiness.

He sat up and reached for his pants. Tony's. He tossed them on the chair in disgust and got up to search for his own.

He remembered Tony's teasing him the night before about being in love with his "wife." At the time he had wanted to kill the man. Well, that hadn't changed. But this morning the words gnawed at him.

Love.

He could not think of anything he had ever done right for the people he loved. Few as they were. For a long time, it had seemed the best he could do for them was to stay as far away as possible.

March and Maggie Jackson had changed that. A little. In their home, he had managed to be a friend without causing too much damage. He had even begun to forge a relationship with his son.

He shrugged into his shirt and sat down to pull on his boots.

But a house in the city or even a ranch like the Jacksons' would become a prison as soon as he crossed the threshold. He had to escape, and the sooner he left the better it would be for him.

He grimaced at the self-serving thought. He might as well admit to himself that the sooner he left, the better it would be for Jordan. She would not want him around, reminding her of what had happened between them.

Now that his physical health had returned, he should take care of other business. Lucifer Jones. If Jones really led the band terrorizing Larimer County, it was Elijah's fault. No, not fault. He could not have killed Pauly in cold blood that day in Longmont. Although, if he had known for sure that Jones's men were responsible for Yves Sevier's murder and Marie's rape . . .

He had no doubt Longmont's marshal would have paid him little more heed than he had Jordan.

Not fault. Responsibility.

Lucifer Jones had to be stopped before anyone else got killed. And with due respect for Malachi's tracking skills and Napoleon Cox's brutality, neither of them had the gun-fighting expertise to take on Pauly's six-shooters.

That was his realm.

And so were the mountains where he would be hunting. He had always found a measure of peace in the wilderness. Whatever it was that bound him to Jordan, the mountains would ease it.

Something had to.

He washed his face in the bowl on the nightstand and ran a damp hand through his hair.

Tony had seemed willing to sell Elijah the sorrel gelding

he'd been riding. The horse was a decent beast. He couldn't approach Achilles for stamina or speed, but he was sound and steady and surefooted. And he didn't bite. Elijah could make do with him until Maggie decided Rover was fit to leave the ranch.

He needed to leave. The peace of the Rockies would be a relief. And it would relieve a lot of other people if he left, too. Jordan. Mal. It would make Tony Wayne's life easier not to have a gunfighter around. The Englishman could charm Jordan to his heart's content, and it would ease his problems with the marshal.

Elijah stopped with his fingers on the bedroom door handle.

Marshal Cox. His hackles rose. It wasn't the marshal's antagonism toward Elijah that bothered him. He'd met too many strangers who wanted to kill him to take it personally.

It was more primitive than that. An instinct. It was almost as though the man smelled wrong.

If the marshal came looking for him, he could take care of himself. He almost relished the idea of a game of cat and mouse with the man. The bully deserved a sound thrashing.

What he didn't like was the idea of the marshal being in the same county as Jordan Braddock. Cox was just the sort of man who would take his anger out on a woman. The very thought turned Elijah cold.

If he couldn't be close to protect them, Jordan and Nicky couldn't stay here in the cabin alone. He'd have to make sure they moved down to the main lodge when he left. And he would have Mal keep an eye on them. His brother might be a difficult human being, but he would never allow harm to come to an innocent.

Elijah shook his head. He had become entangled in so many lives in such a short time. A warning to keep moving.

He stepped out into the main room of the cabin just as someone rapped sharply on the front door. He crossed the room quickly, hoping the noise wouldn't wake the women.

The intruder knocked again, more forcefully. Elijah yanked the door open, glaring into the face of his younger brother. This was just the sort of thing he would not miss when he left.

"I know you know what time it is," he said calmly. "I know you know Mrs. Braddock and Mrs. Braddock stayed out late at Major Wayne's dinner party. I know I told you I would not tolerate any more rudeness to either of them. What I don't know is what the hell you're doing here trying to knock down the door at this hour."

His brother gave him that look of disgusted exasperation only Malachi could achieve. "I'm not here to socialize. I'm going hunting for outlaws, and I want to get an early start."

"I'm not holding you back. I said I wouldn't go with you." He intended to do his hunting alone.

"I didn't ask you to."

He wouldn't. Mal would face down a whole gang of outlaws alone rather than ask his big brother for help. It hadn't been that way when they had been growing up. Elijah wondered how they had drifted so far apart.

"Then what do you want from me?" he asked, knowing he should feel relieved. One less obstacle to his leaving.

"I'm not here to see you," Malachi said. "I'm here to see your son."

"My son?" Elijah asked, still calm, but his voice soft with warning.

"Yes." Malachi waited a moment. "May I come in or should I just chat with him from the doorway?"

Elijah raised an eyebrow. "It will be a long shout. Wolf is in Oxtail."

241

Malachi's eyebrow mirrored his perfectly. "That's a stretch, even for you, 'Lije. He's standing right behind you."

Unable to help himself, Elijah turned.

There, mere feet behind him, stood a boy in rumpled clothes and bare feet, his ruddy brown hair mussed with sleep, looking even younger than his thirteen years. His hazel eyes could have been lighter versions of Elijah's.

The boy had one hand on Loki's head, the wolf's tongue lolling in uncontrolled glee at this intruder he had completely failed to warn Elijah about.

The boy scuffed one foot self-consciously. "Hello, Father."

Elijah began to suspect he would not be leaving Battlement Park that morning after all.

# Chapter 16

"I brought some bread and cheese," Malachi said, closing the door behind him. "To make up for waking you." He failed to sound repentant. "Hello, Wolf."

Wolf's eyes traveled between the two men. "Hello, sir. Are you my father's brother?"

"That's right, son." Malachi set the parcel of food down on the end table by the settee and reached out his hand. Wolf shook it. "I'm your Uncle Malachi."

Malachi glanced at Elijah. "Your father's mentioned me?"

"Yes, sir." Wolf nodded. "He's told me stories about when you were growing up. He said you could throw a baseball harder than any boy in Charleston."

"Is that right?" Malachi flexed his right hand. "Did he also tell you I had the worst aim?"

Wolf scuffed his foot again. "Um, yes, sir."

Malachi snorted, turning to Elijah again. "Remember that time the Wilmer boys' gang was chasing you and I climbed up in that peach tree in old Mrs. Baxter's yard? I hauled off with one of those green peaches. I fully intended to kill Clayton Wilmer."

"I remember," Elijah said. "I still have the lump on the back of my head."

"It rescued you from the Wilmer brothers, though. They ran like hell when Mrs. Baxter came charging out her door with that broom."

For a second the two brothers grinned at each other over the memory.

"He also told me you were with the Seventh Cavalry," Wolf continued, "under Lieutenant Colonel Custer. When we heard about . . . we were afraid you'd been killed."

Malachi's laugher died. Elijah saw a deadness in his brother's eyes he'd never seen before.

"Father wired me." Elijah spoke so Mal wouldn't have to. "That you'd been with Reno's men, not Custer's, that you hadn't died."

"We should have," Malachi said, his voice as dead as his eyes.

"I'm glad you didn't." Elijah didn't know which one of them his words surprised more, but a spark glinted in Mal's skeptical glare. "You're my only brother. But I still don't forgive you for ruining my morning."

Malachi's green eyes definitely flashed. "Hell, I haven't even started yet, 'Lije. Now can I speak to my nephew a minute?"

Elijah returned reluctantly to the present situation. "Not until I talk to him first." He studied his son. "Wolf, what are you doing here?"

"I came to see you," the boy said, only slightly abashed at his father's tone. "We got your telegram that said you'd had your malaria again. We thought you'd come as soon as you were well, but then we didn't hear anything else. We wanted to tell you the news, anyway, so Harry and I rode over to make sure you were all right."

"*Harriet?*" The plague of locusts would be next. "The two of you rode here from Oxtail? Alone?"

"We came through the mountains," Wolf said, his eyes brightening. "March said there was a way through Carpenter's Pass. I brought the compass you gave me for Christmas. We only got a little lost, when we were tracking . . ."

The boy trailed off, seeing that Elijah was not fully listening to his story.

"You came through the mountains," Elijah repeated. "Alone."

He hadn't known he could feel such anger and such fear at the same time. "You and Harriet just thought you'd ride over to check up on me."

Wolf nodded.

"What the hell were you thinking of?" His voice crackled. "Irresponsible." He could barely get the words out. "Thoughtless. Childish."

He took a deep breath. "Have you even thought about what you've done, son?"

Wolf's back straightened, his full height barely up to Elijah's shoulder. "I didn't do anything wrong."

"You don't think so?" Elijah had his voice under control now, but not his anger. "You don't think running off without telling anyone where you're going is wrong?"

It did not help his mood to realize where his son might have picked up that particular behavior.

"Have you even thought about what Henna and Jed are going through?"

The Culberts had cared for Wolf since his mother had died in childbirth, and they loved him as much as any of their own four children. Henna would fight off a mountain lion with her bare hands for Wolf.

And he'd pity the lion, Elijah thought. He suspected he'd suffer an even worse fate when he brought the truants home.

"Henna must be going out of her mind with worry."

"Ma said I could go."

Elijah's fists clenched as much in surprise as anger. "Don't say another word. If you lie to me again, Wolf, I don't know—"

"She said I was thirteen, and I had to learn to make my own decisions, like a man." The boy trembled with emotion, but he raised his chin with dignity. "She said I knew almost as much about traveling in the mountains as Pa, and that they could do without me on the farm for a week if I felt I needed to go."

A flash of anxiety crossed the boy's face. "I told her I'd work double hard when I got back, to make up for it."

His eyes met his father's, and Elijah felt the familiar confusion of love and helplessness that sometimes swept over him when he looked at his son. At barely thirteen, Wolf still looked like a boy, thin and wiry. Too young to hold all the seriousness packed into his soul.

Elijah couldn't imagine Henna letting Wolf ride out into the mountains alone, much less letting him ride out to find his father, more dangerous to the boy than the wilderness in her eyes, despite the truce they had built up between them. Yet she knew his son better than he did and had obviously seen what he was only now glimpsing.

Wolf wouldn't be a boy much longer.

Awkwardly, he put a hand on Wolf's shoulder, feeling the sharpness of the boy's bones, the tension in the young body.

"I'm sorry, Wolf. I should not have lost my temper before hearing all the facts."

"I'm not a liar," the boy said with self-conscious dignity.

"I know, son." He did know, should have known. "And I know you would never do anything to hurt Henna."

Wolf nodded, and Elijah squeezed the boy's shoulder before releasing it. He was going to have to start treating his son more like a man. It wasn't going to be easy. He felt a surge of empathy for Henna Culbert.

On the other hand, Henna had already been through this with her oldest son Jake. This was his first time.

"You're not sick anymore," Wolf said then, trying to sound matter-of-fact, and Elijah remembered why the boy had come.

"I am recovered," he agreed. "I should have sent another telegram. I was the one who acted irresponsibly."

"That's all right," Wolf said gallantly. But, of course, it wasn't. He'd broken his promise to be there for the boy's birthday, and then he hadn't even bothered to send another telegram to assuage Wolf's concern.

"A father-son discussion with no threats of eternal damnation. I'm impressed." Malachi had taken a seat on one of the plain wooden chairs by the fireplace and had been so quiet Elijah had forgotten him. "May I talk with Wolf now? No, of course not."

Malachi rose, his attention fixed somewhere behind Elijah's head. "Good morning, ma'am. Please join us."

Elijah knew it would be Jordan on the stairs, even before he turned. Malachi brushed past him to take her hand and guide her into the circle.

"I hope you will accept my apologies for last night, Mrs. Braddock," Malachi said. "My brother's provocation was no excuse."

"No apologies are necessary, Mr. Kelly," Jordan assured Malachi. "Good morning, Mr. Kelly."

He had expected recrimination, regret. He didn't know what he expected. But it wasn't the glint of wry humor in her eyes at the absurdity of their predicament.

If he lived a thousand years, he would still be able to feel the warmth of her heart, the strength of her courage in that look. He felt it in his soul, a breaking or a healing, he couldn't have said which.

"Good morning, Mrs. Braddock." If his heart was not under control, his voice was. "May I introduce my son, Wolf?

Wolf, this is Mrs. Braddock."

"Hello, Wolf. I'm so glad to meet you." And it showed in her eyes, in the way she offered her hand, no hint of reluctance to acknowledge a gunfighter's bastard. If he hadn't already, he would have loved her then.

*Love?*

"You're the artist, ma'am?" Wolf was asking, responding with earnestness to Jordan's warmth.

"More or less."

"The other Mrs. Braddock, the blond one?"

"Yes?"

"She said you took care of Father while he had his malaria."

Jordan flushed. "It was while we were traveling. I did what I could."

Wolf nodded. "I want to thank you for that, ma'am."

"Mal," Elijah broke in, rescuing Jordan from his son's seriousness, "did you say you wanted to talk to Wolf? You were in a hurry."

"I still am," Malachi agreed acerbically. "Why don't you take a seat, son. Major Wayne told me you had valuable information about our outlaws."

"I hope so, sir," Wolf said, trying not to sound too eager.

"Why don't you tell me what you know."

Wolf pushed aside the blanket on the settee and sat down, Loki settling happily at his feet. Malachi and Jordan took chairs across from him while Elijah moved to add a log to the fire.

"Go ahead Wolf," Malachi urged.

"Well, first off, sir, outlaws robbed the Grand Hotel in Oxtail."

"What?" Elijah whirled, the poker in his hand. "When? What happened?"

"Two days ago," Wolf said. "Thursday. They shot Colonel Treadwell and broke into the safe."

Elijah's blood ran cold. It couldn't happen in Oxtail. He realized he'd actually believed that. His family was there, the Jacksons, the Culberts, Wolf. Had he thought they were safe just because he couldn't bear anything happening to them?

"No, not Colonel Treadwell." Jordan's voice shook.

"He'll be all right, ma'am, so Doc Markham says," Wolf assured her. "They shot him in the leg and broke it. Doc Markham says he'll probably have to use a cane. But they killed two deputies who tried to stop them."

Malachi leaned forward. "Do you know if the sheriff thinks these are the same men who robbed the bank in Longmont?"

Wolf nodded. "Colonel Treadwell said the leader was a sniveling, snot-nosed pit viper, which I guess was close enough to what Longmont's marshal said they were looking for."

"Pauly," Elijah said grimly, seeing the same recognition in Jordan's eyes.

"That fellow Lucifer Jones you told Tony about?" Malachi asked.

Elijah nodded. His brother had been in Battlement Park less than twelve hours, but he'd certainly been thorough gathering his information.

"Anything else, Wolf?" Malachi asked.

"Yes, sir. We saw their tracks." He glanced at Elijah. "At least, we saw tracks, and we think it was the outlaws. After Harry caught up with me, she said she knew a shortcut to Carpenter's Pass—"

"Harriet caught up with you?" Elijah interrupted. All sorts of things were falling into place, and he didn't like any of the patterns they made. "She didn't leave with you? She followed you."

Wolf's eyes shifted. "Yes, sir. She said she was worried about you, too."

"She didn't tell March and Maggie she was going with you."

Wolf scuffed both feet on the braided rug in front of the settee. "I don't know, sir."

That was probably the strict truth, though he could undoubtedly have guessed the answer. And so could Elijah. Harriet had a taste for adventure, and if she thought she couldn't get permission for something, she simply didn't ask.

Elijah almost hoped his headache was the malaria returning. Maybe it would finally kill him.

"Go ahead, son."

"Yes, sir. We were following this stream up a ravine, and it was real slow going for the horses—it was hard to get them around the rocks in some places. And we came to this place where the stream flattened out, and I saw horse tracks in the mud by the bank."

His eyes gleamed with remembered excitement. "There were six of them. Well, at least five, for sure. And one of the horses had thrown a shoe."

"What makes you think the horsemen were our outlaws?" Malachi asked.

"Harry thought they might be, because it was the right number of men," Wolf explained. "So we looked at the tracks real closely, so we could try to follow them, and that's when I found this in the stream."

He dug into the pocket of his blue jeans and held out his hand. On his palm sat a thick gold band with a signet set into it.

Elijah stopped himself from reaching for the ring. He let

Malachi rise to take it and examine it first.

"I thought I could take it to Colonel Treadwell and see if it came from the hotel safe," Wolf said.

"I think maybe we should put it in the hotel safe here, son," Malachi said. He handed the ring to Elijah, who showed it to Jordan. He didn't mean for his fingers to touch her palm as he sat the ring there. Yet that was not so dangerous as meeting those eyes, midnight blue with the storm behind them.

His brother's voice brought him back. "Maybe Mrs. Braddock could do a rendering of the ring that we could send to the authorities in Oxtail."

"I'd be happy to do that, Mr. Kelly." Jordan's voice was clear as she handed the ring back to Malachi. "It's a simple design."

Malachi looked back at Wolf. "You said you wanted to see if you could follow the tracks."

The boy nodded. "We did follow them for a while. The ground got really rocky after a while, though, and I think they split up. We decided we better push on to Battlement Park, but we'd gotten off our trail, and we got a little lost. That's why we got here so late."

They'd taken an untried shortcut. They'd tried to track armed killers through the wilderness. They'd gotten lost and then compounded the error by traveling after dark. Their horses could have broken a leg. They could have fallen down a ravine.

"Good work, son," Malachi said.

Elijah looked at Wolf, the boy glowing with pride, and swallowed his lecture. How did parents survive their children's growing up?

"Do you think you could take me to the place where you lost the tracks?" Malachi asked. "Don't say yes if you're not sure. We don't want to waste time."

"I can," Wolf said confidently. He looked at Elijah. "I memorized the landmarks just like you taught me, Father."

Unable to bear Wolf's grown up dignity a moment longer, Elijah moved over to ruffle his hair. "Did you, now?"

Wolf dodged his father's hand, but his grin was pleased. "Yes, sir."

Malachi nodded. "All right, Scout. Why don't you let me buy you a quick breakfast, and we'll head on out."

Elijah took half a moment to wonder at the man being so thoughtful and astute with his son. What had happened to his rude, obnoxious, insufferable brother? There was one guaranteed way to bring him back.

"I'm going with you."

Malachi's face closed up with an almost audible snap. "No, you're not."

"I am."

"This is my hunt."

Elijah looked his brother in the eye. "I'm the one who walked away from Lucifer Jones in Longmont. I'm the one with friends in Oxtail. If you take me with you, Mal, I won't get in your way. That's a promise."

"And a threat," Malachi noted dryly. "If I don't take you with me, you'll be a pain in the ass."

Jordan's cough didn't quite cover her laughter.

"You are gaining the services of a highly respected gunslinger, suh," Elijah noted with what dignity he could muster. Anything to keep that humor glowing in Jordan's eyes. He didn't know how she could smile at him that way this morning. He didn't deserve it. But it filled his dry soul like fresh spring water.

"All right," Malachi consented grudgingly as he rose from his chair. "But let's get going. I don't want that lunatic marshal catching wind of this and interfering."

"You can't just go and leave me behind."

The figure standing at the bottom of the stairs might have passed for Wolf's older brother, in the same blue jeans and button-down shirt, similar dark hair peeping out from under a broad-brimmed hat, darker eyes flashing with similar youthful pride. She might have, except for the tight curves the masculine clothing didn't hide.

In the midst of his irritation at the slender troublemaker, Elijah suddenly realized that she and Wolf had just made it impossible for him to leave Battlement Park and the web of entanglements holding him there. Oddly enough, instead of the noose tightening around his neck, he felt as if the governor had just announced a reprieve.

A condemned man should know better than to feel this . . . what? Hope? He looked at Jordan. No. He could not hope. But he could live fully each moment he had left.

"So, are we ready to go?" the girl in jeans demanded.

Malachi looked at Elijah. Elijah remembered he had said he would keep out of his brother's way. He almost grinned.

"Miss Harriet, this is my brother, Malachi Kelly. Mal, meet Miss Harriet Jackson. She's all yours. Come on, Wolf, Mrs. Braddock, let's go get our breakfast."

# Chapter 17

*Dear Will,*
*    As much as I love you, you are a stubborn jackass.*

Jordan gritted her teeth and crumpled the paper. True as the words were, they were not going to convince her cousin's husband to come collect his wife. She needed something that would overcome his pride, something that would bring him running from Denver so fast Nicky would have to see how much he loved her.

She tapped the end of the pen against her teeth a moment. She needed something to make the two idiots realize how damn lucky they were to have each other. She had to make them understand how precious life was, how precious the time they had. If only she had this time they were wasting!

Something hard lodged in her throat, but she fought it down. She would not waste her own time by crying. She had already had three more days than she had expected. Elijah had not left yet. Between Wolf's arrival and the hunt for Pauly the Bandit King and his gang of outlaws . . .

She had it!

*Dear Will,*
*    I hope all is well in Denver. We are managing quite well,*
*all things considered. It is so interesting sharing living quarters*
*with a gunfighter and his son. Wolf is a quiet, thoughtful boy,*
*and he can sing like an angel. Nicky is trying to teach him to*

*dance when Elijah will play for us in the evening. Elijah's brother Malachi is quite a good dancer, but Nicky is on a crusade to teach him not to swear so much.*

*Nicky is also making a project of our friend Miss Harriet Jackson. In the evening Harry is the perfect lady in her sweet green muslin (though she refuses to giggle at Major Wayne's charming stories as Nicky does), but during the day she dons blue jeans and rides with the men, tracking bandits. Malachi tried to stop her, but she challenged him to a shooting contest with her rifle and won, so he had to give in. Nicky moans in despair over her, but is thinking of trying a pair of blue jeans herself.*

*I'm not too worried about the bandits, though they have killed several people now. Nicky and I are careful to lock the door when the men are all gone during the day. Elijah has left us his pistols, and Malachi advises us to save the last bullets for ourselves if we cannot hold the outlaws off, so you do not need to worry about us being kidnapped or raped.*

*I have quite a few paintings to finish up, which keeps me busy, but Nicky is not so lucky. She has run out of yarn for knitting baby clothes, so she threatens to take up target practice with the pistols. It might be a good idea, just in case.*

*We miss you, dear Will, but know you are terribly busy. Nicky thinks I don't know she cries herself to sleep at night wishing you were here, but she tells everyone how proud she is of you, getting ahead so fast in a city like Denver.*

*Please give my regards to Mr. and Mrs. Hedgepeth.*

*All my love,*
*Jordan*

Jordan grinned wickedly as she blotted and folded the letter. If that didn't lure Will in like a fat trout, she didn't know what would.

Perhaps she had failed to mention that Tony had hired a dozen ranch hands to help protect his hotel guests while he was out with Malachi's posse. Perhaps Malachi's advice about saving a bullet for yourself had been a story from his cavalry days and not advice for her and Nicky. But the sentiment of the letter was true.

Elijah had shown her how to load and fire his Colts, just in case. Nicky was bored and did cry herself to sleep, though the cabin rang with music and laughter in the evenings, something Jordan would never have expected.

Nicky hadn't exactly said she wanted a pair of blue jeans, but she and Jordan had dug out Jordan's borrowed pair of March's jeans and tried them on in secret. When she was able to ride again, Jordan might even give them a try. Dying from embarrassment over her clothing no longer carried the threat it once had.

And the men treated Harry like a lady, despite her unconventional attire. Not that Harry didn't know how to play the part. She could flirt almost as well as Nicky. She never giggled, but she had a charming sly smile. She could hold her own against Malachi's bluntness, cut Tony's wit in two, and she hung with fascination on Elijah's every word.

Jordan had not had a moment alone with Elijah in the past three days. Even if she'd dared to risk it, she couldn't have gotten past Harry, who followed him around more faithfully than Loki.

"Jo-jo!"

Jordan started guiltily, remembering the letter in her hand. She stuffed it in her dress pocket and turned to see Nicky in the cabin doorway. Her cousin had to make the trip to the outhouse ever more frequently, and her back had begun to ache if she stood too long.

She needed to be in Denver.

"They're coming," Nicky said, shutting the door behind her. "Thank goodness. I was about ready to hunt down Mrs. Jones, just for her charming conversation, for heaven's sake."

Jordan heard the hoofbeats on the path outside, and her pulse jumped. Every day she put the thought of guns and outlaws and trackless wilderness out of her mind. She could get so focused on her painting that she forgot who she was, much less where.

But when the sun lowered in the sky and the outlaw hunters came home, fear burst full bloom in her heart. If anything had happened to . . . to *any* of them . . .

The door popped open and Wolf and Loki jostled each other into the cabin, boy and wolf shedding leaves and dirt in their wake. Jordan couldn't bear to correct them, since Wolf held up his muddy boots to show her he'd remembered to take them off.

"Any luck?" she asked, knowing if there had been any real news, good or bad, he'd already be telling her.

"No, ma'am," he said, padding in his stocking feet to the bedroom he now shared with his father. "The trail's too old to do us any good now. Uncle Mal's hoping we'll find something fresh that will lead us to their hideout. We saw Marshal Cox out there today, but he wasn't having any better luck."

Wolf's attitude said he wasn't surprised. Jordan knew he considered his father and Uncle Mal the best trackers in Colorado. So did Tony Wayne, which meant it probably wasn't far from the truth.

"I don't see why you keep going out," Nicky said, taking a seat on the settee. "Those outlaws are probably long gone by now."

Wolf shook his head. "Uncle Mal thinks they're just lying low. He thinks if we stop looking, they'll plan another robbery, and somebody else might get killed."

Jordan remembered Pauly's ice-green eyes, and a chill settled in her bones. For once she and Malachi were in agreement.

"Are you going down to the stable to help Ben with the horses?" she asked, changing the subject.

"Yes, ma'am. I'll take my clean clothes with me and change for supper down there." Wolf disappeared into the bedroom.

Jordan knew Ben wasn't happy that the younger boy got to ride out with the trackers while Ben had to stay back at the Fox and Hound and work. Still, Wolf had smoothed things over between them with his willingness to help Ben with his chores in the evenings.

Jordan realized that was Wolf's way. She would not have blamed him if he had resented her for being here with his father while Elijah missed Wolf's birthday. She had worried that he might see her as a threat or an intruder. She certainly received that impression from Harriet Jackson.

But Wolf had treated her just like everyone else he met. He waited for an adult to reach out to him, but once assured of a friendly reception, he was quick to respond and to offer help for any project.

He was much easier to be around than his father.

The door opened again, letting in Elijah and Harry, as windblown and redolent of horse as Wolf had been.

"There you are," Nicky said lazily, as if she hadn't been waiting on the edge of her seat for their return. "Doesn't it seem like they get back later every evening, Jo-jo? We could starve to death."

Elijah eyed Nicky's comfortably rounded figure. "I can see the danger."

Harry tossed her hat onto the hatrack, and her long, dark hair fell down around her shoulders.

"Don't give in, 'Lije," she said, making a face at Nicky. "You should see Maggie now. It only gets worse."

As Elijah laughed, Jordan felt a twinge of some dark emotion she refused to identify.

"You smell like a horse," Nicky told Harry, holding her

nose. "Go change. Maybe you can persuade Mrs. Jones to fill you a bath after dinner."

Harry snorted. "And maybe the sky will fall. I don't think that woman approves of me."

"I don't think Mrs. Jones likes anyone," Nicky said. "Tell Tony you want a bath. He'll make sure you get it."

"Tony? Oh, jolly good." Harry rolled her eyes.

"Just watch out for tea leaves," Jordan added. "All that hot water might be too much of a temptation."

Harry choked on a laugh, shooting a surprised glance at Jordan. "I'll go change. I'll be just a minute."

She disappeared up the stairs.

"Excuse me, ladies." Elijah ducked into his bedroom. Jordan heard Wolf's voice, a counterpoint to Elijah's lower rumble. Then Wolf dashed out, his clean shirt tucked under his arm.

"See you later, Wolf," Jordan called.

"You better hurry, or I'll eat your gingerbread," Nicky warned. The chef made gingerbread every night, and Nicky and Wolf were the only Fox and Hound guests who weren't thoroughly sick of it.

"Don't worry, I'll save you a piece." Wolf grinned and bolted out the door.

Jordan left her desk and moved to sit next to Nicky on the settee.

"He's still here," Nicky said, checking the cuffs on her sleeves.

"Hm?"

"Elijah," Nicky said. "He's still here. Waiting. You need to tell him how you feel."

"What? What do you—" Jordan hadn't said anything about what had happened with Elijah to Nicky, nor had her cousin mentioned it before. She had managed to forget that

259

Nicky knew. "You don't understand."

Nicky raised one eyebrow. "You thought he'd leave, didn't you? Don't bother denying it. You were sure he'd go. But he hasn't. What are you going to do about it?"

Jordan glanced around to make sure they were still alone. She lowered her voice. "He had to stay. His son's here. He's been hunting the outlaws."

"Pshaw." Nicky tossed her curls. "He could leave that wild goose chase to Malachi and Tony. And he could take Wolf right back home. He's not leaving because he's not sure he wants to. You have to convince him he doesn't."

"I don't want him to stay." Jordan's voice broke.

"Oh, very convincing."

Jordan glared. "It isn't anything you need to worry about."

"Busybodies must run in the family," Nicky said dryly. "Tell me that wasn't a letter to Will you were hiding in your pocket just now, and I'll leave you alone forever."

Jordan gave a strangled laugh. "Brat."

"Coward."

"Harpy."

"Lily-livered church mouse."

"Snot-nosed shrew."

Jordan and Nicky looked at each other, eyes shining as much from emotion as from suppressed laughter. Nicky reached over to give Jordan's hand a quick squeeze.

"Do it, Jo."

Jordan just shook her head.

"Are we ready to go?" Harry demanded, one delicate gloved hand resting on the newel post at the bottom of the stairs. Each evening Jordan was amazed at her transformation from jean-clad tomboy to perfect lady. She'd only had room to bring one dress, but it looked as fresh that evening as when she'd arrived. Not so much as a sun freckle on her nose marred the effect. "I thought you were hungry, Nicolette."

"It's too late," Nicky said, dragging the back of her hand across her forehead. "Even as we speak, I perish."

"Oh, for heaven's sake," Jordan mimicked.

This time, Harry laughed outright, even meeting Jordan's gaze.

"Here," she said, moving over to the settee. "You grab one arm . . ."

Together she and Jordan hauled Nicky to her feet.

The bedroom door opened. Jordan didn't need to turn her head to know how good Elijah looked in his starched white shirt, his dark hair damp at his temples from washing his face. She looked anyway.

His eyes met hers, holding almost a question. The same silent query she knew her eyes almost asked him. The same look they had shared a dozen times, a hundred times since Saturday morning.

*Are you all right? Do you forgive me?*

Jordan glanced away before her heart could reply. *There's nothing to forgive. I love you.*

"We have an emergency," Harry said. "We have to feed Nicky before she expires."

"Harriet and I will walk on ahead. You slowpokes can catch up," Nicky said, jabbing Jordan's rib with her elbow.

"We're not in *that* much of a hurry," Harry said, her voice sharply gay. "I think you need our protection, 'Lije, after that incident with the mountain sheep today."

Elijah shook his head. "I need a word with Mrs. Braddock. We'll be along directly."

"Don't take too long," Harry tried again. "There may not be much left if you dawdle."

"We'll only finish off the good stuff," Nicky said. "You

two take all the time you need."

By force of will, she dragged Harry toward the door. As they jostled through it, Nicky flashed Jordan a coy grin, but the look Harry threw her was anything but friendly.

"Don't let her get lost, 'Lije" Harry called over her shoulder. "It's quite a wilderness between here and the lodge."

Nicky gave her a little shove, and they were gone.

"The porch?" Elijah suggested. "It's too beautiful out there to be inside."

And being alone together inside was too dangerous.

Reminding herself to breathe, Jordan preceded him out the door. The sun had just begun to touch the snowy peaks with color, the air still felt soft and warm against her skin. If the cabin was too intimate, the porch was too romantic.

Even with the whole of Battlement Park surrounding them and the wide expanse of the sky above, even with Elijah leaning on the porch railing five feet away, he was too close, her feelings too intense for the breeze to whisper away.

Jordan leaned against the railing, too, looking out on the meadow below and the mountain above. She wondered how she would capture the soft hint of lilac in the sky, the blush of rose on the snow.

She wondered how she would paint at all after Elijah had gone. Even now, his presence magnified her awareness of the glory around them. He had the same effect as the twilight, sharpening outlines and deepening colors, making the air sing with radiance.

She snorted at her own mawkishness. She'd manage. She'd managed before. She knew Elijah glanced at her, but she wasn't about to explain.

"I apologize for Harriet," he said finally. "She has no call to be rude to you."

Jordan took a deep breath, wishing she could draw some of

262

the soft, peaceful light into her soul. "She doesn't think you should be wasting time on an eastern greenhorn like me."

"I've known her since she was a wild brat in pigtails," Elijah said. "She's learned how to curl her hair and how to muck a stall without complaining, but she can still act like a child."

"She's almost nineteen." Jordan pointed out. "I was married by her age. I was a widow at twenty. She loves you."

Elijah glanced at her then, eyes distant, thoughtful. "Harriet's brother-in-law Lucas was one of the best friends I ever had. March is another. He and Maggie and Lemuel and Harry are more my family than any relations of my mother and father. I couldn't care about Harriet more or worry about her more if she was my own sister."

"I don't think that's how Harry feels."

"It's how I feel."

Those cool eyes held steady on hers, and a funny tickle ran through Jordan's stomach. He cared very much that she understand this. He might be warning her he couldn't love anyone the way Harry wanted to be loved. Or he might be telling her something else altogether.

She didn't know which thought scared her more.

"You asked me once why I don't wear my guns anymore. I think I should give you the honest answer."

She had to laugh. "That's a change of subject."

"Not really." He leaned more deeply into his elbows, eyes turning back to the mountains. "It was that business in Laramie three years ago."

"The misunderstanding."

He snorted and pushed himself off the railing. "It was damn near murder.

"I'd had two men try to kill me in two months, for no better reason than I was Preacher Kelly and killing me would make their reputations. It should have frightened me. It did.

But it pleased me, too. Because I won. I was the best, and they proved it. 'Only by pride cometh contention.'

"I told myself it wasn't my fault. Those men wanted to shoot me; I was only defending myself. There was nothing I could do about it. But late one Saturday afternoon I was walking to the train station in Laramie, and a voice behind me yelled out, 'Hey, there, Preacher, reach for the sky.' "

His right hand touched his hip, eyes seeing the past. "I wasn't expecting it, wasn't ready, realized I didn't want to die that day. I don't know that I've ever reacted so fast. So fast I didn't even recognize the man who'd called out until he hit the ground.

"It was Silas Gregory, an old friend of Mal's from the Cavalry. He ran a general store there in town. He'd yelled to me as a joke." Elijah smiled, no humor at all in his eyes. "Si's way of saying hello."

Jordan didn't want to hear more, but she knew he needed to tell it. "You killed him?"

"Si didn't die. I hit him in the upper part of his right arm. He still goes around telling everybody who'll listen what dead aim I've got, hitting him in his gun arm." Elijah's laughter crackled mirthlessly in the cooling air. "I've never had the nerve to tell him I was aiming for his heart."

"And you took off your guns so it wouldn't happen again." Jordan paused. "As Pauly said, it might not have deterred the killers. That took a lot of courage."

"Courage?" Elijah's eyes turned flat. "Si Gregory will never have full use of that arm again, but he refused to press charges. He personally went around town pulling down the wanted posters an overzealous deputy put up. He is the one with courage."

Elijah breathed deeply of the sweet air. "I don't want you to have any illusions about me. I crippled Si out of pride. I abandoned Wolf for most of his life out of fear. I don't want to hurt you the same way. I would have left Saturday morning, if Wolf hadn't come."

Jordan glanced away, fighting back the moisture in her eyes as pain shot down her ribs. A long story to make his point, but no sense in tears. She'd prepared herself for it. And there was nothing to say to it.

Orange light blazed on the mountaintop, as if the snow were on fire.

"Wolf's a great kid," she said, not daring to look at Elijah. "When he was so warm to me from the beginning, I thought it was because I'd had so much experience with my nephews and nieces. But now I've gotten to know Wolf better, I don't think it has that much to do with me at all."

She would keep talking until she could stand to think again. "He doesn't offer to help out just to be polite. He's genuinely generous. He has a knack for making other people comfortable. I don't think he even realizes it. It's just natural to him."

"I've noticed that, too." Elijah's voice grew softer. "I wonder if it's because he knows what it's like to be an outsider. The Culberts treat him just like a member of their family. He knows how important that is."

Something Elijah had never known in his own family. Something he'd never been able to give his own son.

Jordan closed the space between them to put a hand on his shoulder. Without turning to face her, he lifted a hand to hold hers there.

"It's all right. You don't owe me anything." Her voice was edged with warmth and sorrow. "I thought you would leave that morning. I always knew you'd have to leave."

He looked at her then. She would hardly have recognized the gunfighter she'd met the autumn before. She could see past his profession to the man he was. She wished she could see all the way to his heart.

"Are you sorry I stayed?" He still had a gunfighter's unfathomable eyes.

"No," she said. *Idiot.* Her heart squeezed. "Yes. It would have been easier."

He brought her hand down to the porch railing, turned his gaze on that.

"I almost thought you—" He stopped. She could see the tension in his shoulders. "I've missed the time we spent together, out on the mountain. This week, with everyone crowded around me . . ."

"I know. It's too much for you."

He squeezed her hand, hard. "Not that. I've been thinking maybe I could stay here a little longer." He turned to her, his eyes more hunted than hunter in the twilight. "I could try."

"No." Jordan jerked her hand free. He looked as though she'd struck him, as though he thought he deserved to be struck, and her tears finally fell. "No, Elijah, please. I couldn't bear it."

With a soft curse, he pulled her close, his strong arms crushing her to him, holding her head against his shoulder. She felt his heart pounding, his breath soft against her hair.

"I'm so sorry," he rasped. "I'm so sorry, Sparrow. I never meant to hurt you."

His hand tangled in her hair, pulling it free from her careful knot. His cheek, rough with a day's beard, scraped against hers. She could hardly breathe, he held her so tightly. She didn't care, as long as he didn't let her go.

With all the fatalism of a drowning victim begging for a drink, she turned her head, her lips brushing along his cheek until they reached his mouth. With a sound almost of desperation, he kissed her, devouring her, claiming her.

Desire bloomed in Jordan's belly, burning along her nerves. Desire and need and fear and grief. And something so tender it made her shake.

He smelled of sweat and soap, pine and gunpowder, and she knew as long as she lived she'd remember that smell, remember the taste of his mouth, remember the way it felt to be held in his arms. He held her as if he would never let her go.

In the charmed, soft lavender light of the evening, suspended between day and night, it felt like eternity could fit in that brief moment.

"Father! Father!" Wolf's voice, squeezed high with anxiety, scattered the magic. "There's been an accident. Come quick."

# Chapter 18

"What's wrong, Wolf?" The gunfighter glinted once more in Elijah's eyes, but his hand held Jordan's tight as she pulled away.

The boy pounded up the porch steps, his sides heaving. "It's Mrs. Braddock. She fell, down near the stables. Ben ran to get Dr. Gottfried, but she was calling for Mrs. Braddock. The other Mrs. Braddock. You, ma'am."

Jordan clenched Elijah's hand so hard she felt him wince. "Oh, God. Is she badly hurt, Wolf? What happened? Is the baby all right?"

She tugged her hand free and ran to the stairs, grabbing Wolf to pull him along with her.

"I don't know what exactly happened," Wolf said, his young face pinched with worry as he followed her down the stairs. "I heard Mrs. Braddock yell and Harry shouting, and when Ben and I ran out, Mrs. Braddock was on the ground crying. Harry sent Ben for the doctor, and I thought I better come get you and Father."

Jordan gathered her skirts and ran for the path, Elijah and Wolf close behind her. Panic bubbled along her nerves. If Nicky had seriously injured herself . . . If something happened to the baby . . .

She should have taken Nicky home to Will immediately after arriving in Battlement Park. She should have insisted on a room for them in the lodge, where Nicky wouldn't have had to negotiate the steep trail to the cabin every day.

She should have been at Nicky's side instead of in Elijah's arms.

If God would just make sure Nicky and the baby were safe, she would carry her cousin home to Will, she would leave Battlement Park without a second thought. She would leave Elijah, her own heart behind if that's what it took.

Elijah grabbed her elbow as she stumbled over a rock. "It won't do her any good if you break your neck on the way," he said, his imperturbable calm restored. Except she had seen it perturbed, and she knew the price he paid for that necessary composure.

"Don't let me fall," was all she said back, pounding down the trail.

As she neared the stables, she saw a flash of yellow, Nicky's dress irrepressibly bright even in the fading light. She burst out of the trees into the yard in front of the stable. A crowd already clustered around the figure on the ground, Tony and Ben and Mrs. Jones and Malachi.

She reached her cousin's side as Dr. Gottfried released Nicky's wrist.

"Jo-jo!" Nicky's blue eyes were huge in her pale face as she looked up at Jordan.

Jordan dropped down beside her, and Nicky grabbed her hand. "What happened, Nick? Are you hurt?" She looked up at Dr. Gottfried. "Is she going to be all right?"

Dr. Gottfried pushed his round glasses up his nose.

"Ja, ja," he said, though his face looked worn and worried. "She will have some colorful bruises, I think. Nicht wahr, Mrs. Braddock?"

"I thought—" Nicky gulped and clenched Jordan's hand. "I thought I felt a cramp . . ."

"You probably pinched a muscle when you fell," Dr. Gottfried said, patting her shoulder. "Or maybe the baby, it kicked. You will lie down. Then we will see. Frau Jones will bring you some warm milk."

Jordan looked up to see resentment and something else flash across Philomena Jones' pallid features. The house-keeper opened her mouth to object, but thought better of whatever she had been about to say. Instead, she grabbed Ben by his shirt and dragged him toward the stable where she shook him and snarled something in his ear.

Jordan felt a strong urge to give Mrs. Jones a good shake of her own, but she turned back to Nicky instead. "Can you walk?"

Nicky bit her lower lip and nodded.

"Balderdash," Tony said. "Excuse me, Mrs. Braddock." He gently edged Jordan out of the way and bent down beside Nicky. "Put your arms around my neck. That's a good girl."

Before Jordan could object that he was going to fall and kill them both, Tony had lifted Nicky up in his arms as though she were still the dainty miss she'd been just seven months ago. The others scattered out of his way, following as he carried her toward the Fox and Hound.

Jordan caught up with the doctor. "Dr. Gottfried?"

He looked at her and took a quick breath, his thin mus-tache twitching. "I think she will be all right, Frau Braddock. I so hope. We will keep close watch on her tonight. But I think she does not need so much excitement until the baby is born, ja?"

"Yes," Jordan agreed.

She glanced behind her. Elijah wasn't far behind, but for once she did not catch his eye. He had his arm around his son's shoulders, bending to listen to something Wolf was say-ing.

Her heart caught at the sight, so different from the scene behind them. As her gaze flickered toward the stable yard, she saw Mrs. Jones pinch Ben's ear until his head bent down.

The woman looked up to see Jordan watching. Her expression didn't change as she stared for a moment, then let Ben go, giving him a slap on the back of the head before following the others.

"She can't treat him like that," Jordan growled. "I don't care if she is his mother."

Wolf's head snapped around to look at her. "Mrs. Jones? She's not Ben's mother."

Jordan frowned at him. "But she . . . are you sure, Wolf? I thought Ben said . . ."

"Ben lives on a ranch about three miles up the park. His ma's run it with his older brothers since his father died a couple years ago. Ben's job here gives them cash when the cattle market's not good."

No, Ben hadn't said anything. She'd just assumed. Jordan's spirits perked up a little. She would have a quiet word with Tony about Philomena Jones' treatment of Ben. That ought to improve life for the boy.

She turned back to follow Nicky, her cousin cradled carefully in Tony Wayne's arms. Families were such fragile treasures. And the soon-to-be newest member of hers needed all the help she could give. She had to get Nicky home immediately.

Besides, what she had tried to tell Elijah earlier was truer now than it ever had been. The longer she was around him, the deeper it would hurt to lose him. Even now, the thought was almost more than she could bear.

If he could not leave, she would have to. As soon as Dr. Gottfried said Nicky could travel.

"I'm staying right here, Jordan Braddock! I won't go back to Denver."

271

Jordan stepped into the cool, quiet hallway with a guilty feeling of relief.

"You can't make me!"

She almost smiled as she shut the door behind her. Nicky's loud pouting was a sure sign her cousin was fully recovered from her fall. Dr. Gottfried had ordered her to stay in bed all the previous day, just to be safe, but he'd pronounced her well enough to travel by tomorrow morning.

The rest was up to Jordan. Whatever Nicky might say, she was going home, and Jordan would have Tony lift her into the Fox and Hound's coach kicking and screaming if she had to.

"Is she still taking your head off?"

Jordan turned to see Harry carrying a tray piled with sweet rolls the chef had made as a treat for Nicky, his best customer.

Jordan shook her head. "She's not too happy."

"Hmph." Harry balanced the tray with one hand while she grabbed a roll with the other. "We're all worried about her and want what's best for her. She doesn't have to be such a brat."

"She's scared," Jordan said. She might not have recognized that fact a few short weeks ago, but her perspective on her cousin had changed. Her perspective on a lot of things had changed.

"Scared that her husband doesn't love her?" Harry took a dainty bite of sweet roll. "That's not worth endangering the baby for."

"The fall scared her," Jordan explained. "I think she's afraid to travel. She's afraid something else might happen."

Harry took another bite, her brown eyes thoughtful. "Why doesn't she just say so?"

Jordan thought of all the unsaid things between just herself and Harry and had to laugh. "We can't all be Malachi and say whatever we think."

Harry grinned, too. "Thank God. All right, I'll take these in to the dragon and see if I can sweeten her up. When are you going to leave?"

*Now. Never.* Jordan shook her head. "The sooner, the better, I think. I'm going to find Tony right now and see if we can arrange to take his coach to Longmont tomorrow."

Harry saluted with the roll. "I'll see what I can do to convince her it will be for the best. If I don't survive, just send whatever's left to my brother."

"Good luck."

Harry nodded, stuffed the last half of the roll into her mouth and opened the door. Jordan beat a hasty escape down the hall.

She suspected that Nicky's well-being was not the only reason for Harry's eagerness for them to depart. Still, she was glad the young woman had taken the day off from outlaw hunting to help her convince Nicky to return to Denver. She was having a hard enough time convincing herself to leave, much less her cousin.

She crossed the large, open entrance room, and walked down the opposite hall to Tony's office at the far end. She knocked on the open door and glanced in. The office was empty, but a cup of tea steamed on the heavy oak desk.

Jordan smiled as she took a seat in front of the desk. It only took a glance to see why Tony spent as little time as possible in his office. The desk took up most of the floor space, and what was left was cramped by the sturdy, dark bookshelves along one wall. The chair she sat in prevented the door from opening all the way. The desk chair backed against the only window, which looked out into the gloomy branches of a spruce tree. Jordan hoped she wouldn't be stuck there long, and she was just visiting.

She wondered if Tony would get terribly upset if she stole

his tea. It would be too cold to drink if he didn't return soon.

"You stupid, lying, foul-mouthed slut!"

Jordan jumped in her chair, heart thudding in surprise.

"I'm stupid? You're the one who let that gunfighter make a fool of you."

Philomena Jones. There was no mistaking that sly, resentful voice, or the gravelly snarl of Marshal Cox.

"You keep smart-mouthing me, I'll knock you halfway to Christmas."

A door slammed open just outside in the hall. The linen closet, Jordan guessed. She wondered if she should step out into the hall, let them know they were being overheard. She had little fondness for Mrs. Jones, but she couldn't stand by if the marshal intended to hit her.

"Try it," Mrs. Jones said, no fear at all in her voice. "See what my son does to you then."

"The whoreson devil's whelp."

Jordan pressed her fingers to her lips, stifling a nervous chuckle at the idea of Marshal Cox being afraid of Ben the stableboy. She should have known that the eager, gentle boy was no son of Philomena Jones. She did give the woman credit, though. She knew how to stand up to Cox.

"I think you better stop talking about my boy that way," Mrs. Jones said, slamming the linen closet door shut once more. "I don't know why he puts up with you as it is. What good are you to him? You're nothing but a witless blowhard."

"I'm keeping that damn posse off his worthless tail, ain't I? Keeping his neck out of the hangman's noose."

Jordan stopped picturing Ben. This conversation was starting to make her skin prickle with apprehension.

"Maybe. Maybe not." Mrs. Jones' voice fairly purred. "What if I told my boy you were helping Deputy Kelly, acting like a jackass on purpose while secretly giving him information?"

"You wouldn't dare, you ugly cow." Jordan heard more fear than certainty in the marshal's voice. "And you know it ain't true. I've got information that snot-nosed brat needs. He needs me."

"Tell me, and maybe I'll keep my mouth shut about you."

"It's not exactly something I can blurt out all over the damned hotel."

"Major Wayne's office. That baron's wife from Bavaria found a mouse in her room. He won't be back for a while."

Without even thinking about it, Jordan dropped off the chair and threw herself behind the desk. Fear oozed down her throat. She didn't know what the two were talking about, but it wasn't good. And they wouldn't like her hearing any of it.

Cox's boots thudded loudly on the office floor. The door slammed behind him. Jordan feared he would hear her breathing echoing in the tiny room.

"So." There was a thud as Mrs. Jones dropped a pile of linens on the top of the desk. "What could you know that's so important? You're not even speaking to Major Wayne, how could you know what the posse's up to?"

"I'm keeping an eye on them." The desk creaked as Cox sat on the edge of it. Jordan tried to squeeze further underneath.

"An eye on him." Mrs. Jones made a sound of disgust. "Staying nice and safe out of sight while he hunts my son and his boys like dogs. And what do you think will happen to you if he catches them? You think you'll be safe then? You think they'll just forget to mention that bigshot Marshal Napoleon Cox rode with them and kept the law off their backs?"

"How can they catch your boy?" Cox asked with bitter sarcasm. "I thought the devil's imp could outsmart any posse, turn invisible if he needed to. I thought he was Lucifer himself. Don't tell me he might actually need my help."

Jordan's heart nearly stopped. Lucifer. That was Pauly's name. Lucifer Jones. Philomena Jones. How could she not have connected the two before?

"He's not a devil," Mrs. Jones was saying, the familiar sound of grievance back in her voice. "Smug, rich sons-of-whores in Longmont gave him that name, Lucifer, because he wouldn't bow down to them. My Polydorus is a good boy. He's just taking what's owed us. My husband struck that silver mine by—"

"Shut your yapping trap," Cox growled. "I've heard it all before. Some rich cattle baron cheated you out of your fortune, blah, blah, blah. Save your breath. Your son's a no-good, murdering renegade, but just as long as he keeps money in my pockets, I don't give a damn.

"Now, unless you want him dangling from a rope, you'll tell him what I got to say."

"And what's that?"

"So, you're interested now?" The desk creaked again as Cox leaned back, obviously feeling things were going more his way.

"Spit it out," Mrs. Jones snapped. "I've got twelve beds to change before I start the laundry. I'm not having my head bit off waiting on a fool like you. I'll tell Polydorus what you got to say."

"When are you meeting him?"

"None a your business."

Jordan remembered Mrs. Jones bringing Ben a hard-ridden horse, the first time she'd met the boy. He'd asked if Mrs. Jones wanted him to take care of the horse as usual. She'd snapped back, put him in his place. No wonder. She didn't want Jordan, or anyone else, knowing she rode out on one of the hotel's horses on a regular basis. Maybe that's what she'd been doing down at the stables when Nicky fell—arranging with Ben to have a horse ready for her to meet her son.

Marshal Cox hawked, but he had no where to spit. "These boys working for Wayne, they may be scoundrels, but they're damn good trackers. They mighta found the rendezvous point if I hadn't messed up the tracks. You better tell that boy to lie low for a while. Try his hand back up by Cheyenne or maybe down to South Park—Fairplay, some of them mining camps."

Tony could send telegrams to those places, warn the local law enforcement to be on the lookout. But it would be better to catch Pauly before he left the area.

Jordan thought of Elijah's panther-like stealth. If he could follow Mrs. Jones to her meeting with her son . . .

Mrs. Jones laughed, a dry, reckless sound. "You think they got him scared? You think those self-satisfied fools are going to scare my boy off? What do you think they'd do if they come back here one evening to find the place burned to the ground? Just what do you think they'd think about that?"

"What?" Cox sounded as shocked as Jordan. "The Fox and Hound? There's six cowboys with rifles protecting the damn place."

"Polydorus and his boys are five. Six if you count you." Mrs. Jones obviously didn't.

"That's insane!" Cox shifted on the desk, agitated. "They can't come here. This is my territory. I'm protecting the place. I can't have a shootout here."

Jordan heard Mrs. Jones lift the linens from the desk. "I'm just saying, 'what if.' That's all."

"Damn it, woman! You tell me what's going on, or I'll—"

Jordan never knew exactly what happened, but she heard

Cox's boots hit the floor and the sound of a sharp slap against someone's face. There was a clatter on the desk, and then Tony's teacup exploded against the wall behind her. Shards of china and drops of lukewarm tea sprayed across her dress.

"Look what you've done, you big fool!" The linens dropped again. "Major Wayne will have a fit if he sees this."

Jordan knew exactly what would happen next, and felt the sick, sinking dread she felt in dreams when she stepped off a steep bank and knew she was going to fall.

"Get me a broom out of the closet," Mrs. Jones ordered, shoving papers out of the way on the desk. Tea dripped on Jordan from the desk's edge.

"Get it yourself," Cox said.

Jordan twisted her head to look at the window. It was latched. There was no way she could get it open and throw herself out before they caught her.

Mrs. Jones muttered something unintelligible, but undoubtedly uncomplimentary. Her shoes brushed along the wood floor, coming around the side of the desk.

"Good glory!" The housekeeper's breath hissed in, then shrilled out, "What are . . . She's . . . Cox!"

Jordan looked up to see that Mrs. Jones' pale face had turned the color of bone china, her mouth opening and closing in dismay. The sight was almost satisfying enough to make Jordan forget her own terror. But not quite.

"What the hell are you going on about, woman . . . Hey!" A big hand grabbed Jordan's hair and hauled her out from her hiding place. Cox spun her around and shoved her back against the desk. Looking into his red face, fury quickly replacing the shock in his eyes, Jordan thought he might break her neck right there in Tony's office.

"She heard everything we said." Philomena Jones

sounded as though she couldn't believe it. "What are we going to do?"

Jordan knew that was a legitimate question, but she didn't really want to know the answer.

"Run," she said, her voice not nearly as steady as she wished it to be. "That's all you can do now. Tony will be back any second. You'd better start now."

At the mention of Tony's name, the murder ebbed a little from the marshal's eyes, though he didn't let her go. Jordan considered screaming, but if no one had heard the yelling and the china crashing, they weren't going to hear her before Cox stopped her mouth. Possibly permanently.

"We've got to get rid of her," Cox said. Jordan could see that the hesitation in his voice came from questions about methods, not morals.

"Not here!" The thought brought Mrs. Jones back to herself. "I'm not cleaning up any more of your messes."

"*My* mess?" Cox turned on Mrs. Jones. "We're in this together, lady. You and me and your precious little boy."

"Tie me up and run," Jordan advised, hoping he couldn't feel her limbs shaking through his hold on her collar. "You don't want them after you for murder. They'd hunt you—"

"Shut up!" Cox shook her, jarring her back against the desk. "You think the thought of murder bothers me? Just keep talking, and you'll find out."

"Fool." Mrs. Jones dropped to the floor to start wiping up the teacup mess with her apron. "You're a great one for talking. Just get her out of here. Miss High-and-Mighty. Miss Gunfighter's Whore."

She looked up at Jordan, eyes burning with malice. "She's always riding off into the mountains, isn't she? Doing her little pictures. Why can't she go for a ride today? Maybe she'll get lost and not come back."

"How the hell do I get her out to the stables without her screaming her head off?" Cox demanded.

"Do I have to do all your thinking for you?" Mrs. Jones got back to her feet, equally disgusted with Cox and his prisoner. "You're the one carrying the guns. Tell her you'll shoot her if she screams. Tell her you'll shoot whoever comes to help her."

She looked Jordan straight in the eye. "He'll do it, too. Your gunfighter friend. Your oh-too-precious cousin. That worthless stableboy. You open your mouth, you'll die and so will your friends. You keep your mouth shut, you'll die, but maybe they won't. You choose."

"She'll scream."

Mrs. Jones, still watching Jordan, shook her head. She smiled. "No, she won't. And if you hurry, maybe nobody will see you leave with her, and I won't have to fix that for you, too."

Obviously skeptical, but without any better ideas, Cox yanked Jordan away from the desk.

"All right. You walk with me. We see anybody, you smile. You forget to smile, I start shooting. I got nothing to lose, right? You understand me?"

Jordan nodded, hardly able to hear his words through the buzzing in her head.

"Give me your arm. Do it!"

She did, and he shoved her toward the door. Her legs wobbled beneath her, but she stayed upright as he yanked the door open and angled her through. The hallway was empty.

Cox looked back over his shoulder. "You tell your boy I'll meet him at the rendezvous tonight. He's going to have to give me something extra to take care of this little problem."

"You push him all you want," Mrs. Jones said, acid on her tongue. "It's your funeral."

With a curse, Cox yanked the door shut and dragged Jordan down the hall.

"Keep up," he muttered, his eyes darting up and down the long corridor. "And smile, you stupid slut."

Jordan heard a murmur of voices. There would be people sitting in the lobby, reading the two-day-old paper from Denver, having a cup of morning coffee or tea. Surely someone would notice something was wrong. Someone would come to her aid.

Maybe Cox wouldn't shoot. He certainly couldn't kill them all.

Cox brought her to an abrupt halt, turning toward a door. Jordan heard the clatter of dishes and pots behind it. The kitchen.

"There's an outside door through here," Cox said, thinking it through. "The hired help won't even wonder at a couple of friends going for a ride. Smile."

He shoved the door open, and they walked through. The two young men washing dishes from breakfast and the young woman rolling out dough for the chef's dill meat pie didn't even turn around.

Cox pulled Jordan past rows of gleaming copper pots and huge iron stoves and around the final counter to the back door that led outside to the icehouse.

He nearly ran her right into Nicky, who stood in the doorway talking with the Norwegian chef.

"Ah, the other Mrs. Braddock!" the chef exclaimed with a wide smile. "Such a pleasure. You like the sweet rolls also?"

The puffiness under her eyes showed Nicky had been crying, but there was nothing soft or weepy in the look she gave Jordan.

"Quit following me around. I'm not going to run away, for heaven's sake." Nicky paused when she noticed Cox. "What are you doing here?"

The marshal's hand tightened on Jordan's arm. His face reddened, but under the easily-lit anger, Jordan suddenly saw fear. And she knew, with certainty, that he would indeed try to shoot his way out of the hotel if he had to. That he wouldn't hesitate to kill the chef, the dishwashers, her, or Nicky.

She knew in her bones that at that moment he was on a knife-edge, the violence in him already wanting to reach for his gun. If she didn't find a way to ease his fear in the next few heartbeats, he would shoot Nicky, killing her and her baby without a second thought.

"Marshal Cox very kindly offered to take me for a ride," she said, hoping Nicky would hear the bite of fear in her voice as righteous irritation. "Since I'm going to have to cut my vacation short to take you back home where you belong, I thought I ought to take the chance to have one last morning in the mountains."

Pink stained Nicky's cheeks, and her eyes sparked. "You want to patronize your petty, selfish baby cousin now? Go ahead. Forget I was the one who helped save your precious gunfighter's hide from the law by being your chaperone. Forget what else I covered up for you."

She gave Jordan a meaningful glare. "I don't care. I didn't ask for you to look out for me, and I'm old enough that I don't have to do what you or anyone else tells me. Go take your ride. Take one every day this summer. Because if you go back to Denver, you're going alone."

Nicky pushed past her and stomped back through the kitchen, her back straight as a ramrod despite her slight waddle. The chef, his cheeks reddening beneath his ginger stubble, muttered his apologies and hurried away to supervise the pies.

Cox paused a second as though not quite believing his luck, then he jabbed Jordan forward through the door and down the steps. Only the icehouse stood between them and the stable.

"I'm impressed," Cox murmured. The fear had ebbed from him. He sounded almost cocky. "I wouldn't have thought you had it in you. Keep this up, and no one has to die."

*Except me.* But Jordan found that some of her own fear had drained away as well. Facing the danger to Nicky had forced her to let go of the debilitating terror that had paralyzed her.

She glanced at Cox. He was bigger, stronger and better armed than she was. But he was also an unimaginative bigot who assumed his very presence kept her terrified and weak. She would have the element of surprise if she fought back.

When she fought back.

Jordan closed her eyes, biting her lip until she tasted blood. She wasn't weak unless she let her fear make her so. She had faced train robbers, bank robbers, a gunfighter, a bounty hunter, and a wolf, not to mention a full complement of her own ghosts, all since last November. And this blowhard of a bully thought he could scare her.

She opened her eyes, seeing the stable ahead. She had to wait for the right time. She'd only get one chance. She'd probably lose, only her wits against Cox's six-shooters. But she'd give him a battle he'd never forget.

# Chapter 19

Elijah didn't notice the rustle in the bushes up ahead until much too late.

"Loki!" he warned, but the wolf had already launched himself from his hiding place, his gray bulk hurtling past them, just inches from the sorrel gelding's nose.

The horse stumbled, snorting with surprise as he righted himself. He hesitated for an instant, then heaved an almost human sigh and started back up the narrow path.

Loki peered up at Elijah, his face wrinkled, his tongue flopping anxiously to one side, his silver eyes searching for answers.

"He's got you figured out," Elijah told the wolf as he rode past. "I know Achilles fell for that trick every time, but once was enough for this fellow."

Loki whined sharply.

"I know. I miss him, too." Elijah leaned forward as the sorrel picked his way up a steep part of the trail.

Such easy words to say. He did miss Achilles. He missed the big bay's alertness and endurance, though he was growing to appreciate the sorrel's steady nerves more every day.

He did not relish describing Achilles' fate to the Jacksons, though he missed them, too—March's good sense and Maggie's sharp tongue. He missed them and Lemuel and the Culberts, even Henna, Wolf's foster mother. He would fiercely miss Wolf after he took him home.

But each step ridden away from them would not feel like a step toward the hangman's noose.

He would miss the glories of Battlement Park when he left, though he would have all the wilderness of the West to console him. Perhaps it was the people he would miss. Ben and Dr. Gottfried and Nicolette. Maybe even his brother and Tony Wayne.

Or maybe not.

Yet, he was used to this, these invisible ties that constricted his heart when he left, but loosened with time and distance, allowing him breathe again. He had survived every loss in his life, and the more he kept to himself, the fewer the losses were, the less pain he caused.

He had never let any of the tentative ties harden, tighten, bind him. Until he'd met Jordan, he had been able to ride away from anyone, anywhere, anytime, without a backward glance.

His horse snorted again as Elijah absently pulled him to a halt.

It wasn't true.

Wolf. How could he not have seen it before? He would never be able to ride away from Wolf for good. His son's hold on his heart was stronger than an iron chain.

And if March or Maggie ever called on him for help, he would be there as fast as he could ride.

Elijah thought of Malachi, obtaining a notarized letter from the marshal in Laramie to rescue his brother from bounty hunters. However many years they had been apart, however obnoxious Malachi could be, Elijah would never hesitate to do the same.

The ties had been there for years, so loose and flexible he had failed to notice them, but as unbreakable as a heart's vow.

Each time he left Wolf, March, Maggie, Henna . . . they all

let him go without trying to hold on, they let him go knowing he might never come back. He knew that. He loved them all the more for it.

Yet he had never realized that something in him was tethered so tightly to them that the only eventuality that could keep him from returning to them was death itself.

He waited. Silence surrounded him, a clear, bell-like silence that went deeper than the crunching of the sorrel catching a quick bite of grass, than the sound of Loki panting nearby, than the song of a bird not far off.

He waited to feel the ropes around his heart. He waited for the fibers to scrape across his nerves, for the nooses to tighten. He waited for the suffocation and desperation of a man losing his freedom forever.

He took a breath, feeling his lungs expand, feeling something tight and dark breaking in his chest. But it wasn't his heart.

Elijah looked around him, at the aspen leaves quivering along the ridge line ahead, at the sky vaulting over the mountaintops above, at the twitch of his horse's ears as it chewed its sharp-smelling snack.

He wasn't sure his eyes had ever seen anything so clearly in his entire life. He wasn't sure his heart could take it.

Loki's soft question turned his head back to the wolf.

"I don't know," he said slowly. "I don't think we're going to find those outlaws in this ravine. There's no way out over the mountain ahead, and they're not stupid enough to box themselves in. We could go back and join Mal and Wolf."

He'd suggested they split up this morning, sending his son off with his brother, giving himself time to think. He should have realized thinking was bound to get him into trouble.

Loki settled onto his elbows.

"You're right. Wolf and Mal are probably not having any

better luck than we are." He took another deep breath. Still no constriction.

The sorrel lifted his head from his patch of grass and slowly, carefully, turned in the narrow track so he was facing back the way he had come.

Elijah looked down at his slack reins and back up at the bright, silent sky.

"Oh, hell." Another quick glance upward. "Sorry." Another breath.

Loki sat up, whined again, his tail spraying pine needles across the path.

"Let's go then."

He nudged the sorrel back down the mountain's shoulder, the horse's hips swaying, Loki trotting ahead, his tail held high. Elijah's stomach twisted awkwardly.

There was no sense in going back to the Fox and Hound, no sense in forcing Jordan to listen to him, when he didn't know what he could possibly say to her. That one night was not enough with her? One week. One month. One year.

One lifetime.

His throat tightened.

He remembered clearly the aching grief in her voice two nights before when she had said she could not bear his staying. Yet she had kissed him, held him, as if she couldn't bear to let him go. What would she say if he promised *never* to leave?

But she had to leave. She had to return Nicky to Denver. And they had to travel soon. The longer they waited, the more dangerous the trip would be for Nicky.

Of course, he could follow her to Denver.

Now he couldn't breathe. Suits and respectability. Streets of comfortable homes. He couldn't live in Denver, not even for Jordan.

He just wasn't sure he could bear to live without her.

The hands clenching his reins were slick with sweat. He couldn't breathe, and it was a good thing he hadn't eaten much for breakfast. He'd never felt this bad walking into a gunfight.

His father's favorite response to any difficult situation—from a fed-up slave-owner trying to burn down his church to a three-foot cottonmouth slithering through the open back door one wet summer morning—had been, "perfect love casteth out fear."

A wicked grin twisted Elijah's lips. "I'm deeply disappointed," he drawled to no one in particular. "Here I thought I was so close to perfection."

"You've got to be kidding."

Elijah closed his eyes, giving silent thanks that he had not stumbled across any murderous outlaws that morning. It would not have turned out well. He opened them again to see Harry Jackson on a rise ahead of him, her chocolate-colored mare's coat streaked with sweat, her own hair tangled in loosened pins down her back.

She rode astride, but hadn't changed out of the morning dress she'd borrowed from Jordan. It was a good thing Jordan was taller than she was or he'd have been able to see more than her ankles.

"Miss Harriet, you are a scandal."

She frowned, but only succeeded in looking more pleased with herself. "Who's a scandal? You're the infamous gunfighter. I could have shot you eight times before you even looked up."

"But since you didn't, and I'm the one holding the rifle, why don't you tell me why you're out here all by yourself when you promised me this morning you would never ever do anything that stupid even if you did get bored babysitting

Nicolette Braddock."

"I'm looking for you." Seeing his expression, she didn't waste time flaunting the fact that she'd found him. "Nicky sent me. She said she'd ride out here herself if I didn't do it for her."

He reminded himself that it had been his decision to turn around. He had no one else to blame that Harry had caught him. "You're telling me that you and Jordan couldn't keep Nicky Braddock off a horse?"

Harry's face changed, and she glanced away. "That's kind of why she wanted me to find you. Jordan's not there, and Nicky's gotten worried about her."

Elijah moved his horse closer to Harry's. "Harriet, why don't you tell me what the hell's going on."

Harry shrugged and made a face. "It's probably just Nicky feeling guilty because she and Jordan had a fight. It's not like she went off riding alone. She had the marshal with her."

The hairs on the back of Elijah's neck prickled.

"Nicky got all worked up about Jordan riding out with him and something about a tea cup, and you know how emotional she—"

"Jordan left the Fox and Hound with Marshal Cox?" Elijah's heart began thudding in a rhythm that felt suspiciously like panic.

"Yes. I guess she told Nicky she wanted to get out into the mountains one more time before she had to take Nicky back to Denver, and Nicky said—"

"And Nicky didn't think something was wrong right away?" Elijah pushed his sorrel past Harry's mare, forcing her to turn and ride with him.

"Because Jordan went riding with a marshal?"

"Cox is a thug." And Jordan had been part of the "Zechariah Kelly" conspiracy that had made Cox look like an idiot.

Cox hated them all, Elijah had no doubt of that, and he suspected the marshal hated Jordan most of all. The man didn't like women to begin with.

Jordan was no fool. She knew what the man thought of her. She would never choose Cox for a riding companion.

Yet she apparently had done just that. Elijah didn't know what could have made her do it, but it couldn't have been anything good.

"How long ago?" he demanded, resisting the urge to spur his horse toward the hotel. He needed information first.

"I don't know." For the first time, Harry sounded worried. "I guess maybe a couple of hours now. It took me nearly an hour to track you down. Do you think there's something wrong? I thought Nicky was overreacting."

"What exactly did Nicky say?"

Harry shrugged again, suddenly looking very young. "Nicky was pretty hysterical, and I wasn't really paying close attention—"

"Damn it, Harriet!" Elijah caught himself. It wasn't Harry's fault. She didn't know Cox. "Just tell me what you do remember."

Harry's forehead furrowed. "I told you about their fight. Nicky went looking for Tony, I guess to tell him he'd have to shoot her to get her on that coach tomorrow, or something equally melodramatic.

"Then I didn't understand the next part very well. Tony wasn't in his office, but the housekeeper was there. You know, the one who looks like she'd be happy to slip poison in your tea . . ."

"Mrs. Jones."

"Yes. Mrs. Jones said something nasty, and Nicky thought she'd scared her, that maybe she'd caught her about to steal something from Tony's desk or something. But when she looked closer, she saw the woman was just cleaning up a broken teacup. She said there were bits of china everywhere."

Elijah struggled to control his voice. "What the hell does that have to do with Jordan?"

Harry shook her head. "Nicky was practically incoherent by that point, she was so upset. It was something about Jordan's dress. I guess she'd seen tea stains on it, but hadn't thought anything of it until she saw the broken cup.

"She asked Mrs. Jones if she'd seen Jordan that morning, and the woman said she couldn't keep track of the guests and do her job, too, so Nicky asked about Marshal Cox, and Mrs. Jones got really upset, said the man was a stupid fool who couldn't do anything right, and pushed Nicky out of the way. Nicky followed her down the hall and saw her run out of the building, maybe toward the stable.

"Nicky went looking for Tony, but Dr. Gottfried said Tony had had a run-in with Baroness Irmina and had run away to join the outlaws—I guess he meant join up with you and Malachi, but he has an odd sense of humor—so Nicky sent me."

None of it made any sense.

There was no pattern, nothing to tell him what had happened, only discrete events that did not fit together, though each carried its own hint of menace.

Something violent had happened in Tony's office. Jordan had left the Fox and Hound with Marshal Cox. She had deliberately hurt Nicky's feelings, something he could not have imagined her doing. Nicky's questions had frightened Mrs. Jones, sending her running out of the lodge, possibly searching for Cox. Tony had disappeared.

No pattern. But the pattern didn't matter. At the moment none of it mattered except that Jordan was gone, and if she was with Cox, she was in danger.

"Harriet, how's your horse?"

Harry patted her mare's neck. "She's warm, but she's all right. We can go all day at the ranch, chasing colts and fillies down."

Elijah glanced around at the deceptively peaceful mountains. He had advised Tony to warn all his guests not to ride alone and not to ride far from the lodge until the outlaws were brought to justice. But he and Mal and the others had been searching all through these mountains for almost a week and had seen nothing more dangerous than a marmot. Harry should be all right.

"Nicky was right," he said. "There's something very wrong. I don't know what it is, but I've got to find Jordan."

Nicky's worry—or his—must have infected Harry, because she didn't make any comments about Eastern ladies who couldn't take care of themselves.

"What I need you to do is find Malachi."

Rebellion flashed across her face. "That could take hours. I can shoot and track as well as anyone. You're just sending me—"

"Don't argue with me." His tone left no alternative. "You can't track like Malachi can. I can't track like he can. I need him. I need you to get him for me. If you don't think you can find him, you need to tell me so I can make other plans."

Yes, he wanted to keep Harry from danger—and out of his way—but every word he'd said had been the hard truth, and it must have shown, because she finally nodded.

"I'll find him. Don't worry. I remember him saying last night where he planned to search today."

Elijah brutally silenced the inner voice that said it probably didn't matter if she found him or not. If Elijah didn't find Jordan in the next couple of hours . . .

"Tell him I'm starting from the stable at the Fox and

Hound," he said already edging his horse away from hers. "I need to know what horses they took. Harry—"

She looked at him, wide-eyed at his use of her nickname.

"—Be careful."

"Don't worry. I've outrun vicious outlaws before."

"Don't get cocky!" This was a bad idea. But it was better than having her follow him. "If you see Cox, don't confront him."

She rolled her eyes.

"I mean it." And there was something else he needed to say, and there was no diplomatic way to say it. "If you see Tony, and he's not with Mal . . . Don't tell him what's going on."

She stared at him. "But . . . *Tony* . . ."

"I can't make a mistake. I don't dare trust anyone but you and Mal. Do you understand?"

She swallowed hard and nodded, and he turned the sorrel's head down the path.

" 'Lije?"

He glanced back. Her eyes were bright.

"You be careful, too. I . . . I'll be praying you find her safe."

He held her gaze for a second longer, then clapped the sorrel with his heels, letting the savvy horse set his own fastest pace down the difficult path.

Prayer. The only one he could manage was please, please please.


Water.

Jordan was long past caring that her dress scrunched up to her knees across the Mexican saddle, leaving her pantaloons hanging out in full view. She had felt only a burst of anger when, once safely out of sight of the Fox and Hound, Cox had given in to a fit of rage and smashed her easel and paint box.

She had only a dim awareness of the ropes digging into her wrists and ankles. She could care less that Cox had connected her ankles with a rope that passed under Smoke's belly. If she slipped off to the side, she would be dragged beneath the horse and trampled. The idea had ceased to bother her much.

The sunburn suffusing her face and searing the back of her neck was merely a minor irritation.

She would be able to endure it all if she could just have one sip of water.

She touched her lips with her tongue and sucked back a whimper. She wouldn't cry. She wouldn't beg. The last time she'd asked Cox for a drink, he'd told her that if she died of thirst, it would save him the trouble of killing her.

Smoke lurched climbing over a ledge of rock, and Jordan grabbed for the saddle horn with numbed fingers. She wasn't dead yet. With the sun hovering just above the western peaks, and the cool promise of evening flowing down from the ice fields, she could hang on until Cox was forced to stop for the night.

He'd have to kill her then, or untie her. And if he made the mistake of untying her first, she had a plan. For hours she had tried to focus on that and not on her family, not on all the places she'd never see, all the things she'd never do.

Mostly, she had tried not to think of Elijah. It was like trying not to breathe. Each mountain view, each creak of the saddle, each scent of horse and leather reminded her of him. Exhausted and sick with thirst, she'd jerked awake twice thinking she'd heard his low, slow drawl whispering her name.

She kept remembering Thursday evening when they had stood leaning against the cabin's porch railing and he had offered to try to stay. She had known she was doing the right thing when she said no. Her answer must have relieved him as much as it had her.

Better to know, to get it over with, than to hope.

But now she wished she had said the wrong thing. Wished she had said yes. She wished she had shown the courage that Elijah believed she possessed and told him what was in her heart.

During the long, horrible day's ride, Jordan had learned two unexpected lessons. The first was that something fundamental had changed within her since Elijah had offered to guide her to Battlement Park. Her heart had come back to life. She cared again, cared deeply about the life around her and about what might happen next in her own life.

Even in the darkest depths of her grief, when oblivion would have been a blessed relief, she had been terrified to die. In a strange way she couldn't explain, she was no longer so afraid, even with death riding before her in the form of her red-faced captor. But she found she wanted desperately, passionately to live again.

The second lesson she had learned was that as much as she regretted all the things she would never have a chance to do, she had very few regrets about the life she had lived.

Some people might have found her life simple or dull, but she had loved all the small, perfect moments. Helping Pete deliver a difficult litter of puppies just before dawn, hearing their tiny cries, the exhausted dam licking them clean. Falling in love with Jackson Braddock when he taught her to ice skate when she was sixteen. Aunt Rue giving her her first set of oil paints. Bringing Frank breakfast in bed the night after the milk cow calved and spending the rest of the morning there with him.

If she had to die today, there was only one thing she would go back to change. She would tell Elijah the truth, that she hadn't just given him her body that night they had spent together. She had given him her heart. She would tell him that there was someone in his life who loved him despite his past, despite his profession, who loved him with all her heart even if he had to leave.

The change in Smoke's gait warned her of danger, and she ducked her head in time to miss the tree limb that swiped at her. They were crossing a broken landscape of rocks and scree interspersed with stunted spruce and pine. Difficult to track over.

Passing the next tree, she reached out with her tied hands and grabbed a brush of needles, breaking off a sappy twig and letting it fall to the ground. She had done that every chance she got during the day. Cox had told Mrs. Jones that he was going to meet up with Pauly. Anything she could do to help the Kelly brothers follow her trail might lead them to the Bandit King eventually.

She had to hope so.

Smoke stopped abruptly, lurching Jordan forward in the saddle. Cox had halted just ahead, in a little stand of pines. Without even glancing back at his prisoner, he dismounted and eased forward through the trees, obviously scouting the way ahead.

Jordan looked at Smoke's reins, looped around the big black gelding's saddle horn, and her heart began to pound. She couldn't ride like Elijah yet, but she rode well enough now to know how smart her horse was. Smoke didn't need her to hold the reins. Smoke didn't even need her to know the way back to the lodge.

She just needed to know what Jordan wanted.

Jordan could barely see Cox through the trees. He was crouching down, looking out over some kind of drop.

Digging her fingers as best she could into Smoke's mane,

Jordan thumped the mare's side as hard as she could with her right knee, and again, sharply. The mare's head swung back to look at her.

"Good girl," Jordan whispered, the words as dry as her throat. She nudged again with her knee.

Snorting, Smoke turned sharply left, yanking on the reins. Cox's big gelding's ears twitched. Smoke yanked again. The black didn't so much as turn his head. The reins held.

Jordan considered maneuvering Smoke close enough to loose her reins from the black's saddle, but it wouldn't do any good to get Smoke free if Jordan couldn't take the gelding, too. Cox would catch her before she got a quarter of a mile.

Smoke tried to turn again, but Jordan could see it wasn't going to work. She eased up with her knee. But Smoke was frustrated now. Her head whipped like a snake striking, biting the gelding's behind.

The black's head snapped up, his back feet shifting right. Smoke lowered her head and backed up, pulling the reins taut. Eyeing the mare warily, the gelding took one step sideways with the pull.

"Good girl," Jordan breathed again.

Smoke pulled the black sideways another step, and another. His head shifted, as he made the decision to turn toward them.

A dead branch snapped, the sound turning all three guilty heads. Cox tramped toward them, no longer worrying about silence.

Jordan's brief hope died. She waited fatalistically for the explosion of rage when he saw what she'd done. But as he reached them, Smoke's head dropped to a patch of thick green grass at her feet, and she began to munch, for all the world as if she'd backed up merely to reach the snack. A strange shiver ran up Jordan's arms as Cox threw himself back into his saddle with barely a glance at her.

They started forward again, quickly reaching the steep embankment Cox had looked out from. Down below, in a small hollow of a ravine, stood what looked like an old hunter's cabin, its logs weathered gray, its roof warped with moisture and old age.

From the bank, the cabin looked as though it had been abandoned for years, but as the horses picked their way across the tiny creek bisecting the cabin's little clearing, Jordan saw signs of recent use. Horses had stood along the creek banks recently, though not that day. Something the size of an army tent had sat just to the side of the cabin, sat there long enough to turn the grass brown. A worn-out saddle blanket lay in front of the cabin door, for all the world like a welcome mat.

This might originally have been a hunting cabin, but Jordan didn't doubt it currently served as one of Pauly's gang's hideouts. In a hidden ravine a half-day's ride from even the remote settlement of Battlement Park, it was no wonder the law hadn't stumbled across this cabin. The gang must have more accessible hideouts, but the saddle blanket mat suggested they felt safe at this one.

Cox dismounted and tied his gelding to the cabin's porch railing.

"If that whore gets my message to her misbegotten brat, he might get here tonight," he said, moving over to wrench on the knots near Jordan's right ankle. "Then he can shoot you and get you off my hands."

He dropped the rope, letting it fall under Smoke's belly, and looked up at Jordan with a mixture of disgust and brutal threat that made her skin crawl.

"You better pray he gets here tonight. Now get down off that horse."

Jordan's dry throat still wouldn't swallow. "Untie my hands," she croaked. "Or I'll fall."

With swift violence, he grabbed her arm and yanked her off Smoke's back, sending her tumbling hard to the ground. Before she could catch a breath, he reached down and grabbed her by her hair.

She moved just as swiftly. Even as he wrenched her to her feet, Jordan reached out with her aching, swollen hands and snatched one of his pistols from his gunbelt.

Instinctively, he let go of her hair to reach for the empty holster. The shock in his eyes at her success must have echoed Jordan's own surprise.

She stumbled back, raising the gun to point at Cox's head. She had it by the stock and could reach the trigger with one trembling finger, but she realized with a rush of dread that she couldn't move her numbed thumb far enough to cock it.

His red face drained pale, Cox hadn't yet realized her predicament. Jordan stumbled back, giving herself a couple of steps on him, then, with all the speed she could muster, she jerked the gun up to her mouth, reaching for the hammer with her teeth.

Cox lunged then, one hand grabbing his left gun, the other reaching for Jordan.

Jordan dodged backwards, her teeth finally catching the hammer. She cocked the pistol, but fell, landing hard, the breath knocked from her lungs. But she still held the gun.

Desperately, she swung the gun up, but too slowly, much too slowly. Cox's foot was swinging toward her hand as she wrapped her finger around the trigger. The heavy boot connected as she pulled. The recoil jerked against her arms, throwing the gun loose as the sound shattered the air around her ears.

Cox stumbled back, almost falling, but she knew she'd

missed. It was his kick that had unbalanced him. Her gun had fallen a couple of feet away. She fought the pain to reach for it, but Cox was already pointing his other six-shooter at her head.

"You stupid slut," he snarled. His chest heaved with rage and fear, but his hand held steady. His finger hesitated on the trigger. "Why should I wait for that snotty little boy? Why should he make all the decisions? Why should he have all the fun?"

Cox lowered the gun. His teeth showed, but the expression wasn't a smile. "I wonder if it would be better to strangle you slowly or shoot you and watch your brains splatter all over the ground."

With her last ounce of courage, Jordan curled her lip at him. "Can't you decide anything for yourself? No wonder that housekeeper walks all over you. No wonder you take your orders from women and boys. You—"

"Shut up!" Cox raged, his eyes slitting like a beast's. He lifted the gun again, his finger firmly on the trigger.

Jordan shut her eyes as the blast of a pistol shot exploded around her.

# Chapter 20

Elijah knelt on the ground, eyes closed, clutching a cluster of green pine needles in his hand. The sharp scent of fresh pitch filled his nostrils.

She was alive.

Or she had been, not long ago. He opened his eyes, glancing up at the fast-sinking sun. Cox would have to stop for the night soon.

Elijah knew he wasn't far behind the two horses he had followed from Battlement Park. He had closed the hours-long gap between them, due in equal parts to his grim determination, to Jordan's efforts to mark her trail, and to Cox's slow travel, dragging a prisoner behind him.

Elijah could almost taste how close he was. Every instinct screamed at him to hurry, but he clamped them down. Jordan was still alive. If Cox intended to kill her before camping for the night, he would have done it already. It wouldn't do Jordan any good for Elijah to blunder into Cox's camp in a blind rush. He needed to move slowly now.

He was better with a gun than Cox. He didn't have to see Cox shoot to know that. It was in the very way the marshal carried himself. But Cox had the advantage. He had Jordan.

Elijah needed the element of surprise.

He rose from his crouch and looped the sorrel's reins around a low branch of the pine. He grabbed his rifle and patted the horse's neck. Once again he had reason to appreciate the gelding's mellow nature as the horse sighed softly and settled in to wait for his return.

Elijah took one last glance behind him. He had left an easy trail for Malachi to follow, but there was no sign of his brother. He'd have appreciated even Loki's company, but the wolf had disappeared before he'd reached the Fox and Hound's stable near noon. He'd have to go on alone.

With just the tips of his fingers, he touched the stock of one of the Colts slung low over his hips. He hadn't worn the guns in three years. Even now, thinking of Laramie, he felt a faint shiver of revulsion for them.

Yet he had continued to practice with them. They felt almost as natural a part of him as his own hands, and he knew they would serve him well. He had told Jordan he didn't wear them because he didn't like to kill.

He wouldn't mind killing Napoleon Cox.

Moving swiftly, he crossed another patch of rocky ground to enter a copse of stunted pines. He would need to be critically aware of his surroundings, in case Cox was worried about being followed. He would need to—

The sound of a pistol shot blasted off the mountainside around him in a thousand splintered echoes.

In the second it took him to recognize that the shot had not been fired at him, he abandoned stealth and sprinted forward through the trees toward where the sound had originated.

He skidded to a halt at the edge of an embankment. Still sheltered by the trees, he could see down into a clearing in the ravine below. His hunter's eyes took in the scene instantly. The cabin, the horses, one of them Smoke, Marshal Cox standing with a gun in his hand, a figure lying prone on the ground . . .

*No!* The word wrenched through him, though no sound

came from his throat. Yet even as the sick dread washed over him, he saw her move, heard the faintest hint of her voice on the breeze that carried toward him.

And he saw Cox raise his pistol, pointing it toward her head.

Raising his rifle to his shoulder had never before taken so impossibly long. Even as he sighted down the barrel of the gun, he heard the pistol fire.

The sound blurred his vision . . . no. Cox had moved, spun around. He was shaking his hand, no longer holding the gun. Elijah dropped the rifle barrel, his gaze searching anxiously for Jordan. She was struggling to sit up, defiantly alive.

On the other side of the clearing, opposite Elijah's position, five men had appeared, as suddenly and silently as ghosts. The slight figure in the center held a six-shooter dangling from one finger. Casually, he flipped the gun back into position and with practiced impudence blew across the end of the barrel.

Even if he hadn't been able to see the shooter's face, the young man's self-confident swagger would have given Elijah all the clues he needed to recognize Lucifer Jones. Pauly the Bandit King, as Jordan called him.

Once more the young outlaw had saved Jordan's life. But he'd increased the numbers against Elijah by five.

Slowly, smoothly, Elijah lowered himself to the ground, out of sight. He would have to wait to see how Pauly handled Marshal Cox, then he could begin to reformulate his rescue plan.

Five against one. Not bad odds.

Jordan wondered if she'd finally hit bottom. There honestly did not seem to be much to choose from between being shot by Marshal Cox now and being rescued by the man Cox intended to have shoot her later. Perhaps she had finally reached the point where things could not get worse.

"What the hell did you do that for?" Cox complained, leaning over to pick up his dropped gun. He grabbed the one next to Jordan and stuck that in his gun belt, too. "You could have shot my hand off."

Pauly shrugged, spinning his gun several times before dropping it back in its holster. "Better than shooting your head off, which I would have done if you'd killed her."

Cox glanced down at Jordan and spat. "You want to do it yourself, go ahead. I don't care."

He was sulking. Jordan winced. She'd almost been killed by a sulky bully. At least Pauly had style.

"No one's going to kill her," Pauly said. "Now untie her and help her to her feet."

Cox's mouth hung open in disbelief. "Somebody's got to kill her," he sputtered, reaching down to yank Jordan to her feet. "She knows I'm working for you."

Pauly's pale green eyes didn't blink. "Your stupidity is no excuse for killing an innocent woman. Untie her and give her something to drink."

"I'll be a wanted man!"

"You *are* a wanted man," Pauly said coolly. "Did you think I wouldn't find out what you did in Topeka?"

Cox's naturally red face paled.

"It was bound to catch up with you eventually. You'll have to give up your soft bed in Battlement Park and sleep cold like the rest of us." Pauly gestured to his other men, who had faded back into the woods and were leading out their horses.

"She knows where this cabin is!" Cox objected, shaking Jordan hard. "She'll lead the law right here."

"Another miscalculation on your part," Pauly said, his cold eyes settling on Cox. He considered a long moment. "I wouldn't make any more tonight if I were you."

He turned toward the cabin, paused, and looked back. "I thought I told you to untie the lady."

"Lady?" Cox exploded, the color starting to return to his face. "This whore? I don't know what you're thinking, Jones. This slut made a fool of me with that gunfighter lover of hers. She spied on me, and she just tried to shoot me. There ain't no way I'm letting her go back to turn me in to the law."

He wrapped an arm around Jordan's shoulder, his hand dropping to rest on her breast. Yet even as he leered down at her, Jordan thought he was using her as much as a shield against Pauly's hair-trigger temper as he was trying to frighten her.

"I don't mind if we don't kill her right away," Cox continued, looking around at the other four men for support. They stood frozen beside their horses. Jordan recognized the big bear of a man from the train and the gawky young Teapot.

"We'll have a bit of fun with her first. You can't complain about our treatment of a lady, Jones, since she ain't no lady."

Pauly turned slowly, cocking his head to one side. "I don't care if she's a two-bit whore or the Queen of England. As long as you work for me, you'll treat her like a lady."

Cox spat again. "You can't enforce that."

His hand squeezed Jordan's breast, and she wavered between vomiting and fainting. Disgusted with herself, she settled for jabbing her elbow hard into his soft gut. He grunted, but he squeezed harder until she stopped struggling.

"I can't?" Pauly widened his stance, his hands casually far from his guns.

Cox's tone lost some of its insolence. "Your own ma said to kill her."

Pauly's green eyes glittered. "Liar."

"What? But . . . but I . . . but she—" Cox stuttered to a

halt, floored by being called a liar when he had, for once, told the simple truth.

"She said—" Jordan swallowed dryly and tried again. "She said that his stupidity was his own problem, and you wouldn't put up with it much longer."

Cox's arm slid up to her neck, and he jerked her back. "Shut up, you stupid, lying slut!" His breathing rasped against her ear. "That's not what she said at all. She was supposed to meet you this afternoon, Boss. She was supposed to tell you what's going on."

But Pauly was laughing, his body loose again. "That's what you get for offending a lady, Cox," he said. "A woman's tongue is as sharp a weapon as any you've got.

"Luckily for you, that posse you can't control got in my way, so I couldn't meet my mama and she couldn't tell me what she really thinks of you. Thanks to your stupidity we've got some plans to change tonight. So untie her, like I told you, and let's set up camp."

"You're right, we got some plans to change," Cox said, dragging Jordan toward the four other outlaws, still waiting nervously by their horses. "Me and the rest of the gang are tired of all your fancy-pants rules. It's time you let the boys have some fun. When was the last time they got a night drinking in town or a soft girl to bed?"

Pauly looked at "the boys."

"You're not having fun?" His voice sounded mildly hurt. "You don't think you're getting your fair share out of our partnership?"

"Oh, it ain't that, Pauly," Teapot spoke up eagerly. "You always done treat us good. Gave us our share of everything. But maybe the marshal's got a point. We don't get a good time in town like we use to."

"You mean," Pauly's voice was still mild, "before we were

wanted men? Before we had a price on our heads?"

"Well, yeah." Teapot shifted his feet. "But you know, Pauly, boys'll be boys." He grinned in relief at coming up with that profundity.

Pauly nodded, strolling a little closer, a lock of blond hair falling over one eye. "You do have a point there, Teapot. You do have a point. The rest of you feel similar here?"

The other outlaws, older and wiser than Teapot, shifted uncomfortably. The big, bearish one shrugged. "I reckon lettin' off a little steam now and then wouldn't hurt too much."

Pauly nodded again, scuffing a boot in the grass. He glanced at the group of them through the screen of his hair, his eyes wide.

"You just want to let off a little steam." His head tilted up, his eyes almost soft in the last rays of the lowering sun. "And what would that entail, exactly?"

He waited, one hand fidgeting on the buckle of his belt. "What do you mean by letting off a little steam?"

The faintest hint of steel in his voice stilled all but Teapot. "Well, like the marshal said, maybe a night in town?"

"Like the marshal said." Pauly considered this. "You think the marshal has some good ideas? You think maybe he knows better than me what's good for this outfit?"

Even Teapot wasn't stupid enough to answer that one, but Pauly shook his head in sorrow as though they'd answered anyway.

"You think I ought to be more like the marshal, running to someone else to make all my problems go away? But who would I run to, boys? You?"

"Now, Pauly, you know that ain't—"

"What, Teapot?" There was nothing soft about the eyes that turned on his youthful friend. "That ain't what? What you meant to say? Then what did you mean? You think the marshal knows better how to have fun, that's all? Maybe the marshal ought to just plan our recreation?"

Teapot's mouth flapped a couple of times. "Well, no, Pauly, I don't really know. I don't—"

"You all like the marshal's recreational plans?" Pauly demanded, his gaze slicing across the whole gang now. Cox's arm tightened on Jordan's neck.

"Has it been too long since you had a good drink? That brandy we took from the hotel in Oxtail wasn't good enough for you?" Pauly's voice rose just slightly. "No, that can't be it. Is it a soft girl, then? Is that what you're missing? You think that would be good enough entertainment for you?"

The last rays of the sinking sun turned his eyes flat as stones on the bottom of a riverbed. "What do you think? You think it would be entertaining to do what the marshal said tonight, to rape and kill this lady here?"

He let the silence drag after his question, let the men listen to their own harsh breathing. Jordan felt a chill on her skin that had nothing to do with the coming twilight.

"Cowards!" Cox snarled. "Stupid, lousy cowards. What's he going to do? Shoot you all for telling the truth? Sure, they wouldn't mind that at all Jones. A little skirt before bed. They sure didn't seem to mind with that little piece of squaw up in Laporte."

Even the men's breathing stopped then.

"What?" Pauly asked finally, shaking his head as though to clear it of confusion. "What about Laporte? We didn't do anything to that girl. Those were ugly rumors the law made up to turn folks against us."

Jordan followed his gaze to the members of his gang. Pale as ghosts, they stared hard at the ground. One, an older man with a vicious scar across his right cheek actually cringed back toward his horse as if he'd been struck.

"You let him *rape* her?" Pauly's disbelieving voice rang through the little clearing. "You let . . ."

He paused, gathering his breath, though his eyes had lost all calm. "When? Jesus Christ. When I was on lookout? Making sure nobody shot us full of holes while you were supposed to be loading the horses? Did all of you know about this? Did you watch it? Did you rape her, too? Which goddamn ones of you were involved?"

Cox's laugh was harsh against Jordan's ear. "What are you going to do, Jones? Kill them all to find out? Too bad if you don't want to know what the world's really like. 'Boys will be boys.' "

Pauly's cheeks burned red, though the rest of him had gone deathly pale. He looked as though he might be sick.

"Go on then," he said, his voice a thin hiss. He waved his arm at his gang. "Go on. You want to follow his way, you want to be like him, you go with him."

He strode toward them suddenly, yanking a pistol out of its holster.

"Go on!" he shouted. Grabbing the pistol by the barrel, he struck Teapot across his jaw, sending the gawky youth staggering back into his horse. "Get out of my sight! You make me sick."

Cox laughed again, his arm easing from Jordan's throat.

"Come on, boys," he said. "You heard him. It's time for us to strike out on our own. Time for a man to lead you, not a boy. Teapot, get me my horse."

Teapot blinked and stared at the marshal, then at Pauly.

"Did you hear me?" Cox snarled. "Get me my horse, boy."

Teapot blinked again and shook his head. None of the other men moved.

"Damn it!" Cox shouted. "Go get that horse, or I'll plug you where you stand."

"What?" Jordan broke in, knowing there was no hope if Cox rode off with her. "Are you afraid to get it yourself?"

Cox's arm, veins standing out on the bulging muscles, jerked against her, forcing the air from her lungs. "Shut up, or I'll break your neck!"

"Get the horse, Teapot, or I'll shoot you myself." Pauly's quiet voice silenced the clearing once more. "I want you all gone."

Teapot shook his head again.

"I'm not kidding," Pauly said, his right hand resting lightly on his gun belt. "I'll kill you."

Teapot sniffed heavily, but he didn't move. "I ain't deserting you, Pauly. You shoot me if you got to." He wiped an arm across his face, brushing away tears.

"Shit," Cox said in stunned disbelief. "Of all the sniveling, stupid . . ."

He shifted, and Jordan felt him reaching for his gun. Once again he'd misjudged and dismissed her. Savage as a cat, she turned and bit his arm, dropping heavily to the ground when he jerked away.

For a second after the shot rang out, Jordan thought she had miscalculated horribly. Teapot slumped over, gasping, and fell to the ground.

On her knees, Jordan scrambled around to look at Cox. She wished she hadn't. Pauly's bullet had struck him square in the forehead. He fell more slowly than Teapot, but more heavily, his gun not even fully out of his holster.

She turned again to see Pauly grab Teapot by his shaggy hair and haul him to his feet.

"Jesus, Teapot. I guess if I was going to shoot you, I would have done it years ago."

Teapot snuffled again and wiped his nose on his sleeve. "I guess I knowed that."

Pauly looked over the rest of the outlaws, who mostly managed to look back at him this time. "Set up camp then, if you're staying."

"What do we do with him, Boss?" the bear asked, pointing at Cox. "Bury him?"

Pauly gave a careless shrug, the cool back in his eyes. "Don't waste the time. Take him out to the rock fall and dump him. Scavengers'll take care of it."

The outlaws began to move, released from their paralysis. The big man hefted Cox behind his saddle with hardly a grunt and headed back into the woods. One of the others lifted a canvas tent from his horse, and two more began to gather kindling to start a fire.

None of them glanced at Jordan. She had an eerie feeling that she could just quietly disappear and none of them would dare to notice.

Pauly, however, crossed over to where she knelt, a large knife appearing in his hand as he walked. For half a second she thought he meant to kill her as casually as he had Cox, but with a quick slash of the knife he loosed her wrists. She clenched and unclenched her fists, trying to drive blood into her numbed fingers.

One cool, slender hand took hers and helped her to her feet.

"I apologize," Pauly said, with a short bow over her fingers. "I apologize for the conduct of my men and that you had to be a witness to such violence. As poor as the circumstances are, I can honestly say it is a pleasure to meet you again, ma'am. I trust you are not seriously injured?"

Jordan was glad when he released her hand, because then she could let herself shake. "Water," was all she could say.

311

"Well, damn. Pardon me, ma'am." He grabbed a canteen from the nearest horse and offered it to Jordan. "Drink it slow."

The water was warm and tasted like leather and metal and green algae, but she couldn't have been more grateful if it had been fresh from the spring in the Garden of Eden.

"I hope you will take my word of honor that I don't mean you any harm," Pauly said. "I was not brought up to treat ladies rough. But you understand that if you try to escape before I can rest my men and make sure of our safe retreat, I will be forced to kill you?"

Jordan nodded. "I understand."

"Good." Pauly took back the canteen. "Why don't you take a seat in the cabin and recover from your ordeal. We will share our supper with you. Then you can tell me what happened to make Cox bring you out here. Go on, now, ma'am."

Jordan nodded again and began walking stiffly toward the cabin. Even now, she didn't like to turn her back on Lucifer Jones. But she didn't dare defy him, either. She didn't trust him not to shoot her however she behaved, but until she had regained some strength, her only option was to play along with his gallantry.

Jordan took a deep breath as she reached the few worn steps up to the cabin, trying to assess her situation.

She was weak from hunger and exhaustion and a sunburn that felt like fire. She was at the mercy of a homicidal youth who had just shot a man as casually as he might swat a mosquito.

She had to admit, things were looking up.

The cabin door closed behind Jordan, but Elijah did not lower his rifle. He could lie on hard ground hunched over his rifle sight for hours if he had to. In three feet of snow. With a mountain lion chewing on his leg.

Elijah grimaced in disgust at himself and lowered the rifle barrel to get a broader view of the clearing below. It was five against one, but he had the advantage of surprise and high ground. He could easily pick off two of the outlaws before the rest could even take cover. Adding in some pistol shots, he might even convince them he had them outnumbered.

Pauly wouldn't fall for that. Pauly might be young, but he wouldn't be leading the older men if he was anybody's fool. Elijah might be able to pick him off first, though it would be a touchy shot at the moment with Pauly moving in and out of the horses. But Pauly was the only one he was sure would not harm Jordan.

At least, he wouldn't harm her as long as his whim of chivalry lasted. As long as Jordan didn't provoke him.

Elijah grimaced again. He hadn't heard every word from down below, but it appeared she'd certainly done a fine job of provoking Cox.

He'd never hesitated in such a situation before. Do the job. Take out the opposition, whether they be fugitives from justice or a rival gang of hired guns in a range war. Take them alive, if possible, but kill if they made it necessary.

Jordan's presence changed everything. He cursed silently. She changed his whole damn life.

Yet despite the indecision, despite his focus on the men making camp below, his ears warned him of company from behind.

In one fluid motion, he rolled to his back, Colt in hand, ready to fire.

Loki crouched fifteen feet away in the shelter of the pines, his tail slashing wildly through the fallen needles, his lips pulled back in a cocky grin. The faintest hint of a muffled jangle told Elijah the wolf had not come alone.

"Stay." He mouthed the command, and Loki's tail slashed faster.

Rolling back to his stomach, Elijah stuck the Colt back in his holster and grabbed his rifle before scuttling back into the trees, well out of sight of the outlaws in the ravine. Loki's cold nose snuffled his ear.

"Good boy," he whispered. He hugged the wolf tight before rising to his feet. "Quiet now."

Loki kept close to his heels as Elijah hurried through the trees. His sorrel gelding glanced up as he passed, but made no noise.

Elijah moved as fast as he dared, careful not to trip or let his boots send a rock flying. He trotted around a curve in the trail and skidded to a halt before a raised shotgun and two Smith and Wesson Schofield pistols.

# Chapter 21

"It's about time," Elijah growled as the two men lowered their guns. "Leave your horses here, and try to be a little quiet about it. You sounded like a herd of elk charging up here."

"That's gratitude for you," Tony remarked dryly, swinging off his blood bay hunter and tying him to a tree.

"That's my brother," Malachi agreed, following suit. " 'Follow me out into the back of beyond so I can abuse you.' "

"Harry told you what's going on."

Tony snorted. "Harry told us next to nothing. Just that we had to follow you and that it had to do with Mrs. Braddock. We might have dismissed the whole thing, but Harry was acting bloody strange. That is, stranger than she usually acts."

Elijah looked at the Englishman's open, amiable face. He had to know. Now.

"I told her not to talk to you if you weren't with Malachi. I guess she wasn't sure how much to say if you did happen to be with him."

Tony's eyebrows rose.

"Marshal Cox took Jordan Braddock out riding this morning. They have not returned. You disappeared from the Fox and Hound about the same time."

"I say, that's a bit circumstantial." Only a faint flush on Tony's cheekbones betrayed his emotions. "There must be some other reason you cautioned Harry about me."

Elijah kept his gaze on Tony's eyes, his hands loose. "I

have been wondering why these outlaws have attacked towns and settlements all around this area, but have stayed away from Battlement Park. I have been wondering how they have found it so easy to stay out of our sight. Almost as if someone has been warning them of where we planned to be."

Tony crossed his arms over his chest. "I have been noticing the same thing. However I don't really see any way to prove to you that I am not involved."

"You don't need to," Malachi broke in, his face redder than Tony's. "Hell, 'Lije, you should have come to me. He's my friend. I would have vouched for him. I'd trust him with my life. Or do you think maybe I'm involved, too?"

Tony's stance relaxed slightly at his friend's defense. "It's all right, Mal. I'm sure he'd take your word for his own life. He just couldn't risk it for Jordan Braddock's."

"What? 'Lije?"

Elijah flicked a glance at Malachi. His brother stared at him.

"A woman?" The faintest of smiles touched Malachi's lips. "Hell. I never thought it would ever catch you, 'Lije. You're in love with her?"

Tony laughed. "Your powers of observation never cease to astound me, Mal."

Elijah felt his own color rise, but he couldn't have answered his brother's question. He didn't know anything about love. He just knew he couldn't let anything happen to Jordan.

"Well, Tony obviously hasn't got her," Malachi said.

"I know you don't think I'm very serious, Elijah," Tony put in. "Maybe I've looked at hunting outlaws as a bit of a game, but I want them caught. I may not have chosen my current occupation as hotel manager, but I feel responsible for my guests, and Mrs. Braddock is one of my guests. Not to

316

mention that I'm damned fond of her.'"

Elijah waited, letting the silence hang around them, judging Tony's posture, his voice, the look in his eyes. Malachi trusted him. He had to trust him or shoot him.

Tony met his gaze steadily.

"You're a good actor," Elijah said finally. "But not that good."

Tony's lip twitched. "Thanks. For once my boyish innocence comes in handy."

"That, and the fact that I already know who's been spying for Lucifer Jones," Elijah agreed calmly, reaching down to scratch Loki's head.

"What? Who?" Malachi and Tony demanded at once.

"Napoleon Cox."

"That bastard." Tony paused. "There, I haven't even asked if you're sure. I wasn't happy when the town hired him, to be honest, but there was no reason to object other than I just didn't like the fellow."

His brown eyes hardened. "I confess it won't bother me at all to bring him to justice."

"You won't get that chance," Elijah said. "He's dead."

Malachi slapped his horse's neck. "Christ. Give a gunfighter a gun . . . If you've gone and killed him, what the hell do you need us for?"

"I didn't kill him."

"Then who did?"

"He pushed our Pauly the Bandit King one step too far."

Malachi blew out a deep breath. "The outlaw gang. They've got Jordan."

"Yes."

"Hell, I'm sorry 'Lije." Malachi ran a hand through his hair. "Is she all right? How are we going to get her out of there?"

317

"There are five of them," Elijah warned. "You don't have to come with me. This isn't your fight."

"The bloody hell it's not," Tony said mildly, releasing his rifle from his saddle. "We've been hunting these scoundrels all week. You think we're going to let you have all the fun?"

Malachi rolled his eyes. "My brother's just giving us an out so he doesn't have to feel bad when we get shot to hell. Come on, 'Lije. What's the plan?"

Looking at the resolve in the faces of his companions, Elijah felt a faint quickening of hope in his own heart. He pushed it aside. He couldn't let his emotions get involved. He had to focus on this job, just like any other job. Only then would Jordan have a chance.

"All right," he said. "I'll give you the situation, what I know and what I guess."

He crouched down on his heels and brushed clean a patch of earth, scratching out a diagram with an old twig. "There's a ravine not far from here that's set up like this. Creek here. Cabin here."

Tony hunched beside him, and after a second, Malachi did, too.

"Maybe you better hurry, 'Lije," his brother said. "You want to be here all night?"

Elijah smiled, a panther's smile. The indecision was gone. "Yes, I do. Don't get too excited, boys. Unless something changes, I think we'll wait until it's nice and dark before we get shot to hell."

Elijah stared up into the stars, so bright and sharp here in the mountains that you could cut yourself on them. He knew he should be asleep. Malachi was keeping watch on the outlaws' camp, and there was another good hour until they planned to get into position to execute their rescue.

Elijah had long ago trained himself to rest like a cat, able to fall asleep anywhere at any time, regardless of physical discomfort, able to awaken in an instant knowing exactly where he was and why.

Tonight the stars were too bright, the scent of the pines too pungent, Loki's snoring too loud. Elijah nudged the wolf, who shifted, snuffled, and started snoring again.

It didn't matter. The truth was, Elijah's muscles refused to relax. His mind refused to slow. He had reviewed the plan a hundred times. A thousand. It wasn't good enough. It was the best he could do.

The outlaws slept outside the cabin, three in the tent, one out of sight under a tree, one sitting watch on the cabin porch. Jordan slept alone in the cabin.

Pauly had brought her out to share the outlaws' supper and use the bushes. She had been unharmed. And brave, though she must have believed herself all alone. Her ordeal had not crushed her, which improved the chances of rescuing her safely.

They would wait until just before dawn. Malachi would be the one to slip up behind the cabin. Elijah would have preferred to do it himself, but Malachi could move every bit as quietly as he could, and Elijah was the deadliest shot of the three. It was necessary to keep his rifle trained on the outlaws.

If there were a window at the back of the cabin, Malachi would attempt to enter through it and steal Jordan away. If not, he would creep around front and take out the guard silently with his knife.

If anything went wrong, he was to get inside the cabin and cover Jordan while Elijah and Tony apprehended the gang.

The plan was simple. It took advantage of surprise. It got someone close to Jordan to protect her. It was a fine plan.

Except for the million and a half things that could go horribly wrong.

Elijah closed his eyes firmly on the stars. *Sufficient unto the day is the evil thereof.*

The thought didn't really help. And when he closed his eyes, he could see Jordan, wrists tied, Cox's hands on her. If he had no other reason for hating Lucifer Jones, he would hate the man for robbing him of the chance to break every bone in Cox's body.

He remembered the night he and Jordan had stood on the cabin's porch, her shadowed eyes the color of the twilight sky. She had told him to go, not to hurt her anymore. Yet when he had taken her in his arms, she had held him as tightly as he had her.

"You're in love with her?" Malachi had asked him.

It wasn't because of her beauty that he wanted her. It wasn't the smell of lilac in her hair. It wasn't her kindness or her courage, though they had drawn him to her from the beginning.

When he was with her, he had a heart again. A soul.

He knew the answer then. Yes. He loved her. With everything he was, everything he could be.

*Terrifying.* His heart should be pounding, his head aching. She was in grave danger. He wasn't capable of giving her the life she deserved. Loving her was possibly the worst choice he'd ever made in a life of bad choices.

Yet a feeling strangely like peace settled over him anyway, easing into his muscles, loosening the tension in his mind.

He was just drifting into a light, soothing sleep when all hell broke loose.

Jordan's eyes snapped open to darkness. Night pressed in on her from all sides. She couldn't hear Nicky and Harry breathing, couldn't move her hands, couldn't remember where she was or why she didn't want to know.

She stifled a sob of terror and waited, picking out the shapes of paneless windows in the faint glow from starlight filtered through trees. She wasn't in the cabin at the Fox and Hound. She wasn't in the room at the lodge she had shared with Nicky and Harry the past two nights.

She tried to sit up, and discovered once more she couldn't move her hands. They were tied to the frame of the decrepit cot she lay on.

Pauly. Lucifer Jones and his gang. Marshal Cox dead. She was in a cabin in the middle of nowhere, prisoner to a gang of murderous outlaws.

She blew out her breath and relaxed back onto the cot. The human imagination was an amazing thing. She never would have thought her nightmares could be worse than this reality. She couldn't remember the dream that had awakened her, but consciousness was actually a relief—except for the rope abrading her raw wrists, the dead sheep smell of the blanket, her full bladder, and the thought of bedbugs, lice, and spiders.

She should have stayed home in Connecticut, moved in with Aunt Rue and Uncle Hal. She could almost see the bright green leaves of the maple tree out the window of the room she'd grown up in. She could almost feel the worn smoothness of the quilt her mother had made. She could almost smell bacon frying and hear Pete's dogs barking out in the kennel.

She choked back a shocking laugh. Pete and Henry Junior would die of jealousy if they could see her now.

A scrape of sound froze her into sobriety. Once, when the guard changed on the porch, someone had opened the door to the cabin, looking in on her. She didn't think any of the men would dare defy Pauly, but just the fact of her own helplessness had been enough to choke her with fear.

This sound was different. Furtive. She turned her head, trying to gauge where it originated from. The window, she thought. The back window.

She could barely see the window's outline, much less anything outside it, but as she watched, part of the darkness outside became more dark. The darkness moved slowly, almost silently, flowing through the window.

Jordan's heart pounded hard in her chest. A mountain lion. Or a bear. Tony had told her stories of bears climbing in through the windows of remote ranch houses, hoping to raid someone's pantry. Or it might be a member of Pauly's gang, defying him, after all.

Yet she couldn't scream. She could only watch as the darkness landed on the cabin floor with a faint thud. Something pale on the window sill. A hand. Definitely human. But not large, Jordan thought as the figure turned, trying to get its bearings.

She couldn't just wait for it to find her.

"What do you want?" she choked out, hardly a whisper.

The darkness whirled, showing the palest ghost of a face. A light, familiar voice asked, "Jordan?"

"Harry?" Her whisper squeaked.

Harry's hand found Jordan's leg and moved up toward her head. "Are you all right? Can you walk?"

"My hands are tied to the bed."

"I've got a knife. Hold on."

Jordan felt cool fingers searching her right wrist. Metal flashed.

"Be careful!"

Harry grunted assent, sawing at the heavy rope.

"What are you doing here? How did you find me? Is Elijah with you?"

"Sh!" Harry shifted the position of her knife. " 'Lije, Mal, and Tony are just up the ravine. Wolf and I did a little reconnoitering and found this cabin had a back window, so we thought we'd get you out before the boys attack the outlaws in the morning."

Jordan's mind flicked through Harry's words. "Harry, tell me 'the boys' know you and Wolf are here."

Harry paused in her sawing momentarily. "They will soon enough."

Jordan whispered a very unladylike curse.

"What? Are you sorry I'm here?"

"Just hurry the hell up."

Harry chuckled and redoubled her efforts on the rope. It finally broke, and Jordan pulled her hand free. Harry leaned across her to attack the second one.

A sudden creak on the cabin's porch froze them both.

"You asleep, Carson?" Pauly's cool, amused voice.

"Whuh? Uh, no, Boss."

"Glad to hear it. Get your horse together. We're heading out."

Jordan and Harry both breathed Jordan's unladylike word. Harry started back on the rope, but the darkness made it too dangerous to cut any faster.

"You think they're looking for us, Boss?"

"Sure, they're looking, Carson. You worried?"

Carson's laugh was only a little nervous. "Well, they ain't found us yet. What are we gonna do with the girl?"

"Take her back to her hotel." Cool. Casual.

"Boss? You mean ride into Battlement Park?" There was an incredulous pause while Carson thought about that. "Ohhhh. They're all out lookin' for us. Ain't that right, Boss?"

"That's right, Carson. No one's going to be expecting a few extra guests at the Fox and Hound. Maybe our kind aren't welcome there. That's just too bad."

Jordan jerked on the rope while Harry sawed. It wouldn't break.

"Harry," she hissed. "Stop. Get out. You've got to warn Elijah what they're up to."

"I'm almost through."

"Just give me the knife and go."

The porch creaked again. "Get saddled up, Carson. And bring the lady's horse over here for me."

"Gotcha, Boss."

*"Harry!"* Jordan whispered urgently. "Go! I don't know what he'll do if he catches you—"

The door squealed as it swung open. Lucifer Jones stood framed in the faint light, a hand on his hip.

"Ma'am?"

His eyes hadn't yet adjusted to the deeper darkness. Jordan felt Harry push the knife handle into her free hand before whirling around to face the door.

The sudden explosion of sound was deafening. A chunk of door frame disintegrated six inches from Pauly's head.

"Jesus!"

He dived around the side of the doorway as a bullet hit the door. Shouts sounded out in the clearing. A shot fired wildly into the night.

"Go!" Jordan shouted, punching Harry in the shoulder.

"He'll shoot you!" Harry objected, taking aim at the doorway once more. "I can't just leave you. Besides, 'Lije'd kill me. I should have brought my damn rifle. I'd've had him."

"Harry . . ." Jordan's mind raced. Harry wouldn't leave to save herself. "Harry, where's Wolf?"

"With the horses."

"And what will he do now that he's heard gunfire and you're not back?"

"What? He'll . . ." Harry cursed.

"You've got to make sure he's safe."

"Ma'am," Pauly called from the porch. "Tell your company to throw down her firearm, or I'll be forced to shoot both of you."

Gunfire sputtered from out in the night.

"I don't have time to argue about it," he warned. "I don't mean to brag, but I don't have to see you to hit you. Tell her to throw me the gun."

"Give me the gun," Jordan ordered. "And run like hell."

Harry's breath sounded ragged by her ear. "Jordan . . ."

"Do it!"

"He loves you, you know. Elijah."

It didn't matter. It didn't matter if he loved her. She was going to die. And even if she didn't, she had to leave. And if she didn't, he would leave. And . . .

It didn't matter. None of that mattered. He loved her. Somehow she knew it as clearly as Harry did. Something warm filled her heart and wouldn't let go.

"Harry," she whispered, her own voice as broken as the girl's, "tell him I love him, too."

"Ma'am—"

"She'll throw it!" Jordan promised.

Jordan dropped the knife to her chest and grabbed Harry's arm. With a sob, Harry thrust the gun in her hand. Harry squeezed her own hand around Jordan's, then dashed for the window. As Harry dove through it head first, Jordan threw the gun toward the doorway. It struck the frame and bounced out onto the porch.

"Damn it!" Pauly dodged around the door frame and fired at the window, but it was empty. He ran over to it and fired out several rounds.

He looked back at the cot, the starlight just catching the

green in his eyes. The sudden flash made him look eerily demonic.

Jordan brought her free hand out from under the blanket and curled it in a fist on her chest, trying to pray. But he didn't shoot her.

"What an inferior rescue attempt." His breath came fast, but his voice was calm. "They send in a girl not fast enough to cut you free and not a good enough shot to kill me. And the rest of your friends are too far away to pick us off in the dark."

He stepped closer to Jordan, out of the window's light. Somehow she could still see his eyes.

"Not organized by your friend Mr. Kelly, I imagine. Not from what I've heard about him." He cocked his head, eyeing her. The shooting outside had intensified, but he paid no attention. "I wonder, though, is he out there? Tell me, ma'am, are we up against Preacher Kelly's guns? Is it time for us to say our prayers?"

"I don't know," Jordan said, her own voice nearly as calm as his, though her limbs were shaking. "Harry was acting on her own. She didn't even know the others were out there."

She saw the flash of teeth as Pauly smiled. "That explains the confusion. He is here, then."

"I doubt it," Jordan jumped in, too fast. She hadn't expected him to believe her. "We had a fight a couple of days ago. He said he was leaving Battlement Park for good. He's probably in Wyoming by now."

Pauly laughed, a curiously infectious, light-hearted sound. "I'm sure if that were true, Marshal Cox would have gotten around to mentioning it before I killed him. It's all right, though. I don't blame you for trying to protect him.

"Here, let me finish your friend's work. We need to get out of here before a stray bullet finds us."

He leaned across her, and with a flash of silver released her left arm from its restraints. He took her right elbow and helped her to her feet.

She took a deep breath and braced herself for when he let her go. She had managed to shove Harry's knife into her skirt pocket. The blade had split the seam, but the hilt kept it from going all the way through and falling to the floor. She could feel the blade bumping against her thigh, thinly protected by her bloomers.

"Boss!" Feet pounded on the porch, and Teapot's gangly form showed in the door frame.

"Are we ready to ride, Teapot?"

The boy nodded violently. "Sure, 'course we are. I got your horse, right in the trees there." He gulped air. "They're shooting us up. They done hit Carson, maybe bad. We can't hold 'em back much longer."

"You don't have to." Pauly pulled Jordan toward the door. "You get back to the boys, Teapot. Tell them to ride to the old Darby place. We'll meet there."

Teapot's nod slowed to a confused shake. "Meet us? Ain't you comin' with us, Pauly?"

"I'll take the lady, Teapot. They want her worse than us. At least Preacher Kelly does. You can get away from the others. I can get away from him."

"By yourself? That ain't right. Let me go with you."

"You don't think I can take him?"

At the cool steel in Pauly's voice, Teapot's head shake intensified. "That ain't what I meant!"

"Then do what I told you."

A bullet splintered through one of the porch pillars, and all three of them jumped.

"Go on, Teapot! And . . . be careful."

Teapot blinked. "Yeah. You, too, Pauly."

"I'll see you at the old Darby place."

With that promise, Pauly yanked Jordan past his gangly confederate and down the porch toward the woods. A bullet whistled past Jordan's head, and she picked up her speed as they jumped blindly off the end of the porch and stumbled through the underbrush into the trees.

She heard a soft nicker from the horses, and was surprised both at how easily she recognized Smoke's voice and how comforting it was to hear it.

As they reached the animals, she readied herself to reach for her knife, but Pauly never let go of her arm. Instead, he grabbed her left hand and brought her wrists together.

"I am sorry," he said quietly, wrapping a binding around them. "I don't like the necessity of doing this, but I do need to ensure you won't escape before Mr. Kelly catches us. I think my bandanna will be easier on your wrists than that rope."

He finished his knot, his fingers deft and competent even in the dark, and lifted her hands up to Smoke's saddle horn. With a quick boost from the bandit king, Jordan found herself once more tied up on the back of her horse being led into the wilderness by a brutal criminal—a criminal endowed with a great deal more intelligence and cunning than Marshal Napoleon Cox.

But this time her feet were free, she had a knife in her pocket, and she knew Elijah was close on her trail. Not to mention Harry and Wolf.

Jordan buried her face in her bound hands and fought back hysterical laughter. She might not survive another rescue attempt.

# Chapter 22

"You may think you're lucky you survived that. You aren't. Just wait until I get through with you."

Elijah glanced back at where Harry and Wolf cowered together in the faint light cast by Malachi's smoky pine torch. Shoulders hunched, eyes downcast, they looked as if they'd been beaten. Another time, he might have felt sorry for them, but at the moment he was angrier than Malachi. He left them to his brother's wrath and climbed the steps to the cabin.

In the dark, dusty emptiness he felt rather than saw where the cot sat at the southeastern corner of the small room. He touched the rough wool blanket that had fallen on the floor.

He knew only his imagination felt warmth in the fabric; it had been half an hour since the outlaws had bolted from their refuge here. But when he lifted the blanket to his face, he could smell the faintest whiff of lilac. And turpentine.

His fist clenched on the material until the tension ached all the way to his shoulder. *So close.* So close, and now he had to wait again, wait for enough light to be able to follow the trail. Enough light to look for hoof prints and broken twigs and spots of blood, praying none of the blood was Jordan's.

There was no blood here in the cabin, at least. He ran his hand down the cot to be sure, but the smell of blood would be filling his nostrils if Pauly had shot Jordan or cut her throat after Harry had escaped through the back window.

Besides, he felt that she was alive, some melody just below

the range of hearing that had not disappeared from the music of the night. At this point he didn't care if it was wishful thinking. He would believe it until he knew for certain either way.

He stepped back out onto the cabin porch. The stars had dimmed. There would be light soon. Not nearly soon enough.

He saw Tony speaking to Malachi and moved to join them. As Elijah reached the group, Tony was rolling his torch in the wet grass.

"Putting it out of my misery," Tony said, wiping smoke tears from his eyes. "Bloody worthless, if you ask me. But I think I have a general idea of what we're up against. It looks like four of the outlaws headed north with an extra horse. Cox's, I assume. At least one of them's hurt pretty badly; there's quite a bit of blood.

"The two other horses went in that direction." He pointed southwest. "I don't know why they'd split up so unevenly, but it does make it a bit harder on us to catch them all."

The hair on Elijah's arms prickled, but he said nothing. He would wait for more information.

Malachi bent down and put his torch out, too. In the heavy gray obscurity of pre-dawn light, Elijah could see all his companions' faces. They looked as grim as he felt.

Wolf cleared his throat. "I think I know why—"

"I suppose we'll send these two back for reinforcements?" Tony said, speaking over him.

"You suppose wrong," Malachi growled. "We're going to tie them to a tree and come back for them when it's all over. With any luck, the outlaws will come back and find them first."

"Ease up, Mal," Tony said mildly. "The bandits started breaking camp before we even got into position to make our rescue attempt. Harry and Wolf didn't start it; they only made things worse."

"Please—" Wolf began.

"We're the ones who found those tracks over the pass from Oxtail," Harry spoke up defiantly. "We've been helping you track these outlaws all week. Then you tell us we have to stay back at the Fox and Hound while you get to bring them in? It's not fair. I'm as good a shot with a rifle as any of you—"

"Like you are with a pistol?" Malachi asked.

"It was dark!" Harry's voice cracked with anger. "We had a good plan, and it would have worked if we'd had another minute. I'm sorry it all blew up like that, but it's not my fault or Wolf's. You should have let us help from the beginning."

She turned on Elijah. "I've faced down outlaws before, or have you forgotten? If you thought we were so worthless, why did you let us help you all week? Why did you let us do all that hard work—"

"Because I thought you could follow orders," Elijah broke in, his anger slicing through her words. "Because I thought you were mature enough to act for the good of the whole group instead of showing off. One of the worst failures of judgment I've ever made."

"Father." Wolf's voice cracked, too, but it wasn't from anger. "I'm sorry."

Elijah looked at the boy. Only sheer bravery had given Wolf the strength to speak, his eyes aching with regret at what he'd done. Elijah's heart broke for him. But he couldn't soften what had happened.

"You could have gotten killed," he said coldly. "And if you don't care about your own life, you might think about this: you could have gotten Jordan killed. You could have gotten me and Mal and Tony killed. If we don't catch these outlaws, they will kill more people. No apology is going to change that."

"They were leaving here, anyway," Harry objected.

Elijah turned the full force of his anger on her. "We had the element of surprise until you alerted them that they were being followed."

"Father."

Elijah kept his gaze steady on Harry, staring down her bravado until she bent her head and tears began to roll down her cheeks.

"Father!"

Elijah turned back to his son, shocked to have to blink back his own tears. "Wolf, I can't soften—"

"I think I know why the outlaws split up!" Wolf paused a second as everyone fell silent. "When things went wrong at the cabin, Harry and I thought maybe we could get behind the outlaws across the ravine from you and trap them with crossfire."

With Harry's extra pistol and Wolf's .22. Elijah felt the blood drain from his heart, but he brusquely gestured Wolf to go on.

"But the outlaws started riding out then, and there were bullets flying all over. I got separated from Harry, and two horses rode by within a few yards of me. It was so dark I couldn't really see them, but it was one of the outlaws with Mrs. Braddock."

"How can you be sure?" Malachi demanded. "You said you couldn't see them."

"I heard their voices," Wolf said, unruffled. "I heard Mrs. Braddock say something about the outlaw turning himself in. That's why I couldn't risk a shot. I might have hit her."

"They made the tracks heading southwest," Elijah said. It was what he had expected.

"Yes, sir. I tried to follow them, but I couldn't keep up without making too much noise. The outlaw said you would catch them soon. I must not have heard right. It sounded like he wanted you to."

"It's got to be Jones," Malachi said. "He thinks we'll let the rest of his gang go while we track down Jordan."

Elijah wanted his brother to keep thinking that. He broke in before Mal could analyze the situation any further. "That's not what we're going to do. I'll track Jones. You and Tony go after the gang. Don't face them down yourselves. Just track them until they go to earth. Harry and Wolf will go back to the Fox and Hound and send Tony's cowboys out after you.

"I'd rather not have to rely on the two of them, but we haven't got much choice at the moment." He glared at the two penitents. "Do you think you can handle that?"

"We'll—" Harry cleared her throat. "It will be fastest if we lead them back here."

"It will be fastest," Elijah ground out, "if you damn well lead them all the way to Mal and Tony. You got yourselves into this mess, you can damn well see it through."

"You've got to be kidding!" Malachi howled. "It's too dangerous. I'm liable to kill them if the outlaws don't. They can wait at the hotel, and even that's too close."

Elijah shook his head. "If the ranch hands Tony hired to protect the hotel had included a decent tracker, Tony would have had him out helping us this past week. Wolf and Harry are the only ones who can lead those men to you in time to do you some good."

A simultaneous flush crept up Wolf's and Harry's cheeks, but something in their eyes changed. They'd do what he asked, and they'd do it well. If anything happened to them, he'd never forgive himself, but they were both old enough to live with the consequences of their actions, which meant they were old enough to deserve a chance to redeem themselves.

"You'll stay out of the fight, if there is one," he continued. They both nodded quickly, still chastened. "If you get yourselves killed, I will hunt you to hell and make you wish you could die again. Do you understand me?"

"Yes, sir," Harry said, with barely a hint of impertinence.

"Yes, sir," Wolf agreed.

"Then *why are you just standing there?*"

The two jumped and whirled and ran to collect their horses. Elijah watched Wolf for a long minute, the boy's wiry body moving with renewed confidence as he checked his saddle and whispered something in his horse's ear.

Elijah wanted to stop time, just for a moment, just for long enough to cross over and take his son in his arms, to tell him he loved him, that he was proud of him, was proud of the man Wolf would be.

But the moment passed, and Wolf and Harry were on their horses and picking their way across the creek back to the steep bank of the ravine. He wanted to shout to them to be careful, not to fall into a hole.

He held his tongue and let them go.

"Show me where the trail starts, Tony," he said, walking over to grab the sorrel's reins. "There's enough light to get started."

"I'm going with you," Malachi said, following him. "Even Tony can track five horses. You'll need my help."

Looking at the somber faces of his two companions, Elijah saw that they knew. They'd figured out that Pauly had taken Jordan specifically to compel Elijah to follow, to force a confrontation to prove Lucifer Jones' gun against Preacher Kelly's.

He rested a hand on Malachi's shoulder. "Those are four desperate killers. They know we'll be after them. I can handle one cocky boy."

"Who's got Jordan as a hostage." Malachi shrugged off Elijah's hand. "Hell, 'Lije, you won't be thinking straight. You need help, even if it's just your obnoxious little brother. Quit thinking about your stupid pride, and start thinking about Jordan's welfare."

"That's exactly what I'm thinking about." Elijah swung into his saddle. A month ago he would have left it at that. But looking down at his brother, Mal's mouth set as mulishly as ever, he realized that Malachi was right about his pride getting in his way.

"I am thinking about Jordan," he said again, gathering the sorrel in. "If I track Pauly down alone, he'll let her go. It's not my pride, Mal, it's his. Whatever the outcome, she'll be all right."

After a long moment, Malachi nodded and looked away. He slapped the sorrel's neck. "Hell, I know you'll be back, anyway. I couldn't get lucky enough to get rid of you for good."

Elijah grinned. "The feeling is mutual, suh."

"Oh, jolly good," Tony muttered, grabbing the sorrel's reins and leading Elijah toward the trail he'd found. "That's fine for you, but I don't grate on anyone's nerves enough to make sure I get back in one piece."

Elijah and Malachi both laughed then.

"Don't you worry about that, Major," Elijah assured the Englishman. "Don't worry about that at all."

The high meadow had a beauty it would be almost impossible to capture in paint. It lay just at the edge of the timberline, twisted limber pines easing the bite of the keen breeze blowing across it, a rock field defining its upper limit. Tiny flowers studded the muted greens of the meadow like stars in a smoky sky. A small mountain tarn, fresh and cold as the ice bank that fed it, reflected the blue of the sky from its place high in the rocks. An eagle circled above it all, his sharp eyes ignoring the ground squirrels popping up around the meadow's rocks, not liking the presence of the two horses and two people, however harmless they might look at the moment.

The sun felt hot on Jordan's head, though Pauly had untied her wrists so she could use his bandanna to protect her sunburned face and neck. She sat on a rock on the high side of the meadow. Her captor wanted her clearly visible from every direction.

Pauly sat in the shadow of his horse a few yards away, making toneless whistles out of blades of grass. He'd already cleaned his guns.

Harry's knife hung heavy in Jordan's pocket. It wasn't a big blade, but she had no doubt it would kill if she could thrust it into Pauly's heart. Of course it might break on a rib. Better to aim for his neck.

And that's why she sat still, though her hands had been free more than half an hour. She reminded herself that Pauly was a killer. She had seen him shoot Marshal Cox in the head without any sign of regret or remorse.

Yet he had saved her life twice. And he looked so young, bent over his blades of grass, half a smile on his face. She could lure him close easily enough, but she didn't know if she could drive the knife home.

Except that he meant to kill Elijah.

Her eyes searched the forest below them for any sign of movement, though she knew she wouldn't see anything, even if he were coming.

If. Pauly was so sure Elijah would come. Alone. If she could see him, just one more time . . . yet she prayed he wouldn't come.

She couldn't let him walk into a trap. Even if he could see the trap for himself. It would be so easy to pick Pauly off with a rifle shot where he sat exposed at the center of the meadow. Easy enough to ensure that Elijah would never do it.

Jordan took another quick look around. Everything seemed so still and peaceful. Even the bumblebee attracted to the lavender color of her dress hummed with laziness. It was now or never—things could only go downhill from here.

Slipping her hand into her pocket, she wrestled out the knife. If Pauly grabbed her, she might find the nerve to stab him. At least she could slash his arm, make it harder for him to shoot.

Gathering her skirt in her left hand, she took a deep breath and launched herself off the rock. Angled away from Pauly, her path led her downhill, and she picked up speed fast. She heard Pauly's shout, but couldn't hear him coming after her; her heart was pounding too loudly.

She had thought she'd make it to the trees, but they suddenly seemed terribly far away. Her legs ached from riding and hunger, and her skirts tangled around her like a net.

She pushed her feet harder, gasping, clutching the knife in a hand slippery with fear. She wouldn't make the trees. She had to turn and face him so he couldn't grab her knife arm. She had to—

A gunshot boomed across the meadow. Stunned, Jordan tumbled to the ground, the landing or the shot making her head ring.

She couldn't believe he'd shot her. It had never occurred to her he wouldn't just chase her down. Maybe he'd seen the knife and decided she was too much trouble. Even so, she'd have thought he needed her alive to force Elijah to fight him. On the other hand . . .

On the other hand, it was taking much to long for being

shot to hurt. Pauly's bullet might have killed her instantly, except she distinctly noticed the ache in her lungs from her run and felt the individual blades of grass pressing against her face.

Footsteps strode deliberately across the thick meadow covering to pause in front of her face. Jordan opened her eyes to an unnervingly familiar pair of black boots.

She suddenly became acutely aware of the picture she made lying face down in the grass, of the faded indigo bandanna over her ragged hair, of her sunburn and the grass stains on her cheeks and down the front of her ruined dress.

She had been a hair's breadth from death for over twenty-four hours, and she was worried about her red nose and green cheeks. No wonder vanity was considered a deadly sin.

A long, brown hand found hers clutched around a clump of blue asters and pulled her gently to her feet.

He looked as good as she had feared he would, no grass stains on his white shirt or planed cheekbones, that deadly humor burning gold in his eyes.

"Sparrow," he murmured softly, his voice tickling against her ear so she thought she might fall into it. "You do have a knack for dragging me into interesting situations."

"*Me?*" Jordan found her legs could hold her up quite well after all. "I think you're forgetting just who's been getting whom into what. Besides, you didn't have to come after me. I had the situation under control."

Elijah merely raised one dark eyebrow and handed her the knife he'd rescued from the ground. It did seem rather small now that she got her first good look at it.

"I thank you for your intervention, sir." The light, cool voice sent a chill up Jordan's spine. "She might have stuck me good with that."

Jordan turned to see Pauly not a half-dozen paces behind her.

"It is not wise to underestimate Mrs. Braddock," Elijah said, his voice suddenly cold. "Napoleon Cox made that mistake."

Pauly shrugged. "I killed Cox. She had nothing to do with it."

Elijah shrugged back, deliberately mocking him. "And if you think that, you're making the same mistake he did."

After a heartbeat's pause, Pauly laughed his infectious laugh, his green eyes lighting briefly. "You're as cool as they say, Preacher. It will be a pleasure testing my guns against yours."

"It would be better for you to give your guns to me and turn yourself in. I don't miss."

Pauly laughed again. "I'd a whole sight rather go to hell shot by Preacher Kelly than sent by a hangman's noose. Besides, I don't miss, either, and I've never met anybody faster than me. I'll give you a minute with your lady."

He turned his back to them and sauntered over to his horse.

Jordan whirled on Elijah, knowing her cheeks burned even redder than the sunburn with fear-driven fury.

"Damn you and your stupid sense of honor! Why did you fire that stupid warning shot? Why didn't you just shoot him?"

"You were running right at me, Sparrow," he answered with that maddening calm of his. "I couldn't get off a clean shot. It came close enough to stop him in his tracks. Now I get another chance."

He pulled the Colt from his right holster, checked the mechanism, checked the barrel, checked the chambers.

Dread squeezed Jordan's throat closed. It was really happening. All this polite bravado was leading up to these two men pulling guns on each other and shooting until one or both of them were dead.

"Elijah, you don't have to do this. Please." She touched his arm as he reached for his other gun. She waited until his eyes met hers. "Please don't do this."

"It has to end, Jordan. He has killed and hurt too many people."

"Not you." She heard the tears in her voice, but didn't let them fall.

She had prayed for one more moment with Elijah, one chance to say what she had been too much of a coward to tell him before. This was that moment. Maybe it was all she got.

"Not you, Elijah. I can't bear to lose you."

He let go of his gun then, reached out to cup her cheek with his palm.

*Maybe this was all she got.* "Please, Elijah. I love you."

His lips brushed hers, so tenderly that her tears spilled over. And then she was in his arms, and she thought only the tightness of his embrace kept her heart from breaking.

"Tell me when it's over, Sparrow," he whispered hoarsely, and she thought maybe his tears mixed with hers. "Tell me again when it's over."

He kissed her again, claiming her this time, with a fierceness and passion that might have frightened her a month ago, a day ago, but that now only answered her own. She touched him, his face, his hair, his chest, knowing she couldn't memorize enough of him, knowing she couldn't hold him safe in the moment.

"He won't let me walk away," Elijah said, finally breaking the kiss. "I have to face him."

"He wouldn't shoot you in the back," Jordan argued, desperate. "His honor—"

"Is anything that suits him." Elijah brushed the hair back from her damp cheeks. "As long as he's breathing, he won't let me walk off this mountain alive."

She knew he was right. Pauly needed to prove himself against a real gunfighter, needed it for his reputation and his own self-respect. If Elijah refused to fight, he would call him a coward and shoot him anyway.

But she clung to Elijah as though somehow she wouldn't have to let him go, wouldn't have to face the possibility of losing him in the next few minutes, a possibility that spun in the summer air like the toss of a coin.

"I would rather face him myself than watch you do it," she whispered.

"I know." He kissed her forehead, then pulled back to meet her gaze. "Yours is the courage, not mine. Whatever happens, you have to promise me to ride safely back to Battlement Park."

Jordan shook her head, the tears streaming again. "If anything happens to you—"

"If anything happens to me, you'll get on Smoke and let her lead you back." He tilted her head, forcing her to look at him. "You'll get Nicky back to Denver. You'll see your little cousin born. You'll get home to your aunt and uncle and all the family that loves you. You have to promise me that, or I won't be able to do this."

Whether he meant it or whether it was blackmail, pure and simple, she couldn't risk being a distraction when he faced Pauly.

"All right. I promise."

"Thank you."

She sniffed. "But you better stick around to make sure I keep it."

She realized she knew him well enough to see the smile he

tried to hide. Just as she could see the pain behind it.

"Mr. Kelly!" The light voice, the casualness of it only slightly forced, carried clearly through the thin air. "It's time."

Elijah brushed his lips across Jordan's once more, and somehow she let him go.

She watched him walk away, up the slope toward the rocky side of the meadow. It took several paces before he settled into his natural, cat-like stride. She could almost see everything human falling away from him as the feral grace of a predator took over his movements. She knew that when he reached his destination his eyes would be as flat and deadly as Pauly's.

He slowed as he reached ground level with the outlaw and turned to face him. They stood maybe twenty paces apart, point-blank range for two gunfighters.

Suddenly dizzy, Jordan sank to her knees in the grass. They were going to kill each other. And there was nothing she could do. Nothing, except pray.

Silence hovered over the mountain. Even the wind and the bumblebees fell quiet. The two men faced each other, one fair and loose, with all the speed and accuracy of youth and fervent practice, the other dark and disciplined, with the wary confidence of experience.

Their hands hovered, flexing above the guns in their holsters, waiting for some invisible signal to set them in deft, deadly motion.

# Chapter 23

Elijah heard through the silence to the pulse beneath. Training, discipline, the knife edge of life or death honed his senses so that he heard the grass reaching for the sun, heard the snow melting, heard the mountain breathing. He heard his own heartbeat, aware that each one might be his last.

And if his heart stopped, what would happen to Jordan? If Pauly let her go . . . If Smoke could find her way back to the Fox and Hound . . . If she didn't succumb to dehydration and hypothermia overnight . . .

Alarm shocked through him as he realized his attention had drifted infinitesimally from his focus on the gunman facing him. That millisecond could have meant the difference between killing and being killed.

Images flashed through his brain. Jordan, Wolf, Malachi, Harry . . . The family a gunfighter couldn't have. And this cocky boy across from him whom he didn't want to kill. A mirror of who he might have been if he had enjoyed the killing, if it had infected him and taken control of his life.

How different could he claim to be, just because he used his guns for work rather than pleasure? Yes, he no longer wore them. But he practiced with them still, kept his skills sharp. Sharp enough?

" 'For thy name's sake, O Lord, pardon my iniquity; for it is great.' " He knew what people said, that he quoted scripture to freeze the blood of his opponents. But it wasn't true.

He knew how much he needed forgiveness.

The outlaw would make his move any second now. Elijah could see it in those flat, dead eyes that thought they gave nothing away.

" 'Look upon mine affliction and my pain; and forgive all my sins.'"

Those eyes jerked to the left suddenly, distracted by a noise from the boulder field above them. They snapped back in consternation, but Elijah only raised a slow eyebrow.

*I could have had you.* Let him swallow the iron taste of uncertainty.

The sound crashed nearer. In his peripheral vision, Elijah saw the rabbit spurt out of the rocks, dodging in a zigzag pattern across the meadow. Behind it, a gray fury of white teeth and yellow eyes.

Pauly broke all eye contact then, spinning to fire at the wolf.

Elijah saw the bullet strike the turf by the animal's shoulder. The wolf spun out of control, flipping head over heels another six feet.

"No!" Jordan screamed as Pauly raised his other gun, her voice pulling Elijah's gaze from his opponent.

"Stay back!" He shouted, waving her off. "Jordan, stop!"

She halted her desperate scramble toward Loki, her eyes turning to Elijah with the fear that she'd distracted him, giving Pauly his chance.

But the outlaw was grinning, mocking the wolf's snarls.

"A friend of yours, ma'am?" he asked Jordan. He fired left-handed this time, loose and from the hip. The bullet dug a furrow in the shallow soil by Loki's right flank.

*Goading me,* Elijah realized grimly. And it was working. His breath quickened at the confusion in his furry companion's eyes.

"Leave him," he ordered. "This is between you and me."

Pauly fired again, kicking up a rock up to clip the wolf's jaw. Loki yelped and jumped, his hindquarters spinning. Another bullet whirred past his ear.

Jordan stepped forward again, her ridiculously small knife clutched in her hand.

"Damn it!" Elijah shouted, moving toward the outlaw. "Turn and face me, you—"

But he stopped when he saw Pauly's face. The outlaw's eyes were wider than Loki's, his teeth showing just as white in his fierce snarl. Even from a distance, Elijah could see that the knuckles clutching the man's guns were white.

Pauly was no longer trying to miss the wolf. He couldn't hit him.

The outlaw fired with his right hand, stepped closer, fired again.

"Jones! Stop!" Elijah shouted again. Pauly had echoed Elijah's boast that he never missed, and Jones was still young enough that for him it might even have been true. But he hadn't hit Loki. Couldn't hit him. He'd lost his touch, lost his feel for the guns. And it had him spooked. Badly.

Another shot. Loki backed and snarled.

"Jones! Look at me." If Elijah couldn't distract him, he might get off a lucky shot. Or he might panic and fire on Jordan.

The outlaw's face contorted. He fired again and again.

"Pauly," Jordan called, the sound of his nickname pulling the young outlaw's gaze to her. "Don't. It's all right, Pauly. Let him go. He doesn't want to hurt you."

For a long moment he stared at her, though he didn't seem to see her. Then, his eyes dead calm, he spun, all his loose grace returning. He raised both guns toward Elijah's head, fingers tight on the triggers.

One more shot rang out, but this one found its mark. Pauly's eyes brightened briefly in surprise, then turned dark as he slumped to the ground. He didn't even have time to raise a hand to the incongruously small red stain creeping down his chest.

Elijah looked down at the Colt in his hand. He couldn't remember drawing it. Couldn't remember firing it. It had happened too fast. Faster than a man with his guns already drawn could pull the trigger.

The fastest he'd ever drawn. The best shot he'd ever taken. A man he had to kill.

And it made him sick, down deep into his bones.

Loki twitched, looking from Elijah to the inert body and back again. Slowly, he rose from his crouch. His ears rose up and he shook himself, his skin snapping loosely around his jaws. Tail motionless for once, he moved to sniff Pauly's body.

Elijah breathed for the first time since he'd fired. Loki was alive. Jordan was alive.

Jordan followed Loki, crouching beside Pauly to check for a heartbeat, as if he had been a sick boy and not a brutal killer. For he'd been both.

She rose and looked at Elijah, tears darkening her sapphire eyes. She came toward him then, but he stepped back.

"No."

She was so alive, and he held death in his hands. Turning away from her, he pulled his arm back, and with all the strength in his body, he heaved his Colt up into the rock field high above them. It splashed into the tarn, shattering the reflection of heaven.

Then Elijah set to work to make a grave.

Jordan added some kindling to the fire she had started.

Sunlight still dazzled in her eyes, but the air would cool quickly when the sun dipped behind the next mountain range. She watched the dry pine blaze up, then looked over to where Elijah toiled over Polydorus Jones' grave.

He had used Pauly's knife and a flat rock to scrape a ditch out of the meadow turf. Now he was piling rocks over the shallow grave to keep predators away.

The work had taken him all afternoon. His shirt long discarded, she could see the muscles in his back strain under the weight of the rocks he shifted.

She had asked if they shouldn't take Pauly's body back to Battlement Park for his mother to bury. Elijah had barely registered surprise at discovering Philomena Jones was the outlaw's mother. He told her that Mrs. Jones had ridden away from the lodge after her confrontation with Nicky, and he suspected the woman would not return.

When Jordan pressed him, he had said he didn't have any desire to drag the body along with them on the long, hot ride facing them the next day.

But watching the way he pushed himself, refusing her help, refusing food, she thought convenience was not his motivation. Elijah was giving Pauly the burial Elijah would have wanted if the gunfight had gone differently. Up in the mountains. Free.

She thought Pauly would have appreciated that, a tribute from a fellow gunfighter.

Loki settled by her feet with a heavy sigh. Even the wolf had been solemn that afternoon, keeping a quiet watch on the humans, ignoring the teasing chatter of the ground squirrels.

Jordan reached down to scratch his ears, and his tail thumped gently in response.

She watched Elijah set another stone, then pause, glancing at the grave and up at the sun. He bowed his head a moment, then turned to grab his shirt. He climbed up into the rock field to the snow-melt tarn and knelt down to plunge in his arms and face.

Jordan shuddered. She knew just how cold the water was from her efforts to clean up earlier in the day. She added a bigger branch to the fire.

She scratched Loki's ears some more, both of them listening as Elijah finally made his way toward them down through the rocks. He crouched on the other side of the wolf, his hand sliding up Loki's back to meet Jordan's hand. He wrapped his fingers around hers.

"I can't do this anymore," he said, watching the fire, low sunlight slanting across the planes in his face.

She watched him, waiting to see what he meant. Being with her. Being alone. She could feel the warmth of him, alive, against her fingertips, and for now that was all she needed.

Even in the slippery light of late afternoon, he looked drawn, drained, worn by more than his labor. But when he looked at her, she could see the light that even his gunfighter's eyes couldn't hide.

"A gunfighter can't have a home or a family. If I ever doubted that, I learned it well here in this place. Sparrow, you meant more to me today than winning or dying, and if you can't afford to lose, you shouldn't be playing this game."

He held her hand so tightly her bones ached, but she squeezed back, her heart aching.

"I've never had a home. Frankly, the idea terrifies me." He didn't quite smile, pushing on in a husky drawl. "I'm a worn-out drifter. I've hurt everyone I've ever cared about. I have nothing to offer you."

"Elijah." She could barely say his name through the tightness in her throat. "You don't have to—"

"Shhh." He reached across Loki to press a finger to her lips. He did smile now, a half-teasing smile that didn't hide the fear in his eyes. "Can't you leave off your kindness long enough to let a man propose?"

She stared at him. "Pardon?"

"I'm nothing but an ex-gunfighter with one pistol and a borrowed horse. But I've found my heart again. You found it for me. Would you have me, Sparrow?"

"Ex-gunfighter?" That was as far as her mind could venture for the moment.

"I said a gunfighter can't have a family. But I've suddenly discovered I've got Wolf and Malachi and March and Maggie and Harry and Loki—"

The wolf looked up with a bright eye.

Jordan knew Elijah must be able to feel her hand trembling. His eyes held hers, more compelling than the first time she'd met him, on the train, when he'd appalled and fascinated her. Panther eyes. It would be about as sane as marrying a panther.

"I thought my heart would simply stop if Pauly killed you today," she said, struggling with the words. "I wished it. It would be so much easier to walk away from you now than to risk losing another husband."

"Yes."

He brushed his thumb across the back of her hand, and the word whispered up her veins into her body. Yes. It whispered in the wind that brushed suddenly against her ear. The last rays of the sinking sun sang it across the snow dazzling on the mountaintop.

*No.* She shook her head as he pulled her to her feet.

Her lungs filled with the scents of pine and fire, wolf and man, warm rocks and cold water. Something light and free was opening in her heart. Yes. Something even grief and fear couldn't touch with darkness.

*No.* It would hurt. Sometime. Somewhere. Loving always hurt. You couldn't control a panther, anymore than you could control a wolf. You couldn't keep him safe.

But even her ghosts refused to chill her, bringing only a whisper of laughter and the touch of a summer breeze. Would she give up the years she had had, just because she had lost them?

Of course not, but this was different. This was not a man who would return with her to New England and settle into a gentleman farmer's life. This was not a man who would take a sensible approach to danger.

Ex-gunfighter? He'd only thrown away one of his guns.

*No.* Definitely not.

"Sparrow?"

"You said to tell you how I felt when . . . when it was all over."

"It's all right." He glanced down at their hands. "Things change, when the danger is over."

"Not this," she said, waiting for him to look into her eyes again. "Elijah, I love you. Yes."

"Yes?"

"Don't look so shocked!" She narrowed her eyes at him. "If you were hoping I'd say no, I can change my mind."

Slowly, that familiar, dangerous smile crept across his mouth, the hawk taking his prey. "Oh, no, Sparrow. No, you can't."

Cupping her head with his free hand, he leaned over to kiss her. His lips pressed against hers with a knowledge and a certainty that pushed her past all hope of escape.

With a groan, Loki heaved himself to his feet and extricated himself from between them. He threw himself to the ground a few feet away with a disgruntled sigh neither of them noticed, as Elijah pulled Jordan into his arms.

Warmth and love and need washed through her, overflowing her heart. But she had to ask. She loved him too much to hold him where he didn't want to be held.

She leaned her head back to look into Elijah's eyes. "Are you sure?"

He brushed a thumb across her cheek. "I love you."

"I know." She could see it in his eyes, and it made the night air sing. "But that doesn't mean this is right for you, for your heart. For your peace of mind."

That smile wreaked havoc on her insides. "I think this is about the only thing that will allow me any peace of mind. When you're out of my sight, I have to spend all my time worrying about you. You need someone to keep you out of trouble."

"Somehow the idea of you looking out for me doesn't make me feel better," Jordan said tartly. "Since I've met you, I've been attacked by a wolf, taken hostage during a bank robbery, threatened by bounty hunters, kidnapped by two different outlaws . . ."

"See what I mean?" he murmured, pulling her closer, so she could feel the length of his body against hers. "You have a nose for trouble. But I'm willing to take you on anyway. In fact, I'm looking forward to it."

"As I recall," Jordan said, stoically resisting the brush of his breath against her neck, "I'm the one who rescued you from Billy Calhoun and tricked Marshal Cox into sparing your neck. You don't even have enough sense to take your malaria pills on your own."

He leaned back a little and raised one eyebrow. "Did I say I'd mind if you looked after me?"

She thought about that a minute. "No."

"Good." The grin was turning wolfish. "Because I'm

looking forward to that, too."

She couldn't keep her lips from curving in reply. "I certainly hope so."

But his expression grew serious again. "What happened here today . . . Loki could be dead. Pauly was good enough, he could have killed me. I'm getting a second chance, Sparrow. To live my life right. I wouldn't have asked if I wasn't sure. You're what I want."

He touched her brow, her hair. "I know you have to take Nicky back to Denver. After that, we could return to Battlement Park. I have money saved. You could have your summer to paint."

Jordan raised her eyebrow, mimicking him. "I'm sorry. I've lost enough husbands. I intend to hold on to you for a while—I'm not going to let you die of boredom. Although —" She glanced at his half-empty gun belt. "Battlement Park is going to need a new marshal."

"True." Definitely a panther's eyes. But they softened as he thought. "There might not be much to the job once Mal and Tony catch up with the rest of Pauly's outlaws. But I could do some mountain guiding on the side."

"Tony would love to have someone reliable to take his guests out," Jordan agreed. "I'm sure he'd—"

"I am *not* going to work for Mad Anthony Wayne," Elijah said firmly. "I'm making a significant concession agreeing to live in the same county with him. Don't ask too much just yet. I'm new at this."

Jordan laughed, her heart so light she thought it might fly away. "I don't care what we do. Mountain guiding. Cattle ranching. Well digging. Or where we do it."

"As long as it's close to Nicky and Will?"

"And in the mountains."

"Not too close to town."

"But close enough to ride in for turpentine when I run out."

Elijah shook his head. "You are so beautiful."

Jordan snorted. "I'm sunburned and grass-stained and I haven't brushed my hair since yesterday morning."

"And the light in your eyes is like the light in the mountains, changing every moment. Blazing, gentle, deep as the twilight."

Looking into Elijah's eyes, she saw that same tender light in them. Love and desire and the knowledge that if all they had was each moment, this moment was enough.

If this was their moment, it was perfect.

"Meanwhile," Elijah murmured against her ear. "We have this whole evening together alone."

"Mm." Jordan pulled him even closer. "It would be a shame to waste it." She tilted her head back to kiss him, slow and soft as the grace of the settling evening.

"Father!"

They started apart, turning, to see a horse trotting across the meadow toward them, a boy on its back. Wolf's ruddy dark hair was plastered damply around his dirty face. He was pale with exhaustion, but his eyes shone with relief at the sight of his father.

"Wolf!" Elijah ran forward to meet the boy as Wolf swung off his horse and threw himself into his father's arms. Jordan watched the surprise on Elijah's face quickly give way to an emotion he tried to hide.

Loki reached them barely a moment later, the boy and man able to turn their rough affection for each other on him, sending him into a whipcord dance of ecstasy.

Elijah pulled back a step to watch his son tumble with the wolf. Only Jordan saw the glint of moisture in his eyes.

"What are you doing here, son? You and Harry were supposed to ride for reinforcements. What happened?"

"We brought the men from the Fox and Hound," Wolf assured him, rising, one hand still on Loki. "Just like we promised. But we hadn't even reached the cabin when we ran into Uncle Mal and Major Wayne returning with the outlaws. I guess they weren't much trouble. Two had been shot up pretty bad, and the other two were pretty young. Uncle Mal said they didn't put up much of a fight without their leader."

As Jordan reached the two, Wolf looked up at her. "I sure am glad to see you safe, ma'am." His welcoming grin faded. "I'm sorry Harry and I put you in danger."

"Oh, Wolf." To her surprise, he let her hug him, his wiry arms squeezing her tight before letting her go with the pleased embarrassment of youth. "You gave me courage, Wolf. I knew I'd be all right with all of you coming after me."

"But you weren't supposed to be coming after *me*." Elijah frowned. "I thought you'd learned your lesson."

Wolf scuffed his boots in the grass, glancing up at his father out of the corners of his eyes. "I brought fresh bread and ham and a jar of plum preserves Nicky—Mrs. Braddock—sweet-talked out of the chef."

Jordan sighed dramatically. "My hero."

Elijah scowled at her. "This is going to be harder than I thought."

"Families always are."

Elijah tousled Wolf's hair. "Go unsaddle your horse, son. We'll discuss appropriate punishment after we've finished off the plums."

The boy grinned. "Mrs. Braddock made me promise to get them to you. She was so worried, I couldn't refuse."

"Wolf," Elijah growled, "don't push your luck."

"Yes, sir!"

"Is Nicky all right?" Jordan asked, anxious herself. "Doctor Gottfried said she shouldn't have too much excitement—"

"I think it's too late for that, ma'am," Wolf said, grabbing his horse's reins. "I guess her husband arrived on the coach this morning, and I don't think she's stopped talking since. Except maybe when they were kissing."

"Wolf!"

He grinned again. "She says it's all your fault, ma'am. Some letter you sent him. She promised to kill you if you got back alive, but I don't think she means it at all. I guess they'll be in Battlement Park until the baby comes."

He tugged his horse's reins, leading it over to where Smoke and the sorrel were munching their suppers.

Elijah reached for Jordan's hand. "He needs to go back to Henna. To the Culberts. They're his family. But if we're so close, sometimes he could—"

"Of course."

"I guess we won't have our evening alone tonight."

She shook her head.

"Tomorrow."

She glanced up at him sideways. "Tomorrow we'll be back in Battlement Park with all our family, and I've lost my chaperone."

"You won't need one." A gunfighter's steel filled his voice. "I don't intend to waste another night like this. There must be a preacher of some kind in Battlement Park."

"Besides you?"

He stared at her, shaking his head. "You're not a sparrow at all. You're a sparrowhawk."

She had wings; she was sure of that. And when he kissed her again, she knew she could fly.

If this was their moment, it was perfect.